A DANGEROUS DESIRE

He was so near that she could smell the clean scent of the Hungary water on his face, and she could feel the warmth of his breath caressing her cheek.

"If I let you kiss me, Patrick, I will not want you to stop," she told him, her voice scarce above a whisper. "Please—do not shame me again."

"You cannot tell a man you want him also, and expect to make him go, Ellie," he said softly. Putting his hand on her shoulder, he turned her around once more, "I am telling you I love you," he whispered. "I am telling you I want you above everything."

It was as though she were brittle, as though if he touched her further she should break, and yet she had not the will to refuse him.

Secret Nights

ANNOUNCING THE

TOPAZ FREQUENT READERS CLUB
COMMEMORATING TOPAZ'S
1 YEAR ANNIVERSARY!

THE MORE YOU BUY, THE MORE YOU GET

Redeem coupons found here and in the back of all new Topaz titles for FREE Topaz gifts:

Send in:

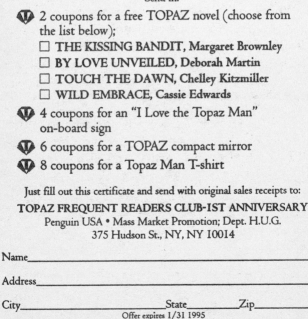

- 2 coupons for a free TOPAZ novel (choose from the list below);
  - ☐ **THE KISSING BANDIT**, Margaret Brownley
  - ☐ **BY LOVE UNVEILED**, Deborah Martin
  - ☐ **TOUCH THE DAWN**, Chelley Kitzmiller
  - ☐ **WILD EMBRACE**, Cassie Edwards

- 4 coupons for an "I Love the Topaz Man" on-board sign

- 6 coupons for a TOPAZ compact mirror

- 8 coupons for a Topaz Man T-shirt

Just fill out this certificate and send with original sales receipts to:

TOPAZ FREQUENT READERS CLUB-1ST ANNIVERSARY
Penguin USA • Mass Market Promotion; Dept. H.U.G.
375 Hudson St., NY, NY 10014

Name_____

Address_____

City_____State_____Zip_____

Offer expires 1/31 1995

This certificate must accompany your request. No duplicates accepted. Void where prohibited, taxed or restricted. Allow 4-6 weeks for receipt of merchandise. Offer good only in U.S., its territories, and Canada.

SECRET NIGHTS

by

Anita Mills

A TOPAZ BOOK

TOPAZ
Published by the Penguin Group
Penguin Books USA Inc., 375 Hudson Street,
New York, New York 10014, U.S.A.
Penguin Books Ltd, 27 Wrights Lane,
London W8 5TZ, England
Penguin Books Australia Ltd, Ringwood,
Victoria, Australia
Penguin Books Canada Ltd, 10 Alcorn Avenue,
Toronto, Ontario, Canada M4V 3B2
Penguin Books (N.Z.) Ltd, 182–190 Wairau Road,
Auckland 10, New Zealand

Penguin Books Ltd, Registered Offices:
Harmondsworth, Middlesex, England

First published by Topaz, an imprint of Dutton Signet,
a division of Penguin Books USA Inc.

First Printing, July, 1994
10 9 8 7 6 5 4 3 2 1

 Topaz is a trademark of New American Library,
a division of Penguin Books USA Inc.

Printed in the United States of America

A special thanks
to my pharmacist, Robin Stith,
who provided me with
the perfect poison.

Author's Foreword

Most of us who enjoy reading about the English Regency see it as the gay, glittering era before those staid, repressed Victorians came upon the scene and spoiled the fun. When we think of the Prince Regent and his time, we tend to think of the reckless pursuit of pleasure, the grand social whirl of endless balls, routs, and country parties where innocent misses transformed reluctant rakes and rogues into adoring suitors.

That was the facade. But beneath the veneer of this sophisticated upper social crust, there lurked a much darker society in turmoil. Displaced by machines or made superfluous by the end of the Napoleonic Wars, many desperate people turned to crime and vice to survive. Opium dens, thieves' kitchens, brothels, and gin shops thrived in London's stews and alleys.

Brought together by rumor, mobs formed spontaneously, looting and destroying houses, torching occupied carriages, and generally wreaking havoc until the Horse Guards showed up and began shooting. Then the rioters fled, melting into dark alleys, leaving behind the bodies of their comrades, waiting to be incited another time.

In the absence of an effective police force, criminals multiplied despite the fact that not only murder but also the theft of anything valued above five shillings, the defacing of public property by so much as a chip of stone, as well as two hundred or so other acts were all punishable by death.

And the gallows were busy. In one September alone, fifty-eight felons were hanged in London—while the wealthy watched over elegant meals conveniently served at windows! Crowds, sometimes eighty thousand strong, pushed, shoved, and trampled one another to death while whistling and jeering at the condemned.

But it wasn't just riffraff who were hanged. Joseph Wall, once a colonial governor, was tried in London for sexually assaulting a Miss Gregory, shooting men from a cannon, and having a soldier whipped to death. To pay his gaming debts, a Scottish doctor profited from dispatching wealthy patients before discovery. A woman who ran a home for orphans was found to have killed her charges. A lovesick swain robbed and murdered to satisfy a greedy mistress, then upon finding her unfaithful killed her also. A misogynistic doctor poisoned unsuspecting females until one lived to tell her tale.

At the same time, good people such as Mr. Wilberforce and Hannah More saw the social ills and suffering, decrying them, taking up the causes of the downtrodden, earning for themselves the sometimes derisive name of Methodists for their troubles. Unfortunately, far too few in a nation still smug from victory over Napoleon were ready yet to listen to those who sought social reform.

Against this turbulent, almost schizophrenic background of wealth and poverty, indulgence and deprivation, piety and vice, I have set my story of an obsessed father, an ambitious young man, and the woman torn between them.

—Anita Mills

London: October 15, 1815

"Not guilty."

Mr. Justice Humphreys cleared his throat in surprise, then repeated the verdict, adding, "The jury has found Mrs. Magdalene Coates not guilty of the murder of Margaret Parker." Almost as soon as he spoke, he rapped his gavel, indicating that the long ordeal was over. "Having discharged its honorable and lawful duty, the jury is dismissed."

Humphreys had confirmed the finding so somberly that it took a moment to assimilate it. Then a low murmur of disapproval passed through the disappointed crowd in the public gallery. The accused, a heavyset woman, slumped briefly, then sat back, wiping her streaming eyes. Beside her, Patrick Hamilton sorted a pile of papers, then inserted them into the worn leather foldover.

It was over, and he wanted to leave before she played out a public scene of gratitude. Rising, he straightened his barrister's robe as Maddie turned to him, scarce giving him time to hold his wig before she grabbed his free hand and pumped his arm vigorously.

"Ye did it, Mr. Hamilton—ye did it! Godamercy, but ye've given Maddie Coates 'er life, and she'll not ferget it—no, sir—not ever! Ye got ter come 'round ter celebrate—aye, we'll tipple a bit o' Boney's best brandy!" Her voice lowered as she added, "And I got a mite o' good stuff I'd share wi' ye—t'morrow, if ye was a mind ter. We'll put it in the pipes—lessen you was wantin' ter eat it—and—"

"Boney's brandy will quite suffice," he murmured. As she looked up at him, tears streaked her heavily rouged cheeks, sending red lines all the way to her sagging jowls. "Thankee—oh, thankee," she whispered, succumbing to the overwhelming emotion she felt.

Patrick disengaged his hand carefully. "You were innocent, Maddie," was all he had a chance to say before she was surrounded by a group of equally painted women. As "her girls" enveloped the now notorious madam, he ducked away.

Glancing warily to the emptying gallery, he was all too conscious that the disappointment there might well turn into outright anger. Having come for blood sport, some were always determined to have it, and there was nothing quite like a London mob. But this time, they appeared merely disgruntled.

"Here now—get away wi' ye!" he heard Maddie say angrily.

He turned back in time to see perhaps the loveliest female of his memory. While blondes were definitely the fashion, this one was possessed of hair somewhere between spun gold and copper that framed the face of an angel with eyes of the deepest, brightest blue.

"I have come to see Pearl," the young woman said, her voice enticingly husky. "We have spoken before. She is ill and in need of a physician's attention."

"And I say she don't want nothin' ter do wi' ye!" As she said it, Maddie grasped the arm of a thin, pale creature, pulling her away from the beauty. "Why don't ye leave well enough be? I take care o' me gels and see as they are healthy enough, I do! You and the interfering Methodists!" she snorted contemptuously. "Don't want me ter make an honest livin', do ye?"

Ignoring Maddie, the girl spoke to the sickly looking girl, "If you wish to leave, you can come with me. This is England, and she cannot own you."

"The gel's bound ter me, I'm tellin' ye!" Maddie snapped.

Before Patrick could intervene, an older man took the lovely girl's arm, saying sharply, " 'Tis enough, Elise! Enough, I say! It ain't your business to interfere."

Maddie turned her attention to the old man. "Aye, take her wi' ye—and don't be lettin' her near me gels again, fer I ain't one ter tolerate interference wi' me business!"

"Ask Pearl," the young woman insisted. "She hates what—"

"That don't matter," the old man interrupted her testily. "Come on now—this ain't no place for this, you hear me? Got to get you out of here," he muttered as he dragged her away. "Elise, what was you thinking of?"

"This is England—people are not owned," the girl retorted.

"Law's on her side," he answered gruffly, pushing her into the crowd. "Besides, she ain't nothing to you."

She argued further, but Patrick could not hear her above those who shouted at the keeper of the gallery. Looking back once, she hesitated as though she still wished to say more, then a wall of humanity closed behind her. Patrick still stared after her, wondering enviously how the man could have acquired such a fancy piece. Then the cynic within him gave the obvious answer—the old gent was undoubtedly rich enough to afford her.

For a moment he considered asking Maddie Coates about her, for Maddie, ever alert to stocking her own establishment, seemed to follow the career of every working girl from the lowest tart to the fanciest courtesan. And she was not beyond advertising that this girl or that "was once under the protection of Lord So-and-so," naming the name. But with a face like hers, he mused that it would be a long time, if ever, before that exquisite bit of fluff wound up in a place like Maddie's.

"A brilliant defense, sir—brilliant," Chief Prosecutor Peale acknowledged ruefully behind him

"Aye," Edward Milton, Peale's associate, muttered grudgingly. "If you'd have asked me, I'd have said the old whore was gallows bait."

"Common sense said she did not do it," Patrick

Hamilton murmured, turning back to them. "But alas, what is common sense when the public clamors against it, eh?"

Peale flushed for a moment, then consoled himself. "Well, if it had been any other, I should have regretted the loss considerably more. You, sirrah, have no peer in the examinations—no peer," he repeated, as though his defeat could not be his fault. Settling his shoulders, he nodded to Patrick. "Do you come 'round to White's with us?"

"No. Too much work by half, I'm afraid."

"More of the unwashed?" Milton inquired sarcastically. "Is there none so impure that you will not defend?"

"Being a procurer, unsavory as that may be, does not preclude Mrs. Coates's right to be considered innocent of murder," Patrick countered.

"Dash it, but the woman's a disgrace—runs a—an utter den of iniquity!" the junior prosecutor sputtered. "Innocent of this or not, she's still done enough harm to hang."

For a moment Patrick looked to the group of cheaply perfumed women, then a faint smile played at the corners of his mouth. "Actually, I believe the place is called a brothel."

"And you, sir, are an equal disgrace to the barrister's profession!"

"Ned," Peale said sternly, " 'tis enough. Today the verdict was his."

"But—"

"Enough." Thrusting out his hand to Patrick, the chief prosecutor forced a smile. "You waste your talents on the riffraff, you know."

Smiling, the younger man shook his head. "I should rather count it that I gain justice for any able to afford me." Out of the corner of his eye, he could see Maddie and her girls moving toward him. "Good day, gentlemen," he murmured quickly.

As he left, he could hear Milton still complaining. "How could you say it, sir? The man's naught but an actor in robes—he belongs on the boards in Drury

Lane, if you was to ask me. His is but an act of legal chicanery, sir.''

Peale's eyes followed their courtroom adversary before he answered. "He has style—and substance, Ned—style and substance. And with his ambition, he's going far, Ned—far. You can wager on it, if you've a mind, I tell you.''

"Surely you do not think he's looking to the bench?'' the younger man demanded, scandalized.

"No, no—to politics, dear boy—to politics. All he needs is the right mentor. Indeed, but I have heard that Dunster—'' Peale caught himself and shook his head. "Well, I daresay we shall know if a certain notice appears in the papers, won't we?'' he added mysteriously.

"Dunster! The Earl of Dunster? Why, he holds the Home Secretary's portfolio!''

"Precisely, Ned—precisely. You may mark where you heard it, dear boy—Patrick Hamilton is going to advance beyond bar or bench,'' the older man predicted smugly.

"With Dunster's backing, he can aspire to a peerage! I mean, Dunster's got the Regent's ear!'' Milton gasped, utterly aghast at the thought.

Throwing a fatherly arm about his junior's shoulders, Peale nodded, "And who can fault Hamilton for going where we shall never be privileged to tread, Ned?''

Right now, Patrick was simply going home. Nearly too tired to think and yet too exhilarated to rest, he was going home to bathe, change clothes, then return to his office.

Outside, he hailed a hackney, climbed inside, and settled back against the hard seat. Within half a block, he'd removed his barrister's wig and combed his flattened Brutus with his fingers. For a moment he closed his eyes, savoring his victory.

Maddie Coates was a free woman, free to return to her lucrative flesh trade in Covent Garden. Maddie. Magdalene. Again the faint smile played at his lips, for the irony was not lost on him—Magdalene Coates

had been aptly named for the career she'd carved out
for herself. Only this Magdalene had no savior to lead
her to righteousness. Truth to tell, he doubted she
had any religion at all.

But he'd won her acquittal, and he had a deep
sense of satisfaction from that. He'd taken a case everyone warned him could not be won, and he'd done
the seemingly impossible. That, coupled with his usual
fee, made the victory sweet. He leaned his head back
against the top of the seat and smiled to himself. His
usual fee. "Me money or me life," Maddie Coates had
summed it up so succinctly. To which he'd countered
her life must surely be more precious than her gold.

She'd pay it, he was certain of that, and he felt not
the least compunction for taking such an exorbitant
sum. She'd make it up, probably by raising her girls'
prices to cover both his defense and her well-known
predilection for opium.

But more than anything, his aggressive defense had
added as much to his reputation as to his purse. And
one got the other, after all. Before he reached his
thirty-first birthday he intended to be not only richer
but also well placed for the political career Peale predicted. Next election, he'd stand for a seat in the
Commons, and with Dunster's support, he might one
day gain a ministerial portfolio for himself.

He'd already come far for the youngest of four sons
born into an obscure branch of an ancient and illustrious Scottish family. But by the time he'd been born,
his father had nearly nothing left to settle on him, so
he'd known from early childhood that he'd have to
make his own way. After his first glimpse of Mrs. Jor-
dan in *She Would and She Would Not,* he'd had his heart
set on a stage career.

Unfortunately, every member of his family from the
distant Duke of Hamilton to his own less than fond
parent had irately disabused him of the notion, and
finally he'd been pushed toward law. But he still
yearned to emote upon the boards, only now his sense
of the dramatic would have to be displayed on the
stage of politics.

The hackney rolled to a halt in front of his brick-faced Georgian townhouse, and the driver hastened down to open the door for him.

"Made good time, we did, sor," the fellow said hopefully.

For answer, Patrick tossed him a full guinea, prompting a wide, gap-toothed grin. Turning to go up the stairs, he heard the man call after him, "Look fer me the next time, will ye? Or ask fer Willie Simms!"

" 'Tis generous to a fault you are," Hayes, his footman converted to butler, sniffed disapprovingly as he took the hated wig.

"One never knows when one might need a hackney—or a hackney driver," Patrick murmured. "And they are much more convenient than having to put the horses to the tilbury, you must admit."

"Aye, I suppose," Hayes admitted grudgingly. "But they don't add anything to your consequence, if I may say it."

"How long have you been with me?" Patrick asked, smiling.

"Since you was going to Cambridge, sir."

"Then you must surely know what a thick hide I have, eh?"

Scarce inside, Patrick reached beneath the neck of his black gown to loosen his cravat. "Tell Wilson I'd have a bath," he ordered, "and while it is being drawn, I'll take a glass of port while I read the post."

"Of course, sir," Hayes replied. "And would you have a nuncheon laid for you?"

"No, I've not time to sit down to a meal. Just have Thomas bring up bread and meat to the library, I'll eat while I read."

The butler's lips thinned with disapproval for a moment, then he sighed. "Very well. And shall I tell Mrs. Marsh to prepare dinner about eight?"

Patrick shook his head. "I'll be going to the office, and God only knows when I shall be done. As I have sadly neglected the rest of my practice for the Coates trial, I doubt I shall be home before ten."

"You must take time to eat."

"If I get too hungry, I can always stop off at Watier's or White's."

"Humph! You work too much, if you was to ask me," Hayes muttered, following him into the book-lined room. Drawing the heavy draperies back for light, he added, "Don't know why you keep a cook, unless 'tis for the rest of us."

Patrick ignored him, choosing instead to drop his tall frame into his favorite leather chair. Retrieving the basket of letters and calling cards, he leaned back and closed his burning eyes briefly, then he squared his shoulders and began opening half a week's mail.

Recognizing Kate Townsend's neat, elegant script, he felt a momentary pang beneath his breastbone. Resolutely, he chose to read her letter before the others. "Always take the worst medicine first," his mother used to say. He broke the wax seal with the edge of his thumbnail, opened the single sheet, and began to read.

Dear Mr. Hamilton,

Words can never express my gratitude to you for your efforts on my behalf. I can only pray that one day you shall be as completely happy as I am, for that must surely be a compensation beyond gold.

As for us, Bell and I are firmly ensconced in our new home here in Cornwall, where the weather is lovely and the sea so close we are lulled to sleep at night by it. The sunsets are truly spectacular and well worth a trip from London to view them. I do not think that ever in my life I envisioned myself so fortunate as I am now. With your help, I have achieved everything any female could possibly desire.

Bell assures me he is content here, saying he does not miss playing Adonis to tonnish beauties at all. He has become the country gentleman, and the life seems to suit him quite well.

I would that you could have been here when we went to church, for word of my scandal preceded me. It was as though everyone wished to pretend I was not there, yet could not quite manage it, for none could keep from admiring my handsome husband. But life is simpler here, and Bell says they will all eventually forget I was the wicked Countess Volsky who divorced her Russian husband, and I shall merely become Viscountess Townsend, mother to a handsome brood of children. Indeed, I hope to have further news on that head soon.

We do hope you will come to visit us, and we shall do all possible to make your stay agreeable, for we both count you the dearest of friends. Until then, you must know you are with us always in my prayers.

She had signed it as "Your most grateful client, Katherine Winstead Townsend."

He noticed she'd left out Volsky's name, which did not surprise him. If ever there had been a woman betrayed by a husband, it was Kate. And her determination to be rid of him had precipitated one of the worst scandals of his memory. It had been actually worse than when the Earl of Longford had shed his adulterous wife some years earlier, possibly because Townsend had been involved in that affair also. Only this time, the usually faithless Bell had actually fallen in love with Kate, and even Patrick believed the passion would prove a lasting one.

For a moment he allowed himself to remember her, to see her face in his mind again. She wasn't a beauty—in fact, she was not even what most men would call pretty—but he'd been drawn to her. She was possessed of fine dark eyes and a genuine smile, and she had great strength of character. As far as he was concerned, Townsend did not deserve her.

There had been a time during her trial when Patrick had actually considered offering for Kate Winstead himself, a time when she'd stood alone and nearly friendless. But Bell had come back for her, saving him from folly.

He sighed and set aside her letter. He ought to be grateful to Townsend, damned grateful, in fact. Marriage to a notorious divorcee would have been fatal to his ambition. A politician needed a spouse as pure as

Caesar's wife, as the saying went. Attractive and well born enough to help him—someone possessed of as much ambition as he. Someone like Jane Barclay, the Earl of Dunster's dark-eyed daughter.

Aye, now there was blood as blue as any, Patrick mused, sipping his port. And if France had been worth a Mass to the Protestant Henry of Navarre, then Jane Barclay's hand was well worth his own conversion from Whig to Tory. Even Liverpool's unpopularity as prime minister had not shaken the Prince Regent's support of the party, making it unlikely they would go out of power.

Briefly Jane's image floated before him. There was no question about it, she was quite pretty—a trifle preoccupied with her father's consequence, but definitely well born and well connected. He ought to consider her discreet pursuit of him a blessing, and he did.

But as he considered Jane dispassionately, her dark hair and eyes faded to that of the girl in the Sessions House. Elise, the old man had called her. For a moment he allowed himself the luxury of imagining that prime article in his arms, of wondering what it would take to steal her away from her aging lover, then he sighed regretfully. Given his work schedule and his impending engagement to Dunster's daughter, it was highly unlikely he'd see the beauty again, unless it was across a dimly lit theater sometime.

Forcing his thoughts away from the two very disparate females, he began sifting through his remaining mail, separating tradesmen's bills into one neat, orderly pile, scented billet-doux into another for his secretary's attention. Near the bottom of the tray, he spied a printed card that intrigued him: *Bartholomew Rand, Purveyor of Quality Bricks.*

As though one might not recognize the name by itself. As though there could be anyone unaware of the vast Rand Brickworks at Islington. Or that Rand was as rich as a nabob, having provided the bricks for scores of elegant mansions and grand houses. And since the terrible war with France had ended, old

Rand stood to gain even more wealth, for now there was also a pent-up government desire for public building.

Curious, he turned over the card and saw the ill-formed scrawl, reading, "I shall wait upon you at three in your office to discuss a matter of mutual interest." Nothing more. Not even a day or date. At first irritated with the man's rather high-handed message, Patrick considered ignoring it, but then his curiosity prevailed. What could someone like Bartholomew Rand need with a criminal barrister? he wondered, now intrigued.

"Hayes!"

"Yes, sir?" came the prompt response.

"This card—" He held it out. "When did this arrive?"

The butler moved closer to peer at the name, then answered positively, "It was carried 'round before noon, sir—rather early to be civil, in fact. And so I told the fellow that brought it."

"Damn," Patrick muttered. "What time is it?"

Hayes glanced at the clock for a moment. "Half past one."

There was scarce time for a bath, and yet for all his interest, Patrick reasoned that he ought not appear too eager. "Send James down to my office with a message for Mr. Rand," he decided abruptly. "He is to be told that three o'clock is inconvenient, but if he wishes to wait, I shall attend him there between half after three and a quarter 'til four."

"Humph! He's not apt to be liking it, if you was to ask me. That man of his was as arrogant as they make them—telling me as I was to send into court for you."

"He can learn patience," Patrick murmured, rising. Indicating the remaining letters, he directed, "Let Mr. Sinclair determine what is to be done with these, will you?"

The butler's eyebrow rose slightly. "All of them? Even the ones from the females?"

"Given his amorous tendencies, I'd say he'd enjoy writing my response to them." As Hayes's eyes mir-

rored his shock, Patrick smiled. "Any woman bold
enough to drench her letters in perfume lacks discretion, don't you think?"

"As to that, I am sure I cannot say."

"Ah, yes—there is Mrs. Hayes," Patrick murmured.

"Precisely."

Patrick hesitated, then made up his mind. "And
when Mr. Sinclair is come in the morning, he is to
see if there are any roses left to be had. If they are
reasonable, I'd have him send them to Lady Jane Barclay in Mayfair." Moving to the writing desk, he found
paper, pen, and ink. Leaning over, he dipped his pen
and quickly wrote *With my sincerest compliments, Patrick
Hamilton.* "Here—have him enclose this, will you? And
make sure he understands to include the title on the
outside, for she gets rather peevish if one forgets to
address her as Lady Jane," he remembered. "Otherwise she will find some way to remind me that her
father is an earl," he added dryly.

"And is he to specify a particular color? Or would
you prefer to have those in best bloom?"

"I don't care."

"Made into a posy?"

Patrick considered it, then shook his head. "No—
she can put them on her dressing table, where they
may last longer." Seeing that his butler apparently
disagreed with him, he smiled. "Too much attention
makes the female of the species take the male for
granted, old fellow."

Obviously displeased, the portly older man fidgeted in the hard, straight-backed chair. Finally, when he could contain his growing ire no longer, he rose to pace restlessly within the small confines of Patrick Hamilton's reception room.

"I've half a mind to leave," he growled. "If he thinks he can keep Bat Rand waiting ..." His voice trailed off. "Five more minutes, sirrah—five more minutes," he threatened the law clerk behind the desk.

John Byrnes looked up. "It is not yet a quarter to four," he reminded Rand mildly. "And if you wish, I am sure that Mr. Banks, our solicitor, would be most happy to accommodate you."

"Don't want any damned solicitor! D'ye think I ain't already got ten of 'em?" the old man demanded angrily. "No, sir—I said three—*three*! Not half after! I expect to be attended when I ask it, I tell you!"

Rand's voice boomed through the small room, making the clerk wish Banks would come out. Returning to his work, the young man reflected that he'd not expected to entertain a brothel madame nor the surly, rough-mannered man now before him when he'd sought employment with the much-admired Hamilton. Everyone had said the barrister was a man on the way up, a man capable of making his assistants as successful as he was. But so far he'd not seen it—Banks had been there two years and he'd passed more than six months with the barrister.

The door opened, admitting Hamilton. With his tall, surprisingly muscular figure clad in a flawlessly tailored dark blue superfine coat, plain waistcoat, and buff-colored trousers, his light brown hair brushed into a perfect Brutus, he appeared the epitome of the fashionable gentleman. For the briefest moment, his hazel eyes took in the situation, then they met Rand's without betraying anything. Bartholomew Rand, Purveyor of Quality Bricks, had been the old gent with the girl in the courtroom.

"My apologies for your wait," he murmured, extending his hand. "Patrick Hamilton, sir. I collect neither Mr. Byrnes nor Mr. Banks could assist you?"

"Eh? No—no, though the little fellow was polite enough, I guess." Rand's manner changed on the instant, and as he shook Patrick's hand, he smiled broadly. "Pleasure to know you, sir. Been watching you for nigh to a year—would have made your acquaintance earlier today, in fact, but for that little dustup. Had to get Elise out of there before she was mobbed, you know. Got to forgive her though—gel's got a soft heart."

"Oh?"

"My daughter, you know," Rand explained, nodding. "Aye, I told Mrs. Rand just this morning I was thinking of engaging you. Always get the best, I say— and you are the best, sir—the best."

"Thank you," Patrick acknowledged politely, adding casually, "You are to be congratulated—Miss Rand is quite lovely."

"Oh, she don't take much from me," the older man admitted openly. "Looks like her mama, and a good thing that is, ain't it? My folks was all unremarked for their looks, I can tell you." His smiled broadened into a knowing grin. "Aye, you was taken with her, wasn't you? Well, you wouldn't be the first as was—no, sir."

Not wanting to betray an interest, Patrick changed the subject. "Did Mr. Byrnes offer you a drink perhaps?"

"Eh? No, but he wasn't the interfering sort, at least," Rand conceded.

"As a general rule, he is to inquire as to both your comfort and your business."

"Wouldn't have done him any good if he was to ask," the old man retorted. "I got to see for myself before I open the budget about my affairs. I like to keep things close." Leaning nearer, he added, "I don't suppose you got somewheres as we can be private, eh?"

"Of course." Patrick crossed the small reception room and held open the door to his inner office.

The brick merchant stepped inside, and his smile faded briefly as he scanned the room shrewdly. Then he nodded approvingly. "Don't waste your blunt, do you? I like that."

As he shut the door behind Rand, Patrick followed the man's gaze. With naught but mahogany bookcases, a sideboard, a cluttered desk, and two chairs, the office was extremely plain. But it suited him. Smiling, he murmured sardonically, "Unlike Mr. Banks, I'm afraid I don't hang any letters of recommendation on the walls."

"Don't need 'em," the older man assured him, sitting heavily in a chair. "Ain't a soul breathing in London as ain't heard of Patrick Hamilton, sirrah! 'Hamilton will take those cases as cannot be won, and afore God, he'll win 'em,' 'tis said."

"I'm afraid you flatter me."

"Why?" Rand asked bluntly. " 'Tis the God's truth, ain't it?"

Without answering that, Patrick took his seat and turned over a large sand-filled glass, then sat back, his hands folded over his plain buff waistcoat. "You behold an intrigued man, sir."

"One of them as wants me to get to business, eh? Well, in the ordinary way, I'd be wanting to, but just now I'd rather be getting to know you." For a moment the man's bluff affability slipped as he looked at the small hourglass. "Eh, what's that?"

"It merely tells me when half the hour is passed. In consult, my fee is measured by time. Mr. Banks requires five pounds for his work, and I expect no less than twenty. Beyond the consult, if I choose to defend a client, I'm afraid I require a great deal more than

that based upon the nature of the charges filed
against him.''

"I'll say one thing, sir—you are dashed plain-
spoken, ain't you? Well, I like a man as can tell me
straight out, so's there ain't no mistaking what's expected, eh?''

"Yes.''

"But there ain't need for that glass, is there? Any
as knows Bat Rand knows as he's got all the gold as
you could ask.'' He stopped to dab at a deep scratch
on his neck, then rubbed his balding pate with a fine
lawn handkerchief before asking, "You ain't got any
wine, have you? A bit of sherry or hock even—I ain't
too proud to drink most of it. And put away that
demned thing—a profitable arrangement ain't made
in half the hour.''

Rising, Patrick went to the sideboard, opened a
door, and drew out a bottle and two glasses. "Which
is it—port or Madeira?''

"Please yourself, sir—either one'll wash the dust
from m'throat. Like I told you, I like all of it well
enough.''

When Patrick turned around with the filled glasses,
he noticed that the brick magnate had removed the
sand timer from the desk and placed it on the floor.
Before he could say anything, the fellow grinned.
"Caught me out, didn't you? Well, all you got to tell
me is the tariff, and I'll pay it—I ain't one of your
fancy gentlemen as dodges the tradesmen, no sir.
When I deliver the bricks, I get m'money on the
spot—and you can expect the same from me.''

"An admirable trait.'' Handing one glass to Rand,
Patrick sat down and took a sip from his. It was, he
knew, considered the best port to be had in London.

Rand drank deeply, then nodded. "Good stuff,
damme if it ain't.'' He met Patrick's gaze. "Got you a
wonderin', ain't I?''

"Yes.''

"Been followin' you for a good bit of time—saw you
first when they was hearin' the Volsky mess, in fact.
You was brilliant, sir! When they was a-tellin' it like

she was a demned adventuress, you was a-getting her a fine settlement from that Russian."

Patrick's expression did not change. "Scarce my usual business," he said. "I merely took it on as a favor to a friend of Lady Townsend's. Under ordinary circumstance, I should have referred the matter to Mr. Banks."

"But there was money to be made there, eh?"

"More than you might expect," Patrick admitted. "And I wished justice for Lady Townsend."

"Come to think of it, I did read it somewheres as she snared Viscount Townsend, wasn't it?" Rand recalled. "Well, if you was to ask me, I'd say each deserved the other." The older man peered at Patrick from beneath heavy brows that nearly met above his rather red nose. "Then there was the Coates thing." Leaning closer as though he were a conspirator, he asked, "Did you really believe the mort innocent?"

"I believe the murderer was a man," Patrick answered.

"You don't say it!" For a moment Rand seemed shocked. "No!" Then, "But how was you to think that?"

"The dead girl's weight."

"But the Coates woman is fat! And the watch said—"

"If you had attended the arguments earlier, you'd merely have heard him say he saw a stout female just after he heard something hit the water, and he presumed that female to be the murderer."

"Aye—Mrs. Coates."

"Not necessarily. In the course of examination, the watch admitted the fog was so heavy that he could scarce see the next street lamp, and whoever passed him had a hooded cloak pulled over the head. I'm inclined to think he saw a man."

"Aye, but she passed right by him! I read it in the papers! He saw her, sir—he saw her!"

"He saw *someone*, Mr. Rand. But when pressed, he had to admit he did not see Mrs. Coates's face."

"But the Coates woman had reason, didn't she?"

the old man argued. "The girl had run away from
her, they said. And you heard her today—she ain't
going to let that other girl go neither. Woman's a
demned flesh peddler, that's all—no skin off any of
us if she was to hang," he muttered.

"If any had bothered to inquire of Mrs. Coates's
female employees, it would have been learned that the
Parker girl wished to return to her, that life on the
street was more difficult than she expected."

"Employees!" Rand snorted. "Her tarts, you
mean."

"Moreover," Patrick continued, unperturbed, "it
might also have been learned that Mrs. Coates suffers
from an inflammation of the bones. It is her physician's considered opinion that she could never have
lifted Margaret Parker's weight." Patrick paused much
as he would have before a jury, then drove home his
winning point. "But you see, Mr. Rand, you have
made the same assumptions, based on little more than
contempt for Magdalene Coates's profession, that the
prosecution did. In truth, because Maddie is a madam,
you failed to note that no one asked any questions
that might have exonerated her."

"You don't say! Well, I wasn't there for all the arguments, of course—just went to hear the verdict read."
Setting aside his empty glass, Rand wiped his mouth
with his handkerchief, then stuffed it back into his
coat. Leaning forward, he asked curiously, "What
d'you think will happen about it all now?"

"Nothing. By tomorrow, Peg Parker won't even be
a memory."

"Aye."

"And unless the murderer is caught while killing
again, he will never be brought before the bar of
justice."

"How'd she afford you—the Coates woman, I
mean? I'd heard—well, you said yourself you wasn't to
be had on the cheap, you know."

Patrick took a sip of his port. "That, sir, is a matter
of confidence."

At first, Rand appeared taken aback, then a low

chuckle rumbled somewhere beneath the wide expanse of his waistcoat. "Damme if you ain't as good as they say! Without you, it would have been 'damn the evidence and hang her!' "

"Probably. But we are afield. You wished to discuss some business, I believe," Patrick prompted him.

"Now I ain't about to be rushed," Rand protested. "Like I said, I got to know you first." Leaning toward Patrick again, he said, "But I'm liking what I see, sir— d'you know why?"

"No."

"I can tell you got a passion for what you are doing." As Patrick's eyebrows lifted, Rand nodded. "Aye—passion. Like I said, I heard you at the Volsky trial. Went home and told Mrs. Rand you was worth the gallery ticket—I been to plays where the demned actors ain't had half the feeling, I can tell you."

"Thank you."

The older man held out his empty glass. "I'd have another, if you was to offer it." As Patrick took it and rose to pour him the drink, Rand conceded, "Oh, it ain't much—my business here, that is—nothing like what you are used to. I just want to know as I got the best in everything."

While pouring the port, Patrick reflected that he could see what made the man successful. Rand practiced flattery as though it were an art. Returning to his desk, Patrick handed the older man his refilled glass.

"Go on."

"Bat Rand don't do anything halfway." Setting his glass on the desk, the older man reached into his coat to draw out a leather money folder. As he handed it across, he watched Patrick. "Go ahead—there's five hundred quid in there, and that's but the beginning."

For a long moment, the younger man regarded him soberly. "Mr. Rand," he asked finally, "are you accused of a crime?"

"Eh? No, of course not! Just want a bit of insurance, that's all. Ain't to say I won't need you someday, is there? A man of wealth ought to have more'n a decent lawyer," Rand insisted.

Patrick eyed him skeptically. "A criminal barrister? Mr. Rand, I assure you I have not the least competence in civil law. You are better advised to seek a solicitor, and I do not hesitate to recommend my associate. Mr. Banks is as thorough as—"

"Dash it, but you took the Volsky woman's case, didn't you? A man don't have to kill nobody to engage you, does he?"

"I believe we have discussed Lady Townsend already."

"Only meant she wasn't in the way of your ordinary client," Rand said hastily. Leaning forward again, he sobered visibly. "Look—I ain't forgot how the Luddites burned the looms and ruined businesses. Well, bricks—millions of 'em—is my living, don't you see? What if it was to happen to me? What if I was to have workers as despises the hand as feeds 'em."

"If you notify the Home Secretary's office, the militia can be brought to defend your brickworks."

"The militia be damned! They don't come until all's done, as far as I can see it," Rand scoffed. "I'd rather tend the matter in my own way."

"I cannot countenance a crime before it is committed—or after, for that matter," Patrick said dryly.

"What if I was to defend my business, and what if a rioter was to get killed?"

"The circumstances would have to be considered, but in most cases, the law is on your side."

"Circumstances be damned also, sir!" The older man's expression softened suddenly, and he coaxed, "Take the money—I'd rather pay you than a damned militia."

A faint smile played at the corners of Patrick's mouth. "Mr. Rand, if you were to actually be accused of harming anyone, I'm afraid I should require a great deal more than five hundred pounds."

"And like I was telling you, I got it—whatever you was to ask, I got it. All you got to do is name the price. Tell you what—your time's short, ain't it? Listen, you come to dine with me tonight in Marylebone—got the biggest house there—and we'll discuss the matter at

length over more port," he coaxed. "Meet m'family—
Mrs. Rand's one of your people—born Quality, I
mean. And Elise—the gel you saw—is a great admirer
of yours." Afraid Patrick might decline, he added slyly,
"My only issue, you know."

"No, but—" Patrick hesitated, torn between the opportunity to see the intriguing Miss Rand again and
the prospect of an interminable evening among
strangers not of his class.

"Got all the fine manners, too," the old man declared proudly. "She wouldn't have been with me, but
when she heard I was going to hear you, I couldn't
keep her away."

"And I rather thought she'd come to see—er—
Pearl, was it?" Patrick murmured sardonically. "Yes, I
think the girl's name was Pearl."

"Oh, that don't signify! Told you—m'gel's got a soft
heart, that's all. Besides, who's to say it wasn't you as
drew her down there? Mebbe she was a-wanting to see
you a bit closer, eh?" Rand winked. " 'Tis a handsome
buck you are, Hamilton, and you got to know it."

"As a general rule I regard work and pleasure
rather like oil and water," Patrick said.

"And you don't mix 'em. Aye, but you've seen my
gel, and you will, eh? Good, good. Look forward to
it." Rising with an effort, the old man held out his
hand again. "See you about eight—or later, if you was
to wish it. Damme if Emma and Ellie won't be pleased
when I tell 'em you are coming, sir."

As tired as he was, as little as he relished the prospect of dressing again for dinner, Patrick considered
the girl and relented. "Then eight it is, sir."

"Good. I can promise you a fine dinner, too. I got
a Frenchy cook by the name of Jacques Millet as was
in Napoleon's own kitchen once. Why, you won't
know but what you are eating like a royal duke, I swear
it." His business concluded, Rand started for the door,
then turned back briefly. "My gel's going to be in Alt,
sir—Alt," he predicted.

After the old man left, Patrick settled back in his
chair and contemplated his half-filled glass. Earlier

he'd dismissed any hope of ever seeing the fair Elise again, but given a freak circumstance of chance, he was now going to dine with her. Not that he could have any real interest in that quarter, he reminded himself, for no matter how wealthy her father, he couldn't afford to ally himself with a female of inferior social standing.

"Mr. Hamilton—sir?"

Patrick looked up. "What is it, John?"

"Mr. Johnson declined to wait, sir—said he'd be 'round tomorrow, and he wouldn't talk with Mr. Banks either, saying he needed someone who could conduct a defense before the bench. I collect it is something concerning his brother's arrest for larceny—it seems he was a footman caught inside Lord Brompton's house in possession of a piece of Lady Brompton's jewelry."

"If he was caught in the act, about all I can do is plead him," Patrick decided.

"Mr. Johnson was hopeful that perhaps you could get him transported. Otherwise, he is very much afraid his brother will hang."

"I'd say it is a certainty he will."

The clerk cleared his throat. "He says his brother was wrongfully discharged for dallying with the lady. The brooch in question was supposed to be a parting gift from her."

"Ah, now that could make the difference. I doubt Brompton will wish to chance washing his linen in court. I suppose," Patrick mused, "I could suggest to Peale that it is in everyone's interest to avoid embarrassing Brompton."

The young man cleared his throat again. "And Mr. Johnson was wishful of knowing if you could be paid later, sir. I did suggest that he visit the cent per cents, but I am not at all certain he can afford a moneylender."

Patrick drummed his fingers on the folder containing Bartholomew Rand's money. Finally, he sighed. "When Mr. Johnson returns, you may inform him that I shall speak to Mr. Peale, and if it can be arranged between us, I will plead for his brother." He stared unseeing for a moment, then sighed again. "God grant that Mr. Justice Tate sits on that one; otherwise, if it should be Russell, Johnson can count his brother as good as hanged already."

"Oh?"

"Last session he sentenced a twelve-year-old boy to the gallows over a bucket of paint," Patrick recalled dryly. "Anything else?"

"Mr. Banks finished researching Lord Pender's case, sir, and has prepared a summary for you."

"Did he include the depositions?"

"Yes." Byrne hesitated, then blurted out, "I have read them, and I think Mr. Thirske perjures himself. What he told Mr. Banks yesterday does not at all agree with what he said to the magistrate."

"One day, John, you are going to practice before the bar," Patrick predicted.

"Thank you, sir."

"I don't suppose you have seen the *Gazette,* have you?"

"I put it in your drawer."

Leaning over the desk, Patrick found the paper. "Ah, yes. That will be all for the moment." He unfolded the newspaper and scanned the front page for the previous day's account of the Coates's trial. It wouldn't show that she'd been acquitted, but it would still provide diversion from the usual announcements and scarce-veiled *on dits.*

To his disgust, there was nothing of interest beyond the lurid account of another murder, once again a prostitute, judging by the reference to "the soiled dove." He read on, drawn in by the writer's clever mix of righteous indignation and condemnation. "The poor unfortunate," one Fanny Shawe, had apparently fallen victim to a dissatisfied client, resulting in a vicious attack that left her dead, her body dumped into the Serpentine. She'd apparently attempted to fight, for no fewer than fifteen slashes to her arms and face had been counted. Either that, or her killer had vented a great deal of fury upon her body.

"One more thing, sir," John Byrnes murmured apologetically from the door.

"Yes?"

"I almost forgot—Lord Leighton stopped by to see you."

"On business?"

"No. He wished me to tell you that Lady Townsend is supremely happy."

"I know—she wrote me also."

Byrnes's gaze dropped to the *Gazette*. "Shocking business—that poor girl, I mean."

"Yes."

"He seems to like the river, doesn't he? The killer, I mean."

Patrick refolded the paper and set it on a corner of the desk. "It almost reminds me of the Peg Parker thing, but in that case, there was little struggle."

"Third girl to be discovered in the Serpentine this year," Byrnes remembered. "Except for the suicides, that is." When Patrick said nothing, he added, "You'd think they—those girls—would be more careful, wouldn't you?"

"A hazard of the profession."

"I suppose." Byrnes sighed. "Well, in any event, I'm off—unless you need me, of course."

"No, not at all. I'll walk out with you. We shall leave Mr. Banks to toil alone, poor fellow."

"Oh, I think he likes being shut up with the books, sir."

"And you, John—what do you like?" Patrick wondered.

"I should wish to be precisely what you are," the clerk answered without hesitation.

Patrick heaved his tired body up from his chair and twisted his head to ease his aching neck. He could hear the vertebrae in his neck pop beneath the back of his stiffened cravat. His eyes were almost dry from lack of sleep, telling him he ought to be going home to bed. Instead, he was looking forward to seeing a

Cit's daughter, who was probably possessed of more hair than wit.

Aloud, he said, "You'd best lock the door—Henry can let himself out when he wishes, but I doubt he will want to speak with anyone who should wander in."

" 'Tis a wonder he does not go blind from preparing papers, sir."

"Being a solicitor is a good, solid profession," Patrick reminded the clerk.

"I should still wish to be a barrister." Retrieving the office door key from a coat pocket, John Byrnes waited for him to step outside. "A man cannot burn both ends of the candle forever," he observed as Patrick passed him. "Though you and Mr. Banks seem to think so."

"Two more weeks, John—two more weeks," Patrick promised, "and then I shall enjoy hunting grouse with Lord Dunster in Scotland."

"And upon your return, I expect we shall be wishing you happy," the younger man said matter-of-factly.

"Where did you hear that?"

"Everywhere—'tis common gossip in the Bailey, sir." The clerk grinned. "I've got ten quid on it myself." He looked up, his expression sobering suddenly. "But if you do not mind my saying it, sir, I should think it a shame if you ceased the practice of law."

"Actually, I have been thinking of standing for Parliament."

"I know. There's wagers on that also, sir," Brynes acknowledged. "But I still think it wrong for you to be anywhere other than arguing in the Bailey."

"I shall take that under advisement," Patrick murmured dryly.

"I hope so," the clerk declared sincerely. "I truly hope so."

"Reading again, Puss? It ain't nothin' to do with Holy Hannah, is it?" he asked suspiciously. "Ought to be like other females—readin' novels and that fellow Byron."

Elise Rand looked up guiltily. Her father stood in the doorway, a nearly empty glass in his hand. One glance at his florid color told her that he'd already imbibed more than he ought.

"But you don't like Byron," she reminded him mildly.

"Don't like his politics, that's all."

"You called him a faithless libertine, I believe," she added, smiling.

"So what's that?" he demanded abruptly.

She sighed. "I am caught out, I'm afraid. It is *The Christian Observer.*"

"Methodist pap!" he snorted.

"Not entirely," she responded mildly. "Mr. Wilberforce not only has supported the abolition of slavery, but he has also wished for the emancipation of Catholics."

"And Catholics is Papist fools! As for Wilberforce, he ought to keep his Methodism out of Parliament! He's naught but an infernal meddler, I tell you! Next thing he'll be wanting is women in politics!"

"They are already there, Papa."

"You know my meaning, Puss—no need to be roundabout with me! I was meaning the next thing you know he'll be wanting 'em to vote!"

"Is that such a bad notion, Papa?" she asked, feigning innocence.

"Eve was made to serve Adam!"

It was no use provoking further argument with him, and she knew it. He had little use for any sort of reform at all. "I am only reading what the man has to say, Papa."

"Aye, and afore long you'll be wantin' to go to the demned meetings, won't you?"

"I have already heard Mrs. More and Mr. Wilberforce speak, and while I tend to agree with them, I am well aware you would threaten to disown me if I actually joined them. And," she added impishly, "I have not heard either of them suggest that females ought to vote—though I cannot think it would not be a good notion."

"What? Now you see here, missy! You'll not—" He caught himself and peered suspiciously at her. "Humph! Well, I collect you was funning with your papa, wasn't you?"

"Yes."

Somewhat mollified, he muttered, "Well, you ain't going to any demned meetings, gel—see as you don't forget that." He drank from his glass, then regarded her almost soberly for a long moment. "What was you thinking of today, anyway?"

She knew he meant the scene in the Sessions House courtroom, but decided to feign ignorance. "Today?"

"Sly puss, ain't you?" He walked closer, until he stood over her. "You ain't got no business with the Coates woman."

"But did you not see the condition of Pearl—of the thin girl with her? Papa, I think she has consumption!"

"It ain't none of your affair, Puss."

"But that woman will not seek medical attention for her," she argued. "It doesn't mean anything to Mrs. Coates if Pearl should die—no doubt she will merely go to the poorhouses and buy another girl to sell for a few shillings to the tumble."

"Puss!" he remonstrated sharply. "You ain't supposed to say that sort of thing! And where in the deuce did you meet that sort of female?"

"What difference does it make?" she countered, unrepentant. "And I've heard you say something very like that."

"I want you to talk like a lady, that's the difference—and don't you be forgetting it. Now—where did you meet the tart? I ain't asking but once!"

Her chin came up and her bright blue eyes met his. "I was handing out leaflets in Covent Garden, if you must know." As his color darkened ominously, she decided to appeal to his conscience. "Papa, she buys those girls! It is as though they are slaves!"

"Shows what you know of it!" he snorted. "If they wasn't there, they'd not eat, Elise. You think they'd be better begging in the opium dens?"

"Surely you do not condone the practice of—of selling female flesh to—to the worst of men!" she sputtered.

"Course I don't condone it! Now, damme, you are putting words in m'mouth! But there's been bits of fluff since the Garden of Eden!"

"Where? 'Twas only Adam and Eve then, Papa."

When it came to matters of religion, he knew he was on decidedly shaky ground. "You was knowing my meaning, Puss," he muttered defensively.

"Have you ever been to a brothel, Papa?" she asked him directly.

"Course not," he lied. "But that ain't to say as they don't serve a purpose."

"I'd like to know what it is—besides pandering to the worst sort of perversion."

"It ain't your affair," he reminded her testily. "There—must be the third time I've said it, and that's the end!" Reaching out with his free hand, he snatched the paper from her lap, then flung it into the fireplace, where it was quickly consumed by the flames. "A pox on Hannah More, on Wilberforce—aye, and on the tarts also! A man's got a right to peace in his own house—and don't you be forgetting it, missy."

"But I cannot—"

"And you ain't bringing one of 'em here to reform neither, that's all there is to the matter. I still ain't forgot as how I had to pay off that chimney sweep's master afore you was arrested," he recalled with feeling. "As though I wanted the little heathen underfoot."

"And he is in Mrs. More's school, which is where he belongs. Surely you would not wish him to die of soot sores, would you?" she countered reasonably.

"Don't want to hear of it," he muttered. "Just don't bring me anything else, or I shall deliver it back to its rightful master—or mistress, as the case may be."

"You would not."

"Aye, I would." He stared down into her upturned face, then looked away as his manner changed. "Aye, you are a good girl, Ellie—the joy of m'life. Aye, a good girl," he repeated almost soberly. "But you've too kind a heart. You ought to be worrying about a house and husband instead of the riffraff."

"I thought Mama was the joy of your life," she reminded him. "I am the bane, as you will recall."

"Never said it."

"In the carriage today."

"Was vexed with you, that's all. Always wanting to do good instead of what you was made to do. A female is meant to be married, you know. You are two and twenty, Puss—if you was a nob, they'd be a-calling you an ape-leader ere now."

"But I am not a nob, am I? I don't have to pretend as though I know nothing of the world around me—and I don't have to waste my time doing nothing."

"With my money, Puss, I could have made you a lady. There was Sir Richard Hanford—or Darlington even."

"There was Ben."

"Aye, but—" He glimpsed the pain in her eyes and backed off. "The boy's dead, Ellie," he said gruffly. "Ain't anything as I can do about that." He touched his scratched jawline gingerly. "London streets ain't safe for anyone."

"And after what happened to Ben, I find it a wonder you venture out at night."

"Know where to go, that's all."

"And thrice you have been robbed this year."

"Aye." He shook his head as though to clear it, then remembered his original purpose. "I ain't speaking of the dead, Puss. I've been patient—gave you time to mourn the boy, didn't I?"

"I don't think I want to speak of this," she decided.

"Two years I've let you grieve yourself into a reforming Methodist, and I ain't said a word," he went on.

"You've said a great deal—and I am not a Methodist," she retorted.

"Beginning to think like one—always reading their trash, ain't you? First you was enamored of the demned Jews, and now 'tis the More woman, ain't it?"

They were back to Ben, and she knew it. "I could have wed him, Papa, but you wanted me to wait."

"The boy wasn't like us, Ellie."

"He was kind and caring—and he loved me."

"That's not what I meant, and well you know it. I meant they wasn't Christians."

"And we go to services so very often, don't we? 'Church is for matchin', hatchin', and dispatchin',' you were wont to say. If I was to become one of Hannah's converts, I doubt you would know of it, for you would never be there. But I have not, so you need not worry."

He was oversetting her now, and yet he could not stop. "I didn't say as you couldn't wed him, did I? I told him he could have you, as sorry as I was about it."

"What difference does it make now?" she wanted to cry. "You found something wrong with every wedding date until it was too late! You waited until Ben was dead before you even said one good thing about him!"

"The Roses wasn't happy about you, neither," he muttered. "Sam and I was agreed as you should wait." When she didn't argue, he went on, "And I've been sorry ever since the boy was killed. But what's done is done, ain't it? I ain't got no control over the thieves as prowls the streets, do I? Look—you are alive, Ellie. You got to forget—you got to." He looked away to avoid the reproach in her eyes. "Now I got this fellow as is coming over, and I'd like you to be nice to him. Oh, I ain't expecting as you'll throw your cap over the windmill for him, but—"

"There is not the least chance."

Moving behind her, he dropped an awkward hand to her hair. "You always was a beauty, Ellie—always. Even when you was a little chit, you was. There was people as would stop on the street to stare at you."

"As though I were an exhibit at the Tower."

He knew he'd already bungled the matter badly, but once he'd opened his budget, he was willing to gamble a bit. "I've hopes you'll take a liking to this fellow," he said, his voice coaxing.

She stared at him, disbelieving her ears, then she shook her head. "Papa, I cannot."

"Aye, you can. Dash it, but he's good *ton*—moves in the first circles, don't you know? Got enough money to keep you in first style, too."

"I am a Cit, and I am proud enough of it."

"Ellie—Ellie—" His own voice lowered, and his hand tightened on her shoulder. "You are my pride. My only issue, Ellie, but I ain't sorry for that. Oh, I wished you was a son when you was born, but once you began to grow, I quit repining, I swear it. And I ain't blamed your mama for it neither. I was always proud enough that she was born Quality, that I could say Bat Rand got himself a gentlewoman."

Releasing her, he went to the desk and drew out the bottle he kept there. Pulling the cork with his teeth, he opened it and unsteadily poured port into his glass. It overflowed, spilling, spreading a dark red stain on the carpet. He downed half a glass in one gulp, then refilled it. Turning back to her, he blinked as though to clear his mind.

"Now, where was we?"

"Mama was a gentlewoman." Even as she said it, she relented. For all that they'd never seen eye to eye on Ben, she still loved her oft irascible parent. She smiled and shook her head. "You are coming in the back door, aren't you? You want me to feel guilty enough to encourage this man, don't you?"

He appeared wounded for a moment, then he grinned. "Always was a downy one, wasn't you? If you *had* been a boy, we'd a ruled the biggest fortune as London has seen, wouldn't we?"

"But you are halfway there without me," she reminded him.

"All right—all right." He lifted his hand, then let it fall. "You caught me out."

"It wasn't very difficult."

"I need him, Puss."

"Who?"

He tossed off the remainer of his port and turned to find his bottle again. His back to her, he mumbled something unintelligible.

"Papa, you are more than half-foxed."

He swung around at that, sloshing more wine onto the floor. "I want you to be nice to him, and that's all. You just got to do the pretty for 'im! You know— wear the fancy gown, put up your hair—and—" He groped for a word and did not find it. "Well, you are a female, ain't you? Play over the fan with 'im."

"Papa, I will not!"

"Hamilton—"

"The Scottish peer?" She choked. "He must be fifty—and he's a stranger to me!"

"Lud, no! Fellow you saw this morning." He blinked again, then turned his attention to his wine. As the port dribbled down his chin onto his waistcoat, he drank greedily, emptying the glass again. He sat it on the edge of a table, where it teetered, then fell onto the carpet. Wiping his chin with his coat sleeve, he ignored it. "I want him, Puss—man's the best demned barrister in London—best to be had anywheres."

"Oh—*Patrick Hamilton*." For a moment, she recalled the man who'd defended the awful Coates woman. "Papa—"

"The man's but nine and twenty—I made my inquiries—and he don't even have a lightskirt. You ought to like that."

"Papa, I don't—"

"Told you—you just got to encourage him a bit,

that's all," he mumbled evasively. "But I wouldn't take it amiss if you *was* to set your cap for him, Ellie—I don't deny it."

"You *are* foxed, Papa—utterly foxed," she decided, disgusted.

"Just a few glasses of wine, Puss—the nobs, they drink the clock around, you know."

"You are not a nob. And neither am I."

"Your mama—"

"Mama was a parson's daughter," she reminded him. "She never claimed—"

"She was gentle-born, and don't you ever forget it! Oh, the Binghams wasn't titled, but they was landed gentry," he maintained stubbornly.

"Grandpapa Bingham—"

"Was a younger son," he finished for her. "And poor as a mouse in his church, but that don't take anything from your mama, you hear me?" When she didn't answer, his anger faded, but the mulish set to his chin remained. "The old gent made me wait until I was fixed well enough to provide for her, too, I can tell you. Bartholomew Rand wasn't good enough for Miss Emmaline Bingham until he could settle five hundred pounds on her," he recalled. "As if the Reverend Bingham had so much as one fifth that in his living," he added resentfully.

"Whether she was Quality or not doesn't signify," Elise said finally. "All that matters is Mama has always been a lady, titled or not."

"Aye, but she was gentry," he insisted. "The old gent's papa had land in Hertfordshire and tenants as farmed it for him. What was wrong with the reverend was that he had the ill luck to be born down the line a bit, that's all."

She could only recall a couple of visits to her grandfather's rectory, so it scarce seemed worth discussing. Besides, she'd knew it never changed anything to argue with him when he was in his cups. "Mama was gentry," she murmured, acquiescing.

"Aye. Even if Old Bat here ain't what you'd want for a papa, you got good blood on one side."

"No, I have the best from both sides, Papa."

For a moment he eyed her suspiciously, then his face broke into a pleased smile. "You mean it, don't you?"

"Yes."

"Now, where was we?" he asked again. "Oh—Hamilton—I got him coming to look at you. You got a pretty face—beautiful even—I got hopes—" His brow furrowed as he tried to remember his purpose.

"If he is born to the gentry, I daresay he's not looking for a Cit's daughter, Papa. And I assure you I should not want him if he were."

"Handsome devil," he argued.

"Unprincipled," she shot back. "He defended Mrs. Coates, lest you forget it."

"Jury said she was innocent."

"Of murder only! What could you possibly want with Patrick Hamilton, Papa?"

But he wasn't listening to her. As though she'd not asked, he went on, "I got you—and I got more'n a hundred thousand quid to interest 'im. Why, there's royal dukes as would make bricks for that." He swept the room with bleary eyes before returning his attention to her. "There's high-born nobs as ain't got what I got. And I made it all by myself—I wasn't born to it." Once again, he laid his hand on her shoulder. "Got to impress Hamilton, that's all," he mumbled.

This time she reached to clasp his hand. "I know you wish the best for me, Papa," she said. "And I know you love me. But if you are in some sort of difficulty—"

"Aye, you love the old man, don't you?" he asked, his voice thickening.

"Yes."

"You're m'blood, Ellie—you got me in you." His fingers tightened around hers, holding them, while his free hand stroked her hair. "Pretty little gel—pretty little gel," he crooned.

"But, Papa, about Mr. Hamilton—I don't see why you cannot merely engage him. I don't see why I—"

"Got m'heart set on him."

"But I don't want anyone but Ben," she told him desperately. "I don't want anyone."

"All you got to do is try, Puss—for your papa, you got to try."

"Papa, *are* you in some sort of trouble?" she asked directly.

"No—but that don't say I couldn't be."

"Enough to need a criminal lawyer?"

"Told you—a man never knows—well, sometime I might be."

"But not now?"

"I ain't saying."

"You know you are already more than half-disguised, don't you?"

"No, I ain't—scarce got started—"

"You are—and if you'd have my opinion of it, you are better advised to send a note 'round, saying you are unwell. He won't think much of you if you have drunk yourself into a stupor, will he?"

"Just a little port, Ellie—just a little port. Good medicine, that's all." His hand caught her arm, pulling her against him. "Come on—give your papa a squeeze, eh?" She seemed to hesitate, then she laid her head against his chest and slid her arms to hold him. He smoothed her hair, then patted her arm. "My girl," he said softly. His other hand rested on her crown for a moment, then he let his arm fall to his side. "Might not always be here, you know."

She ducked away, then bent to pick up the paper that had slid off her lap. She sighed. "I have the distinct feeling I am being bamboozled."

"Course not." Pleased that he'd apparently won, he added, "You are a good gel, Puss. Aye, a good gel, but you got to get this reforming nonsense out of your head, that's all." Moving away again, he found his nearly empty bottle. "Not enough for a demned mouse," he mumbled more to himself than to her. With that, he walked unsteadily from the room.

She sat very still, wondering what had caused this latest queer start of his. For the past several months, no more than six at most, he'd begun drinking more, acting more unpredictably. Twice he'd had to be brought home by the watch, and once he'd managed to make it home unaided after being robbed and beaten. Still he would go out to crawl his pubs alone, insisting he could fend for himself, that he knew how to take care of himself. And it did no good to remind him that Ben's throat had been slit, for he'd had such contempt for kind, gentle Ben. He'd point to his own scars and scratches and say he'd at least fought to keep his purse.

No, she still could not think of Ben without wishing to cry. Determined not to give in to yet another bout of blue devils, she forced him from her mind, then rose and made her way upstairs.

Molly, her maid, awaited her. "Ye'd best hurry, miss—yer papa says ye're to be down to dine by half after seven," the girl chided her. "And how I am to do it, I'm sure I don't know," she added, shaking her head. " 'Heat the tongs,' he says, 'and see as she wears her best.' "

Rather than throw herself at a man like Hamilton, Elise considered begging off with a coward's headache, but she knew her father, no matter how drunk, would not stand for it. If he could yet stand unaided, he'd come up and get her. Whenever he got any maggot in his brain, he tended to become obsessed with it.

"Perhaps the peach muslin will do," she mused half to herself.

" 'Silk,' he told me, 'see as she wears silk,' " the maid insisted. "I thought p'rhaps yer blue one—the one as has the sars'net shawl over it, don't ye think?" But as she spoke, the girl eyed Elise speculatively. "Aye—ye got to show a bit of yer shoulders," she decided. "Ye got lovely shoulders." Moving past her mistress, she reached into the wardrobe, drew out the gown, and held it up. "Makes yer eyes as blue as the sky, don't it?"

Elise eyed the dress skeptically. "Molly, it is far too grand for dinner at home. It looks like something I should wear to the opera."

"The master said—"

"I know what he said, but—"

"Shows yer neck to advantage also," the girl declared. "With yer mama's sapphires—"

"I think it shows a great deal more than my neck—and if I wear anything with it, it will be my own pearls."

"Yer papa—"

"Molly, I have no wish to flaunt my person or papa's gold before a stranger in my own house."

"But it does become ye—the gown, I mean," the maid reminded her. "And we got to hurry, ye know. Like I said, the tongs is hot, and we ain't got time to tarry. Now, if you was to sit down, I can do yer hair right proper. But ye got to get out of that, so's we don't muss what we've done."

Telling herself there was no reason to rip up at Molly for doing what she'd been told, Elise removed her day dress and sat before her dressing table. As the girl began brushing the tangles from the thick, red-gold hair, she stared at her reflection in the mirror. "What else did Papa say?" she asked casually.

"That he wants ye to make a grand impression on the gentleman," the girl answered, giggling. "Said he was right handsome—the gentleman, that is."

"He's a barrister, which ought to tell you he's not a gentleman. Most of them merely twist the law this way and that for a price."

"Well, it don't make any difference what he is—'tis time and enough for ye to be thinking of a mister."

"I am content enough to be an ape-leader, I assure you."

The maid rolled a section of hair around the hot iron and held it, counting silently. As she released it, she declared, "Woman wasn't made to live alone."

"Did Papa say that also?"

"No, but 'tis God's truth, ain't it?"

"You forget I was betrothed to Benjamin Rose."

"Aye, and a pity it was," the girl clucked sympathetically. "I shed a tear for ye, I did. And then when he—" She caught herself guiltily. "Well, I wouldn't wish anyone dead, even if he wasn't right for ye."

"Molly, I don't mean to listen to it," Elise warned her.

"Well, it don't make any difference now, does it?" the maid countered. "Seems as God did the choosin', I'd say."

"Ben Rose was the kindest man I have ever known."

"Aye," she agreed. "He was that, I suppose. And patient enough to wait for yer papa to set the date, wasn't he?"

"He respected Papa—for all that they were different, he respected him."

"Well, if he was wanting to wed ye, he oughter have taken ye to Gretna," the girl declared, sniffing. "Been right romantic, wouldn't it a-been?"

"Ben was not that sort of man, and well you know it. He would never have embroiled me in a scandal."

Molly sensed the wistfulness in her mistress's voice and forbore saying anything more. But privately she thought Benjamin Rose had been too kind for his own good. He probably hadn't even put up a fight when the cutpurses had killed him.

As the girl continued to work quickly, taking first one piece of hair, then another, making a riot of reddish-gold curls, Elise forced her thoughts away from Ben to her father. As much as she loved him, she felt resentment that he could expect her to cast out lures to anyone, and especially to a stranger she expected to dislike. Her gaze met her own in the mirror, reproaching her. He seldom asked for much from her, she had to admit, and for some reason, an association with Patrick Hamilton was exceedingly important to him. But why?

The maid picked up the brush again and pulled the curls back from Elise's face. "Yer pardon—it ain't right for me t'be impertinent, is it?"

"Since when? Molly, you have always been impertinent."

"Aye, but ye like the way I do yer hair, don't ye?" Molly countered, working to pin Elise's hair at her crown. Deftly, she freed a few wispy tendrils to frame the oval face. "Well?"

"Always."

"Aye, I got a something to work with," the maid

went on. "My sister Bess, the one as is a lady's maid to the Misses Banks, well, she's allus complaining. Ain't one of 'em as don't have something wrong with 'em. The oldest one's got bad teeth, the middle one's got straw fer hair, and the youngest one's throwing spots. Ain't nothing she can do for 'em, she says." Picking up a strand of pearls from a silk-lined box, she began threading them through the crown of blond curls. "Me—I got you, miss. If ye'd go about more, I'd be set to work for anyone—why, they'd be a-throwing the gold at me to make me leave ye." She stepped back to survey her handiwork and smiled happily. "There—we done it, miss—just look at ye."

The girl in the mirror seemed a stranger, a lovely, distant stranger. Behind her, Molly reached for the rouge pot and haresfoot, and as Elise watched, she gave the appearance of life to the stranger. The maid viewed the mirror critically for a moment, then dipped her fingertip first into a small container of hair pomade, followed by the rouge pot. With great care, she reddened Elise's lips. The girl in the mirror frowned.

"Just a wee bit of color—ye want Mr. Hamilton to think ye got blood a-flowing through ye, don't ye?" Molly said, wiping her hand on a cloth.

Elise made a face at herself. "I look like a Cyprian."

"No, ye look lovely. If he ain't at yer feet, I ain't Molly Woodson. Now all we got to do is dress ye."

As the maid moved to shake out the blue dress, Elise stood. Stepping behind her, Molly carefully eased the gown over her head and waited for her mistress to thrust her arms into the sleeves. Then she pulled the shimmering silk down over the slim hips, smoothing it as it fell.

"Now for the shawl," Molly murmured, enveloping her in the thin silk. "But ye got to drape it just so— aye, like this, I think." Catching a glance at Elise in the mirror, the maid declared happily, "If you ain't a vision, I don't know what is, miss. I'll get yer pearls."

But Elise stood still as a statue, staring at herself. *I don't wish to do this,* she thought almost desperately. *I don't want to flirt with anyone again—not now—not ever.*

Patrick mounted the steps of Bartholomew Rand's impressive Marylebone mansion with an almost eager anticipation. For much of the afternoon, his thoughts had turned far too often to Elise Rand, and now he would have the opportunity to see her again, to discover if she was even half as lovely as he'd thought her.

It didn't matter if she was, he told himself, for there was no room in his life for a Cit's daughter, not when he'd all but tipped his hand to Dunster, and the earl expected his imminent offer for Jane.

Now if Elise Rand were a widow or a bored wife, and if there was not the matter of dancing attendance upon Lady Jane, he could envision a definite affair in that quarter. But she was neither, and the mushrooms within the middle class tended to demand more than a slip of the shoulder, particularly when the female in question was possessed of an immense fortune. Unmarried women of wealth, he reflected regretfully, rarely succumbed to any offer short of a wedding ring.

A stiff, correct butler came to the door, looked him over discreetly, then stood back to admit him into a wide, marble-tiled foyer that seemed almost as cavernous as something designed by the Prince Regent. It was dominated by a huge double staircase, and the whole was illuminated by a chandelier worthy of an opera house. He looked around him, torn between awe and contempt for such an obvious display of the old man's money.

The butler cleared his throat, and when Patrick's attention returned to him, he gestured politely for the barrister's hat and cloak. "None of the family is yet down," he announced, "but I am to direct you to the front saloon. Shall I send a footman to attend you, sir?"

"No—I don't need anything."

Patrick started toward the saloon, then stopped to take one last look at the grandness Rand's bricks had bought. Above him, a slightly husky female voice told someone, "I don't care—I won't toadeat Mr. Hamilton, no matter what Papa says. I've no wish to even meet him. After all, he defended that awful brothel keeper when she ought to have been hanged."

"Elise!" another woman complained. "Oh, how I wish Bat would not speak so plainly before you. Gently bred females don't know of such things."

"Fiddle, Mama. Why must we pretend to be fools to please some silly notion of propriety? It is outside of enough that we always have to find clever ways of speaking when it is a given that we are speaking of harlots. At least Papa calls them the whores that they are."

"Elise, if you go on like this when Mr. Hamilton arrives, I vow I shall have need of my salts."

"Fiddle, Mama. Why should you care what Mrs. Coates's barrister thinks of us?"

"Mr. Hamilton is connected to the dukes of Hamilton, dearest," the other woman reminded her. "And if you are uncivil, your papa will blame me for it, when in truth the fault is his. If he would not—"

"By now, I doubt Papa will blame anyone for anything," the girl retorted. "It would surprise me if he were able to come down."

"You are out of reason cross tonight," her mother chided.

"With reason, Mama," Elise Rand countered. "I am dressed like the veriest Cyprian to meet a man in whom I have not the least interest. Where *is* Papa, by the by?"

"Simpson is making him presentable."

"I don't envy him the task."

"How can you say such a thing?" the woman protested.

"Because when last seen, my father was well into the wind and still had a bottle in his hand," came the exasperated reply.

"Elise!"

"Well, 'tis the truth. And one of us is going to have to tell him he drinks too much ere he is in his grave."

There was a nervous titter, followed by, "Well, in any event, I expect we'd best not wait for Bat, lest Mr. Hamilton should arrive and think us inhospitable."

As Patrick looked up, the two women reached the top of the stairs. When the younger one started down, he could only stare again, and for a moment, his breath caught in his throat. His earlier brief glimpse of her, haunting as it was, had not nearly done her justice.

As she took each step, the tips of her blue satin slippers could be seen beneath the skirt of her blue gown. His gaze moved upward slowly, noting her slender figure, her graceful carriage, her nearly perfect face. And again, her brilliant blue eyes were utterly arresting. When she inclined her head slightly, her red-gold hair shone as though it reflected the light from the hundred candles above. No, he'd not been mistaken at all—the girl was truly a Diamond of the First Water, an Incomparable absolutely worthy of the epithet.

She saw him and was for a moment nonplussed. Her face flushed becomingly, then she murmured wryly, "Oh, dear," followed by, "my wretched tongue—you heard everything, didn't you?"

He ought to play the gentleman and deny it, but he nodded. "Yes." Then, flashing his most devastating smile, he declared, "But I assure you I am perfectly willing to be toadeaten."

Instead of covering her face demurely with her fan, she looked him up and down nearly as boldly as he had her. "Well, at least you do not lie overmuch," she said finally.

"Alas, but I am a barrister and therefore prize the truth," he countered.

She inclined her head slightly, then a faint smile formed at the corner of her mouth. "Ah, yes, but then we must remember Shakespeare's opinion on the worth of lawyers, I think."

"I cannot say he held them in much esteem," he admitted cheerfully. "I should hope that you do not already wish me dead on such short acquaintance."

"No, of course not. Actually, I don't wish you anything."

"Except at Jericho?"

Her smile widened, warming those eyes. "As you are already here, I doubt it would do any good to wish you there, would it?"

"I shall try to take that for encouragement," he murmured.

"Please don't—I assure you it was not meant to be."

"Are you always so frank, Miss Rand?"

"Not always, sir—only when the occasion demands it."

She came the rest of the way down, while her mother hovered somewhat anxiously behind her. "Really, Mr. Hamilton, but I cannot think what you must—"

"Mama, there is no need for dissembling now—Mr. Hamilton has already overheard my worst." Stepping off the last step, Elise met his gaze steadily. "But I suppose I ought to beg your pardon for at least *some* of it."

"About your opinion of my client—or about your refusal to throw yourself at my head?" he asked lightly.

"Should I have called her a purveyor of flesh instead? Or perhaps a manager of impure wares?" she riposted, ignoring the second half of his question.

"Well, actually no matter what you choose to call her, Miss Rand—as an English citizen she has a right to be defended in a court of law."

"With such feeling?"

"One must persuade a jury, after all."

She sighed. "I suppose I ought to know better than

to fence words with a barrister, shouldn't I? Very well—shall I offer you a bargain?"

"Cry friends?" he suggested.

Again, a smile played at the corners of her mouth. "No. The most I am prepared for is civility."

"Really, Elise—" Mrs. Rand protested weakly. "What Mr. Hamilton is to think—that is, sir, you must forgive her—but Bat—my husband, that is—has always encouraged her—" She hesitated, then looked anxiously upward. "Well, there has always been an easy discourse between them, I'm afraid."

"Until Ben, Mama." Looking at Patrick again, Elise explained, "What she means, Mr. Hamilton, is that when it suits him, Papa treats me like a son—otherwise, he bullocks me shamelessly, which is how he treats most females." Elise cast another sidewise glance at her mother. "That is what you wished to say, isn't it?"

"Not precisely," the woman said weakly.

It was Patrick's turn to smile. "And what do I contribute to your bargain, Miss Rand?"

"You don't stare—and you don't make bad poetry of my eyes or my hair. Nor do you flirt, sir."

"You make it sound like a common dinner-table occurrence."

"Common enough that I never wear sapphires anymore, I'm afraid." The corners of her mouth twitched. "My hair, however, usually defeats them—one of Papa's clerks wrote of my 'rose-gold halo,' which was a great deal of nonsense. There is nothing angelic about me, you see."

"And for my restraint, what shall I get in return?" he inquired softly.

"The civility I have already mentioned."

"Mr. Hamilton, I don't know what to say," her mother tried again. "Usually she is possessed of manners. Indeed, but I have never—"

"We have never had Mrs. Coates's lawyer here before," Elise finished for her.

Studying the girl before him, thinking that the slight huskiness of her voice made him think of a great deal more than her eyes and hair, he murmured regretfully, "And I had such hopes of being toadeaten."

"Not before pigs fly, sir."

"Very well, then." He held out his hand as he would to a man, daring her to take it. "As much as I am distressed by the message, I must admire your candor, Miss Rand."

Elise hesitated, then nodded. Reaching out, she clasped his warm fingers, shaking them. "Done."

At that moment, Bartholomew Rand appeared above them, and his voice boomed downward. "You are already met with my family, I see! Well, sirrah—no need to stand on ceremony, is there?" he demanded heartily. He started downward, negotiating each step unsteadily. It was obvious that he was drunk.

"Think I got a pretty little gel, don't you, Hamilton?" he said, his voice thick, his words slightly slurred.

As Elise Rand flushed, Patrick answered, "A true Toast, I'd say."

Mrs. Rand, torn between decorum and potential disaster, hurried up the stairs to meet her husband. Possessing one of his arms, she tried to steady him, saying, "Put your hand on the rail, Bat."

"Don't need it! Ain't an invalid, Em!" He shook loose, nearly missed a step, and caught the banister with both hands, muttering, "Don't know why the females in m'family don't think I can hold m'wine."

One foot caught an edge, and he pitched forward. As his wife watched helplessly, he slid down several steps. Patrick ran upward to catch him, and as Rand fell into his arms, the old man blinked up at him. "Gout—got the demned gout," he insisted. "Knee gave out."

Mortified, Mrs. Rand cast a stricken look at Patrick. "Please, sir—he is unwell. Elise, call a footman to help."

"Help me where?" Rand demanded. "Damme if you will! Got company—Hamilton's here, ain't he?"

"Papa!"

There was no mistaking the reproof in the girl's

voice. Her father seemed to collect himself, drawing his portly body erect with an effort. "Wouldn't disgrace you, Puss—swear it." Once again, he looked at Patrick. "Females—surrounded by 'em sir." Then, still trying to recover his dignity, he spoke slowly, carefully, attempting to control his uncooperative tongue. "Got to present m'daughter—Miss Rand. Puss, come do the pretty for Hamilton. Fellow's a lawyer—best demned barrister—"

"I know—we are already met."

"Taking little thing, ain't she?" Rand mumbled to Patrick. "Paid to make her a lady—watercolors—demned dancing fellow—had to let him go, though."

"I can see she is accomplished."

"I waltz miserably," she murmured. "Poor Mr. Tweed did not last beyond 'sapphire stars embedded within an alabaster sky,' you see," she added with a straight face.

"Ah, the turned-off dancing master."

"Yes."

"Demned fellow wished to take liberties—wrote silly verses," Rand recalled, frowning.

"Quite understandable."

"You wretch," she muttered at Patrick under her breath. "You will encourage him."

But her father's attention had turned to his wife. "Met Mrs. Rand, too, ain't you? Em—Emmaline—was a Bingham, y'know. Been reforming me for nigh to twenty-five years, ain't you, m'dear?" He blinked his eyes and shook his head again to clear his thoughts. "Why ain't we in the demned parlor, Em?"

"I am sure I don't know," Mrs. Rand answered grimly. "But if Mr. Hamilton—"

"Come on, Hamilton—got to sit down. I told Old Starch—where's Old Starch?" the old man demanded.

"Mr. Graves is behind you, Papa."

"Eh? Oh—good name for 'im, eh? Got the manner of an undertaker, don't he?" Leaning closer to Patrick, he whispered loudly, "The stiffer they are, the more y'got to pay for 'em, eh?"

Rand's wife took his arm, guiding him toward the

saloon. As she neared Patrick, she spoke low, "He usually isn't like this, I assure you."

"Ain't like what?" her husband demanded truculently.

"Foxed," Elise Rand answered for her mother.

"I ain't foxed! Tell 'em, Hamilton—tell 'em as we ain't begun to drink! I got good port—best Madeira— anything you was to want—best there is, too!"

"Allow me," Patrick offered, holding the door.

"Got Old Starch for that," Rand protested. "Pay 'im for it. The demned cook, too. Aye, the Frenchy has done himself proud, and I ain't spared a penny. 'Make me something as Boney would've liked,' I told him." Lurching away from his wife, he swept a room grand enough for one of the royal dukes with his hand. "Can't say there ain't a fortune in making bricks, eh?"

"It is impressive," Patrick acknowledged politely.

"Impressive! Five thousand pounds says it is—five thousand pounds in one demned room!" Lurching to the mantel above a blazing fire, he picked up a Sevres vase. "Humph! Useless gewgaw, ain't it?" he asked contemptuously. "'Em calls it art, sirrah—art! Only difference between art and nonsense is money, I say."

"Bat, I am sure Mr. Hamilton has no wish to know how much we have spent on anything," Mrs. Rand told him dampeningly.

"Eh?" For a moment, he seemed bewildered, then he mumbled, "Just want 'im to know I can afford what I want, Em—that's all. You ain't offended, Hamilton?"

"No," Patrick lied.

"Mr. Hamilton has come to dine, Papa, not to buy any of our furnishings," Elise said. "If you will but sit down—" She led him to a chair and held on as he sank into it. "There."

"Even the chairs is dear," the old man grumbled. Then he looked at Patrick almost sheepishly. "Aye. Going to have a good dinner, ain't we? Celebrate—" His brow furrowed deeply, then cleared as he remembered. "Got to celebrate as you got the whore off, don't we?"

"Bat—please!"

"Can say what I think in m'own house," Rand grumbled. "A whore's a whore, Em."

"Bat, I am sure Mr. Hamilton does not know what to think. Mr. Hamilton," she tried desperately, "would you care for something before dinner? Perhaps some tea . . ."

"Tea!" Rand exploded. "He'll have the port! Good God, woman! What was you thinking of? *Tea!*"

"She was thinking you've already had too much," Elise spoke up calmly. "And I daresay Mr. Hamilton thinks we are the Cits he expected."

"Ain't. Your mama—"

"Was a Bingham," she finished for him tiredly. "I know, but we are Cits, Papa, and I expect Hamilton wishes to escape our clutches already."

"Actually, I don't wish for anything of the sort," Patrick countered.

"Then I suppose you find this amusing," she decided acidly. "But Mama is quite right—he can be most charming when he is sober."

"Now where was I? Damme if you ain't made me lose—oh—the whore as got off—"

"Bat!" Now there was no mistaking the anger in Mrs. Rand's voice. "You will not speak thus before your daughter!"

"The Coates woman, then," he muttered, unrepentant. "Ain't anything I'd say as she ain't already heard from me." Nonetheless, he turned to Elise. "Was that better, Puss?" he asked her.

"Yes."

"Best there is, ain't you, Hamilton?" Rand looked to him expectantly. "Tell 'em."

Embarrassed for him, Patrick managed to say, "I have enjoyed a measure of success."

"Success!" Rand snorted. "The old whoremonger was hanged without you!"

Mercifully, the butler interrupted them, announcing, "Monsieur Millet informs me dinner is ready to be served, sir." Unable to stand unaided, Rand tried to push away from his chair, then fell back. Reaching a hand toward his daughter, he mumbled, "Got to have help, Puss. M'gout—"

Before the girl could go to her father, Patrick grasped the old man's arm and as he pulled him upward, he thrust a shoulder beneath him. They both staggered from Rand's weight, until Elise caught her father from the other side.

"I think we'd best call a footman to get him to bed, Mama."

"No! Best demned peas to be had—apricot tarts—got to feed him—got business after."

"I cannot stay overlate," Patrick demurred. "I have to be in court in the morning."

"More whores, eh?"

"Proper barristers do not discuss other people's business," Elise said dampeningly. "Come on—let's get you up to your bed."

"No—ain't going. Hamilton—knee's gone—help me to the food."

With an effort, they managed to get the old man into the dining room, where he nearly overturned his chair before they got him into it. As liveried retainers began serving, he stared glumly into his port. It wasn't until the turtle soup was placed before him that he roused. "Best demned turtles to be found anywheres. Aye, and best demned joint coming, I'll wager you on it. Best demned peas, too."

"You have already mentioned the peas, Papa."

"Oh."

"And the tarts."

"You like apr'cot tarts?" Rand asked Patrick. "You got to—all the nobs—"

"I have a fondness for them," the younger man admitted.

"Aye. Then we got to eat 'em, don't we?"

Despite his host's condition and the subdued manner of the Rand women, Patrick found the meal quite excellent. Across from him, Elise Rand ate in silence, her attention seemingly on her plate. As he ate, Patrick took the opportunity to study her, wondering how the old man had managed to fend off a legion of suitors, for despite her plain speaking, she was as rich as she was beautiful.

"Do you have a townhouse—or do you merely lease one for when you are here during the social seasons?" Mrs. Rand inquired, breaking the silence.

"I own a house, I'm afraid, for I have to be in town much of the year."

"And do you have a country estate?"

"A modest one," he answered. "I have but recently bought a place in Kent."

"Well," she admitted wistfully, "I have long wished to have a house in the country, but Bat insists that his business is here."

"He lets us visit Mama's brother at the vicarage, and he thinks that is quite enough of rusticating, I'm afraid," Elise said.

He guessed she was not just out of the schoolroom—she had too much aplomb and too sharp a wit for that—but neither did she appear to be on the shelf. He supposed she was perhaps a year or two past twenty. Wondering idly what she thought of him, he sipped his wine as he continued watching her.

He'd been on the town far too long to take whatever anyone told him at face value. There was no question in his mind what the old man wanted—none at all. The retainer, the dinner invitation, all of it, were but lures to draw Patrick in, to intrigue him with the girl. As he looked at her, he wondered whether she protested too much, whether she and the old man had their caps set on him.

If so, it wasn't the first time someone had set the parson's mousetrap for him, and he'd already proven himself more than adept at extricating himself from the matrimonial ambitions of a number of heiresses. He'd been an *eligible parti* long enough to recognize nearly every possible blandishment designed to attach him.

Elise pushed her peas about her plate without eating them until her father noticed. "Eh, what's this? You don't like 'em? Paid the greengrocer—"

"I know, they are quite dear," she said tersely.

"Would you care for some more of them, Bat?" her mother asked quickly.

"Take some—" He stopped to belch loudly, then lifted his glass. "More port, boy!" he called out to one of the servants.

When she dared to look up, Elise was well aware that Hamilton studied her. He was a handsome man, no doubt about that. The light from the center candelabra made his brown hair shine softly. He turned his head briefly to address her mother, showing a profile as strong and well defined as that of a statue—straight forehead, chiseled nose, good chin. When he looked back to her, the light caught hazel eyes far too beautiful to belong to a man.

But even if there had never been Ben, even if she'd met the barrister under different circumstances, she would not have thrown her cap over the windmill for him. As handsome as he was, Patrick Hamilton was of a different class, and no matter how much her papa wished otherwise, money could not bridge the gap between a merchant's daughter and the poorest younger son.

"Tell me, Mr. Hamilton, how do you choose your clients?" her mother asked him, trying to draw him into conversation again.

"Usually I believe in them—or I believe the punishment does not fit the crime."

"Oh. Well, I am afraid I know nothing of the law, sir."

When he turned his attention to her again, Elise met his gaze steadily until he began eating once more. The next time he looked up, his hazel eyes betrayed a glint of amusement that irritated her.

"Mr. Hamilton, are you in the habit of staring at females?" she asked acidly.

"Only the pretty ones," he assured her, smiling. "And—" He let the word hang for a moment, then finished with, "—I could ask a similar question of you, Miss Rand."

"You do not keep your bargains very well, do you?" she told him tartly, fixing her gaze on her plate. As

she carried a bite to her mouth, she was acutely aware
that she hadn't deterred him at all. Defiantly, she
forced her thoughts to Ben, trying to bring his face
to mind. It would not come.

"Puss!" her father called out, startling her.

"What?"

"Wash th' matter with th' food? First the peash, and
now you ain't eathing nothing."

"I'm not very hungry."

He turned bleary, reddened eyes to Patrick. "Hate
a sh-shinny female," he mumbled.

"You wouldn't wish me fat," she countered evenly.

Once again, an uneasy silence settled over them,
broken only by an occasional, polite inanity uttered
by Emmaline Rand, while her husband abandoned his
food in favor of his wine. Every time he drained his
glass, he held it up to be refilled, until Patrick wondered how long it would be before the old man
slipped under the table. Not that it was an unusual
occurrence for a man of any class, he conceded. Despite his best intentions, he found his gaze straying
again to the fair Elise.

"Well, lookee at that!" Rand shouted drunkenly.
"Moon—moonin' like they wash calflingsh, eh? I got
fifty thoushand saysh you can 'ave 'er, boy!"

Humiliated, Elise flushed to the roots of her hair.
She rose angrily, dropping her napkin on the floor.
"Enough, Papa—I have had enough! I have no wish
to be thrown at anyone—and so I have told you!"

"Sit down, missy!"

"No!" Her cheeks hot, she looked to her mother.
"Good night, Mama—your pardon, Mr. Hamilton,"
she choked out. With that, she turned on her heels
and marched from the room.

"Missy! Elise!" His own face in high color, the older
man tried to shove back his chair, but could not.
"Afore God, you'll come back! A—ash-amed of you!"

"*You* shame me, Papa!" she shot back.

For a moment Patrick was rooted to his chair, then
he rose hastily, hoping to catch her before she went
upstairs. "I daresay she is merely overset," he mur-

mured low to her mother. "I assure you I thought nothing of it."

"Mr. Hamilton, I have never been so mortified in my life," the woman answered. "I can only offer my deepest apology, and—"

But Patrick was already nearly running for the door. "Miss Rand—wait!"

"No!"

At the bottom of the staircase, he caught up to her, taking her elbow from behind. She jerked it angrily, but he managed to hold on.

"I would you left me alone!"

"Miss Rand, there is no need to flee—the man was in his cups, nothing more."

"Nothing more?" Her voice rose incredulously. "When I would not flirt with you, he threw me at your head! And you—you stared at me like I was one of Elgin's marbles!"

"The same could be said for you, couldn't it? Look, I didn't expect—"

She rounded on him. "You expected us to behave like fools, and so we have! Well, you have had your amusement, Mr. Hamilton, and now you are free to go home!"

"Miss Rand, don't—" Afraid she meant to cry, he attempted to comfort her, smoothing her shawl where it lay over her shoulders. "Please."

She swallowed visibly as she met his eyes. "Mr. Hamilton, there is no need. I—I am quite all right, I assure you. I am merely humiliated."

Again, the husky quality of her voice enticed him. His hands slid from her shoulders down her arm, taking the silk shawl with them. As it fell to the floor, he drew her closer, savoring the smell of dried lavender on her warm skin.

Her eyes widened in shock as his lips brushed hers, then she pushed him away. Turning, she fled up the steps and did not stop until she looked back from the safety of the top.

"How dare you, sir? For all that I am born common, I am not one of your fancy pieces!" With that, she gathered her dignity stiffly and disappeared into the upper hallway.

"Miss Rand," he said too softly for her to hear, "there is nothing common about you at all." As he heard a door slam somewhere above, he reluctantly turned back to the dining room.

Mrs. Rand still sat in her chair, but her husband had slumped forward, and his head rested in his plate. As Patrick entered, she sighed unhappily.

"There is nothing I can say, is there?" she managed, her voice low. "Graves has gone to fetch two footmen to help him upstairs."

"I think I'd best leave."

"Yes." But as he turned to go, she spoke again. "I wish you could have known him before—well, before—"

"I have seen men in their cups, Mrs. Rand," he said gently.

"But he was not used to—that is, *before* he was beaten and robbed, Bat never drank so much, Mr. Hamilton."

"There is something about having a man's purse lifted that makes him feel rather mortal and vulnerable," he observed soberly. "Perhaps that has happened to Mr. Rand."

"He despises weakness, Mr. Hamilton."

"I daresay he will eventually recover."

She looked up at that. "If he does not drink himself into his grave first, sir."

"How long has it been?"

"Since the first time? Five—perhaps six months, I think. There were two times not far apart, then, well, it happened again, but not so severely, only yesterday. Thankfully, they got nothing, and he suffered no more than scratches when he fell. The watch said—" She caught herself. "Well, it doesn't signify, in any event. He was gotten home safely."

Two sturdy fellows, both in livery, arrived to lift their master from his seat. As they righted him, he seemed to rouse, then was heartily sick. It was a good time to withdraw. While Emmaline Rand bent over her husband to dab at his face with a napkin, Patrick took his cloak and hat from the rack in the foyer and let himself out.

At the curb, he looked back at Rand's grand house. Upstairs, a woman stood watching the street, her slender body silhouetted against the window. Certain it was Elise Rand, he raised his hand to her. But instead of acknowledging she'd seen him, she closed the shutters, and he heard the sound of the latch clicking into place. Beyond having no wish to flirt with him, she obviously did not want to continue any acquaintance.

Weary almost beyond reason, he mounted the step of his carriage and flung his body into the seat. Leaning back, he closed his eyes and saw Elise Rand in his memory. She was considerably smaller than her temper, he guessed she could not be more than a couple of inches above five feet, but she'd felt uncommonly good in his arms. For a moment he remembered smelling the clean scent of lavender on her skin, then he caught himself. For a man noted for sense and reason, he was behaving more like a mooncalf than one about to promise himself to the Earl of Dunster's daughter.

In the house behind him, Elise Rand watched from a crack in the shutters while Hamilton's carriage rolled slowly down the nearly deserted street. As the coach turned the corner, her fingers crept to her mouth, and she remembered the warmth of his breath against her cheek, the intimacy of his lips touching hers, and her thoughts turned again to Ben, recalling his all-too-few kisses. But despite his lower birth, Ben Rose had been the greater gentleman, she reminded herself.

"**W**ait around the corner for me, if you please," she ordered her driver crisply. "I shan't be above ten minutes."

"Got to go with ye," a liveried coachman insisted, jumping down to the street.

The fewer tales carried home the better, but even as she thought it, she knew her father was going to be mad as fire anyway. As if he were not already angry enough about Hamilton. But, looking at the narrow building that housed Magdalene Coates's infamous establishment, she wavered. Too many stories had come out about how innocent females had been coerced into prostitution.

"All right," she decided. "I may need you to carry her things."

Determined, she screwed her courage to the sticking point and marched to the door. Behind her, the coachman eyed the building skeptically. "Sure ye got it right, miss? It don't look like no place fer ye ter be."

"Yes."

Before she could bang the knocker, a beefy fellow opened the door, looked her up and down, then started to close it.

"Wait! I'd speak with Pearl—please."

The doorman paused, but the expression on his face was utterly inhospitable.

Elise licked her dry lips. "All right. You may tell Mrs. Coates that Miss Rand begs a word with her."

"She ain't receiving."

"I shall make it worth her while."

He eyed her curiously. "And how'd ye do that?"

Glancing down the street first, she furtively dug into her beaded reticule and drew out a money purse. Smiling at the doorkeeper, she held out a gold guinea. "For you—if I am allowed to see Mrs. Coates."

He took the money, then assessed her person more boldly, his eyes lingering on the swell of her bosom before returning to her face. "Ye ain't her kind."

"I should hope I am not, but I have come to her on a matter of business." Daring to step closer, she tried to calm the rapid beating of her heart. "Tell her I wish to purchase one of her girls. And—and if you think to attempt anything, I have brought Will with me."

Unimpressed, he shrugged. Turning around to speak to someone she could not see, he apparently argued about something. When his attention returned to Elise, he opened the door wider.

"Sorry, miss, but there's a gentry cove with 'er."

"Please." She licked her lower lip again. "Tell her—tell her I can afford whatever she asks."

He shook his head.

"Listen to me—the girl Pearl is in need of a doctor—and I will see she is seen by a good one. Otherwise, I fear she will die of consumption."

"Ain't no cure fer it."

"But can you not see? It will spread amongst all of you."

"Not ter me. She don't let me 'ave any of 'em."

Nonetheless, he disappeared, leaving his post unattended, and she took the opportunity to follow him inside. Behind her, her father's coachman muttered something profane, followed by, "This ain't no place fer a respectable female, miss."

The big man hesitated outside a closed door, then rapped on it loudly. From inside, voices stopped in midsentence, then a woman called out.

"Told ye I wasn't ter be disturbed!"

"Aye, but ye got a fancy mort a-callin' on ye! Got th' Lunnon mint on 'er back, if ye was ter ask!" the fellow shouted through the closed door.

"Me arse she does!" But there was the scraping of

chairs within, the sound of footsteps on carpet, then the door cracked open, revealing Magdalene Coates's shrewd eyes. "Where? Oh, 'tis ye, is it?" she said nastily. "Out wi' ye! I ain't got nuthin' ter say ter the likes o' ye!"

"I have money."

"Fer what? Me gels don't—" The woman's words died as she watched Elise hold up several banknotes. "what was ye a-wanting?" she said instead.

"I want to buy the girl you call Pearl."

"Gel's a bit beneath the weather."

"I know. Now—may I come in?"

"Aye," the woman muttered grudgingly. She stood back, letting Elise and the Rand coachman pass into the room. "Tom, ye were ter watch as none came in," she grumbled.

"Tried, missus—did."

"Another time and ye'll be turned off, ye hear?"

As he slunk back to his position, Elise looked around the room curiously, thinking it garish yet oddly opulent. Everything was dark and heavy, with red moire-covered walls, red couches trimmed with heavy gold tassels and gilded legs, red velvet window coverings. And there was a surfeit of gold paint everywhere, while above it all hung a chandelier nearly half as large as the one in her father's foyer.

"When ye be done gawkin', ye can talk."

But Elise's gaze had rested on long, trouser-clad legs, and as she watched in horror, they unfolded, and Patrick Hamilton stood. A faint smile played upon his mouth as he bowed. When his eyes met hers, they seemed to mock her.

"An unforeseen pleasure," he murmured politely.

"Not to me, I assure you. But no doubt you are quite familiar with the place." Turning her back on him, she addressed Magdalene Coates. "I spoke to Pearl on the street when we were handing out pamphlets."

"As if yer papers was going ter feed a body!" the woman snorted.

"Pearl indicated then that she wished to leave

your—er—employ, Mrs. Coates, but I understand she is bound to you. If that is the case, I am prepared to give you what you paid for her."

"Ain't that kind o' ye! Ye hear her, Mr. Hamilton? The fancy mort is wishful o' robbin' me!"

"Ten pounds," Elise said firmly.

"Oh, did ye hear it? Ten quid! A gel can bring me more'n that in a night!"

"Not if she is dead. Besides, I should think that cough would drive your—um—your custom away."

"She ain't takin' any just now, but—"

"Mrs. Coates, I have heard her cough, and I assure you—"

"Gel's got the ague, that's all," the madam maintained stoutly. "I don't keep 'em if they was ter stay sick."

"She needs a doctor."

"Doctor! Humph! Gel's more in need of a birchin' than a physicking, if ye was ter have the truth. Cough's made her lazy."

Elise sighed. "All right—how much do you wish for her?"

"Ye was with the stout gent, wasn't ye? Aye, ye was. Well, now—" Maddie eyed the younger woman speculatively. "I got ter have more—much more'n ten quid." Her gaze raked over Elise's clothes as though she were estimating their worth to the penny, then she smiled. "I paid fifty quid fer her."

It was a lie, and both of them knew it. Girls came out of the poorhouses for a few shillings every day, bought like the horses at Tattersall's for vastly less money. Elise decided to gamble.

"I'm afraid I don't have quite that much in my reticule, Mrs. Coates. I could perhaps afford twenty pounds."

"Twenty pounds! Not fer yer life! Twenty pounds says she stays, missy—fifty says she goes, and that's that, it is."

"Er—if it is merely a matter of funds, perhaps I may be of assistance?" As he spoke, Patrick drew out a leather money folder and counted out the full fifty pounds.

Elise knew she'd been caught out, but she had no wish to be indebted to the lawyer for anything. "That won't be necessary," she retorted. Opening her reticule again, she dug into her money pouch. "All right—fifty pounds it is, but you are a disgrace to—"

"Me profession?" the madam supplied sarcastically. "Well, afore ye go a-lookin' down yer rich nose at me, missy, I can tell ye as I take in more'n a night than ye see in a quarter."

"Where is Pearl?" Elise asked, ignoring the woman's gibes. "I'd take her and everything she owns with me now."

Magdalene Coates walked to the bellpull that hung beside a heavy hanging. Her back to Elise, she gave it a hefty jerk. "The old gent as was with ye ain't going ter be happy with ye, I'll wager," she warned the young woman.

Aware that Patrick Hamilton was watching her, Elise lifted her chin defiantly. "No, he will commend me for rescuing the unfortunate creature, I am sure," she lied. "But in any event, I shall be taking her to London Hospital."

"Fer the poor," the madam scoffed. "Now if ye was ter really care, ye'd be a-taking her ter a better place, wouldn't ye?"

"Where I choose to take her is none of your affair now, is it?" Elise countered evenly. "The worst pit must surely be better than this."

"Oho now! Would ye listen ter her, Mr. Hamilton? And what would a gentry mort be knowin' as ter how I live?"

He did not intervene, but Elise felt he was vastly amused by the whole proceeding. "Where is Pearl?" she snapped. "I have not the whole day."

" 'Fraid m'place will rub onter her fancy gown, ain't she?" Maddie whispered loudly to the lawyer.

Uncomfortable with the scene, Patrick reached for his beaver hat. "My thanks for the Madeira," he murmured. Setting the hat upon his head, he adjusted it jauntily, then picked up his walking stick. "Until we are met again, Miss Rand. Mrs. Coates."

"I don't think so," Elise muttered.

"But we ain't done yet," the madam protested. "I was a-wantin' ter pay ye—I got most of the blunt I owe ye—and who's ter say as I'll have it later? Ye'd better take it with ye."

It was a point to be considered, given the woman's reputation as an opium user. Patrick wavered, then nodded. At that moment the door opened again, and the doorkeeper ushered the thin, wan Pearl inside. The girl wore only a shapeless dress of faded muslin, without any wrap about her narrow shoulders. Before Elise could protest, Maddie Coates herself went to the brass rack inside the door and took down a heavy shawl. Not looking at Elise, she draped it around Pearl.

"Good riddance ter ye," she muttered. "Ye can go wi' yer fancy mort like ye was wantin'."

The girl tried to speak, only to be overcome by coughing. The bark was deep and hollow, drawing Patrick's attention. As he took in the yellowish skin and the sunken eyes, he felt a deep pity for her. She was not long for this world.

Elise reached to take what appeared to be no more than a dress bundled into a rag. "Come on, Pearl," she said briskly. "We shall see you are better fed and cared for. I am taking you to London Hospital." As she said it, she glanced defiantly at the madam.

But the girl quaked. "Not Lunnon—not the Lunnon, miss!"

"Why not?"

"It ain't far from the poorhouse," Maddie Coates answered for her.

"Don't never want ter go back," the girl insisted, whimpering pitifully.

"All right, then—the Royal Hospital in Chelsea," Elise decided. "Good day, Mrs. Coates. Mr. Hamilton."

With that, she took Pearl's arm and hastily thrust the girl through the door. The footman hesitated, then followed.

"Come back when ye ain't with her, me fine buck, and Maddie'll fix ye up with a girl as knows what she's made fer!" the madam shouted after him. "Humph!" she grumbled, turning back to Patrick. "Don't know why the preachin' fools don't leave well enough alone. It ain't going ter make no difference if she was to get ter a doctor," she declared with feeling. "What's he goin' ter do fer her, I ask ye?—give her a bleedin' or a physickin'? At least I gave 'er clean sheets, and I wasn't lettin' the' customers at her."

"Then why did you sell her?"

The woman shrugged. "Fifty pounds is fifty pounds, ain't it?" A slow smile turned her rouged cheeks into round apples. "Besides, I got your bill ter pay, ye know." Moving to a carved wooden cabinet, she unlocked it and drew out a heavy box. Lifting the lid, she took out a bag and began carefully counting out a goodly sum of money. Frowning, she stopped and brought a wad of banknotes to him.

"Well, it ain't quite all I owe ye," she admitted. "But ye'll get the rest within the week, I promise ye."

"All right." He slipped the money beneath his coat.

"Aye, I'll get yer money," she said, her expression suddenly odd. "I think I know where ter get it."

"Don't lift any purses," he advised her. "My services come dearer the second time."

She smiled secretively. "Old gents get queer starts, don't ye know," she murmured. "Aye, they do. And I got one as wouldn't want me ter blabber."

"Maddie, don't do anything that could get you into more trouble."

"Eh? No, I got real rich coves as spends their gold wi' me." She leaned closer, nearly whispering, "I had this one old gent, rich as a nabob he is, but he wasn't wantin' the regular—and me gels didn't like 'im at all." Her expression grew distant, her voice low. "Had a fancy for Peg oncet, but she was afeared of 'im, so I put a stop to it." Abruptly she changed the subject. "Well, it don't matter now, anyways, as Peg is dead, and I got me bills ter pay, don't I? Tell ye what—ye go on, and Big Tom'll bring ye the rest o' what I owe ye tomorrow."

"I know a heave-ho when I see one," he said.

"Well, if ye was wantin' ter stay, I got a gel upstairs as can make ye think she's Quality, I swear it. Pretty hair, pretty face, and pretty manners—got white hands like a lady. I don't let any but the gentry coves have her, ye know," she added slyly.

"Not today. Besides, if I were to take my fees in trade, I'd have an office filled with sheep and chickens, I'm afraid."

The woman grinned broadly. "Aye, ye don't have ter pay fer the gels anyways, do ye? Ye got 'em all a castin' out lures to ye, don't ye? Well, then off with ye, and let me tend ter matters."

"Good day, Maddie. Try to stay away from the opium until I am paid, will you?"

"Ye'll get yer money—ye will."

As he emerged out into the gray day, he could see that Elise Rand and the girl still waited at the curb. The footman, who'd not uttered a word inside, had disappeared, probably to fetch a carriage. He would have gone on without saying anything further to them, but the corner of his eye caught a careening coach headed toward the women.

"Watch out!" he shouted.

But neither of them saw it. Without thinking, he lowered his shoulder and ran at them, hitting Rand's daughter with such force that she struck the pavement hard and rolled with him in a tangle of arms and legs as the vehicle jumped the curb. The coach teetered precariously, then fell. There was a sound of splitting wood and the neighing of frightened horses. One of the wheels spun in the air above Patrick's head.

Elise Rand lay still beneath him, but he could feel the rise and fall of her breast beneath his chest, and he could hear her gasp for breath. Gingerly, he rolled off her and sat up, narrowly missing the iron-clad wheel.

"Are you all right?"

Her blue eyes widened as she stared up at the underside of the coach. She turned her head toward where Pearl lay and saw the bloody gash on the girl's forehead. With an effort Elise crawled to her.

"Pearl!" The girl did not move. Elise shook her, but there was no response. With that, she sat up, leaned her head on her knees, and began to cry softly.

Patrick moved between them and cradled Pearl's head against his leg. Leaning over her, he listened carefully to her chest, then straightened. "She's alive."

Elise swallowed hard. "Are you certain? She doesn't—"

"She took a bad blow, but she'll survive that at least." Gently easing the girl off, her stood up and dusted his hands on his buff trousers. "Near thing though."

"Yes—yes, it was." From where Elise sat, he looked so very tall. Forcing a painful smile, she managed to struggle to her feet. "Thank you, sir. 'Twas a very brave thing—I expect I owe you my life."

Her expensive walking dress was torn, and her red-gold hair straggled about her face. She reached to touch a bleeding scrape on her cheek carefully, wincing.

"You'd better get home and tend this," he said, dabbing at it with his handkerchief.

"Miss! Whatever—?" her returning coachman gasped. As his eyes took in the overturned carriage, he shook his head. "Gor blimey—ye nearly bought the ticket." Then he looked down at Pearl. "Lud a-mercy."

"Yes, she is going to be all right, Will," Elise said without conviction. "But we've got to get her to the hospital."

By now, a crowd had gathered, and several were clamoring that the driver ought to be punished, but the fellow had apparently fled down an alleyway. A few stout men climbed over the wrecked coach, then one shouted, "Ain't anybody inside!"

"Can you lift her, do you think?" Elise asked her coachman anxiously.

"Aye, miss." To demonstrate, he bent down and picked the slight girl up, staggering slightly as he shifted her over his shoulder. One of her arms hung limply at her side, and her feet dangled below his waist. "Which hospital?"

"The Royal, I think."

"Lunnon's closer."

"Yes, but she has no wish to go there." Holding out her hand to Patrick, Elise met his gaze briefly. "I am in your debt, sir."

He didn't want to let her go. "While Will is taking the girl, I'd see you home, Miss Rand."

"Someone has to admit her, and I expect there will be a charge." She glanced to where Will was already laying the girl onto the velvet seat of her father's carriage. "I expect I ought to go with her."

"If you do, you'll be ogled by every jack in the place." He reached under his now dirty coat and drew out his money. Peeling off several banknotes, he walked over and handed them to the coachey. "Give them this so they know she is not a charity case."

"Aye, sor. But—"

"They'll require her name." Elise turned to Maddie, who'd belatedly come out of her house. "I'll need her full name, I expect."

"She don't have none," the woman answered. "She was a foundling—'twas me as named her Pearl. I got girls as is called Opal, Jewel, Ruby, like that. I called her that 'cause she was so pale. There's men as likes the delicate ones, ye know."

"No, I wouldn't know," Elise muttered. As Will stood waiting, she decided, "Yes—well, perhaps we ought to say she is a Smith, then." She looked down at her torn dress, saw the street grime on her arms, then sighed. "I expect I'd best bathe ere Papa sees me," she decided. "Otherwise I shall be quite in the basket."

"If Miss Pearl don't stay, where am I ter take her?" Will inquired nervously.

"I doubt they will release her today. But if there is not a bed for her—" Elise hesitated, knowing full well that her father would not take the girl in. She looked up at Patrick hopefully.

"No, Miss Rand, I will not."

"Well, I did not expect *you* would, but I thought perhaps you might know of someone, and—"

"No."

"For a moment I forgot who you were, didn't I?" she muttered.

"Gratitude is such a fleeting thing, isn't it?" he chided her.

"Alas, but I am rather vexed just now," she retorted. "Will, you are to go on, and I shall try to come to the hospital later to see how she fares. You'd best stay with her until I get there." She walked to her father's coach. "Pearl, you are going to be all right," she promised the limp girl. "As soon as I can, I shall come to see you."

The coachman eyed her balefully for a moment, then heaved himself into the seat across from the girl. "Ye ain't going ter let yer papa turn me off, are ye?"

"Of course not. Hopefully, he will not notice anything is amiss, but if he does, I will make certain he knows the fault was mine." Turning back to Patrick, she exhaled heavily. "Well, I'd best not tarry."

"Afraid Rand will read a peal over you?" Patrick asked gently.

"Well, I have hopes he will not be at home."

He took her arm and started toward his hired hackney. "You could say you were set upon, I suppose."

"Mr. Hamilton, I am not given to telling lies."

"Nonsense, Miss Rand. You are, after all, a female."

"Of all the impolite things to say," she declared sourly as he gave her a boost into the coach. Sinking back against plain leather squabs, she waited for him to take the seat across from her. Her eyes took in the stark interior curiously. "One would think you did not prosper," she observed.

"I'm afraid I leave ostentation to those above and below me."

"A set-down, Mr. Hamilton?"

"No more than yours," he countered cheerfully. "Actually, I find it easier to hire a hackney than to put my pair to my gig, particularly when I am going to have to leave them standing somewhere."

"Then how are they properly exercised?"

"I have a boy who walks them every day, and I take the whole rig out on weekends when court is not in session."

"You must surely be the first gentleman I've met who will own that he works for anything," she murmured.

He leaned back against his seat and regarded her quizzically.

"I would you did not do that."

"I could say I was paying court to your beauty."

"You'd best save your Spanish coin for those who can appreciate it."

A faint smile played at the corners of his mouth. "You cover yourself with quite a shield, don't you?"

"Mr. Hamilton, I am on the shelf."

"And determinedly so."

"Yes."

"Why?"

"That, sir, is none of your affair."

"But it is a sad waste." As she turned her head to stare out the hackney window, he could not help admiring her fine profile and the way the light filtered through stray strands of her unusual hair. "Someone played fast with your heart, didn't he?" When she did not answer, he said softly, "I cannot think you were jilted, Miss Rand."

For a moment she continued to stare silently, then she swallowed visibly. "Only by death, sir."

"Then there was someone."

"Yes." Almost defiantly, she turned her face toward his. "His name was Benjamin Rose," she said evenly.

If she expected him to show surprise, she was destined for disappointment. He merely digested the name and nodded. "Samuel Rose's son."

"Yes. Does that shock you?"

"No. Sam Rose is a good man. I've sent more than one client to him."

"Papa called him a heathen cent per cent and

worse," she recalled bitterly. "For two years, he would not hear of it, and then when he finally realized I would not change my mind, he allowed the engagement to proceed. Not the marriage—only the engagement. But," she acknowledged, "Ben's father felt much the same way as Papa."

"Why didn't you elope to Gretna?"

She stared unseeing out the window again, this time looking backward in her mind. It was a question that did not bear the asking, yet this time she answered it. "Because Ben had too much honor," she whispered. "He believed Papa would come to understand."

He felt acutely sorry for her. On impulse, he reached across to cover her hand with his. "I read the newspaper account of what happened," he said gently. "And I am truly sorry."

"Everyone is sorry—even Papa—but that changes nothing. Ben is still dead." When she met his gaze again, her eyes were dry yet haunted. "They slit his throat, sir, and left him to bleed to death alone. For a purse of less than fifty pounds, they murdered him in the street. Everyone is sorry, but no one has paid for it but Ben and me."

There had been no witnesses as he recalled, and given the lack of any real constabulary, he knew no one would ever hang for the crime. "I'm sorry," he said again.

She looked down where his fingers held hers. They were warm, strong, alive. And the ache in her breast was nearly too much to bear. "Thank you," she managed.

He released her hand, and leaning back again, he tried to keep his voice light. "And so now you have devoted your life to the poor and downtrodden, eh?"

"There is too much evil in this world, Mr. Hamilton."

"And you believe Hannah More has the answer to it?"

"No. The answer, sir, must lie within ourselves." She studied him soberly for a moment. "You are like

Papa, aren't you? In your books, one must either be a crazed reformer or a profligate.''

"And you?" he asked softly.

"I am a selfish person whose life was touched by Ben," she answered. "As I saw how Papa treated him, I came to realize that we all wish to think ourselves better than others. Somehow it is better to be born poor in the Church of England than to be born rich and Jewish or Catholic. But I am not at all certain that God cares for the difference. Sometimes I think He must look down upon us and shake His head at our follies."

"You sound like a Methodist, Miss Rand."

"Well, I am not. Not that there is anything wrong with them, sir," she hastened to add. "I just happen to admire Hannah More and what she has done to alleviate the suffering of this world."

"What are you going to do with Pearl? Presuming she lives, of course."

"I could not leave her in that place—I could not. We were handing out pamphlets in Covent Garden last week, saying that everyone deserved food and shelter," she recalled slowly. "She came up to me and touched my dress so carefully, as though she feared to soil it, and I asked her where she was from. She pointed to that house, then began to cry, and when I asked why, she said it was because of the men, that she knew her soul was lost. She could scarce speak for the cough, that awful cough."

"Consumption," he said matter-of-factly.

"Yes." Elise dared to meet his eyes. "Mr. Hamilton, she is but fifteen."

"There is no cure."

"I know, but why must she spend the rest of her days in a place like that? Even if Mrs. Coates no longer sells her, she is in a living hell, sir."

"And now she will die amongst strangers."

Ignoring the truth of his words, she went on, "She wanted to come with me that day—I know it. But Mrs. Coates's man came and took her back."

He was silent as he considered what she'd said. Finally, when he spoke, he tried to reason with her. "Miss Rand, what you are doing is dangerous. No gently bred female should be standing on the streets in Covent Garden, no matter how noble the purpose."

"You sound like Papa. But no matter what he wishes, I am not a gentlewoman, Mr. Hamilton. I am a Cit."

"A rich one with no business in Covent Garden."

"I have no wish to be wasteful of my time on earth. I cannot sit idly about, doing naught but watercolors. If I were a man, I should not be content to make bricks like Papa, not at all." Once again, her chin jutted defiantly. "I should be a Whig and stand for Parliament. I should introduce and reintroduce the bill against climbing boys over and over again until it passes. And against slavery. And for the emancipation of the Catholics."

"And the Lords would defeat every bill."

"There will come a time when enough people realize that the Lords should not be entitled to stifle every piece of progressive legislation simply because they have been born to titles, Mr. Hamilton."

She spoke with passion, reminding him much of himself in the days when he still believed a younger son could be what he wished, even an actor.

"How old are you, Miss Rand?"

"Twenty-two. Definitely not in the first bloom of youth."

"I wouldn't say that."

"Mr. Hamilton—"

"No, no—I admire you, Miss Rand. You have chosen not to trade on your face to gain yourself some wealthy, titled, and altogether pompous husband." It was his turn to look out the window. "I had different dreams, I am afraid."

"You wished to be a rich barrister."

"No, not at first." His mouth twisted. "I wished to be the greatest actor since Kemble—greater even than Kean. As a youth I would practice alone in the Scottish hills, shouting into the wind to strengthen my voice."

"You do not have a Scots accent," she said softly.

"I read aloud the same passages over and over, trying to sound like a sophisticated Englishman, until I got the hang of it."

"Well, you have succeeded in that. But why did you change your mind and read law?"

"Because I am a Hamilton, Miss Rand. And even a poor Hamilton must remember the illustrious line from whence he has come. Hamiltons," he declared with a finality, "go to Eton, then to Oxford. My great defiance was to choose Cambridge."

"And the law."

"And the law. What is the law but a stage, and what are barristers but actors? The great body of common law provides the script, and we adjust the parts to suit the circumstances. I submit to you, Miss Rand, that we posture as much as Kean."

"And you are exceedingly successful, sir."

"Yes. But now I have my eyes set on another stage." He paused, letting that sink in as he would before a jury. "I am considering a run at Parliament."

"You could do a great deal of good."

"A position of power is perhaps the grandest stage of all." He smiled crookedly again. "All I need is the right wife, a powerful patron, and a platform from which to harangue my fellows."

"I see. And do you have these already discovered?" she asked, smiling back.

"Every one."

"Well, I hope you choose the Whigs, for they are the only ones with any conscience at all."

He didn't know why he said it, why he'd confided anything to her at all, but he shook his head. "I expect to cast my lot in with Dunster."

"But he is a Tory! And they are against everything!"

"But they are in power."

Her smile faded completely. "Then you are no better than Mrs. Coates, are you?"

There was no mistaking the censure in her voice. He stared again out the window. "Thankfully, Miss Rand, I do not have to answer that. You are at home."

Still, he felt compelled to add, "Unlike you, my dear, I am quite practical."

She knew she had no right to rip up at him, no right at all. And she also knew that both of them could have been killed beneath the runaway coach's wheels when he'd chosen to save her. She sighed.

"My wretched tongue again. Too often it takes me where I ought not to go."

"Brutally so."

As the hackney driver opened the door, Patrick jumped down, then reached up for her. She hesitated, then leaned into his arms before sliding to the ground. As he looked into her upturned face, he forgot his anger entirely.

She held out her hand. "I must thank you for everything, sir—my life, the lift home." She looked up again, then dropped her gaze self-consciously. "Yes—well, I doubt we shall meet again, so regardless of how wrongly you have chosen, I shall wish you well."

"If you need my assistance to explain, I can come in with you," he offered, taking her hand.

"No. For all his faults, Papa still loves me dearly." Pulling away, she quickly went up the steps. When she turned back, he was still watching her. "And if he is at home, I shall just have to tell him what has happened." She smiled. "Good day, Mr. Hamilton."

Accompanied by Big Tom, Maddie Coates slipped through the narrow, cramped lane into a dead-end alley, passing those who'd stumbled out of the opium dens to lie in stupor amid garbage and filth. Holding a perfume-drenched handkerchief over her nose to mitigate the stench, she directed her manservant to bang upon an ancient door.

Hinges creaked as it swung inward, then an attendant peered out before silently stepping back to let them pass. It was dim and smoky within, making those who hunched over hookahs as well as those who sat on the floor appear as vacant-eyed wraiths from some nether world. Big Tom whispered to the doorkeeper, who nodded, then directed Maddie to a corner table where a solitary man awaited, his face shrouded by the hood of his cloak.

As she sat down, Maddie's eyes darted with the eagerness of a lover to the small tannish cake on the shingle.

"It looks good, it does."

"It is."

Her heart pounding, she watched him chip off bits of opium, then powder it with a pestle, mixing it with sugar before dividing it between them. His gold ring flashed, an odd bit of light amid the heavy haze that surrounded them. Her hand shook as she took a pinch and carried it to her mouth, where she tasted it. She made a face, then shuddered.

"Oooh, 'tis bitter, it is," she complained.

"The purest as can be had," he told her. "Wait and you will feel it."

She reached into her reticule and brought out a

tiny, blackened spoon. Dipping into the drug, she ate of it determinedly, wanting the pleasure she knew it would give her. Across from her, her companion watched, his expression one of contempt for her.

"Your business, Maddie?" he prompted her. "You said you had a matter of import, as I recall. Something as cannot wait, wasn't it? And you was wanting opium, you said, else you would spill the budget. Well, I brought it, so's you can speak up anytime you was to want."

But her eyes were closed as she tried to feel the first effects of the powder he'd made for her. "Aye," she murmured. "Where'd you get it? 'Tis strong."

"Like it, don't you?" he said, nodding. "And well you ought, for 'tis the best to be got anywheres—had to pay good gold for it." This time, his ringed finger pushed his own small pile of sweetened opium toward her. "Best as can be got, Maddie—purest stuff. Pure as country snow." His voice was low, seductive, but his eyes were narrowed on her face. "Spill your business, and I got more for you."

Already she thought she could feel the pleasant warmth, but despite her anticipation, she sensed there was something different about it. Her tongue tingled oddly. "Aye," she said. "Ye got something else in it?"

"Ain't used to it like that, are you? You been getting the stuff as is more sugar than poppy, eh?"

"I ain't rich like some, ye know." She ran her tongue over her lips. "My business," she began. "Aye, my business," she repeated more stoutly. " 'Tis about Peg."

"Peg?" He seemed taken aback.

"Ye know—the one you was always pesterin'—the one as ye was wantin' me ter swing fer." A slow, sly smile curved her reddened lips. "Ye know the one, don't ye? The one as was once under Maidenhope's protection until she was poppin' with his babe. Aye, ye know which one, fer ye paid extra fer her."

His manner changed abruptly, and he sat back, his eyes malevolent. "Old woman, if I was you, I'd not tell this," he warned her.

"I ain't no older'n ye—most likely younger, if ye

was ter have the truth o' it." She leaned forward to stare beneath his hood. "And I know—aye, I *know.* Ye can fool the watch mayhap, but ye ain't giving the slip ter Maddie, I can tell ye. Ye was the one as dumped her in th' river, wasn't ye?"

"You are a fool," he growled. "A silly fool."

"Oh, but I ain't. I got it figgered out, don't ye see? And don't be thinkin' ye can do with me as ye did poor Peg, for I brung Tom wi' me ter watch as ye don't try ter snuff me out. I wouldn't want ter tempt ye, ye know, so I ain't going nowheres with ye save where there's folks as can see ye." She waved her hand toward the big man, who waited for her by the door. "If ye was ter want ter harm me here, ye'd not live ter the alleyway. Tom—" She blinked again, thinking the opium was taking effect. "Tom's got a sticker as would carve ye like a goose—a big long 'un. Aye, ye'd be carved like ye was a big, fat goose."

"You've eaten too much opium, Maddie," he responded coldly.

The drug was potent, more so than any she'd had before. She tried to focus her eyes and return to the matter at hand. "But if ye was ter do right by me, why I'd be real fergitful, ye understand. I'd—" Her tongue felt too thick for speech. "I'd not tell the magistrate what I know."

"Why, you old tart—you miserable old tart," he sneered, shaking his head. "There's none as would believe you."

"Tart is as may be, ye old devil. At least I ain't killed a body, which is—" She stopped to pull at her tongue.

He looked around uneasily, then laughed harshly. "If you was to tell a constable, you'd be clapped up in Bedlam for sayin' it was me—aye, there ain't a man in London as would believe you. I got money, Maddie, and money buys anything I was to want. I could snap m'fingers, and they'd a be putting you away—*away*, Maddie."

"Ain't anything as says I got ter tell—I might, and I might not, ye know." This time when she dipped her opium spoon, her hand was almost too heavy to lift. "Ye see, I might be persuaded ter keep what I know close—real close—ter me. Then ye could be knowin' yer secret was safe within me bosom."

"I ain't your mark, Maddie."

"Fer a bit o' yer money," she went on, "Maddie'd fergit as how ye treated me gels—or what ye wanted from Peg, don't ye see? Aye, ye do, don't ye? And I figger I got the blunt comin' as 'twas me that nearly went ter the Nubbing Cheat for what ye done."

For a long moment he glowered at her, then spat out, "How much? How much was you wanting?"

"Fer five thousand quid, I'd be real quietlike—why, m'lips'd be tight shut, they would. Aye, be a sort of justice fer Peg, wouldn't it? Ye'd be a-paying fer what ye did ter her."

"I ain't the fool as you'd take me for, Maddie. Why, there's none as would believe such a tale," he said again.

"But being a respectable gent, ye'd not be a-wantin' 'em ter ask ye about it, would ye?" She closed her mouth around the spoon and sucked on it, scarce tasting the bitterness. " 'Tis good, it is," she said thickly, "but next time I'd have—more sugar in it. Got too much opium—" She was feeling it now, the lethargy that wanted to overwhelm her. "Where was we? Oh—money. Aye—money, it was." She dropped her spoon onto the table. "Mebbe they won't believe me, but when there's more gels in th' river, mebbe they'd remember, eh?"

"You'd not stop at five thousand, you old bitch."

"If they wasn't findin' more, I would." It was getting hard to speak, and her limbs seemed to be going numb. "Don't know if I was ter want more o' this," she mumbled. "Real good, but—" As she said it, she felt an enveloping dizziness. "Pure," she decided. "Too pure."

"I brought you what you was askin' for, Maddie."

His voice seemed to be coming from a distance, whispering to her brain. "Too strong by half," she gasped. "Too—strong—by—half."

"You ain't used to the good stuff, eh? Perhaps you would wish for more?" he asked, pushing the remainder of the cake toward her. "Here—you got it all, Maddie—all."

"Cannot—" This time, when she blinked her eyes, they did not want to open. "Sleepy—too sleepy." Her shoulders slumped forward, then she managed to lift her head back one last time. "Too much."

Again, she felt the overwhelming weakness, and she knew she could not fight it. Her head was heavy, her mind confused, and as the blackness enveloped her, she was unable to cry out for help. She scarce felt it when he reached across the table to fold her arms and ease her head onto them.

"Old whore," he muttered contemptuously.

He glanced furtively around them, but most were too befuddled with drug to note anything. Rising carefully, he bent as though he would speak to Maddie, then he straightened, pulled his hooded cloak closer, and went to the door. The big man there glanced to where Maddie Coates seemingly dreamed over her opium, and he shook his head.

"Have ter carry 'er home, eh?"

The hooded man handed him a guinea. "Mrs. Coates said you was to buy a pipe while you wait fer her." He looked back, shaking his head. "It might be hours ere she wakens."

Big Tom considered it for a moment. "Aye, if I was ter tarry a bit, mebbe she'll come 'round enough ter save me the trouble," he decided, brightening. "Got twelve stone ter her, she does."

"And I'd not waste the stuff on the table, you hear? Like I told her, 'tis the best to be had."

With that, he ducked out, leaving Big Tom with the coin. For a long moment the manservant hesitated, then he went back to the dim corner where Maddie slept. Torn between spending his guinea or pocketing it, he took a seat. She wouldn't care, he decided, or if she did, she was too gone from the drug to know it. Reaching beneath her arm, he helped himself to what was left of the pressed opium cake, scarce bothering to cut it with the sugar.

It had been a satisfying morning in the Bailey, ending with a decision not to bind Patrick's client over for trial. Dodging a chagrined Ned Milton, Patrick emerged into crisp autumn air. Without waiting for the privacy of a hackney, he tore off his barrister's wig and loosened the neck of his robe.

"Hamilton!"

Patrick spun around as Bartholomew Rand hailed him, then waited, forcing a smile. The older man approached hurriedly, puffing from the exertion.

"Was waitin' to take you up, sirrah—aye, thought mayhap you'd be a-thirstin' from all the arguments you was making. You was masterful, Mr. Hamilton—masterful. Damme if you didn't have that Milton fellow nigh to apoplexy."

"Thank you. Actually, I was thinking of merely going home for a quick nuncheon," Patrick admitted.

"Aye, you are afeared I mean to disgrace you, ain't you?"

"No, not at all," Patrick lied politely.

"Aye, you are—I can see it in your face." Rand smiled diffidently. "Didn't make m'fortune without knowin' what folks was thinkin', you know. Cannot blame you though if you was to turn your back on me."

"No, I am merely tired, and my day has scarce begun."

"Well, Em and Ellie would have it as I made a fool of myself the other night. Allowed as though they was mortified, but I was hoping you wouldn't cut the connection," the old man went on. "Was in my cups, that's all."

"You are not the first man to drink too much," Patrick assured him.

"Then you wasn't offended?" Rand asked hopefully.

"No."

"Well, then I got just the ticket! Come along to Garraway's—I got me a table there, don't you know? Coffee's good for drowsiness, ain't it? Be a better man in no time." The old man clapped Patrick on the back familiarly. "Got excellent meals at fair prices, if I do say so."

"I have appointments in my office beginning at two."

"Got plenty of time! Carriage's waiting 'round the corner, and I won't be offended if you was to wish to take off your robe in it." When Patrick still hesitated, Rand persisted. "Look, I got to make amends for the other night, don't I? And I owe you for seeing my gel home yesterday—ain't no telling what was to happen to her if you hadn't come along. Near thing it was, or so she said."

"She told you about it?"

"Course she did! Oh, I ain't saying as we don't disagree mightily on this reformist business, but she's a good gel."

Not knowing if Elise Rand had mentioned Pearl to him, Patrick forbore saying anything more than, "I was happy to oblige."

"Got no business there though—didn't mean you, of course, 'cause you're a man—but I ain't liking for her to be where she might be harmed." As he spoke, the old Cit took Patrick's arm, directing him to the waiting coach. "Been given too free a rein, I guess, but as I only got the one, I been inclined to indulge her, probably more'n is good for a gel, if you want the truth of it. But we've been pretty open in the budget with each other, which is good 'cause her mama ain't the sort as understands me or Ellie. M'gel's always come to me when she was in the basket. Not that Mrs. Rand ain't a good woman, mind you," he added hastily. "Proud of her—demned proud of her. I think I told you she was a Bingham, didn't I?"

"Yes, I believe you did," Patrick murmured.

"Good blood there, but none of 'em has got much more than a farthing to pay the porter with, no matter how it pleases 'em to look down on me. But now as I got the blunt, they ain't shy about hangin' on m'sleeve."

"I trust Miss Rand suffered no real harm, then?" Patrick asked, hoping to distract him before he launched on another discourse about his wealth.

"No—though she's a bit bruised where she went into the pavement, but she'll come about. Brave thing, Hamilton—deuced brace—and like I was saying, I owe you for it." As they'd reached the curb, Rand nodded to his liveried coachman, who responded with alacrity, opening the carriage door with a flourish. "Don't go to the coffee houses much, do you?" the old man went on. "Or if you do, I ain't seen you about."

"No, not very often."

"Aye, being Quality, I'd expect you was to prefer the clubs, eh?" Without allowing any time for an answer, Rand rambled on. "Ain't been any of the gentlemen's places—to the nobs I ain't but an encroaching mushroom, you know." He stepped back to allow Patrick to swing up onto a padded seat, then he climbed with an effort to take the one opposite. Wiping his brow with a lace-edged handkerchief, he muttered, "Ain't as young as I was to wish. No, sir, I ain't a young buck like yourself."

"Sometimes I don't feel particularly young anymore," Patrick admitted ruefully.

"You didn't take any harm when you was saving Ellie, did you?"

"No."

"She said you ruined a fine coat."

Patrick shrugged. "Nothing that cannot be replaced, I assure you." As the ornate town carriage lurched forward, he wondered why he'd committed himself to an hour or more of the old man's company.

"I'll wager 'twas Weston's finest, wasn't it? Well, I

don't mean to let you stand the loss, sir. If there's anything Bat Rand does, 'tis pay his honest debts."

"It was an insignificant amount at best," Patrick said dismissively.

"Insignificant? You saved my daughter from being run down, Hamilton! No, sir, I'm standin' you for a new one! What do them as caters to the bucks get for good coats anyways?"

"I'm afraid you'd have to ask my secretary."

"Ain't saying, eh? Well, I mean to find out." The man stared into the passing street for a moment, then looked again to Patrick. "Ellie's dear to me, Hamilton. Oh, she's got her queer starts, but she's a good gel. Pretty, too, but I don't need to tell you that—you saw her."

"Yes, she is," Patrick agreed warily.

"I might've been nigh to beneath the table the other night, but I still got eyes—I could see the way you was looking at her." When it appeared as though Patrick might speak, Rand lifted a silencing hand. "Told you—I ain't one as beats around the budget. If I think something, I'll say it." His pale blue eyes fixed on Patrick's face, and his expression sobered. "I want my gel to be happy, that's all."

"She told me about Samuel Rose's son," Patrick said quietly. "I'm sorry."

The old man's eyes went cold, then were veiled as he appeared to consider the watch fob that stretched across his rounded belly. "I ain't," he said finally. "I wasn't pleased about the boy at all, and I don't mean to say I was. I didn't make millions of bricks so as she could waste herself on no cent per cent. Rose!" he snorted. "Even the sound of it's namby-pamby, ain't it? A demned flower!"

"I rather like Sam," Patrick murmured. "I've sent a few clients to him."

"Borrowing money from 'em is one thing—marrying 'em is quite another!" Rand snapped. Recovering himself, he smiled again. "But it don't make no difference now, anyways, does it? Boy's gone wherever it is they go, ain't he? And I've been real patient with

Ellie, but I got to think of her future. It ain't as I was
going to be around forever, you know."

Patrick picked at a crease in his black barrister's
robe, then returned his attention to the old man.
"There is much to admire in Miss Rand—she is possessed of beauty and kindness, which rarely come together. But if you are wishful of honesty, I will have
to tell you that ere Christmas, I expect to be sending
my own betrothal notice to the papers," he said
gently.

It was as though all the bluster left Bartholomew
Rand. "I see. Aye, that does put a different complexion on what I had intended to say," he managed
finally.

"But even if my interest were not already fixed elsewhere, I very much doubt that Miss Rand would
have me."

The old man studied him for a moment. "What you
was meaning to say is you wouldn't have a Cit's daughter, ain't it? I ain't one as needs sugar with my medicine, Mr. Hamilton."

"Not at all." Patrick's mouth twisted wryly. "If anything, Miss Rand is far too good for me."

"Aye, and you don't know the half," the old man
said, sighing. "Got too kind a heart. Even before the
Rose boy, she was taking in all manner of creatures.
Let me tell you, sirrah, I've had every sort of mongrel
under my roof since she was old enough to cry over
'em. Why, there was dogs as would hurt you to look
upon—aye, and a one-eyed cat even," he recalled with
feeling. "But the worst was a chimney sweep as was so
black 'twas only his eyes as could be seen above the
filth. He had sores, she said. He was being beaten, she
tells me. And he *was* naught but skin and bone, but
I was wanting to give him back to his rightful master."

"But you didn't."

"Even Em agreed with me, but when the man came
to get him, Ellie was in such a taking as I had to let
him stay. The More woman's got him now, making
him pray for his food, I'll wager."

"Something ought to be done about the deplorable way we allow climbing boys to be treated."

Rand's head jerked back, and for a moment he regarded Patrick. "You ain't a reformer surely?" he demanded suspiciously.

"No. In fact, I expect to declare myself a Tory."

"You don't say! Well now, I knew I liked you, sirrah—from the moment I saw you, I knew I liked you!" He leaned across the seat. "Aye, we got to let the females preach a bit, but we ain't for changing the order of things, eh?"

"Even a Tory can have sympathy for the plight of children," Patrick retorted.

"Aye, mayhap so," Rand conceded, "but that don't mean we ought to attempt fixing everything, does it?"

"No."

Apparently satisfied, the old man sat back. "I was hoping to find a husband as would steer Ellie better than I have," he said almost wistfully.

"With her face and form, not to mention her fortune, I should not think it a difficult task."

"No—no, I suppose not. Well, as we are nearly there, I wouldn't take it amiss if you was to want to take off the robe, sir."

"Thank you."

As Patrick unfastened the heavy black overgarment, silence descended between them. It wasn't until he'd struggled out of it that Rand spoke again, this time distantly.

"She was fortunate you was at the whorehouse. Ain't no telling as what could have happened to her."

"Yes."

"I don't know what to do save clap her up at home like she was a demned prisoner." He stared out the window, then sighed heavily. "I thought I had the blunt to tempt you." When Patrick said nothing, he sighed again. "I thought as you would defend the whore, you could be bought."

"Shall I return your five hundred pounds?"

"Lud, no!" Turning troubled eyes back to Patrick,

he shook his head. "If I wasn't to need you now, there ain't no telling but what I might ere long."

Patrick's eyes narrowed. "We are not speaking of your daughter now, are we?"

"No."

"Mr. Rand, if you are truly in need of my services, nothing but the truth between us will suffice. I shall have to know the whole."

"Aye, but now ain't the time," was the evasive answer. "We are arrived at Garraway's."

"Mr. Rand—"

"Oh, I ain't hiding anything," the old man assured him.

A chill, steady drizzle descended from the gray sky as the carriage weaved its way through clogged, muddy streets. Patrick stared moodily out the side window while the girl opposite him maintained a determined discourse, describing Lady Witherspoon's card party of the previous evening.

She stopped midsentence. "You are not attending me at all," she said, accusing him.

He managed to smile ruefully. "I am caught out, aren't I? Then I suppose I must plead the press of business, my dear."

"Well, you are not very flattering either, are you? If you had no wish to accompany me to Hookham's, I am sure I would have understood."

"No, no, you mistake the matter," he assured her smoothly, reaching to possess her gloved hand. "Dearest Jane, when we are at Dunleith, I mean to be all yours."

"Papa's, you mean," she said peevishly. "He will have you out shooting all day, and I shall only have your company for the evening."

"The best part of the day, then." He leaned closer. "Shall I tell him I wish to remain at your side?" he asked wickedly.

She flushed and pulled her hand away. "As if he would listen to you." Sighing expressively, she added, "Sometimes I think I am but his political pawn."

"Not with me, Jane. I think you quite lovely."

Apparently the softness of his voice mollified her, for she sat back against the red velvet squabs of her father's elegant town carriage. Glancing out her own window, she sighed again. "We have been together so little, Patrick, that sometimes I think you must be avoiding my company."

"I'm sorry, but I am one of those sad cases who has to earn his bread, I'm afraid."

"There are times I find myself simply wishing to be *seen* with you, to use your consequence before the world," she mused wistfully.

"*My* consequence? My dear, your father is the earl." Once again, he smiled. "I am the plain mister, lest you have forgotten."

"But everyone knows who you are." Her dark eyes studied him as a slow smile warmed them. "And there is nothing plain about you, Mr. Hamilton—nothing at all, I assure you."

"And I suppose you think no one knows Dunster?" he asked, lifting one eyebrow. "A whisker if I ever heard one."

"But just now I am but Papa's daughter, you see. One day I—" She caught herself and stopped short. "Well, one day I shall be someone's wife—or at least I have hopes of it."

"And that will give you more consequence than being the incomparable Lady Jane?" he quizzed her.

"Yes. Then I shall preside over my own establishment, and I shall be as much the hostess as Countess Lieven, though we ought perhaps to consider a larger—" Again, she caught herself, biting her lip. "Well, I shall mean to be my husband's political partner, of course."

As much as he intended to offer for her, it still rankled him that she could consider him as much as leg-shackled already. Nor could he fathom why it was so important to her to parade him about every opportunity she could find, even when she knew he was extremely busy. And now it was as though she not only hoped to force a declaration even before he went to Dunleith, but she also was desirous of a larger house.

"My dear Jane," he said dampeningly, "my establishment is well situated to my office and to the Bailey."

"Well, I was not speaking of you precisely," she retorted. "But I cannot think that you could wish to continue in your current endeavors forever, Mr. Hamilton. I mean you surely do not intend to associate yourself with the likes of that—that *awful* Mrs. Coates when you stand for Parliament. There I have said it."

"Mrs. Coates is a client merely."

"I know, but she is not the sort—well, she certainly does nothing for your consequence, after all."

"My dear, there are not many peers or peeresses accused of capital crimes, I am afraid. Were I only to defend them, I should starve."

"Yes, but—well, there will be settlements, of course, and I cannot think you will wish to practice law forever. I mean, in the *general* way, a gentleman does not earn his money."

It was time to disabuse her of that notion. "Lady Jane, I do not mean to be led about by my wife—or by her money."

"Well, I did not think—"

"Yes, you did," he declared bluntly.

She knew she'd gone too far, and she sought to retrieve the situation before she lost him. "Mr. Hamilton—Patrick—I assure you that I should never attempt to interfere. But Papa said—that is, he said you would probably not continue in the practice of law when—"

His jaw tightened, but he forced it to relax, telling himself that the last thing he needed was to lose a powerful patron for the sake of his own vanity. Reaching across the seat again, he possessed both her hands with his. Looking into her eyes, he managed to smile.

"Jane, we have talked a great deal of ifs and whens, but I have always tried not to count my chickens ere they are hatched. If you are asking my intentions toward you, that is your right, but until the matter is settled between us, I should very much rather not discuss the rest of my future."

"Yes, of course." Clearly disappointed, she looked at her lap. Tears brimmed, threatening to overflow, as she swallowed hard. "Well, then I suppose I ought to dare to ask, shouldn't I?'' she whispered. ''What *are* your intentions, Mr. Hamilton?''

''When we are at Dunleith, it is my intent to ask you to be my wife,'' he answered quietly.

''Then why must you wait?'' she cried. ''If you would wed me, why cannot you puff it off to the papers while I am still in London? While my friends may yet see it and felicitate me?''

''Don't you think I ought to speak to your father first?''

''But he has already counted your chickens, sir! And he will make no objection, I assure you,'' she managed, trying to calm herself. ''If you want me, I would you asked me now.''

Outfaced, he nodded. ''I'd hoped to do this with a bit more style, my dear,'' he murmured. Lifting her chin with his knuckle, he forced her to look at him. ''My dear Jane,'' he asked huskily, ''will you do me the very great honor of becoming my wife?''

Her tears spilled over, streaking her face. ''Oh, Patrick!''

''And if you say no, I'll take it for a hum,'' he warned her.

''Yes,'' she answered happily. ''Oh, yes!''

He'd been piqued and repiqued, and he knew it, yet he'd not been forced into anything he'd not planned to do eventually, he reminded himself. But as he looked into her lovely, tear-stained face, he felt oddly empty.

''I still would that you said nothing until I have spoken with Lord Dunster,'' he managed, still trying to maintain his smile. ''As you said, there are the settlements to be decided.''

''Oh, Papa means to be *most* generous, Patrick, but I shall leave it to him to speak to you of that,'' she told him coquettishly. ''But we shall both have everything we want, I assure you.''

Despite the wealth he himself brought to the match, he still felt as though he'd been bought and sold. His fingers closed over hers for a moment, squeezing them, then he released her hand.

"Well," she demanded archly, "aren't you wishful of kissing me?"

For answer, he leaned across the space between them to take her face in his hands. With slow deliberation, he brushed her parted lips, then he kissed her. When he drew back, she smiled her triumph.

"Oh, Patrick, I have loved you for such a long time," she said breathlessly.

"I know," was all he could think of to say.

"We shall be quite suited, you know," she went on eagerly. "With Papa's help, you will have a brilliant career, and I shall have quite the handsomest husband in all of London."

"Well—"

"Oh, but you are! Everyone says so, you know—la, but I can scarce wait to see the look on Lady Witherspoon's face—or on that presumptuous Miss Marsden—when it is known that you have chosen me. Patrick Hamilton, I vow I am in alt!"

"Thank you," he murmured dryly.

"I think we should have no more than two children, for I should not like to become stout like so many females," she decided. "After all, you would not wish for a fat wife, I am sure."

"Even if both children should be girls?" he quizzed her.

"Well, we shall have to have an heir, of course," she admitted judiciously. "But we can hope one of the first two is a son, can't we? After all, I shan't wish to be forever increasing, for I mean to be the most dashing Tory hostess you will have ever seen."

"An admirable ambition."

"Now I know you are funning with me," she retorted, "but I am quite serious, I assure you. Everybody will wish for an invitation to my salon."

"I doubt we can get everyone in it, my dear."

"Well, once we are wed, I expect you will see the wisdom of a larger establishment."

"For our two offspring, my dear?"

"For our consequence."

He leaned back, cocking his head slightly as he regarded her lazily. "Have you never thought it might prove impossible to, er—restrain ourselves? That we might err through passion and parent more than a pair of small Hamiltons?"

"Passion," she pronounced definitely, "is for the lower classes. But if you are like my father, who is the soul of discretion, I shall try not to notice when you indulge yourself with the demimonde."

"After we have done our duty to name and fortune?"

"After we have done our duty." She caught the faint twitch at the corners of his mouth. "What amuses you?"

"Your naiveté, my dear—your utter naiveté. First you would have me kiss you, then you would prate of a future devoid of passion." He straightened and sat up. "I'm afraid, Jane, my love, that I have not the least intention of straying from your bed for the sake of your figure."

"Really, Patrick—"

"No, if we take each other, you'll simply have to eat in moderation."

She stared incredulously at him for a moment. "You're quite serious, aren't you?"

"Let us merely say I don't take solemn oaths lightly."

She opened her mouth, then shut it. "Well," she said finally, "I daresay you will not feel that way forever. I mean, Mama says that every man eventually seeks amusement elsewhere."

"And," he went on, ignoring that, "I take leave to tell you that I not only intend that my heir resembles me, but that every child after does also."

"Sir," she said faintly, "I really do not think we ought to be speaking of such things."

His mouth twisted wryly. "Actually, my dear, I believe it was you who brought up the indelicate matter of children."

"Then I must beg your pardon for it," she said, her voice low.

"Jane—" He reached across to lift her chin with

his hand. "I would hope that when we are husband and wife, we can discourse freely on everything. I want more than a female decoration for my establishment—much more. You have said you have loved me forever, and—"

"And I have!"

"Then when we are wed, I shall expect you to prove it." He released her and looked out his rain-streaked window. "We are arrived at Hookham's my dear." Reaching down, he drew out his watch and flicked the cover open. "I pray you will hurry, for I am engaged to meet with clients this afternoon." Closing it, he returned it to his waistcoat pocket, then he opened the carriage door and jumped down, trying to avoid the muddy puddles. "Come on," he said, reaching up for her.

She leaned into his arms, letting him lift her. As she slid down effortlessly, she looked into his face.

"And what will you prove to me? I wonder," she asked softly.

He set her down upon the curb, then offered his arm. "I shall attempt to be an exemplary husband."

As he held the library's door open for Lady Jane, he saw Elise Rand at the desk inside, and his breath caught when the girl turned around, recognizing him.

"Why, Mr. Hamilton, what a surprise."

He recovered quickly. "You thought perhaps that I do not read?"

"Not at all. Actually, I thought you must spend most of your time at the Bailey—and other places, of course," she added knowingly.

Jane's fingers closed possessively on his sleeve. "You must make me known to your acquaintance," she murmured.

Nodding, he smiled at the brick merchant's daughter. "Miss Rand, may I present Lady Jane Barclay? And," he added, gesturing to Elise, "Jane, Miss Rand."

"How do you do?" Elise inquired politely, extending her gloved hand.

"Very well, thank you," Dunster's daughter responded stiffly. Her eyes took in everything from Elise Rand's altogether fetching feather-trimmed blue velvet bonnet to her matching braid-trimmed pelisse to her soft kid gloves and dainty slippers before returning to the girl's blue eyes. "I'm afraid I cannot place you, Miss Rand," she decided coldly.

"I did not expect it, Lady Jane," Elise responded, her voice enticingly husky. "We do not move in the same circles, I'm afraid."

"I did not think so." Dismissing the other girl with an aristocratic sniff, Lady Jane moved toward the desk to inquire whether Hookham's had a copy of "the Austen woman's latest."

Elise's gaze followed her briefly, then returned to Patrick. "Yes," she observed, "she suits your aspirations admirably. Now, if you will excuse me, my carriage awaits me, and I have been informed it is not good practice to keep horses standing any longer than necessary. Good day, Mr. Hamilton."

She stepped outside, then raised her blue umbrella against the light rain. As the door closed behind her, Lady Jane returned, saying peevishly, "They are all out of the one I have not read, so we have come for naught." Seeing that Patrick still watched as Elise Rand disappeared from sight, she caught his sleeve. "Who is that creature, anyway? I vow I thought she was perhaps not what she ought to be, but then I knew you would not introduce me to one of those. Although," she added archly, "I own it surprised me greatly that you did not present her to me first. After all, my father—"

"Is an earl," he finished shortly for her. Turning around, he regarded her soberly. "My mistake merely, but she is Bat Rand's daughter."

"Bat Rand?" she repeated blankly.

"Bartholomew Rand—of Rand Brickworks in Islington."

"Oh, *that* Rand. Well, then I daresay that explains everything."

"What?"

"Her clothes. My dear Patrick, that creature must

have been wearing well over a hundred guineas." She sniffed again. "Why is it, I wonder, that the encroaching Cits must always attempt to flaunt their money beneath our noses?"

"She is not 'that creature,' my dear—she is Miss Rand," he reminded her tightly. "And I daresay she has more money than Dunster and I put together."

"Much good it will do her," Jane retorted coldly, "for she cannot aspire to society."

The image of Elise Rand bargaining with Maddie Coates came to mind, and he could hear again her passionate concern for poor Pearl. "I don't think she would wish to," he murmured. "In fact, I am certain of it."

"Nonsense," Jane insisted. "They all aspire to recognition beyond their station, when in truth they are scarce removed from their own servants." She sniffed disdainfully again as she pulled up her gloves. "I blame the French, you know, for they created this horrid notion of equality between servant and master. We should have helped King Louis scotch their revolution."

"We did not have to—they had Napoleon to foist another aristocracy on them."

"The Corsican upstart? You jest, of course. He took what he could not claim by birth." Her chin came up haughtily. "Napoleon was a peasant," she declared dismissively. "He did not possess so much as a title."

"The same could be said of me."

"No, it cannot, for at least you are born a Hamilton," she said, taking his arm again. "And there is a Hamilton duke." As they emerged out into the steady drizzle, she saw Miss Rand's all too elegant carriage pull away from the curb. "Obviously, she lives far above her station," she muttered sourly. "I wonder that you know her, Patrick."

"I met her when I dined with the old man in his house."

"Yes, well—with that hair, she is a bit too florid, don't you think?"

"I think, Lady Jane, that it makes her a beauty," he stated baldly as he opened her coach door.

"In a common sort of way, I suppose," she conceded coldly.

"No, my dear, you are mistaken—there is nothing common about Miss Rand at all."

This time, they rode the distance between Hookham's and Dunster's mansion in Mayfair in relative silence as she began making mental plans for her wedding and his future. He sat across from her, his thoughts obviously elsewhere, responding only vaguely when she spoke to him.

"I should think we would wish to be married before the next Season, don't you? I mean, then I should come to town again a married lady, and I could be presented at court as such."

"I'll examine my calendar," he murmured noncommittally.

"Your calendar?"

"To see when court is in session."

"Oh."

As she lapsed once again into silence, he thought regretfully of Elise Rand, contrasting her to his betrothed, thinking that even a brush across her lips had provided more passion than a full kiss on Jane's. But now, ambitious fool that he was, he had irrevocably tied himself to Dunster's self-centered daughter. And somehow the notion that she would be a brilliant Tory hostess did not compensate for the price he was going to pay for her.

"What are you thinking of now, Patrick?" Lady Jane asked.

"Hmmm? Nothing much," he lied.

"You are coming in with me, aren't you?" she wheedled. "You know Mama will be like the cat over the cream pot when she hears the news."

"No," he managed, shaking his head. As her smile faded, he added regretfully, "Press of business, I'm afraid. But I expect to call upon Lord Dunster ere the week is out," he promised.

"Well, I hope so, else I shall go home a spinster,

when I have in fact held out all year for you. I could have had Lord Dillingham, you know—or Stand-bridge even."

"Both admirable Tories," he murmured.

"But I have waited for you, Patrick."

He pressed his lips together to avoid a sigh, then nodded. "Well, I hope I shall prove worthy of the wait, my dear."

"Oh, you will, I am certain of it—you will."

But as he stared at the gulf between them, he was not nearly so sure.

Maddie Coates was dead. Patrick stared at the boxed article that leapt from the newspaper page. He read it several times before it sank in—Maddie Coates was dead.

According to the report, both she and one Thomas Truckle, identified as a "butler" in her employ, had been found dead in an alleyway "not far removed from the iniquitous dens of the opium eaters," their bodies stripped of everything of any value. When questioned by the district constable, the area proprietors had at first professed no knowledge at all until someone recalled that both bodies had been dragged from the Red Dragon, a particularly notorious place. Thereupon the owner had allowed that he'd discovered them "asleep o'er their spoons, their faces as peaceful as if they was in heaven."

The article went on to say that there was not so much as a mark beyond that caused by dragging on either person. The constable's opinion, seconded by the coroner, was that both deaths had occurred as a result of the purity of the opium, but there were curious specks within the remaining cake, which was being sent to a chemist in France for examination.

The only other clue the Red Dragon's proprietor had remembered was that "an odd cove—all covered wi' 'is cloak, he was" had been seen sharing the opium with Maddie Coates. When asked why he'd recalled the man, the den owner had insisted it was because the fellow had brought his own stuff and merely paid for the use of the table.

The story ended with the moralistic opinion that

Magdalene Coates had atoned for a lifetime of sin by inadvertently removing herself from this world. No explanation was given for the demise of her equally unfortunate "butler."

But Patrick wondered. As he laid the paper aside, he could not entirely believe that an experienced addict had died by her own mistake. Why had the constable not ordered a search for the odd cove? He knew the answer to that almost before the question crossed his mind—however she departed this world was immaterial to the authorities. For whatever the means of it, Maddie Coates's death was a good riddance.

Poor Maddie. Patrick felt a regret, not all of which came from the balance she owed him. For what she was, she was not a particularly bad sort. He sat there, his mind recalling his last interview with Maddie on the day Elise Rand had bought the dying Pearl from her. What was it that the woman had said?

Aye, I'll get yer money . . . I think I know where ter find it . . . Old gents get queer starts, don't ye know . . . and I know one as wouldn't want me ter blabber . . .

She was going to get money, that much had been clear, but then she'd sort of rambled on, telling him she had a rich old client, rich as a nabob, she'd called him, saying her girls didn't like the man. And that he'd had a fancy for the murdered Peg once.

And now Maddie was dead also. Without having any illusions about what she did for her living, Patrick had actually liked the old madam. Closing his eyes briefly, he could see her facing Elise Rand, the girl filled with outrage, the woman clever enough to prey upon that rage.

"John!"

"Aye, sir?"

"What time is the next appointment, old fellow?"

"Well, as Mr. Johnson's brother has given a slip to his jailer and managed to escape wearing a lady's gown, Mr. Johnson wishes to save his money."

"He must have bribed the jailer with it," Patrick decided cynically. "And I have already pled him not guilty. Who else?"

"Well, there is a Mrs. Fitch coming." John Byrnes looked to the book in his hand, then shook his head. "I told her she merely needed a solicitor, but she wishes for someone famous."

"For what?"

"She is accused of attempting bodily harm over the matter of a pig, I believe."

"Egad."

"I told her I believed it might be settled civilly, but she says Mrs. Hughes wishes her to hang."

"She must have stolen it."

"She says not, sir."

"So say they all," Patrick murmured dryly. "Yes, well, can you attend the matter?"

"I think so, but she hoped to see you."

"Is she on bail?"

"Yes. The hearing is set for the twenty-second."

"Send 'round to Peale, requesting a continuance until after Christmas. Plead hardship, saying I shall be out of town. Anyone else?"

"Well, Mr. Rand was here quite early, but he would not say if he meant to return. Though he did seem a trifle out of sorts, I must say."

"If he chooses not to take an appointment, I can scarce be held accountable for being here. Anything more on the Steele matter?"

"Every statement I have taken damns him further."

"I was afraid of that." Patrick heaved himself up from the chair and reached for his beaver hat. "I shall be out for a while, so you will have to muddle through as best you can."

The clerk's gaze dropped to the newspaper. "A terrible shame, isn't it? She ought to have at least finished paying us."

"She paid enough."

"Do you think it was divine retribution, sir?"

Patrick shrugged. "I don't know. I'm not at all certain I have that much faith in the Almighty's interest in the misdeeds of humanity."

Shocked, Byrnes remonstrated, "How can you think so, sir? Holy Writ says—"

"Holy Writ is filled with contradiction, John." As his clerk appeared on the verge of apoplexy, Patrick relented. "But if you ask if I believe in an Almighty, the answer is yes, I do. My only question is whether He truly wishes to insert Himself into everyone's life all the time. Given that Napoleon managed to waste the youth of a nation vaingloriously, I rest my case."

Somewhat mollified, John Byrnes hastily returned to Maddie Coates. "Did you know she was an opium eater?"

"I knew she paid to have it smuggled into Newgate."

"It does seem odd that her butler was with her, doesn't it?" the clerk ventured.

"I expect she wished protection merely." Setting his hat on his head, Patrick leaned to retrieve his walking stick. "But I hope to discover the whole."

"Then you don't think it was an accidental overdose of opium?"

"I don't know. I did think I might speak with the females in her employ," Patrick murmured.

"An unenviable task," Byrnes said wryly. "Were I you, I should check them for—"

"John," Patrick interrupted him, "I do not plan on riding any of them."

"No, of course not," the clerk said quickly.

But once outside, Patrick considered that Maddie's girls might not be much inclined to speak with him, particularly not if they believed her a murder victim. Not to mention that they might consider themselves threatened by Maddie's "old gent." Nonetheless, he hailed a hackney and swung up into it. Hesitating but a moment, he abruptly changed his mind.

"Marylebone," he ordered tersely. "Do you know the Rand house there?"

"Big brick one?"

"Yes."

"Aye."

Telling himself his purpose was to ask Elise Rand of Pearl and discover whether the girl was still at the Royal Hospital, he settled back against the hard leather-

covered seat. But as the hackney wended its way
through city traffic, he knew he could have simply
inquired at the hospital. What he really wanted was to
see Miss Rand herself.

Old Starch, as Rand called him, answered the door
stiffly, then left Patrick to wait in the same saloon he
remembered from that awful night. Fidgeting, Patrick
sat for a moment, then rose to walk to the many-
paned window. To his chagrin, Bartholomew Rand was
stepping down from his coach, and there was going
to be no way to avoid him. Sighing, he squared his
shoulders and waited for the verbal barrage.

"Well, well, sirrah!" the old man said heartily, coming into the room. "No need to call upon me now,
you know! I was just stopping by for a bit of a chat,
nothing more."

"Actually, I came to inquire if Miss Rand would care
for a turn about the park." Even as he said it, Patrick
felt the old man would know it for a hum.

And Rand was no fool. "In that hackney? No, sir,
you will not—not at all!" Moving back to the door,
he called out to a footman, "Tell 'em not to unhar-
ness m'team, you hear? Tell 'em I said they was to
walk the horses." Turning back to Patrick, he grinned
broadly. "Damme if I won't let you borrow m'own
equippage! Got the best damned rig as money can
buy, you know."

"It doesn't surprise me."

"Been in it, ain't you? Took you to Garraways, you
remember?"

"Yes."

The old man eyed him closely. "Damme if I won't
tell her to go, sir—damme if I won't. Gel don't get
out enough, if you was to ask me. Only goes to the
demned library and out to the demned meetings—
time she was getting out with a fine buck like
yourself."

"As it was not raining, I thought I'd take a bit of
air," Patrick murmured.

"Aye—a man could get as musty as the books in
your office, couldn't he? I sat there nigh to half an

hour this morning, you know—your clerk tell you that?"

"As a matter of fact, he did."

"Well, like I was saying, I didn't want anything of you. Just went in 'cause I like you."

"Thank you." For want of anything else to say, Patrick told him, "Maddie Coates is dead."

"Dead! Well, I ain't going to lie to you and say as it was a shame, 'cause it ain't. Woman was a procuress, that's all she was, and 'tis a good enough riddance."

"According to the newspaper, she and a man named Thomas Truckle apparently overdosed themselves with opium."

"No! Damme if I'd ever heard she used the stuff, but it don't surprise me. Didn't know her, of course," he added hastily. "Just what I read in the papers."

"For what she was, she wasn't a bad sort."

"I ain't into whores, Mr. Hamilton. But they all got the vices, don't they? If they ain't gin sots, they're smoking the poppy, or so I've heard."

"In this case, they apparently ate it."

"Must've needed it in a bad way, eh? When they get to eatin' it, they are more'n halfway to perdition, ain't they?"

"Probably."

"Odd thing though," the old man mused, "she was a fat woman. I thought when they was into the poppy, they dropped weight."

"I think most do. They'd rather eat opium than food."

"Well, I don't know much about it, you know. But it ain't a vice as I'd want. Got enough of m'own, if you was to know it."

The footman Patrick had seen at Maddie's stuck his head in the door, murmuring apologetically. "Mr. Hamilton, sir? Miss Rand said ter inform ye as she ain't coming down. Said she wasn't prepared to go out on short notice."

"Not coming down! Here now, Will, what's this?" Rand demanded. "You tell the gel—no, damme if *I*

won't do it m'self! Not coming down! Nonsense—
utter nonsense!"

"If Miss Rand does not wish to go, I am sure I
should not impose," Patrick insisted, reaching for
his hat.

"No, no—don't go. Thing you got to understand
about Ellie is she don't like presumption—she don't
like to think as a body might order her around."

"Such was not my intent, sir."

"Course it wasn't!" Rand all but roared. "Females!
I tell you, Hamilton, there's times I wish Ellie was a
son—you don't get such queer starts out of boys," he
added with feeling. "But I ain't really repining, 'cause
she's a good gel. Just needs a man's hand to guide
her, that's all."

"Really, but—"

"Sit down, sirrah! I'll have her down in a trice, I
promise you."

Not waiting for any protest, the old man left Patrick
standing. In less that half a minute, his voice could
be heard booming down from above.

"What was you thinking of, missy?" he demanded.
" 'Tis Hamilton, I tell you—the same one as saved
your life! Damme if you don't owe him for that, I say!
Now go on—all you got to do is put on the demned
pelisse!"

Elise Rand's answer could not be heard, but apparently she still demurred, for the old man's next words
were, "Your cloak then! Damme, Elise! The fellow
don't care what you are wearing!"

"Bat—whatever—?"

"All right, Em—you make her see reason! Tell her
I ain't giving her above five minutes at the rouge pot
ere I drag her down! Hamilton is important to me!"

"But not to me!" Elise finally shouted.

"The man saved your life, Puss! And this is your
old papa as has kept you out of rags! Now, for the
last time, I'm telling you to go!"

"Really, Bat, but she is not dressed for it," Mrs.
Rand protested.

"She can demned well throw on a cloak! I'm telling

you the man's nigh to besotted with her—he ain't going to care what she is or ain't wearing!"

"I would you left me alone, Papa!"

"I ain't standing for this, Ellie!"

Finally, Patrick could stand Rand's browbeating no longer. On impulse, he went upstairs, meeting Emmaline Rand in the hallway.

"Do you mind if I speak with her?"

"I doubt it will help, sir, for each is as stubborn as the other. And when he shouts, I fear it only makes the situation worse," she said unhappily. "Now he must win—no matter what, he must win."

He moved to the open door and rapped at the jamb with his knuckles to gain their attention. Elise spun around angrily, then saw him.

"What are you doing here?"

But he looked to her red-faced father. "Er—if I might be private with Miss Rand for a moment? I assure you I mean to do nothing to overset her further."

For a long moment the old man stared back, then slowly his own anger ebbed. "Aye," he muttered. "Gel's naught but pigheaded. Mebbe you can speak to her."

Her heightened color faded as she faced Patrick. "I cannot make him understand I have no wish to throw myself at your head, sir," she said, her husky voice low.

"Miss Rand, I assure you I expect nothing of the sort," he responded gently. "I merely thought to take you up for a carriage ride about the park." His smile twisted diffidently. "Was it my mistake, or did we not cry friends?"

She wanted to cry out that she had no wish to go anywhere with him, but she knew it was not entirely the truth. Glancing at the small watercolor she'd done of Ben, she felt acutely disloyal as she nodded.

"You must think me terribly ungrateful for my life."

"Gratitude makes for unequal friends, Miss Rand."

"Is that what you want? To cry friends only?"

"Yes."

Her father turned to her mother, who still hovered

in the hall. "Told you he had a way about him, didn't
I?" he whispered loudly.

"My hair is down like the veriest schoolgirl," Elise
said finally. "And I look the complete dowd. But—"
She met his hazel eyes for a moment, then looked
away. "But I daresay it does not make much difference, does it?"

"None at all."

"And when I am seen, there's none as could think
that I—"

"No one could mistake you for a Cyprian," he said,
interrupting her, forgetting he'd once thought it.

"How cold is it?"

"As I mean to purloin your father's carriage, I
should say a light pelisse would suffice."

"Yes. Well, London is rather short of company already, isn't it?"

"Not so short that I could not have discovered
someone else," he countered, smiling.

"No, I suppose not. But I cannot think why you are
come here."

"I told you—I thought I would merely share a drive
with a friend."

"Go on, Puss," her father urged her. "Do you good
to get outside when it ain't raining."

"Mama—?"

"I should think it rather pleasant to escape this
house."

"Very   well,"   Elise   decided   without   much
enthusiasm.

Turning to fetch a blue merino wool pelisse, she
put it on with unsteady hands. Guilt washed over her
again, but she put it aside, telling herself that Patrick
Hamilton had no real interest in her and she none
in him.

"I'll have Mary get your bonnet," her mother said.
"And perhaps you can take her with you for propriety," she added.

"I can find one myself, Mama—and as I am not a tonish
lady, I don't need Mary to maintain my reputation."

"Puss!"

"Well, I am not." Her chin came up. "I am two and twenty, and I am a Cit."

"Here now—"

"And I am proud enough of it, Papa."

She found a rather plain felt shako trimmed only with pheasant feathers and tied the narrow grosgrain ribbons beneath her chin. "Yes, well," she managed, sighing, "I expect I am ready, sir."

It was not until he was handing her up into her father's town coach that he asked, "Was it necessary to poll your parents ere you could decide?"

"Yes," she answered simply. Taking her seat, she fixed her gaze on the gleaming brass sconce for a moment. "I suppose I wanted Ben to know that I am not particularly disloyal."

"Ben Rose?"

"Oh, I know he is dead, Mr. Hamilton, but I like to believe he knows I still care."

"Ah, I see the reason behind the military hat," he murmured. "You have made yourself into a citadel."

"Actually, I merely happen to like the style." She forced a smile. "Well, which park is it to be—Green or Hyde?"

"Neither."

"Neither? But you said—"

"I know, and it was as good an excuse as any I could think of at the moment. Actually—" He paused as her eyes widened. "Actually, Miss Rand, I'd thought to visit Pearl."

"Pearl!"

"Maddie Coates is dead. You might have read the tale in the morning papers."

"No," she said faintly. "No, I did not. I was rather occupied with writing a letter to Mrs. More—I have hopes she can be persuaded to find a place for Pearl in the country, where the air is better."

"Do you really think the girl will be able to travel, Miss Rand?"

"Yes—no." She sighed. "But I have prayed she will survive." She looked up at him, her expression sober. "She has had such an awful life, you know."

"And I suppose it has never occurred to you that everything cannot be fixed, has it?" he asked, smiling.

"I know that, sir," she retorted. "I am not a complete imbecile. But I do think that God expects us to attempt alleviating the suffering of our fellow man, Mr. Hamilton."

"Ah, I forgot—the Methodists."

"They do a great deal of good."

"And preach while they dole out the bread, my dear."

"Is it so terribly wrong to wish to make things better? Is it wrong to give people hope?"

"Not if they wish to hear it, Miss Rand. But to make preaching the price of survival seems rather dictatorial to me."

"Yes, well, I suppose a man of your stamp might think so, sir," she countered evenly. "I happen to think that a belief in some higher being can sustain one through life's tragedies."

"My stamp? What the devil is that supposed to mean? My dear Miss Rand, I take leave to tell you that I have helped my share survive."

"And they pay you handsomely for it." She looked at her gloved hands for a moment, then spoke more slowly. "I am not a Methodist, Mr. Hamilton—indeed, I am not nearly good enough to be one."

"You relieve my mind," he said dryly.

"Is everything a jest to you? Do you care about nothing, sir?"

"I care about a great deal, but I happen to think a good dollop of pragmatism is worth far more than a prayer." A smile twisted his mouth. "Come, can we not avoid a brangle every time we are met?"

"You could have asked for Pearl's direction, you know. I would have told you she is still abed at the Royal."

"I thought she might be afraid to answer my questions," he admitted. He leaned back, regarding her intently, then exhaled fully. "According to the newspaper, Maddie Coates died of an acute overdose of opium, taking her butler with her."

"Her butler?" She appeared taken aback. "But how——?"

"That is precisely what I should like to know. I have encountered a number of opium eaters, but she must surely be the first experienced one who did not succumb alone. 'Twould seem odd that Big Tom also perished, wouldn't it?"

"Well, I——that is, I cannot say that I know much about the subject at all. But unless they both partook of something tainted, I should think it quite odd myself."

"Precisely."

"But what has Pearl got to do with it? She was not even there," she pointed out reasonably.

"I don't know. But Maddie started to tell me of one of her clients." As her expression changed to one of disbelief, he tried to mollify her. "I realize this is a rather indelicate matter, Miss Rand, but having encountered you at Maddie's establishment, I did not think you the sort to be unduly missish."

"No, of course not," she managed, "but I must say I am unused to the subject."

"Your pardon, then. In any event," he went on, "she spoke of an old gent whose peculiar appetites got him turned away from the place."

"And you think Pearl might know of this person?"

"Yes."

"But what has this got to do with Mrs. Coates and Big Tom?"

"I think that Maddie intended to bite into the old gent's purse."

"You mean extort money from him."

"Precisely again."

"You think she knew something," she mused, "but if that were so, why did she not speak up during her trial?"

"I don't think it occurred to her at the time. I think something must have happened to remind her of him after the trial ended."

"I see. But if it was not an overdose, don't you think that the authorities would investigate the matter?"

He looked pained. "My dear Miss Rand, Magdalene Coates was a brothel keeper and an opium eater. I do not doubt for so much as a minute that her demise is counted other than a good riddance."

"But that is absurd!"

He cocked his head slightly, his eyes on hers. "Is it?" he asked softly. "Do you count her a loss?"

"No, but—"

"I rest my case."

"But I am not a constable nor a coroner, Mr. Hamilton. If I were, and if I believed she died by other than her own carelessness, I should consider it a matter of justice to investigate the matter thoroughly."

"May the Almighty deliver me," he murmured, grinning. "Never say you are one of those who believe that justice comes down like manna from heaven."

"There is the rule of law, sir," she retorted stiffly.

"The law, Miss Rand, suits the judge—not the judged."

"Do you believe in nothing?" she countered, her voice rising. "You, sir, are a lawyer!"

"And I believe in me. I am the best damned barrister to be had," he declared flatly.

"Yes, so Papa is wont to tell me."

"If I were in danger of facing the hangman, my dear, I should wish to conduct my own defense."

She looked out into the street and recognized the Royal Hospital building. "If you are so filled with your own conceit, sir, I cannot think why you wished to bring this mere mortal with you."

This time, his smile warmed his hazel eyes, making them seem nearly gold. "I suppose I felt the need for company," he murmured, reaching for the door.

"I cannot think why. Perhaps you ought to have asked Lord Dunster's daughter. She seemed quite ready to hold your sleeve, as I recall."

He jumped down, then reached up for her. As she slid into his arms, he could not help feeling a pang of regret. "Lady Jane would frown on poor Pearl. You, on the other hand, are possessed of a great deal more charity."

He was so close that she could smell the Hungary water he'd used after his shave, and for a moment she was acutely conscious of the strength of his arms, of the solid feel of his man's body. As she pulled away, he released her and stepped back.

To cover the sudden awkwardness she felt, she told him, "I shall take your recognition of my charity as a compliment, for it is possibly the kindest thing you have said to me."

"It was so intended."

Straightening her wool pelisse over her plain blue muslin day gown, she passed him and climbed the hospital steps. Without waiting for him to catch up, she approached a man behind a desk.

"We are come to visit Miss Pearl Smith."

The fellow looked up, then without saying anything, he rose and disappeared into a narrow hall. Patrick Hamilton came up behind her.

"Is something amiss?"

"No, I don't think so—I merely told him we intend to visit her." She looked around. "Perhaps he must tell someone."

But a solemn-faced man came back with the hospital clerk. "Miss Rand?" When she nodded, he shook his head. "I'm terribly sorry, miss—indeed, but we have dispatched someone to your house to tell you."

An awful premonition sent a chill through her bones. "Tell me what, sir?"

He looked to Patrick. "Miss Smith passed on a scant two hours ago, poor soul."

"She's dead?" Elise asked blankly. "But she cannot be! She was getting better!"

The clerk shoved a chair behind her, and the other man looked acutely uncomfortable. "Yes, well, I have seen it many times before, Miss Rand. Often in cases like these, where the patient cannot get well, there is a marked improvement just before the end. The mind becomes clearer, the body stronger, and then when the patient is unable to sustain the rally, he lapses rather quickly."

"But she was getting better! I was here but yesterday, and she was sitting up," Elise protested.

"She cherished your visits, Miss Rand," he said soothingly. "She spoke often of your kindness."

She sat down and clasped her hands in her lap. "I cannot believe it," she said hollowly. "I thought with care she would get better."

It came to Patrick that it was more than merely a patronizing charity to her, that she had truly cared about the pitiful girl. His hand dropped to her shoulder, squeezing it comfortingly. "I'm sorry," he said gently. "You did all you could."

"No." A tear escaped her brimming eyes and trickled down her cheek. "No," she whispered. "She died alone, when I could have been here."

"Miss Rand, I assure you she had the best of care," the clerk said awkwardly. "Dr. Adams—"

"In many ways, it was a mercy," the doctor told her. "I have seen far too many struggle, spitting up blood, being frightened of the end. Miss Smith passed on quietly."

"Yes, of course," she managed. Squaring her shoulders, she looked up at Patrick. "At least she did not die in that awful place."

"No."

"Where would you that we sent the body?" the clerk asked.

She hesitated momentarily, then decided, "I'd give her Christian burial, sir. If you will but allow me the rest of the day, I am sure I can speak with Mrs. More. In any event, I should like any charges sent directly to me. You have my address, do you not?"

"Yes."

"Yes, well—there does not appear much else to be done, does there?" Rising, she held out her hand to Adams. "I thank you for the care you gave her, sir." Turning to Patrick, she said, "I should like to go to Mrs. More's, sir. If you wish, I can set you down somewhere."

"No—I'll go with you."

"I cannot think you would wish to."

"I don't think you should go alone."

Outside, he handed her up into the carriage, then swung up to take the seat opposite, where he watched her swallow back tears. For one of the few times in his life, he felt helpless.

"People will say she"—she sniffed audibly—"that she was naught but a fallen creature, but—"

"But she could not help what she was."

"Yes." Turning her face away, she succumbed to weeping. "It was n-not fair," she sobbed against the velvet squabs. "Not fair at all!"

"No, it was not." He watched her shoulders shake until he could not stand it. Sliding across to her side, he drew her against him and closed his arms around her, letting her cry against his coat. With unaccustomed awkwardness, he tugged at the grosgrain ribbons, then cast the shako onto the floor. Shifting her against his shoulder, he smoothed her red-gold hair much as one would with a child. "It's all right—it's all right," he murmured softly.

"It's not all right!" she cried. "She had no chance!"

"Perhaps she has gone to a better place."

"You are like Papa when my dog died!"

"It was not my intent, Ellie," he assured her.

She lay silently against his chest, hearing his heartbeat beneath her ear, feeling oddly comforted despite her words to him. And then she thought of Ben, and she wanted to cry anew, but she could not.

His arm still about her shoulders, Patrick managed to reach his handkerchief and began dabbing at her tear-stained face. "That's better," he said softly. "Much better."

She sat up and wiped her eyes with the back of a gloved hand, then managed shakily, "You think me a fool, don't you?"

"No, not at all."

"I do not usually display an excess of sensibility."

"I did not think anything of it." Knowing the moment had passed, he reluctantly released her and took his own seat again. He smiled crookedly as he regarded her. "Actually, I prefer a little sensibility to a total lack of it."

"You jest, of course."

"Miss Rand, you are a truly kind female, which surely must be a gift of God amongst your sex."

"I did not think you a believer," she retorted, embarrassed by the gold warmth in his eyes.

He looked heavenward. "How is it that everyone would have it that I have no religion?" he asked. "Miss Rand, I am as certain of an omnipotent power as you are. My only question is whether He intervenes, or whether He expects us to muddle through as best we can before He sorts it all out in the end."

"You sound like the American Benjamin Franklin."

"Do I?"

"I think they call that deism, sir."

"For what it is worth to say it, I attend the Church of England, my dear."

"Because you believe—or because it is politic to do so?"

He sobered visibly. "Probably a bit of both."

"You know, I could like you better if I thought you stood for something, Mr. Hamilton. As it is, you do not even believe in justice, do you?"

"Perhaps I have seen too much of it." Pulling out his watch, he flicked open the case, then shut it abruptly. "It grows late, so perhaps you'd best set me down, after all. I can hail a hackney."

"I have angered you, haven't I? My wretched tongue—I am heartily sorry for it."

"No, but today I find myself ill-prepared to face Holy Hannah also."

After she left him on a corner, the carriage seemed terribly empty. She looked back briefly, seeing that he still stood there, and she felt a pang of guilt. He'd been kind, and she'd been the harridan. Then she recalled why she'd not wanted to go with him in the first place. She had no wish to be disloyal to Ben, she told herself, but even as she thought it, she knew it was more than that. What she really feared was Patrick Hamilton the man. Closing her eyes, she could still feel the warmth of his arms around her.

The girl leaned seductively in a doorway, her dirty satin gown loosened at her bosom to expose the twin mounds of full, rose-tipped breasts. As he passed her, she drew her knee up slowly, showing a shapely leg and ankle, as she rubbed her nubile body against the wood door frame.

"Oooh, ain't ye a fine old gent?" she cooed. When he started to pass, she pursed her lips in a kiss. "A tuppence fer a feel, if you was ter want one."

He stopped to peer into her face, then reached out to caress a breast, cupping it, weighing it with his hand. His thumb rolled over her nipple, turning it into a small, hard knob, while his other hand lifted her skirt, slipping beneath to climb upward over the warm flesh of her thigh, finding the soft, furry mound above still wet from her last customer.

He licked dry lips. "How much? How much for all of it?" he demanded hoarsely.

"A guinea ter pop it in," she told him archly. "More if ye was a-wantin' me to suck it." As she priced herself, his fingers toyed with her wet button, then slid inside. "Oooh," she cried, throwing her head back, "ye know what ye want, don't ye?"

"Aye," he croaked. "I'd give you a gold guinea if you was to make me come."

She drew away from his hand and backed from the doorway, pulling him inside a dingy, smoky room. The place was bare save for a dirty, straw-filled mattress, a bucket of water on the floor, and an oil lantern that hung from a hook on the ceiling. She worked alone, and he was glad enough of that.

Closing the door behind him, she bent over to remove her dirty white stockings, rolling them down. When she turned around, he'd shed his cloak and was unbuttoning his pantaloons. She moved closer to rub her body against his. A stocky man, he caught her roughly at the waist, bending her backward to give him access to her breasts.

"Oooh, ye'll drap me," she protested, but he paid her no heed. Instead, he found one of her nipples and began to suck eagerly. "Here now—" Afraid of falling, she caught at his arms. He bit her hard then, causing her to cry out in pain. She struggled as his teeth sank into her flesh, but his hand tangled in her hair, pulling it.

"Owwww! Look, guvnor, Annie Adams ain't—owww, yer hurtin' me!"

He pushed her away then, sending her reeling to the floor. She knelt there, wiping the blood from her breast. "Take off everything," he ordered curtly. "And be quick about it."

She looked up, her eyes wide, then she scrambled on her hands and knees for the door. "Mercy! 'Ave mercy on poor Annie!" she called out before he pulled her back and slapped her hard across the face.

"Shut your filthy mouth, bitch," he snarled. "And take off the clothes, else I'll not pay you."

Unable to escape, she stood up as her hands moved to the open neck of her gown. She slowly pulled the dress down, revealing the bare flesh beneath. As the gown slipped past her rib cage, over smooth hips, to fall in a pool of dirty satin at her feet, she ran her tongue over dry lips and tried to smile.

"How d'ye want it?" she asked him.

"I told you—I want everything." When she didn't move, he added tersely, "Get down—I'm riding first."

She glanced nervously toward the closed door, then nodded. "Now ye ain't going ter hurt Annie, are ye?"

"Not if you was to make me come," he promised. "Lie down, and I'll see you paid."

She regained some of her confidence. "Ain't a gent alive as don't pop 'is cork fer me," she promised.

Lying on her back, her legs apart, she reached up to him. "Let Annie show ye, and we'll make it real quicklike."

Without undressing further, he freed himself and dropped to his knees over her. "Pop my cork, Annie," he said hoarsely. "I want everything as a man could pay for."

"Aye." Still smiling, she reached up between him to fondle his limp manhood, caressing it lightly at first, then closing her hand over it, grasping it, pumping incessantly. "Ye ain't—"

"Keep on."

"But ye ain't—"

"Shut your filthy mouth!"

"Now if ye was ter come inside, I got a warm place fer ye," she said seductively. "Ain't a man as don't get ready there."

"Not yet." His hands fondled her breasts as his mouth smeared wet kisses on her neck. "Keep going," he urged her. "Keep it up."

"But it ain't—"

"Make me come, Annie—make me come," he ordered urgently. "I want you to do it for me." His hands came up to grasp her neck, shaking her head against the hard, dirty mattress. "You got to do it—you got to!"

"Owwww! Yer hurtin' me!" Desperate, she tried to guide the flaccid flesh inside, closing her body around it as tightly as she could. "All ye got ter do is move," she coaxed, "and it'll come."

He rocked and pumped, beating against the wet warmth, his hands still tight upon her neck. "Do it, Annie!"

"Ye ain't lettin' me breathe!" Trying to calm herself, the girl caught at his hands as she struggled beneath him. "Yer hittin' me head!"

"You got to make me, Annie!" he shouted at her.

"And I'm a-tryin'!" She wriggled and writhed, working all the while to hold him inside. Moving one hand between them, she used the other to rake his back, urging him on to no avail. "Mebbe if I was ter get on top," she gasped.

"No!"

"I could suck ye," she said earnestly. "I could try it fer ye."

"I want it now, Annie! I want it *now*! Don't you understand, bitch?—I want it now!"

"Aye, but—"

He worked so hard against her that he panted from the exertion, and still there was nothing.

"But ye ain't going ter come like this!" she cried.

He hit her across the face then, his heavy gold ring cutting her nose and cheek. "Damn you! Damn you, Annie! Aye, you'll make me—you *will*!"

"Look—some old gents—"

She got no further. His hands tightened around her neck, frightening her, and she began to fight him. Her hands grabbed for his face, gouging at his eyes, raking his cheeks with her fingernails as she sought desperately to get him off her.

His face a mask of unpent anger, he yelled at her, "You promised me, Annie—you promised me!"

She fought to tell him he was killing her, but her words were cut off with the air. She was stifling, her lungs were bursting, and his grip on her throat was like iron. Her eyes felt as though they would pop from her head as she made one last futile effort to push him away. Then all went mercifully black.

He continued banging her head as her body became limp beneath his. "Damn you, bitch! Damn you!" He rocked against her unresisting warmth, striving hard, gaining nothing. Finally, he rolled off her and gazed into her blank stare. "Worthless tart!" he shouted at her. "Wake up, damn you, else you'll pay!" Drawing his knife from beneath his waistcoat, he plunged it into her. "Damn you!" When she did not move, he stabbed her repeatedly, cutting into her lifeless flesh, cursing her in his fury. "Damn you! Damn every one of you! You're all the same, ain't you?"

When his anger ebbed, he stared down at his bloody hands, at the wet spatters on his coat, then rose unsteadily to stagger to the bucket of water she probably used to clean herself. He pulled off his jacket, flinging it onto the dusty floor, then removed his ring to wash away the blood beneath. Stooping, he picked up the satin gown and wiped his hands and face with it.

Self-loathing washed over him, making him heartily sick, and he vomited onto the floor. Again, he wiped his face with the harlot's dress.

Someone pounded on the door. "Annie! Annie!" a man called out. "Are ye all right? I heard ye!"

"Go on wi' ye!" he answered thickly, trying to sound like one of them.

"Ye ain't Annie! Yer a cove!"

Panicked, he moved behind the door, hoping the fellow would go on, but instead, the door swung inward, covering him for a moment.

"Annie?" The man looked to where the woman lay, her face vacant, her body slashed across her breasts to the bone beneath. "Gor blimey!" the fellow gasped, dropping down beside the soaked mattress.

He bolted then, running through the open door into the narrow street as fast as his unsteady legs would hold his bulk. Behind him, the man pursued, shouting, "Stop 'im—stop th' cove! 'E's murdered Annie!"

As luck would have it, a curious woman stepped out between them, giving him time to round the corner and hide himself behind a garbage wagon. His pursuer passed him, running into the watch.

"Here now—ain't no need—"

"I got ter find th' cove as killed Annie!" the man cried.

The watch grasped his arm firmly, pulling the fellow into the dim yellow light. "Oh, 'tis ye, is it? Go on wi' ye!"

"'E stuck her like a pig, I tell ye! Th' devil's killed me Annie!" Gesturing back to the open door, the man babbled, "'E's killed 'er, I tell ye!"

"Been tippin' the cup a bit, Johnny?" Taking the fellow's arm, the watchman pushed him back toward the room where Annie Adams lay dead.

"Hit were a right fat cove—I saw him wi' me own

peepers!'' the man protested loudly. "Ye got ter get
'im!''

The old man ran again, scarce conscious of the
watchman's shout of discovery, knowing now that
he ran for his own life. It was not until he reached
the end of the street that he dared slow down. One
block over, he could hear the hue and cry. He leaned
against a deserted building and caught his breath,
then walked slowly away. It had been a near thing, but
he'd managed to escape again.

But as he crossed over to the other side of the
street, they came around the corner, their number
swollen to half a dozen. He started to run, but he was
too short of breath to sustain the pace. Within a hundred feet, they caught up to him.

"Hit's him, I tell ye! 'Tis the bloody cove 'as done it!''

Cornered, he had no choice but to brazen it out.
He swung around and pointed at his pursuer. "Ye
ain't a-murderin' me also! Devil take ye fer killin'
th' gel!''

The watchman was torn for a moment, then ad-
vanced on him. "Where's yer coat?'' he demanded.

He licked his lips. "He was tryin' to rob me,'' he
gasped breathlessly. "I saw 'im kill the gel, and I ran.''

" 'E's lyin'—th' filthy bloke's lyin'! There's blood
on his shirt!''

The expressions of the men around him were men-
acing, ominous as they took in his torn waistcoat and
his scratched face. He backed away, begging the
watchman, "You got t' keep 'em away from me! If
any's lying, 'tis him!''

But the watchman was peering closely at his face.
"That yer coat back there?'' he demanded.

"Aye, but—'' He cast a wary eye around him. "She
was a tart—we was doing it—''

"And the bloody cove killed 'er!''

He licked his lips again and tried to quiet the fear
within. "He came in—was goin' to rob me.'' Nearly
sobbing, he choked out, "I'd give m'gold to the gel,
and so I told him—he turned on her—''

" 'Tis true, Johnny?'' someone demanded.

"Blood's on 'im—not me," Johnny retorted.

Rough hands grabbed him then, dragging him back to the dingy room, thrusting him inside. For an awful moment, he feared they were going to hang him from the exposed beams above. But the watchman turned over the gold ring with the toe of his boot, then bent to pick it up.

"Blood on it," he declared succinctly. Looking across the room, he asked, "Yers?"

"No."

"Hit don't fit me!" Johnny protested loudly. "Make 'im put hit on!"

"Your coat?"

"Aye."

"If it weren't 'im, 'ow'd he get the marks on 'is face?" one of the men wanted to know.

"Your cloak?"

"Aye."

"Damme if it ain't got a hood onter it!" someone discovered gleefully. "We got 'im! 'E likely killed Peg and th' other also!"

"You are lookin' at the wrong man!" he cried. "I can explain—"

"Aye, ye can—ter the constable," the watchman growled. "Ye'd best come along wi' me."

"Listen—I got money—'tis Bartholomew Rand as you've got, you fool!"

" 'E said 'e didn't 'ave any!" Johnny shouted triumphantly. " 'E's the cove as has murdered me Annie—and 'er a gel as was only a-tryin' ter earn 'er bread!" Overcome, he had to stop to wipe at his eyes with his dirty fist. " 'E killed 'er!"

"Old Rand, eh?" the watchman said, looking him up and down. "Aye, ye'll need yer blunt, I'll wager."

"This is ridiculous!" Rand spluttered. "You ain't taking his word above mine surely?"

" 'Tis ye as has got the blood about ye," was all the fellow said. Closing his hand over Rand's arm, he gestured toward the others. "Billy, you watch o'er the body—the rest o' ye come with me t' take 'im in."

Patrick woke up to an urgent note from Bartholomew Rand, requesting that he attend him at Newgate. Making haste to the Bailey to enter a plea in for a client, he encountered Peale, who told him nearly everything about Rand's capture, declaring the constable and magistrate were on their way to providing the prosecution a damned good case. Stunned, Patrick canceled his morning appointments by messages to Byrnes and Banks, then he crossed Newgate Street to the prison.

"Well, it took you long enough," Rand said sourly when Patrick was ushered into the damp, cramped cell. Looking around himself with disgust, he grumbled, "They ain't givin' me a better place until I pay 'em for it. Pigs! This ain't fit fer pigs, sirrah, and they've put Bat Rand into it! Well, I want out—I want you to get me out now! Not tomorrow nor the day after, but *now*, you understand me?"

"I think you'd best sit down," Patrick said quietly.

"Sit down! The devil I will! I ain't staying in this filth, I tell you!"

"The charge against you is murder."

"Murder!" Rand snorted contemptuously. "She wasn't nothin' but a dirty little cock's inn!"

"The charge is still murder," Patrick pointed out evenly.

"She was unfit to take air with decent people!"

"If I speak with Peale, perhaps it can be arranged to plead you Thursday next. Even then, I doubt any of the justices will agree to set bail given the charge, not to mention that there is a continuing investigation."

"Thursday next! Damme if I shall wait for that, sir— damme if I will!"

"Sit down, Mr. Rand."

"I ain't—"

Patrick closed his leather folder and called for a guard. The old man paled, then sank onto the narrow bench, the chains at his ankles clanking against the floor. "I ain't used to being ordered about, Mr. Hamilton," he noted testily. "In my business, I'm doing the ordering."

"This is my business."

"I'm paying you to get me out of here!" Rand snapped.

"I am not here to work against you, but I require a modicum of cooperation, else I shall not be able to represent you," the younger man reminded him. "And I'm afraid I've not much time ere I have to appear in court again. Now—" He took a seat beside Bartholomew Rand. "Now I would that you told me the whole. Otherwise, I shall simply send Mr. Banks to take your statement tomorrow."

"Tomorrow!"

"Tomorrow, sir."

"But there ain't nothing to tell, sirrah—nothing. I ain't done nothing, that's all I got to say."

Patrick looked pained. "You are charged with the murder of a Miss Annie Adams, sir—and according to Mr. Peale and one of the magistrates, there is the possibility that you will also be charged with that of Miss Fanny Shawe."

"Demned free with the 'misses,' ain't they? Miss Adams! Miss Shawe! Why, they wasn't nothing but filth upon the earth, Mr. Hamilton!"

"Did you kill Annie Adams?"

Rand stared hard at him for a minute, then his lip curled. "No, but 'tis a good enough riddance, ain't it?"

"I pray you will not say that in court, sir," Patrick said coldly. "It will not play well with the jury."

"Truth's truth, ain't it?"

"Do you deny all knowledge of Miss Adams?"

"'Course I don't deny it! M'coat and cloak was there, wasn't they?"

"I should prefer to ask the questions, Mr. Rand."

"Eh?"

"If I am to take the case, sir, I shall expect total honesty between us."

"I got enough gold to make you richer'n Golden Ball, Hamilton!" the old man retorted. "Don't go a-dangling 'ifs' between us."

"Honesty, Mr. Rand. If I accepted every client willing to meet my fee, I should be sadly overworked. Now—how did you know Miss Adams?"

"Wish you'd cease calling her a miss," Rand growled. "She was no more a miss than one of them rats as in the cellars."

"Mr. Rand—"

"All right," the old man muttered grudgingly. "I was doing what you'd think there. Gave her a guinea for everything, she said."

"Given the place, a pound seems rather a lot, doesn't it?"

"Dash it, sirrah, but you wasn't borned a fool, was you? I was gettin' over, under, and a tongue-licking, too—there, I have said it, ain't I?"

"Go on."

"Ain't much else to tell."

"There is the matter of Annie Adams's murder. Did you witness it?"

"Aye." Rand looked up at him from beneath heavy brows. "Don't know as what Mrs. Rand and Ellie are going to say to this," he muttered. "It ain't as what I'd like 'em to know."

"No doubt," Patrick murmured dryly. "Now, what precisely transpired last night when you were with Miss Adams?"

"I told you to cease calling her a miss! She was a whore, sir—a demned *whore*!" Seeing that Patrick's patience was thinning again, he raised his hand, then dropped it to his knee. "Well, we was doing the business when—"

"How were you dressed, sir?"

"Dressed? Devil take you for a fool, sirrah! What would you think I'd be a-wearing when I was a-going at her?"

"Where was your cloak? Your coat?"

"My cloak was on the floor where I took it off. I was bang-tailing her, wasn't I?"

"And the coat? Did you have it on?"

"You ain't got no right to ask all my business," Rand grumbled.

"Were you wearing your coat?" Patrick persisted.

"Don't see what difference it makes. I had my pantaloons unbuttoned, and that was all as was needed, if you get my meaning."

"One last time, sir—were you wearing your coat, or had you removed it?"

"Cannot remember," the old man said mulishly. "Cannot think why you was to ask it."

"Your coat was found on the floor by the bucket, sir. As was a ring that fits you."

"Then I must've taken 'em off before."

"You took off your ring first?" Patrick asked, lifting an eyebrow.

"Not the ring. Her Johnny come for the money took it from me, I suppose."

"Then how did you get blood on the coat?"

"Damn it, sir! I don't have to stand for this—no, sir—not at all! You are supposed to get me out of here, not ask all the demned questions as don't concern you! How the devil am I to know what happened, I ask you? All I was doing was putting the cock to the pudding."

"I'm afraid Mr. Peale will ask the same questions of you when you are under oath in court," Patrick said tiredly. "Now did you take your coat off before or after you coupled with Miss Adams?" Referring to notes he'd made after he'd spoken with Peale, he added, "Or did you finish your business at all?"

"Of course I finished it! What do you take me for—a funny boy? I did her up real good, sir—real good."

"Before or after you took off your coat?"

"What's this coat business, anyway?" Rand demanded angrily. "What if I was to say I don't know?"

"Then I hope you are prepared to hang."

"Eh? No, sirrah, by God, I am not," the old man blustered. "I got you, and you are getting me out. Best demned barrister as there is to be had, ain't you?"

"One of the best, in any event." Patrick regarded Rand soberly for a long moment. "But I cannot keep Peale or Milton from making you look as guilty as sin itself if you are unwilling to assist in your defense. Now—did you murder Annie Adams?"

"I already told you I didn't!"

"Then will you explain how your bloody coat came to be on the floor beside the bucket? Or how the water in that bucket came to contain what appears to be blood? Or how a gold ring that fits you was lying there also?"

"I don't see—"

"Because if you took them off before, you will have to satisfactorily explain to a jury of your peers how blood happens to be on them. And if you took it off after, you will have to explain how you found the time to do so."

"She was just a tart, for God's sake! They ain't going to hang Bartholomew Rand over no tart!"

"How did she die, Mr. Rand?"

"They was rolling me, sir! There—I have said it."

"When?"

"When I was a-gettin' off the gel!" The old man sucked in his breath and let it out slowly. "I ain't used to being talked to like this, Mr. Hamilton."

"Are you used to hanging, sir?" Patrick countered. "Somehow I cannot think you truly wish to kick out your life on the Nubbing Cheat."

"No, of course not. But they ain't hanging a man as has got my sort of money," Rand maintained stubbornly.

"Your sort of money will insure that the mob will demand a hanging. Now—honesty, sir."

"It ain't easy to tell it." The old man looked at where his hand rested on his knee. "Thing is, I don't want it to get out and about what I was doing. I got to think of Emmaline.''

''I rather think it out already. Peale has spoken with the newspapers, and I daresay every paper and hand-bill in London will publish an account.''

''Aye, I suppose so,'' Rand conceded finally. ''All right. What was you wanting me to say?''

''I want you to tell the truth. While your guilt or innocence is of no moment to me, I still like to know what sort of cards Peale could have in his hand.''

Rand viewed him with disgust, then returned his attention to his knee. ''I said I didn't kill the whore—ain't that enough? Have I got to wash all m'linen in court?''

''There have been a number of prostitutes mur-dered and thrown in the river lately—I think Peale said there were at least five, possibly seven where there were similarities. In any event, there is a public outcry to end it.''

''Public!'' Rand snorted. ''Rabble's more like it.''

''Rabble, then. Whatever you choose to call them, they are clamoring for a hanging, and once the story is told in the newspapers, it will be your hanging they want.''

''I mean to tell the judge as I ain't done it,'' the old man retorted.

''Unfortunately—or fortunate, as the case may be—you will not be allowed to testify for yourself.'' Patrick waited until Rand looked at him, then he added, ''The only things between you and the noose are me and a jury, sir.''

''I still say they don't hang a rich man.''

''And I am telling you there will not be a ticket to be had to the gallery,'' Patrick declared flatly. ''And if you are convicted, people will come with beds and picnic baskets to see you go to the gallows.''

The old man was silent for a moment, then he nod-ded. ''All right,'' he said again. ''We was finishing the business when the fellow came in and demanded money of me. I said as I didn't have any—that I'd given it to the gel. He pulled me off'n her and started

going at her with his sticker. There was blood every-
wheres, and I was afeared he was going to do me in
with her."

"And what did you do?" Patrick prompted. "Did
you try to help? Did you run for help, sir?"

"Dash it, but I been robbed thrice already! No,
course I didn't go out a-calling for aid! No telling as
who might've shown, eh? No, sirrah, I was in a hurry
to go, I can tell you."

"He stabbed her while you were positioned over
her?"

"I was a-trying to get out of the way."

"But you saw him do it?"

"Aye."

"What sort of knife did he use?"

"How the devil am I to know that?" Rand asked
querulously. "I told you—I was a-wantin' to get out
of there."

"How did you lose your ring?"

Rand toyed with his hand. "Damme if I ain't already
told you that."

"Before he stabbed her or after?"

The old man eyed him malevolently. "How the devil
should I remember that? If you was wantin' to know,
ask the cove as killed her. You ain't got no right to
talk to me as if I was the criminal."

Patrick considered him for a time, then he shook
his head. "No, it won't fadge, I'm afraid."

"Won't fadge!"

"Peale will have your story in shreds within an
hour."

"Then you tell me what to tell 'em when they ask
me!"

"I wasn't there."

"Damn it! I'm paying you to tell me what to say,
sirrah, and afore God you're going to do it!" Red-
faced now, Rand rose to stand above Patrick. "I don't
care what it costs me, you are going to do it! I ain't
no hand with words, Hamilton!"

"Did he stab her with your penknife?"

"It was his."

"He cannot read nor write, I'm afraid."

"Look, I don't care as how you do it, but afore God, you're going to get me freed! And you ain't bouncing me, 'cause I ain't standing for it! You are getting me out today, d'you hear? Today!"

"No." Patrick closed his leather folder and stood, towering over the stocky man. "I don't have to do anything, sir."

"You got my gold! Dash it, but I paid you—you cannot refuse me, sirrah—you cannot!"

"My clerk will see you get it back."

The color drained from Bartholomew Rand's face, and his bluster left him. "You'd desert me?" he said, disbelieving it. "Hamilton, I got gold—whatever you was to ask, I got it."

But Patrick already had his folder tucked beneath his arm. Picking up his walking stick, he started for the iron door. "Counsel done," he told the nearest guard.

"But you cannot—you cannot—" Rand insisted. "How much d'you want? Ten thousand? Twenty?"

"If you wish, I shall be happy to recommend another barrister to you."

"I don't want another," the old man said plaintively. " 'Tis you as I engaged."

"You might send 'round to Parker. He has an excellent reputation."

It dawned on the old man then that Hamilton was indeed serious. "But why?" he demanded incredulously. *"Why?"*

"Because I require my client's active cooperation," Patrick answered. "And because you are lying to me. You may lie to your family or to the magistrate, but you do not lie to me. Good day, sir."

Following a guard, Elise Rand picked her way into the depths of Newgate. Lewd fellows called out to her from behind grate-covered doors, their voices intermingling in a cacophony of obscene words. She held her head high and pretended not to hear them. Her heart raced and her stomach sank within her as she viewed the squalor of the denizens of the prison. In some places, whole families huddled together over a single cooking pot, while in others, mothers in rags clutched babes against their breasts. As she passed one, a jailor winked at Elise's guard, then unlocked the cell and let himself inside, where he could be heard telling a faded flower what he wanted of her.

Someday, Elise reflected wearily, she was going to have to attempt doing something about the wretched conditions, but just now she had to see her father. The farther she went, the greater the stench as the odors of unwashed bodies, rotted teeth, and human waste commingled, nearly gagging her. She had to take out her handkerchief and hold it over her nose.

"You have no right to hold my father among common criminals," she told the guard with feeling. "Surely there must be some other place he can stay until bail is set for him."

He turned around at that, favoring her with a blackened, gap-toothed grin. "Aye, fer a bit o' blunt, Oy might could find 'im sommat better, me fine mort." As he said it, his gaze moved over her insolently. "And 'e ain't gettin' bail, Oy'll be bound."

"What?"

"No bail," he repeated plainly. "But if ye was t'cross me and—"

"I should rather report you," she muttered. " 'Tis bribery you suggest."

The fellow shrugged. "Then 'e can rot 'is rich arse below." Again, he grinned, pointing to another door. "Or 'e cud be tipplin' like he was a dook."

"A what?"

"Dook—like 'e was a royal."

"You mean duke," she decided.

"Aye. Fer a bit o' grease, Oy cud see as 'e 'ad a clean flop, a mite o' fancy bitin'—a fancy piece e'en."

"I would that you spoke plain English," she retorted. Nonetheless, she peered inside long enough to see that a gentleman dressed as finely as any dandy lounged lazily over a card table with another like him, while a servant hovered behind ready to pour from a wine bottle. "This is disgusting," she decided.

For a moment he appeared wounded, then his grin widened from ear to ear. "A bit o' fancy yersel', ain't ye?"

"I am sure I have not the least notion," she told him severely.

"I can get 'im a bit 'igher, if ye was ter be nice ter me."

"I shall speak to the keeper of your insolence." But as she said it, curiosity got the better of her. "What did they do?" she finally asked. "I mean—why are they here?"

"The gent as is in the green? 'E's goin' ter' ang' fer stickin' a sharp as was cheatin' 'im. T'other gent's a-visitin' 'im."

"I don't believe you."

He gave a derisive snort, but nonetheless he fell silent until they reached a cell door. Then he gibed at her father, "Ye got a fine mort as is wishful o' seein' ye—see as 'er gets out whole, will ye?" Producing a ring of keys, he chose one and turned it in the lock. "No more'n ten, or I ain't lettin' ye in agin," he told Elise.

She stepped inside and tried to adjust her eyes to the lack of light as the door was locked behind her. "Papa?"

"Aye, Puss."

Coatless, and with his cravat dangling, he sat on a single rough bench, his legs in irons. When he looked up to her, his eyes were sunk within dark fleshy bags, his expression bleak. She sank down beside him and took one of his hands between hers. Swallowing hard, she blinked back tears and tried to speak.

"Are you all right?" she managed to ask him.

"Well, I ain't exactly in alt," he muttered dryly. Glancing at the locked door, he grumbled, "If he was in my employ, I'd have turned that fellow off, I can tell you."

"You are mistreated?"

"I'm here, ain't I?" he retorted. He looked around the small cell glumly. "It ain't much like home, you know."

"I know." She forced a smile. "I am told I can pay for a better situation."

"Ain't they told you? I'm far too dangerous to move, Puss. I was brung here in fetters," he recalled with feeling, holding out his chained feet. "Fetters!"

"But the jailer said—"

"You ain't giving him a farthing! The dirty nabber'll naught but take m'blunt and leave me here to rot!" As her hands tightened on his, he brightened slightly. "But if you was to grease his fingers just a mite, I daresay he'd bring me a tipple of port." Nodding toward an empty cup, he added, "Demned ale as they give me is enough to make a man puke—ain't fit for the slop bucket."

"I shall tend to it," she promised. Releasing his hand, she rose to hide her agitation. "I would that I could get you out of here."

"Hamilton said they ain't going to bail me."

She turned away. "They say you killed a woman, but I cannot believe it," she said finally. "I know you could not do such a terrible thing."

"A woman!" he snorted contemptuously. "A pugnasty, you mean! And a good riddance, too!" Catching himself, he added quickly, "But 'twasn't me as killed her, Ellie."

"How did you come to be there, Papa?" she dared to ask, turning back to face him. "What were you doing in such a place? You have always condemned that sort of woman."

"Still do," he maintained stoutly. Without meeting her eyes, he sucked in his breath, then let it out. "But I'm a man, Puss."

"And that makes it right?" she demanded incredulously. "What is Mama to think?"

"A man's got needs!"

"But you have a wife—and—and you are so proud of Mama, that I—"

"That ain't got nothing to do with it, Puss!" It was his turn to look away. "Your mama nearly died birthin' you, Ellie—I couldn't risk puttin' another loaf in her oven, don't you see? I took another chamber, trying to stay away from her, but man wasn't made to live like that.'' His voice scarce above a whisper, he went on. ''I lived without for nigh to a year, Ellie, then one night I wasn't wanting to burn alone anymore.''

''But the Adams woman—''

''Don't call her a woman!'' he snapped. ''She was no more than a flea in the straw! But I ain't got there yet—I was telling you how things was. When I first started doing it, I was going to the high-priced whores as could brag they'd had the fancy nobs between their legs, don't you see? I had this one as I set up in Hans Town, but she got greedy.''

''Papa, I don't want to hear this,'' Elise protested.

''Aye, you do—you asked, didn't you? And you and me—well, we ain't got many secrets between us, Puss. You been my pride, you know. I always treated you as you was a son.''

''Yes.'' She smiled crookedly. ''Yes, you have—except when I wished to wed Ben.''

''Fellow was a cent per cent, Ellie! All the Roses was!''

''Yes, well, in any event, I am trying to understand how you are here, Papa.''

''And I'm telling you!'' he snapped. ''Got to do it m'own way, that's all. Anyways, I got myself into the clutches of a harpy as was threatening to tell Em if I wasn't wanting to buy her off. I knew it would kill Em to think I had to have a pot to pop it in.''

''Papa, please! You do not have to tell me everything. I shall quite understand if you wish to merely explain about Miss Adams.''

''Well, it would have killed your mama, like I was saying,'' he went on, unrepentant. ''She'd have wanted to do it for me, and I couldn't take the risk. So I bought the harpy off—demned dearly, too—cost me a house for the creature and a bit o' gold on the side. Well, to get to the short of it, the tumbles wasn't worth Em's discovering about 'em, so I started going to the whorehouses.''

''I cannot believe you have been doing this since I was born,'' she muttered under her breath.

"Had to," he insisted. Casting a sidewise glance at her, he sighed. "Didn't think as you or Em would know."

She closed her eyes and shook her head. "You always said you hated prostitution, Papa."

"And I do, Puss—you got to believe it. But they ain't like you or Emmaline, honey—they ain't noting."

"Annie Adams wasn't even in one of those houses."

"Aye. I quit going to them places, 'cause I didn't want to be seen. In and out, that's all I was wanting, and there's whole streets where e'en a blind man can find a lay, 'specially in the rookery."

"Is that why you have been robbed thrice this year? Because you go to those places?"

"Aye. But this time I nearly bought the ticket, Ellie. The Adams slut had a pimp as wasn't trusting her to give 'im the blunt." He looked up at her now. "Curst fool busted in ere I was done with m'business, and afore I knew what he meant to do, he was a-stickin' her like he was a madman. I tossed m'bloody coat and tried to run for it. Next thing I knew he and the watch was chasing me, and he was saying as how I'd murdered the tart." He paused, waiting for her to say something, then when she didn't, he asked, "You believe your papa, don't you, Puss?"

"Yes, of course I do," she said finally, "but I fail to see how you could even do such a thing with a stranger. You make it sound as though you were shaking her hand rather than—well, than what you were doing."

"Told you a man's got needs—powerful needs. Ain't a man alive as don't do it or think about doing it full half the time."

"I am sure that Ben never would have consorted with such females."

"There ain't no heathen saints, Puss," he retorted. "If he was any man at all, he was wantin' up your skirt." Abruptly his manner changed. "But that ain't to the point now, is it?"

"No."

"If you are wanting to help your papa, you'll go to Hamilton." Seeing that her eyes widened, he nodded. "Aye, the demned fellow's deserted me," he announced heavily. "I got to have him, you know—fellow's m'only hope."

"Deserted you? But *why*? If you are innocent—"

"Humph! You think that matters?" Rand demanded sarcastically. "Well, it don't. There's them as would cheer to see me swing just 'cause I made the gold, and so he told me. Said they'll have the Bailey gallery packed so's they are a-faintin' when the justices is hearing the case. If there was any right to it, I wouldn't be here."

Never say you are one of those who believes that justice comes down like manna from heaven ... The law suits the judge, not the judged ... Patrick Hamilton's words seemed to echo in her ears. "Papa, did you tell Mr. Hamilton what you told me?"

"Didn't get a chance to," he lied. "He don't want to defend me, that's all there is to the matter. Gone namby-pamby on me."

"But he must have had some reason," she countered reasonably. "Perhaps if you offered more money ..."

"Money ain't got anything to do with it. It's politics, Puss."

"I see. Then I doubt I can make him change his mind."

"He likes you—I can see it in his eyes, Puss. If you was to want, you could get him for me."

"Did he make an excuse?"

"Fellow's got ambition, that's all."

"And you told him you did not do it?"

"Of course I did! Look, Ellie," he coaxed, "I got to have him else I'll swing." He caught her hand and drew it against his cheek. "For your papa, Puss—for your papa. You got to get him to save me."

I am the best damned barrister to be had ... I should wish to conduct my own defense ...

"Yes, of course I shall try, but—"

"There ain't any 'buts,' Puss. I got to have him."
He looked up at her. "I got to, else I am gone."

"Yes, well, we did not precisely part friends yesterday," she admitted.

"But he took you up to be seen in the park," he
reminded her. "Dash it, but he's got to be interested."

"Actually, he took me to see Pearl."

"Pearl! Who the devil is Pearl?"

"The girl from Mrs. Coates's establishment."

"Oh." Then he asked cautiously, "Why would he
want to speak with her?"

"He does not entirely believe Mrs. Coates died by
an accident, I'm afraid. I think she must have said
something to him before it happened."

"Preposterous! Why, all the papers is—well, even
the constable said so!" He eyed her closely for a moment. "And just what did this Pearl say?"

"Nothing." She was silent for a moment, then repeated the word. "Nothing, Papa—she was dead. She
died from consumption despite my poor efforts."

"Well, I could say 'twas good riddance, but I won't.
Oh, I know as you was wanting to do good, Ellie,
but—"

"She had no chance, Papa! She was but fifteen, and
since the age of twelve, that woman—" She choked
briefly, then managed to go on, finished with "that
woman sold her to every man with ten shillings to
spare!"

"Aye, 'twas a shame," he agreed.

"Well, it surprises me to hear you say that, for you
have just told me how you have paid for such
services."

"Well, I ain't favored 'em as was that young," he
insisted defensively. "So he thought the Coates woman
was poisoned," he mused. "Queer notion."

"I collect it was because the man called Big Tom
died with her."

"Oh—aye. Well, it don't signify anyways now, does
it? More to the point is your papa here. Now if you
was to smile and flirt a bit with Hamilton, I daresay
you could get him to come back, you know."

"I would doubt that. He is about to offer for Jane Barclay."

"Jane Barclay? Who the devil is that?" he demanded.

"The Earl of Dunster's daughter."

"Eh?"

"Yes, and he means to stand for Parliament as a Tory, if you would have the whole," she recalled with disgust.

"Hey now, missy—none of that! The Tories has got the right of things, and don't you be forgetting it."

"Personally, I think they are without any feeling," she muttered. "And Hamilton is one of them."

He recovered. "Aye, well, that don't say as you couldn't ask him to come see me again, does it?"

She wanted to tell him that she had no wish to see Patrick Hamilton at all, but she knew that would be a lie. The truth was that she was both irritated and fascinated by the handsome barrister. "All right," she said reluctantly. "But if he refuses, we will just have to engage someone else, don't you think? I cannot very well be expected to get down on my hands and knees to beg him, can I?"

He didn't answer.

"Well, there *are* other criminal barristers, you know."

"I don't want 'em. I got to have Hamilton."

"Time's up!" the jailer called out, turning the key in the lock.

"Wait—I am willing to pay," Elise said quickly.

"Not terday, ye ain't." Once again, he eyed her insolently, his grin knowing. "Now, tomorrit, Oy might—fer the right price . . . but terday Oy got me orders." He winked at her. "Already done bent 'em a bit, if ye was ter know hit." He came inside and moved so close to her that she could smell his rotten teeth in his breath. "Ye didn't bring 'im anything, eh? Mebbe a wee bit o' a feel, wot?"

"He is my father," she answered coldly.

"Get away from her," Rand growled. "Just because I am here don't mean as she ain't Quality."

The guard looked her father up and down, then grinned again. "Them as has got gold does the gallows kicks 'bout th' same as them as don't, ye know. Aye, they do." He reached for Elise's arm. "Oy wouldn't want ye ter fall, dearie."

She shook loose and turned to her papa. Bending over where he still sat, she kissed his cheek. His hand came up to smooth her hair, then fell again to his lap. "I shall be back tomorrow," she promised. "And hopefully Mama can be persuaded to come with me."

He nodded. "Aye, Em ain't happy with me just now, is she?"

"No, she is disappointed." Pulling her round cloak close about her, she carefully stepped past the jailer.

"But you will see Hamilton?" Rand called after her.

"Yes," she answered, "though I don't know what good I can do in that quarter."

"He ain't going to turn a taking female away, I'll be bound—he ain't," he said bracingly.

Hurrying up the steps toward more light and air, she was not nearly so sure as he was. After the way she'd ripped up at Hamilton over his politics, she doubted the barrister would even receive her. He'd been angry enough he'd preferred walking to staying in her carriage. No, if he'd refused Bat Rand, he'd certainly refuse her.

Neither the barrister nor his associate was in the office when she arrived, but the clerk assured her that Patrick Hamilton was expected ere the day was out. So she sat there, her thoughts alternating between hope, despair, and impotent anger.

As shocked and disappointed as she was by her father's behavior, she could not and would not believe him capable of actually harming anyone. He was bluff, sometimes to the point of crudity, but he'd never offered the least violence to his family or to anyone in his household. The worst thing he ever did was to attempt intimidation through bellowing, and not even Lizzie, the lowest tweeny in his house, was afraid of him. To a person, every servant was as astonished by his arrest as his daughter.

Time seemed to stand still, or at best creep so slowly that she was having second thoughts about seeing Hamilton. The longer she waited, the weaker her resolve to plead with him. Flirt with him, her papa had said. Well, she could not bring herself to try it, not knowing that he was interested in Lady Jane. No, that was not the real reason, she had to concede to herself. It was that it would be disloyal to Ben. That and the fact she was actually drawn to the barrister's rather unorthodox charm. She had no wish to lay herself open to the awful, almost bewildering pain she'd felt when she'd lost Ben.

Besides, she was not the sort of female who could simply flirt and flee. She prized truth and honesty too much for that. She could not mislead Patrick Hamilton.

"Could I get you something, Miss Rand?" the clerk asked her.

"What? Oh. I am sorry, sir—I was not attending," she admitted ruefully. "I'm afraid I was wool-gathering."

"I should think so, miss. Indeed, I was shocked and saddened to hear of Mr. Rand's arrest." He coughed apologetically. "That is—well, I am sure there must be some mistake."

"There is—there has to be. Indeed, but I would that I could wake up and discover this is but a nightmare. That Papa was at home where he belongs."

"A dreadful business—terrible."

"Yes—yes, it is."

He'd watched her and he'd wanted to speak to her ever since he'd directed her to the chair, and now it was going badly. "I could get you a bit of port," he offered, then reddened when he realized what he'd done. "That is, we do not have any ratafia, but—"

"I don't need anything, thank you."

Despite the fact that he had been pursuing a Miss Hedley for nigh to a year, he could not help staring at the stunning Miss Rand. She was more than a mere beauty, he decided—with that face, figure, and unusual hair, she was an Incomparable. And none of that took into account the enticingly low timbre of her voice. He could scarce believe she was in his employer's office, actually sitting there with him, that he was indeed talking with her.

"I could run down the street perhaps, and get you something more suitable," he offered. "There is a small place frequented by solicitors and barristers that provides refreshment—meat pasties, bread, wines, and ale—that sort of thing. Usually they have a decent wine punch." He was running on, sounding like the veriest fool, but he could not stop himself. "Truly I should not mind doing it, Miss Rand."

He was hovering about her, making her more uncomfortable than she already was. She started to decline again, then decided against it. "Yes, that would be fine—I should like some punch, I think."

"You would? Oh, yes, of course. Well, what would you favor?"

"A cup of punch would be fine," she repeated.

"Oh, yes—of course. And if they do not have it?"

"Then I will take water. You do have water, don't you?"

"Of course we do. But I cannot think you would like it—I mean, water is rather bland, isn't it?"

"Or I could take the port, I suppose—though I've not had any since Papa gave me a taste when I was a child. At the time, I did not think I liked it, Mr. Byrnes."

"No, no—I shall go to Grover's for the punch. I do not mind, miss—not at all."

He started to leave, then turned back to her. "Ah, how did you know my name?"

"It is on your desk."

"Oh—yes it is, isn't it? Well, I shan't be gone very long, but if you were to wish it, I could leave you Mr. Hamilton's copy of the *Gazette*."

"Thank you." She waited nearly until he reached the door. "Don't you think you ought to take a wrap of some sort, sir?"

"Eh?" Flushing, he shook his head. "Oh, it's not far," he assured her. He hesitated a moment, then blurted out, "If anyone else were to come while I am out, would you mind saying I have just stepped out? Just tell him to take a chair."

"I shall be happy to, sir. But where is the paper?"

"I put it on Mr. Hamilton's desk, miss."

"Thank you."

She sat there for several minutes after he'd gone, then she rose and went to find the *Gazette*. Once inside Patrick Hamilton's office, she could not help looking around, wondering why a barrister of such note would wish such plain surroundings. Moving to his desk, she looked for the newspaper, but it did not appear to be there. She lifted up a neat, orderly pile of notes and assorted papers, peering beneath them.

"Ransacking my office, Miss Rand?"

She spun around guiltily. "It was no such thing, I

assure you. Your clerk said I might read your copy of the *Gazette* while I waited for you to come in."

"Speaking of that, I don't suppose you would care to tell me what you've done with my poor, probably bedazzled clerk? He doesn't usually leave the place unattended."

"I collect you mean Mr. Byrnes, and I wouldn't precisely say your office is unattended. He left it in my hands."

"Alas, but he is the clerk—the only clerk in the office, Miss Rand."

"Yes, that did surprise me." Seeing that one corner of his mouth twitched as though he were about to smile, she confessed, "I'm afraid that he is gone to fetch a glass of punch for me, sir. He seemed to feel it incumbent to offer me something since I have been sitting here much of the afternoon."

"He would. If you would pardon me for a moment . . ."

While she watched, he reached up to rid himself of his old-fashioned barrister's peruke and tossed it onto a peg near the door. His hands worked at the hooks at the neck of his black robe, then he pulled it off over his head, revealing a dark blue coat and buff trousers. The robe joined the wig, then he combed his hair with his fingers, tousling the soft brown waves into a semblance of a Brutus. Shrugging his shoulders, he adjusted his shirtsleeve cuffs at his wrists before returning his attention to her.

"A trifle improper, I suppose, but I prefer my comfort." His hazel eyes met hers quizzically. "I don't recall an appointment—was I expecting you, Miss Rand? In fact, when last we were met, I had the distinct impression that you held me in contempt."

"No. No, you are mistaken, sir."

"In any event, if I had been expecting you, it wouldn't have made much difference. I have spent the last hour and a half in Mr. Justice Russell's chambers, attempting to dissuade him from hanging my client."

"I hope you were successful."

"I wasn't."

"I thought you always won, sir."

His faint smile twisted. "Most of the time, I do, but in this particular instance, there is no question of innocence. And so we must either hope for an exceedingly stupid jury or chance the mercy of the presiding justice. Either way he is going to be convicted."

"Doesn't there have to be a trial?"

"Not if the facts are indisputable, and as the poor fool admitted his guilt to all who would listen, there's not much I can do except beg Russell to consider his wife and children. Not a very auspicious circumstance, given the judge."

"Russell has no mercy?"

"Precisely. Now if my client had kept his mouth buttoned, I might well have confused a jury enough to gain an acquittal," he added. "But unfortunately by confessing he has played all my cards for me."

"You make it sound like a game."

"With higher stakes," he acknowledged. Moving to his desk, he opened a drawer and drew out the newspaper. His eyes scanned the front page for a moment, then he held it out to her. "Are you quite certain you wish to read this?"

Instead of taking it, she looked down, seeing the boxed story that began with the words "Murderous Fiend Apprehended, implicated in heinous crime." She shook her head. "It is a lie, you know," she managed.

"Is it?"

Her chin came up. "I have known my father for twenty-two years, Mr. Hamilton, and in that time I have discovered him to be sometimes contentious, usually kind, and almost always fair. He is utterly incapable of such a terrible, terrible thing. Besides," she stated flatly, "he says he did not do it, and that is quite sufficient for me."

"Peale will render him a fool, and a jury will hang him, Miss Rand." As he watched her wince, his expression softened visibly. "I'm sorry, but that is the way I see it."

"Well, you are seeing it wrong, sir!" As his eyebrow

rose, she sought to rein in her rising temper. Taking a breath, she tried to calm herself. "He believes you can save him, Mr. Hamilton." When he said nothing, she blurted out, "Surely you cannot think him guilty! You cannot!"

"I don't know whether he is or not. But I do know he is lying."

"But he isn't! Indeed, but he has told me the whole, and I believe him. If you would but listen—"

"If he told you the whole, you are more informed than I am," he murmured dryly. "I had to pry for every answer, and he was not forthcoming about anything."

"He is not proud of having been there at all, Mr. Hamilton."

"No, I suppose not. With his money, he could have afforded a great deal more than a tumble on a dirty mattress," he responded noncommittally.

"I am aware that he has not behaved as he ought, sir," she said stiffly, "but visiting that sort of female does not make a man a murderer. If it does, half the men in London deserve to hang."

"Spare me the hypocrisy, Miss Rand. Annie Adams was no worse than Pearl, only much poorer." As her eyes widened at the harshness in his voice, he nodded. "She did not deserve to be throttled and butchered like that."

"No, of course she did not—I did not say she did, did I?" she retorted hotly. "I merely said that Papa did not kill her."

He relented slightly. "Exactly what did he tell you?" As he said it, he gestured to a chair drawn up before his desk. "If you do not sit, I mean to be utterly ungentlemanly and take my seat anyway, for I am rather tired. And unlike you, I have a great deal of work to do before my day is over."

She sat down, clasped her hands in her lap to keep from displaying her nervousness, and mentally prepared herself to speak as matter-of-factly as she could. He sat behind his desk, leaning back, his arms behind his head, his feet stretched out before him.

"You have my attention, my dear."

"I am not your dear," she snapped. Recovering, she managed, "I am sorry—I shouldn't have said it quite that way, should I?"

"It was a manner of speaking, merely. But do go on with your tale."

"There is no delicate way to say most of it." She inhaled deeply, then let her breath out slowly. "He said," she began, "that he has been seeing those, uh—those females—"

"The word is whore, Miss Rand—there is no need to be delicate about it now, for I seem to recall having heard you say it before," he said brutally. "But if that is too difficult to repeat, you may call them unfashionable impures as opposed to the fashionable ones such as Harriette Woods and her sisters."

"Those women," she said defiantly. "And you have no right to make fun of me—no right at all."

"Your pardon," he murmured sardonically. "It must be my Tory leanings."

She was well aware that she was getting no help from him, that he was still irked with her, and she knew she had to mollify him. "Well, I daresay there can be good Tories," she conceded judiciously. "And I did not mean to impugn your—"

"Yes, you did. But we are going afield, Miss Rand."

"You are making this exceedingly difficult for me, sir."

"I suppose I am. All right, then. You may go on, and I shall try to stifle my levity. I think we were speaking of your father's explanation," he prompted more gently.

"Yes. As I was saying, Papa turned to those women after my mother nearly died giving birth to me. He did not wish to risk Mama's life again, you see, and he found it difficult to—"

"Live the celibate life?"

"Yes."

"Noble of him."

"Mr. Hamilton," she said evenly, "if you are wishful

of hearing his side of the tale, I would that you also
refrained from an unseemly display of sarcasm."

"Objection taken under advisement."

"I don't know why I have to do this. It would have
been better had you spoken directly to Papa about
what happened."

"I tried—as you will recall, I tried. And I heard a
great deal of bluster and nonsense—and very little
more, my dear."

"I told you I am not your dear. And I have asked
that you cease—"

"I merely said he failed to say enough to convince
me."

Feeling very much as though she were whistling into
the wind, she forced herself to go on. "All right. He
has admitted to me that he has made a habit of seeking the services of"—she met his gaze squarely now,
determined not to let him rattle her again—"of
whores, then—for at least the past twenty-one years.
But while the action was contemptible, his motives for
it must surely be understandable."

"If you can reason that out, you ought to make
someone a complaisant wife," he murmured.

"*Will* you listen? Is everything a jest to you?"

"No. Your pardon. I am nearly too tired to think."

Despite her resolve, her face reddened. "Yes, well,
at first he merely kept a female, but she proved a
greedy harpy, and she threatened to tell Mama if he
did not pay her money sufficient to satisfy her."

"This is quite edifying, my dear, but what does this
have to do with Annie Adams?"

"I am getting to that, sir. I am merely asking that
you attempt to understand him."

He leaned forward to take his sand glass from his
drawer, then he turned it upside down. "You'd best
get done ere the sand is gone."

"What happens then?" she asked nervously.

"I go home to sup." Leaning back again, he rested
his head against his interlocked hands. "Until then,
you have my attention."

"Barely, sir," she muttered dryly. Nonetheless, she

plunged ahead again, trying to speak as calmly as she could. "After he paid her off, he began visiting the—"

"Brothels," he supplied for her.

"Yes." She looked down at her clasped hands. "This is not particularly easy for me to say, sir. I may be a Cit, but I have been brought to speak properly in public, if not at home. If you heard me say it before, it was because I did not know you could hear me. And somehow saying it to you is nothing like saying it to my mother." Sucking in her breath again, she let it out, then nodded. "He was afraid he would be remarked coming out of those establishments, so he turned to the worst sort of female, Mr. Hamilton. Last night, he encountered that unfortunate woman, and she agreed—well, they struck a bargain, and—"

"I suppose one could count murder an unfortunate circumstance," he murmured, "particularly if one were Annie Adams."

"Indeed." She dared to look at him, but for all that he sounded otherwise, he appeared to be regarding her quite soberly. "Yes, well, he was quite frank with me on this head, sir, and there is no way to wrap this up in clean linen at all. He—he said he was with her when her protector interrupted them to demand money," she recounted baldly. "Apparently Papa had already paid her, and there was a quarrel between her and her—"

"Pimp. The word is pimp, Miss Rand."

"Well, I cannot say I have ever heard that one. In any event, the man became incensed and began stabbing her. Papa said he managed to—to disentangle himself—and—" At this point, Hamilton could not quite suppress a smile, and her face burned with embarrassment. "Well, he tore off his bloody coat and ran, sir. The next thing he knew Annie Adams's murderer and the watch were pursuing him, and 'twas he who was accused. The watch would not listen to him, Mr. Hamilton. There—that is everything, I think." Done, she breathed a deep sigh of relief. "So you see he did not do it."

He sat up. "An edifying tale, Miss Rand."

"Then you will not abandon him?"

"I told you—he is lying."

"You cannot know that! There is no way you can know that!"

He appeared pained. "Miss Rand, I never believe a client who evades my questions, for I have found most defendants ready to babble their heads off to convince me of their innocence. Your father, on the other hand, either could not or would not tell me how his coat came to be left near Annie Adams's bucket of bloody water. Or how his ring came to be found there also. He gave me some farradiddle about having had it stolen."

"Why don't you believe it was?"

"It was found with his coat, and both were by the bucket."

"What difference does that make?"

"If he stopped to wash her blood off him, he could not have felt any particular danger from Annie's pimp, which in turn would indicate that she was dead before the fellow discovered him, which is precisely the story John Colley told the watch."

"Maybe you gave him no chance to explain! Maybe you were as disagreeable to Papa as to me!"

"Miss Rand—"

"But I have told you how the coat came to be there!"

"The Adams woman was not only stabbed, but she was also throttled quite brutally. This was a crime of passion, not greed, my dear."

"There! Then he had no reason, for they—well, she was not refusing him, was she?" This time, she could not look into his face. "They had agreed on the money and everything."

"Why would Colley kill her? He only had her, so one must suppose she was his golden goose, so to speak."

"As you took Papa's money, you have no right to turn your back to him!"

"He engaged me under false pretense, Miss Rand. He said it was in the event he had a problem at his brickworks, and I told him at the time that I did not usually take such cases.''

"But you took his money," she repeated.

"And it has been returned."

"He could not have known he would be taken up, sir," she argued desperately.

"He may have thought it but a matter of time. There are, after all, several unfortunate females who have been murdered rather brutally within the past year. Quite frankly, Mr. Peale is meeting with the magistrate to determine if there is reasonable suspicion to warrant an indictment in the matter of Fanny Shawe— or of Peg Parker. And they will search the records to see if perhaps there are others."

"*What?*" she screeched indignantly. "Oh, of all the—"

"I expect they will get around to interviewing the watchman who erroneously identified Maddie Coates as Peg Parker's killer."

"Why are you telling me this?" she demanded furiously. "You know very well he could not have done those things—you know it! And he does not deserve to be held in fetters!"

"You asked why I have refused Rand's defense, and I am merely giving you your answer."

"But you must defend him! You yourself said you were the best damned barrister in London!"

"I am. But there are others of repute."

"Oh, now I see everything clearly! You are afraid Papa's case will be too unpopular for an aspiring Tory, aren't you?" She rose angrily. "You, sir, are naught but a sham! No wonder you account yourself the best lawyer to be had—you do not attempt that which you fear you cannot win! Or else you meet with the justice in chambers and do your dirty little deeds where none can witness!"

He stood also, facing her across a space that might as well have been a gaping chasm. "I am sorry, but I have to believe that my clients tell me the truth."

"But just this afternoon you were arguing for one who didn't," she reminded him bitterly.

"Oh, but he did. He told me precisely what he told the magistrate."

"Do you want my father to say he has done what he has not?" she asked incredulously. "For if that is what you are saying, I'll not countenance it! I am telling you that Bartholomew Rand would not, could not, and did not murder that woman!"

"There is no need to shout at me," he said calmly. "We don't happen to agree, I'm afraid."

She glanced to where the sand was half-gone from the glass, and knowing that she'd failed, she tried to collect what dignity she could. "I think perhaps I ought to just get my cloak and leave. Obviously, I cannot appeal to your conscience," she added bitterly.

His gaze took in her dark blue walking dress, then traveled to her nearly perfect face. "It would take a great deal to change my mind," he admitted.

"What is that supposed to mean?"

"No. I should not have said it." He walked into his outer office and found her hooded cloak hanging on a mahogany hook. Taking it down, he held it out for her. She regarded him sourly for a moment, then stood still as he draped it over her shoulders. As she fastened the braided frogs, he stepped back.

"It is a pity we could not have met under different circumstances, Miss Rand, for I admire you greatly."

"And I would that I could say the same of you," she retorted, drawing on her gloves. "Good day, sir."

As she started out the door, she encountered John Byrnes, who apologized. "I'm terribly sorry it took so long, Miss Rand, but there was a sad crush. I have acquired a jar of punch for you, however, and I can get you a glass out of the cabinet."

"Thank you, sir," she managed civilly, "but my business with Mr. Hamilton is quite at an end. Perhaps he will share the punch with you, for he is in sad need of warming his exceedingly cold heart." With that, she left.

Patrick's eyebrow lifted perceptibly. "Punch, John?"

"Well, she was here quite a long time, sir, and there

was scarce anything else to offer her. I did not think you would mind it."

"No, I suppose not."

Byrnes stared after her before turning back to Patrick. "Miss Rand must surely be the loveliest female I have ever seen," he murmured. "An absolute Incomparable."

"She's above your touch, old fellow." As the clerk's face fell, Patrick nodded sympathetically. "Alas, but she's above mine also."

"Yours, sir?"

"She has money—and far too many principles. Come on, John, let's go home," Patrick said tiredly. "I don't even care if I eat ere I go to bed, but if I don't, I'm afraid my cook will give notice. And I have got to sort out the quarter's bills for Mr. Sinclair before I try to find a suitable precedent to justify transporting poor Findley rather than hanging him. Somehow it does not seem quite right for the state to kill him for butchering his neighbor's pig."

"Should not Mr. Sinclair collect the bills, sir? He's the secretary, isn't he?" Byrnes reminded him.

"Yes, but I keep an incredibly disorganized desk, old fellow. Would you want me rambling through yours?"

"No, I suppose not." Byrnes looked down at the jar in his hands. "But the punch—"

"Take it with you. Perhaps you can share it with someone more able to appreciate it. Just now I feel as though the blood has been drained out of me."

Feeling as though she were living a nightmare, Elise came down early to discover her mother already at breakfast. Taking her place at the table, she stared for a long moment at her father's empty chair, then looked up.

"I suppose you could not sleep either," she said finally.

"No."

"Poor Papa," she murmured, sighing. "It is such an awful place. And to make everything worse, they have got him in irons."

Her mother said nothing.

"I dread telling him that I could not persuade Hamilton at all."

Her mother looked away without speaking.

"Mama—"

"There is nothing to say, is there?" came the toneless reply.

"He needs you, Mama."

"No."

"I know you cannot understand it, but he said he visited those women to save you." When her mother did not respond, she tried to plead her father's case. "He said you nearly died having me, and he could not risk losing you." She cast a sidewise glance, but her mother sat still as a statue, almost as though she did not hear. "Mama, he didn't kill that woman—he didn't."

"I shall never hold my head up again. Never."

"We shall get another barrister, and he will prove Papa innocent—I swear it."

Emmaline Rand stared unseeing at the polished table, then shook her head. "It doesn't matter, Ellie."

"It doesn't matter! Mama, you have got to come out of this! We have got to fight to save Papa's life!"

"No." The older woman sighed deeply, then shook her head. "No," she repeated, her voice scarce above a whisper. "If they will have me, I am going to my family."

"If they will have you?" Elise demanded incredulously. "Mama, what nonsense is this? You are Papa's wife—you cannot mean to desert him now."

" 'Twould appear as he deserted me, don't you think?" Emmaline bit her lower lip and turned away again. "All these years he has lived a lie, Ellie—a lie."

"I know you are disappointed, Mama, but—"

"Disappointed? *Disappointed?* Is that how you would call it?" her mother cried. "I know not how I shall face anyone!"

"Please—come with me today—listen to him."

"No."

" 'Tis the least you can do for the life he has given you," Elise argued. "He needs you, Mama—he needs you."

"He has never needed me," Emmaline declared bitterly.

"He loves you. He has always been so very proud of you, and you cannot deny it. Why, he has boasted to nearly everyone how you were born a Bingham— how you are Quality."

"Because I gave him consequence, Ellie—because I gave him consequence, and that is all." Her mother raised her head to meet Elise's eyes, and there was no mistaking the pain in her face. "I am worth no more to him than this house—than the rug beneath our feet, Ellie—and too long I have denied it."

"That is not true, and you know it! Mama, he has worshipped you!"

"He left my bed for those—those cheap little tarts!"

"He said he did it for you."

"For *me?* I never denied him—not once did I ever deny him! And he has repaid me with this!"

"Mama, you are overset. Please—come to see him with me, and let him explain—"

"He was caught with a whore!"

"But he didn't murder her."

"He has murdered me, Ellie—as surely as he pricked my heart with a knife, he has murdered me."

"If you could see how he is kept, Mama—if you could see how miserable he is, you would know that for whatever sins he has committed, he is paying dearly. He may even pay with his life."

A footman came in and placed a dish of porridge in front of her mother, then withdrew discreetly to get another for Elise. The older woman unfolded her napkin and laid it carefully in her lap, then reached for her spoon.

"He loves you," Elise repeated.

"I am going home to my brother's vicarage, dearest," the woman said flatly. "If you wish, you may go with me."

"Go with you—? Mama, you cannot cut and run! Look around you—look at what he has built for you!" Seeing that her mother's fine profile was like that of chiseled stone, she pleaded, "Please—at least see him once. Once—'tis all I ask, and then if you can leave him, so be it. But you owe him that much at least—you owe him that much at the least!"

The older woman carried the spoon to her mouth, then swallowed the bite of porridge. "I owe him nothing, for I have asked for none of it."

"But surely you loved him once!"

"He left me long ago, Ellie, and I have but now come to know it." Once again, her mother looked at her. "I have listened to too many of his lies to ever believe in him again."

"Mama—"

"He doesn't love either of us."

"He loves both of us, and you know it."

"Does he?"

"Yes."

"As for this house and everything that is in it, they were all his, Ellie—his. He had to have everything, to boast that he had the best. That's all I was—I was but the best he could buy."

"Because he wanted you."

"He wanted to own a gentrified wife, that was all. No, my dear, what he really wanted was—well, I shall not say it. I'm sorry if I have disappointed you, but you cannot know the whole."

"What he wanted was what?" Elise persisted.

Her mother sighed. "Yes, I suppose you are more like him than like me, aren't you? Both of you are so very strong-willed, after all."

"I have always been proud of both of you. If I have been more like Papa, it is that he treated me like I could have been his son."

"And filled your head with a great deal of nonsense, I'm afraid."

"But you were going to tell me why you are leaving him, weren't you? Go on—say it, else I shall believe you care more for saving face than for him."

"I suppose you have heard everything, anyway, haven't you? He wouldn't let me rear you into the lady I wanted, you know."

"He let me think, you mean."

"Except for Mr. Rose."

"Except for Ben. But we shall leave Ben out of this, I think."

"All right, I will say it." Emmaline laid her spoon on the edge of the charger plate. "What your father wanted was a lady by light of day and a whore beneath him at night. And if he said he turned to those women because of your birth, I shall call him a liar."

"He told me—"

"I was too stupid to know it then, but upon looking backward, I can see far too many times when he had excuses for not coming home, for not being—"

"He worked hard, Mama—he worked night and day to provide us with the comforts of his wealth."

"No."

"He honors you."

At that, her mother carefully refolded her napkin

and laid it beside her barely touched porridge. Rising, she looked down at Elise.

"My mind will not budge, dearest. No, I am going home to the house where I grew up, and God willing, I shall never have to come out into the world again."

"No, you are turning your tail and fleeing!" Throwing down her own napkin, Elise stood to face her. "You are a coward, Mama!"

"Your loyalty is admirable, my love, but I fear it is misplaced," the older woman said mildly.

"Well, I don't mean to desert him!"

"If you change your mind, I am sure your uncle Charles will welcome you also."

"Only if I bring Papa's money bags! That's all the Binghams have wanted from him, you know—they've all tried to hang on his sleeve, and well you know it!"

Her mother turned and walked slowly from the dining room, leaving Elise to stare after her. As she heard the woman's steps on the stairs, the girl's anger faded to dejection. Sinking into her chair again, she put her head into her hands and fought the urge to cry. Now she would have to tell him that not only would Patrick Hamilton not defend him, but that rather than face the ignominy of his trial, his wife was leaving him.

Having discreetly avoided the quarrel between mother and daughter, one of the footmen coughed apologetically behind her, then set her plate next to her elbow.

"Cook is wishful of knowing whether you'd be having coddled eggs with the porridge or not, miss."

She sat back and took a deep breath. Looking up at him, she managed to show him a calm that she did not feel inside. "I'm not very hungry, I'm afraid." Pushing the plate and bowl away, she said, "I think I shall merely have a tea tray brought up to my chamber."

"Aye."

"I have to visit my father."

"Aye. And a bad business that is, miss—there ain't a body here as don't feel sorry about it."

"Thank you."

"None of us believes he did it—a pack o' lies it is, or me name ain't Joseph."

"Thank you." She pushed away from the table and stood again. "Yes, well, I shall convey your good wishes to him, and I am sure he will appreciate your loyalty."

"Aye, miss."

There was a small but decidedly unfriendly crowd at the entrance to Newgate Prison, and as she passed them, they were shouting at the guards stationed outside, raising their fists, demanding the death of Bat Rand. Pulling her hood up, Elise hurried inside.

Her father had been moved, but the accommodations were not much better save that the room was a trifle larger, affording him a small, rough-hewn table in addition to the bench. And there were sheets upon the cot scarce wide enough to be called his bed. An empty bottle of something lay where he'd left it upon the floor.

As the door closed behind her, locking her in with him, he rose unsteadily to hobble to her, his face eager.

"I knew as you'd be here—aye, I knew it. You ain't about to forget about your papa, are you?"

He looked as though he'd not slept either, and his unshaven face made him appear even more haggard than before. She forced her brightest smile.

"Well, I could scarce stay away." Digging into her reticule, she drew out a linen-wrapped sweet bun. "Your cook sent this. Indeed, but Joseph said you are missed by everyone in the house."

He took it, but laid it upon his table. "Where's Em?"

"She—uh—she could not come."

"She ain't sick over this, is she? You just got to tell her it'll all work out, that's all."

"She is not precisely ill."

He nodded. "Aye, I see—she's vexed, ain't she?"

"Something very like it."

"I was wanting to tell her I didn't do it, you know."

"I know."

He sat heavily on the edge of his cot. "You ain't giving me the whole—I can see it, Puss."

She didn't want to admit that her mother was already on her way to Somerset, so she evaded him.

"Yes, well, I have been to see Mr. Parker, and he will wait upon you directly."

"Parker? Damme if I didn't say you was to see Hamilton, Ellie!"

"I did."

He stared at her for a time, then seemed to explode at her. "You was to persuade him! Now I know you could do it if you was to have a mind to! I know it!"

"I couldn't, Papa." She drew a deep breath and let it out slowly. "He wouldn't listen to me."

"And why the devil not?"

"He doesn't believe you."

"I see." It was as though all the bluster left him entirely. He sat there, his face betraying his dejection. "And Em's gone, too, ain't she?" When she said nothing, he told her, "You don't have to tell me no fibs, Puss, 'cause I can see right through 'em—always could, even when you was a little chit, you know."

"I know. I daresay that Mama's merely overset, that she will come back when she realizes how much you truly love her."

"Run to the preachy brother of hers, no doubt," he muttered. "Much good he'll do her unless she took m'blunt with her." He sighed. "But the Binghams was all like that, you know. Fair-weather friends, the lot of 'em. Don't you think I knew how it was? The old man, may the devil take his soul, was letting me grease his hands—selling Em, he was—and all the while he was a-telling any as would listen how he hated to do it." He straightened his shoulders resolutely. "Aye, well, I can take care of that later, I suppose. Right now, I got to get Hamilton."

"I don't think you would wish him, Papa," she said quietly. "I told you—he thinks you have lied to him."

"Well, I ain't—and I ain't taking anybody but him. That's all there is to the matter, Puss—I ain't taking anybody else."

"But I have already told you that Mr. Hamilton has declined. Mr. Parker has agreed to see you later today."

"Parker! Humph! And what's he supposed to do

for me, I ask you? Fellow ain't known like Hamilton! Peale ain't afraid of him!''

"Papa, one lawyer must be nearly the same as another, and you have not even seen Mr. Parker."

"Don't need to," he muttered. "A man as goes into court with Hamilton has got an advantage ere he even opens his mouth. I told you—I seen him argue for the Volsky woman, and the Russian's lawyer was done for no matter what he said. Hamilton acted close to his chest, just asking for things real innocentlike—letting the other fellow look like he was winning. Then—" Rand hit his fist in his hand so hard that the pop startled her. "Then he all but killed him. Why ere the other fellow was knowing what was happening, he was a laughingstock. Hamilton asks questions as makes the other side look like fools. And the summations—why he can make a jury cry." Looking up at her, he rested his case. "Now—who knows this Parker, I ask you?"

"Perhaps that can work to your advantage. Mr. Parker at least has an open mind."

"Open minds ain't where it's at, I tell you! I got to have Hamilton if I am to have a chance at cheating the gallows, Ellie—I got to!"

"I cannot very well force him to defend you, Papa," she said tiredly. "Besides, contrary to your belief, he has been known to lose a case."

"Who told you that?" he demanded suspiciously. "The Parker fellow?"

"No. Mr. Hamilton."

"Well, he don't lose many of 'em, I can tell you. Why, when he is arguing before a jury, the man's got a gold tongue—aye, and he's got passion, Ellie. It's just like it was when Kean was troddin' the boards in Drury. Ain't nobody looking at anyone but him. They ain't paying no attention to the prosecutor—nor to the justice's directions. Seen it myself, and damme if I wasn't hanging on every word out of his mouth. Like I was saying it, the man's a genius at making 'em all look like fools." He stared off for a moment as though he were reliving something, then he nodded. "Aye, I got to have that, Puss."

"But you have never heard Mr. Parker speak, have you?" she countered.

"Don't have to. Damme, Ellie, but you ain't listening to me! I got to have Hamilton, I tell you! Anybody else and I am as good as gallow's bait!"

"Papa, I have done my best!"

"No, you ain't! Look at you, Puss—ain't a man in England as you couldn't have at your feet if you was wantin' to have 'im there. You just didn't go about it right, that's all."

"I cannot very well throw myself at his head—and it would not matter if I did. I told you—he is very nearly engaged to Dunster's daughter!"

"Well, he ain't stepped into the parson's mousetrap yet, has he?" he demanded truculently.

"What you are suggesting is offensive in the extreme, Papa," she managed more calmly.

"Now I ain't meaning as you got to actually do anything, Puss—just make him think you was interested, that's all."

"He isn't interested in me."

"Bosh and hogwash! He's breathin', ain't he?"

"We do not even deal civilly together, I'm afraid. Within half the hour, no matter how pleasantly we start out, we are at daggers drawn."

His eyes narrowed briefly, then he shrugged. "All right," he muttered. "Guess I ain't got any right to ask you to turn against your own principles, do I?"

"No."

"Course I don't. Here—come here and give your papa a kiss, eh?"

She moved closer and bent to brush her lips against his cheek. His hand came up to smooth her hair, much as he'd done when she was a small child.

"Aye, you are a good girl, Ellie—a damned fine girl, if I was to say so myself."

"Fiddle, Papa."

"And when I am gone, you got to look after Em and m'business, Puss. I didn't build my fortune to see it wither away from inattention. You got to see to it as there's a Rand Brickworks in Islington to leave to

your children, you know. Aye, and don't you be lettin'
yourself get cheated, you hear? There's plenty of fellows out there as will think they can make you pay
'em for the privilege of selling 'em the bricks, that
you got to bribe 'em ere a Rand brick goes into the
pile. But we make the best demned bricks as is to be
had, and the nobs is wantin' 'em for their houses, so
you ain't got to give 'em a farthing.''

"Papa, you are not dead yet."

"Well, I'm going to be. And I ain't wanting you there
to see me swing neither. When all's said in court, you
got to go to Em's preachy relations until it's over.''

"Papa!"

"Plain as a pikestaff, ain't it? The whore's pimp gets
to tell as how he found me with her, and I don't get
to say nothing. I'll wager you didn't know that, did
you? Well, 'tis God's own truth—I ain't allowed to
testify for myself. So I got to have Hamilton to make
the fellow look the fool. Otherwise, I am as good as
dead right now.''

"You make him sound like God," she muttered.

"Aye. And you know what, Puss? His name is
enough to get me acquitted, 'cause like I said, the
prosecutor is afraid of him and the juries is believing
him 'cause he's Hamilton.''

Caught between her mother and him, she was feeling utterly, completely beleaguered with nowhere to
turn. She tried one last time. "Papa," she said, enunci-
ating each word clearly in the hope he would somehow listen, "I cannot make Mr. Hamilton believe you
are innocent. I am telling you that he thinks you
guilty. Indeed, he thinks you will be charged with Peg
Parker's death also—maybe more.''

"Aye." His hand slid down her arm to clasp her
hand. Holding it against his breast, he swore solemnly.
"As sure as you can feel my heart beneath your hand,
Puss, your papa is innocent of all of it. The worst I've
ever done is to lay amongst the whores.''

"I know."

He released her hand. "I'll talk to Mr. Parker—for
you, Ellie, I'll do it. But you got to promise me as you

won't come to hear the case when it comes to the docket. I ain't wanting you to be there when they say I got to hang."

"Papa, I know a whisker when I hear it," she retorted. "You have got Mr. Hamilton in your brain."

"Mebbe—but I know what I need—better'n you, I know what I got to have."

"And what if Mr. Hamilton were to fail you? What if he represented you and you were to be convicted?"

"Then I'd die knowing as I had the best chance I could have got."

"He is not a worker of miracles, you know. He is only a man, and a Tory at that, which leads me to believe he cannot be infallible."

"Course he ain't—but damme if he ain't the next thing to it. And what's being a Tory got to do with anything? I'm a Tory myself!"

"The Tories never wish to make anything right—all they concern themselves with is staying in power. At least the Whigs want to stop slavery and protect climbing boys from dying of soot sores or worse."

"Aye, they got their heads turned backward, don't they? They forget as what made this country great."

"Slavery?" she asked sarcastically.

"Looking out for England first. The Whigs is always ready to play dead when there's fighting as has got to be done."

She started to rebut his words, then caught herself. "Papa, I don't want to brangle with you. I want to help you, but I don't know how. Please—"

"Aye. Then you got to get Hamilton to at least come back to see me."

"And if he won't?"

"Then I'm dead."

She didn't want to seek out Patrick Hamilton again, but she couldn't very well refuse her father either. "How much am I authorized to offer him?" she asked tiredly.

"Anything he was to want, Puss—anything he was to want."

"Ten thousand?"

"Oh, you ain't getting him for that, I'll be bound. Rumor's got it as he charged the Coates woman more'n that. Aye, they say as he gets as much as half of what a fellow's got for defending him."

"But that is robbery! Surely you cannot wish me to offer anything like that? You would be giving him a fortune!"

"I told you—whatever it takes. My gold ain't much good to me if I am gone."

She regarded him askance for a moment, then sighed. "All right."

"Time's up, miss."

This time it was a different guard who came to let her out, and he was almost deferential. She was about to smile at him, when she saw her father hand him a gold guinea. As her eyebrow went up, he nodded.

"Aye, ye got to grease 'em, and they ain't so bad, eh?" Looking past her to the jailer, he flashed another coin. "I'd take a bottle of hock, if you was to fetch it."

She waited until she was following the fellow up the steps before she asked, "Can you not at least remove the fetters? He is but one old man unable to run. Surely it can be arranged, don't you think?"

"I'll speak ter th' keeper about 'im," the jailer promised. "Aye, fer the right gold, he'll listen ter him. Mebbe he'll even take him into his apartments—and mebbe not."

"If Papa will not, then I shall pay it."

But as she climbed the steps, she felt as though the weight of the world rested on her shoulders. Whether it was a queer start, a maggot in his brain, or pure obstinacy on her father's part, he was utterly determined to have Patrick Hamilton plead for his life in court.

No, she would have to screw her courage to the sticking point and call upon the infuriating barrister again. And God only knew what she could tell him to make him change his mind. Twenty-five thousand pounds maybe—surely that ought to be enough to do it. But even as she thought it, she knew in her heart it was going to take a great deal more than money.

Feeling very much against the wall, she did nothing until Mr. Parker waited upon her at her home. But what he told her did nothing to resolve the terrible conflict within her breast. For one thing, now that the tale of Annie Adams's murder had been covered in lurid detail by the papers, who described her father with words such as "murderous fiend," "demonic beast," and "savage ghoul," Parker had been subjected to more than the usual vilification. On hearing a rumor that Rand would be bound for trial today, an angry mob had formed between the Bailey and Newgate, jeering at the barrister, "Hang the bloody bastard! Cut 'im up like 'e did 'er!" Despite his distinguished legal career and his excellent reputation, the crowd had pelted poor Parker with garbage.

And her father, he further reported, had been uncooperative in the extreme, going so far as to accuse him of being "a demned charlatan" and "a legal leech." Considering the whole of both circumstances, he was regretfully declining the case.

So she'd paid him for his effort, then she'd sat for a long time in her father's bookroom, staring at nothing, searching her soul, hoping for some divine answer, and seeing only the one other possibility. Patrick Hamilton. At least Rand wanted him, which must surely make him more cooperative now.

Finally, she'd risen to go up to her bedchamber, passing her mother's empty room, knowing that Bat Rand had no one he could depend upon but her. When she looked out onto the quiet street, she could see the yellow balls of streetlights still being lit below. And she knew if she waited until the morrow, she would probably lose her nerve.

Crossing her arms defensively over her breasts, she sighed her resignation. As much as she did not want to, she was going to have to throw herself on Patrick Hamilton's doubtful mercy and offer him whatever it took to gain his services. Having made that decision, she went to work.

She bathed, then dressed carefully, choosing a peach silk dress that drew attention to her red-gold hair, having Molly twist that hair into a crown of curls, adding two strands of creamy pearls around her slender neck. Finally, she stood back from her cheval mirror, admitting even to herself that she looked very well indeed.

"Ye couldn't be prettier if ye was a royal princess," her maid declared proudly.

"Thank you. I have hopes you are right, Molly, for I mean to put it to the touch."

"Ye'll be the fanciest one at the party, I'll be bound ye will. All them gentry morts'll be a-wantin' to stand up with ye—and more."

"Just now I expect I am more the pariah," Elise muttered.

The maid stepped back to admire her again, then sighed sadly. "A pity it is that neither yer mum nor yer papa is here to see it."

"I know. Did you tell Joseph to order the carriage?"

"Aye, and he was wantin' to know yer direction."

"I am going to call upon Mr. Hamilton," Elise admitted baldly.

"The mort as was here?" Molly asked, scandalized. "No, ye ain't. Yer papa—"

"It is Papa who asks it."

"Then I'm going with ye."

"No. No, this is something I have to do myself."

"But ye'll be a-givin' 'im the wrong impression! Here now—no ye ain't! Yer mum ain't going ter approve, I can tell ye."

"Mama isn't here." Elise took a deep breath, then

let it out fully. "And if I do not try, Papa may hang for something he did not do."

"Ye ain't going ter call on no fellow by yerself, miss—ye ain't. Why, what is Mr. Hamilton ter think?"

"I don't know."

"Why, he'll think ye a common trollop," Molly answered herself. "That's what."

"I hope not."

"Well, look at ye! All fancied up ter call on one man! Ye'll have no rep, ye know," the maid predicted direly.

"I think I know what I am doing, Molly. And I'd rather see Papa survive than anything."

"Well, Joseph ain't going ter let ye go!"

"I'm not taking him. The driver and a coachman will suffice, thank you."

The maid relented slightly. "Ye ain't going in ter no gennulman's house alone? Ye mean ter take James with ye?"

"Yes," Elise lied.

"Still, it don't seem right. I mean, the nobs has got rules, miss, and ye don't cross 'em but at yer peril."

"I am not a nob, Molly. I am a Cit."

"Aye, but—"

"My mind is quite made up. Now, fetch me the evening cloak that goes with this, will you?"

"Ye'll freeze ter death," the maid predicted direly. "And I got a mind ter speak ter James meself."

"You will do no such thing," Elise warned her severely. "Lest you forget it, with Mama gone, I am mistress of this house."

"Aye, but—"

"It is not your place to pass judgment on what you do not know." Collecting the velvet-lined peach silk cloak, Elise wrapped it around her shoulders and fastened the pearl-studded clasp beneath the folded-over velvet collar. "There." Seeing that Molly still regarded her askance, she managed to smile. "I am not a green little chit just out of the schoolroom, Molly. I am two and twenty, you know."

"But ye ain't been out in the world."

"Molly—"

"All right!" The maid threw up her hands. "I ain't saying anything more."

"Good." As Elise turned around to leave, she saw her watercolor of Ben Rose. Walking over to it, she held it lovingly for a long moment, then opened the table drawer and put it inside. It didn't matter anymore, she told herself resolutely as she closed the drawer. Regardless of what happened, Ben was lost to her forever. And no matter what occurred between her and Patrick Hamilton, it could not touch the heart she'd given to Ben.

In the carriage, she sat very still, rigidly almost, her lace-gloved hands clasped so tightly that her fingers were numb, hoping first that Patrick Hamilton would be at home, then that he would not. Water from an earlier rain splashed up beneath the coach wheels, spraying a tipsy gentleman, who held up his walking stick and cursed at her loudly, but she scarce noted him.

She tried to pray for forgiveness, but her agitated mind would not comply. Finally, she managed to tell herself that she would let God decide which was the greater sin by whether Hamilton was there or gone from his house.

All too soon, her driver had found the address, and as the carriage stopped, the coachman hopped down to open the door for her. "I dunno, miss—it don't look like no party here ter me. Ye want me ter bang the knocker?" he asked nervously.

"Just help me down, please," she said, her voice tightly controlled. "And if I am not out within the half hour, you may leave."

"When was ye wishful o' coming home?"

"I don't know."

"We got ter come back fer ye," the man reminded her.

She didn't even know if Hamilton possessed a carriage of his own. Every time she'd seen him, he'd been either in a hack or her papa's town coach, but that didn't mean anything. Perhaps he'd merely not wanted to leave his horses standing while he attended to business in the Bailey.

"All right," she decided finally. "Wait around the corner out of sight. I may be here awhile, so you are welcome to shelter yourself inside the coach."

"Thankee." But once again, he eyed Hamilton's narrow townhouse dubiously. "They ain't got many as came, do they?"

"Perhaps all of the guests are not yet arrived," she murmured.

"Still, I oughter announce ye."

"I am quite capable of announcing myself. As I am neither a titled lady nor a daughter of the gentry, I don't need to stand on ceremony."

Reluctantly, he let her go, then climbed back onto the box. She waited until the carriage rounded the corner out of sight, then she resolutely climbed the steps to lift the brass knocker. Holding her breath, she banged it loudly several times, then fought the urge to run as her stomach knotted.

"Here now—no need to wake the dead, is there?" Hamilton's butler grumbled, opening the door. He saw her, and his eyes widened, betraying his shock. Obviously, his first notion was to turn her away, but as his gaze swept over her, taking in the richness of her clothes and the pearl clasp at her throat, his expression grew more uncertain.

"You must be lost," he decided.

"Please—is Mr. Hamilton at home?"

"As to that, I cannot say," he answered noncommittally. "If he is, he didn't say he was expecting you."

"Perhaps you could give him this—if he is at home, that is," she added hastily. "And please tell him it is of the utmost importance that I see him."

"He'll be in his office tomorrow, miss." He looked down at her card, saw the name Rand, and decided to risk his master's ire. "If you would step inside, you may wait here while I inquire."

He entered Patrick's book-lined study, and coughed

apologetically to gain attention. Patrick looked up, frowning.

"What it is, Hayes?"

"There is a person to see you, sir—a female person."

"The devil there is. Why didn't you send her away?"

"If you was to see her, you would not ask. Besides, 'tis a sight as has to be beheld."

Patrick sat back and squeezed his tired eyes tightly shut before opening them again. "What sort of female?"

"Looks like a goddess."

"Good God. Yes—well, then I suppose I could take a look at such a creature." He gestured wearily to his disorderly desk. "At least I have everything catalogued for Mr. Sinclair, and I have read until I can scarce see the print anyway." Heaving himself up from his chair, he flexed his shoulders, seeking relief from the ache between, then took the card Hayes held out. "Damn," he muttered under his breath. "Is she alone?"

"Aye."

"That little fool—she's got no business out at night."

"I rather did not think so either. Er—shall I direct her in?"

"No, I think I'd better come out."

Waiting, she studied the tall, rather narrow foyer, thinking it more a snug house than one befitting Patrick Hamilton's reputation as a successful barrister. As she waited, she could hear voices from down the entry hall, then Hamilton himself emerged from one of the doors in shirtsleeves and breeches. He approached her in his stockings, stopping about six feet from her. He regarded her slowly, lazily looking her over from her crown of hair to the tips of her expensive slippers.

"My lamentable memory," he murmured sardonically. "I must have forgotten the, ah, social engagement."

"Please—" It was the only word she could get out as her throat constricted too tightly for speech.

He started to say something cutting, then held it

back, choosing instead to admit apologetically, "You find me rather unfit for company, Miss Rand." His hand smoothed unruly waves. "I've been working, I'm afraid."

"You work at home, also?" As soon as the words were out, she felt incredibly foolish. "I mean I thought gentlemen—that is, well, you *are* gentry, after all."

"Unlanded barristers must pay the tradesmen, my dear. And I have been researching a particularly difficult point," he added, explaining, "There are nearly nine hundred years of English law, and each case is predicated on all that has gone before it. My duty is to draw the court's attention to those best suited to the admittance of discretionary evidence. It is a rather selective business, I'm afraid. And unfortunately there is not much that says one cannot be executed for stealing a pig."

"A pig? Surely not."

"Oh, it is worse than that, I assure you. We civilized English have been known to hang children over a loaf of bread. But you did not come here to discuss law, did you?"

"Actually, I have," she managed. "Uh—if you do not mind it, I should like to be private with you for a moment."

"Private?" Again, his eyes took in her evening cloak. "All right." He stood back, then directed her to the door he'd just come through. "I suppose I ought to be impressed that you have taken time to stop by for my opinion, my dear."

She wanted to snap at him, to tell him yet again that she was not his dear, but she forbore saying it, given the circumstances. Instead, she moved past him into his cluttered study, where his coat and vest hung over a chair, his boots beneath. Behind her, he followed her gaze.

"I have an orderly mind rather than an orderly desk, I fear."

"Yes. I can quite see that, sir."

"It must be a matter of some import for you to attempt bearding a lion in his den, Miss Rand."

There was no mistaking the amusement in his voice. She swung around quickly, catching his rather odd smile. Biting back anger, she looked into surprisingly warm eyes.

"Yes, it is." He was far too close for her comfort, but she dared not move lest she break and run. "I was afraid that if I waited until tomorrow, I should lose my resolve."

"Oh? Now that ought to intrigue me, shouldn't it?"

"Yes—no. That is, I don't know. I'm afraid I don't know how you think, Mr. Hamilton. If I did, this would be considerably easier."

"I told you—with a great deal of order." He stepped closer. "Perhaps if I took your cloak, you might look less like you mean to bolt and run." She stood very still as his hands touched her shoulders lightly, then moved beneath her chin. "You know, my dear, the last time I saw such a face, it was on a deer facing a gun."

"I know you must think this quite odd, sir, but—" Too aware of the warmth of his flesh where his hands worked at the pearl clasp, she closed her eyes and swallowed. "I can do that for myself," she protested.

"A gentleman always takes a lady's cloak," he reminded her.

"But I am not a lady, and no matter what I said before, you are not a gentleman!" she blurted out. "If you were, I shouldn't be here at all!"

He moved behind her to lift the unfastened cloak from her shoulders, and as his hand brushed her bare shoulder, she shivered. He stepped away to fold it and lay it over his coat. "A bit of Madeira? Or perhaps some claret?" he offered politely. "I know I ought to offer you something innocuous like ratafia, but I'm afraid I have none. Unfortunately, I am not in the habit of entertaining females at home. In fact, you are the first to breach these hallowed doors."

"Yes, I suppose you entertain them at Mrs. Coates's, don't you?" she said acidly.

"Now that, Miss Rand, was unworthy of you."

"Yes, it was, wasn't it?" she admitted. "I ought not to have said it."

"No, you should not, but you seem to be peculiarly devoid of convention, so I've not come to expect a surfeit of civility."

He had moved to a small cabinet, where he drew out two glasses and a decanter of wine. Closing the mahogany doors, he unstoppered the bottle and poured the amber Madeira. His back was turned to her, making it seem as good a time as any to broach her business with him.

"You must wonder why I am here," she said awkwardly.

"It had occurred to me to ask about that, but I decided if I waited long enough, you might tell me," he murmured, restoppering the wine bottle. "I had thought perhaps you were on your way somewhere else, and being in the area, you wished to set me on the right path again."

"No. I am only come to see you. It's about my father."

The warning hairs on his neck stood as he asked warily, "Oh? Trouble with Parker also?"

"Do you think my father can be defended?" she demanded. "You can tell me the truth—do you think there is any chance for an acquittal?"

"Did Parker see him?"

"Yes."

"And what did my worthy colleague say?"

"Papa would not cooperate with him, so he has declined the case. That and the fact he was pelted with eggs and rotten food seems to have dissuaded him."

He took a sip from his glass rather than look at her. "Probably wise of him," he murmured. "I hear all of London wants to witness the hanging."

"Papa believes you are his only hope, you know." When he did not respond at all, she decided to rush her fences, "Could you save him, sir? Are you truly that good at what you do?"

He turned around at that. "I don't know," he answered honestly. "Regardless of what he has told you,

I am not a Vauxhall magician able to pull favorable verdicts from my hat.''

"But they say you are the best—even Parker said it!''

"I'll wager he did, if he did not want the case.''

"But you could keep him from hanging, couldn't you? You could perhaps cast enough doubt to gain a lesser conviction. I mean, it is but his word against that—well, against that fellow's, isn't it?''

"Not entirely.'' As her face fell, he relented. "I suppose, given the witnesses, that if I had the right jury and the right justice, I could twist enough words to cast a reasonable doubt—if I wanted to.''

"Then you are saying all is not lost, aren't you?''

"You asked a hypothetical question, and I gave you a hypothetical answer—nothing more.'' He handed her the other glass. "Here—sometimes a little Madeira lifts the spirits.''

"What would it take to persuade you to see Papa again?'' she dared to ask.

"A great deal more than I've been offered, I'm afraid, and maybe not even then. I told you—I want a public career, and I cannot think it politic to represent a man the masses want to hang.''

"Then you are a sham, sir—an utter sham!''

He shrugged. "The English public are a bloodthirsty lot, not overly given to forgiving those who thwart them.''

She drank again, then declared flatly, "I am prepared to offer anything you want if you will defend my father.''

He stopped mid-drink and looked over the rim of his glass. "Anything, Miss Rand?'' he asked softly. "Anything encompasses rather a lot, you know.''

She swallowed visibly, then forced herself to meet his gaze steadily. "Yes,'' she managed nearly too low for him to hear. "Anything.'' As he took a step toward her, she swallowed again. "I thought perhaps twenty-five thousand pounds.''

He stopped. "I don't need your money.''

"But surely you could use it!'' she cried. "You are not rich, are you? We can make you wealthy!''

"No." His gaze dropped to the swell of her breasts, then to the slimness of her hips beneath the peach silk gown, and he could feel the heat rise within him. On the outside at least, she was more than a man dared ask for. "No," he repeated before draining his glass. "The next offer?"

"Fifty—fifty thousand, then!"

"I told you—I don't need money." He went to pour himself another drink.

He was going to make her humiliate herself, she knew it, and yet there seemed no other way. For courage, she gulped the remainder of the heady wine, then reached up to her hair, unpinning it, letting it fall over her bare shoulders. Carefully, she set her empty glass down, her eyes on his back.

Licking her parched lips nervously, she managed to choke out, "There is me! What if I were to offer myself?"

He spun around, spilling wine onto the carpet, then he recovered. "I see," he murmured softly. "Now that does put a different light on the matter, doesn't it?"

She closed her eyes to hide the fear she felt. "If I were to come to you," she asked painfully, "would you defend my father?"

Her words hung between them. Despite the fact that she stood like a statue, he could see the rise and fall of her breasts against the soft silk of her gown. His own pulse raced, pounding in his temples, as he took in what she offered. And he knew he wanted it. His gaze returned to her flaming face.

Unable to stand it, she cried, "Well—aren't you going to say something at least?"

He sucked in his breath and tried to gain control of his thoughts. "God, but you know how to drive a bargain, don't you?" he managed finally.

She forced a crooked smile, then looked away. "I suppose I am my father's daughter, Mr. Hamilton."

Setting his glass down on the cabinet, he crossed the room to her, stopping a scant foot away. "Are you quite sure you want to offer so much?"

Her face hot, she nodded her head mutely, not daring to meet his gaze.

His rational mind told him he was being a fool, but he was too acutely aware of her to care. He reached up with his knuckle to lift her chin, forcing her to look at him. "You know," he whispered huskily, "a man could drown in your eyes, Ellie."

It was as though she could feel the heat of his body, but it was a shiver that went down her spine. "You have not answered me, sir," she said low.

"Paris ought to be worth a Mass," he murmured as his lips touched hers.

A sob formed deep in her throat, then died as his arms circled her, cradling her while he kissed her ardently, urgently, taking her breath away. Her clenched hands still at her side, she closed her eyes, feeling the intoxication of his arms around her, of his man's body against hers. His kiss deepened, parting her lips, possessing her mouth. Telling herself that it was in truth the only way, she slid her arms around his waist, holding him, grasping the soft cambric of his shirt.

When at last he left her lips, he traced soft kisses along her jaw, murmuring hungrily against her ear, "If you want to leave, there is still time, Ellie. Otherwise, I'm taking you upstairs."

Rather than answer him, she twined her fingers in his thick, wavy hair, turning her face back for his kiss. His hands moved eagerly over her body, smoothing the rich silk against her hips, pressing her closer.

He broke away from her, searched her face, then caught her hand, pulling her after him into the deserted hall, up the steep, narrow stairs into his chamber above. Closing the door behind them, he faced her. Seeing that she watched him, her luminous eyes wide with uncertainty, he told himself he had to move slowly, that he had to court her ere he got her to bed. Collecting himself with an effort, he walked to where last night's wine still sat by his bedside.

Pouring a full cup of it, he carried it to her, then drank his own straight from the bottle. "Go on—it will make it easier."

"Is it so awful I have to be disguised?"

"No, of course not. I just thought you might prefer some wine, that's all," he answered awkwardly. Even as he said it, he felt as foolish as a boy embarking on his first grand passion rather than a man who'd had his share of women. He took another long pull from the bottle, then put it down. "Come here," he said softly. When she hesitated, he promised, "For whatever it is worth, I'll try to make it good for you."

It came to her then that she was crossing a line from which she could not turn back. Her conscience warred with her mind, telling her that what she did was very wrong, but she'd already come too far for flight. She gulped down the wine, hoping to bolster her resolve. As he took her into his arms again, her cup fell to the floor.

"Uh—"

"Forget it," he murmured. "Forget everything but this."

Panic assailed her, and she pushed at his chest, then dropped her arms as the heat of his embrace warmed her and she tasted the wine on his lips. One of his hands smoothed her hair as though she were a child while the other worked the hook at the back of her gown, unfastening it. She stiffened.

"Let me undress you, Ellie," he whispered. "I want to see you."

"No!"

He returned to kissing her, tasting of her mouth, her ear, her throat, trying to reassure her. Her flesh was hot, her breathing rapid, and he could feel the pulse in her throat with his lips. This time, when his fingers slid beneath the silk to the bare skin of her shoulders and back, she did not protest until he tried to slip the dress down over her arms.

She was as skittish as any he'd ever seen. Reluctantly, he released her. "Do you want to go home?" he demanded harshly. "If you do, go now."

"If I do, you will not defend my father!" she cried.

"No."

Clasping her hands tightly before her, she tried to control herself. "It is just that I—well, I have never—"

"I know."

He came up behind her to trace along the open silk where he'd unhooked her gown. Something akin to a sob broke from her, and she tried to turn into his arms, to hide her face against his chest that he could not see her, but he wouldn't let her. Instead, he kept her back against him.

"No, it will be all right, I promise you," he whispered. "You won't be sorry if I can help it."

She felt so taut she feared she would go to pieces as his fingers touched her bare skin lightly, moving along her shoulder, then back to her spine, dipping lower. Still holding her from behind, he lifted her heavy hair from her neck and kissed the sensitive skin at her nape, sending new shivers coursing through her.

He could feel the tension within her as he nibbled along her neck and shoulders lightly. His hands slid beneath her arms to the soft rounds of her breasts, cupping them, rubbing over her nipples with his thumbs, hardening them until they strained against his palms. Her body trembled, telling him she liked what he was doing to her. And when one of his hands moved away to pull her gown down from her arms, she whispered her anguish.

"What are you doing to me?"

"Shhhh. We've but begun, Ellie."

As he spoke, his voice soft, caressing, he rubbed against her hips, giving her the feel of him while his hands explored her, touching the soft, smooth skin of her belly, the satin of her hips beneath her gown. Her flesh seemed to quiver beneath his fingers. He had her dress and petticoat loose now, held up only by the closeness of his body against hers. She turned against him, clinging to him as he worked her gown downward. Finally, it fell at her feet.

He lifted her, freeing her from her clothes, then carried her to his bed, where he knelt to remove her slippers and stockings. Working feverishly, he peeled out of his shirt and breeches and rolled into the bed against her. He looked down, seeing the faint bluish tinge to her closed eyelids, the tangle of red-gold hair spilling onto his pillow.

"God, Ellie, but you are beautiful," he said, touching her body reverently. "Truly beautiful." His hand skimmed over her breasts as he watched the nipples harden again. Settling his body lower, he teased them with his tongue, while he explored her until he found what he wanted.

Shocked, she stiffened as his fingers touched her, finding the warm wetness there. But as they toyed with her, stroking before they eased inside, she was utterly unprepared for the exquisite sensation he aroused within her. She threw her head back, arching her body, moving her hips beneath his hand, no longer caring about anything other than what he was doing to her.

Her breath came in gasps as her legs opened and closed around the movement of his hand, until he could stand the wait no longer. Rolling over, he eased his body above hers and guided himself inside.

She panicked momentarily when her flesh tore, then closed around his. As she cried out, he lay still for a moment, whispering soothing words against her damp brow, then he began to move, slowly, deliberately at first, then losing whatever control he had as she rocked and writhed beneath him. He rode hard then, lost in her, striving for the ecstasy her body promised.

Nothing could have prepared her for how he felt inside her. It was as though the very center of her being was where he was, as though she could not get enough of what he was doing to her. Her legs came up, trying to imprison him, as she bucked and thrashed beneath him, straining for more.

Her breath came in gasps, mingling with his, then he cried out and collapsed to lie over her. His head rested against her shoulder as her arms held him tightly. She lay still, vaguely disappointed, thinking she'd not gotten enough of him.

Finally, he separated from her and lay beside her, gasping. As reality sank in, she felt utterly mortified by what she'd done. Now she wanted to crawl away before he looked at her, but there was nowhere to hide.

He turned over and drew her into the crook of his arm, smiling down at her. His fingertip traced her forehead, her nose, her chin.

"I didn't hurt you very much, did I?"

"No," she choked out.

"It wasn't very good for you," he decided, sighing. "You don't even have any notion how good it can be, you know."

"Just now, I feel more than a trifle humiliated. I cannot think how I—" Her voice trailed off, and she had to turn her head away. "I must have behaved like the veriest fool," she managed painfully. "I think I ought to go home."

"Do you now?" he asked lazily. His free hand reached to touch her breast, stroking the nipple until it hardened once more. Knowing that he watched her, she closed her eyes to hide, then felt him roll over her again. "I don't break my promises, Ellie—I promised to make it good for you, and so I shall," he told her huskily.

Later, she crept down his stairs, her wicked body wrapped in her velvet-lined cloak, her hood pulled up over her disheveled hair, and she hurried around the corner to her carriage. It wasn't until she was safely within it that she dared to touch her swollen lips and relive the memory of his touch. She was no better than a harlot, she decided bitterly. But instead of selling her body for gold, she'd pawned it to Patrick Hamilton as security for her father's defense.

Drawing her knees up on the seat, she stared into London's dark streets. Well, she'd made her devil's bargain, and now she would have to live with it. She closed her eyes, remembering how it was to lie beneath him, to feel his body within hers, and regardless of the shame that nearly overwhelmed her, the hunger was undeniable.

He arose late, and by the time he'd bathed, shaved, and dressed, it was nigh to eleven, an unseemly hour given the work that awaited him. But despite having spent half the night in Elise Rand's arms, he felt exhilarated rather than tired when he came down the stairs.

Hayes regarded him reproachfully before inquiring stiffly if he meant to eat. Upon the negative reply, he'd disappeared, a clear indication that he thoroughly disapproved of Patrick's night of debauchery with a female of the bourgeoisie.

As Patrick started to leave, he noticed there were already a couple of letters in the foyer basket. Stopping, he recognized the slanted scrawl of Lord Dunster on the top one, and he felt more than a little guilty. He picked it up, broke the seal, and read the brief note begging his attendance for later in the day.

He knew what Dunster wanted. Already he'd delayed far too long in presenting himself before the earl to ask for Jane's hand. But the tenor of the note wasn't reproachful, so Patrick supposed now would have to be as good a time as any to get the matter settled and over. In fact, since he'd committed himself to Rand's defense, he'd probably have to delay the grouse hunting trip for a few days. But no doubt an announcement in the *Gazette* ought to mollify Lady Jane and her fond parents.

If he were fortunate enough to get it set for the current session, he might be able to have Rand's initial pleading over almost before Dunster got wind of it. There was no question that Jane's father would wish

Patrick to avoid controversy until well after the next election, no question at all. And equally unquestionable was the certain notoriety any association with Bartholomew Rand would bring him.

But a bargain was a bargain, and Elise had more than kept her end of it. No, he was going to have to mount the best defense possible for the old man. And if he managed by some special grace of God to get Rand off, he reasoned, it would surely enhance rather than harm his reputation. If not . . . well, he was not prepared to think of that.

He glanced at the tall hall clock. Fifteen past eleven. No time to stand there woolgathering—no time at all. Looking out the narrow pane by the door, he could see that Hayes had managed to get him a hackney. And there was a steady, gray drizzle.

"Your robe and peruke are already out, sir," the butler announced behind him. "Wilson put them in a box between tissue to keep them neat despite the rain."

"Give him my thanks, will you?"

"And he took the liberty of bringing your cloak rather than a greatcoat, sir—said it would be less cumbersome in a public hackney."

"If he had his way, I should have a town carriage with my name blazoned on it," Patrick murmured, taking the cloak.

"Well, as a man of fashion, perhaps you ought to consider it," Hayes suggested.

"I prefer my tilbury myself. Unfortunately, there isn't much of a place to leave it standing at Sessions, you know—nor is there sufficient room to enlarge my carriage house for anything beyond one conveyance and a pair without evicting my coachman from his quarters," he added, smiling. "So there you have it, I'm afraid."

Hayes looked at the opened letter for a moment, then inquired slyly, "And did Lady Jane like the roses?"

"Yes, she did, as a matter of fact." He looked at

Hayes for a moment. "Ah, I see—you are still out of crease, aren't you?"

"I am sure 'tis not my place to criticize my betters," the man answered stiffly.

"Then see that you don't." His hand on the door, Patrick hesitated. "I don't mean to be at home for dinner, so you may tell Mrs. Marsh she may have anything she likes."

"And if any is to ask, where might I say you are to be found?"

"I am not on leading strings," Patrick reminded him. "And I don't know."

"I merely meant if a client were to express a need, sir."

"I rarely bother with fools taken up by the watch."

"I am sure I only meant if you were at one of your clubs, I might direct—"

"No, you did not."

He turned the door handle and let himself out before Hayes could feign further innocence. But the man hurried after him, holding an umbrella over Patrick's head.

"I am sure I meant no insolence, sir," he protested.

"Of course you didn't," Patrick murmured. "Good day, old fellow." Looking up at the hackney driver, he ordered, "The Bailey."

He'd meant to go to his office, but there was too little time. Instead, he settled into his seat and considered whether he ought to have called upon Dunster before he saw Rand, deciding no, he owed Elise the greater debt. Closing his eyes briefly, he could still see her offering herself in exchange for his services. As long as he lived, he would always remember the pause he'd felt when she'd said, "There is me."

Nor would he ever forget the feel of her warm skin, the sight of her hair spilling across his pillow, the ecstasy of possessing her. Nor the shame she'd felt when it was over. For that and that alone, he was sorry. But not for any of the rest of it. A man could live a lifetime and never come close to having a female like her.

He looked out onto the grim, gray street, then sighed. He'd told the driver the Bailey, but it didn't matter. Newgate was scarce a walk from there.

Reviewing everything he knew of Bartholomew Rand, he realized he ought to believe him. The old man had worked hard, pulling himself from a bricklayer's son to a factory owner worth more than ninety percent of the *ton*. Three hundred thousand pounds, one newspaper had reported. There was something about the fall of the mighty that engendered glee, a sort of validation of one's sense of proper order. Men like Rand weren't supposed to get rich. That was a privilege better reserved to aristocrats and landed gentlemen.

And Rand was surely not the first defendant willing to lie to his lawyer. The old man was probably so used to the power that came with his money that he merely resented having to answer for anything. That much Patrick could accept.

But why had Rand gone to such subterfuge to engage him? Why had he thrown his daughter at a man he did not know? If either answer indicated a need to be prepared *before* he was arrested, then he had to be as guilty as sin itself. Or some sort of fool who really believed he might be facing labor unrest in Islington. And whatever he thought of Bartholomew Rand, the man was scarce a fool.

No, he was canny and manipulative, willing to admit he'd patronized the very prostitutes he'd professed to despise, blaming it not on his own weakness, but rather on his wife. But again he would not be the first client ready to point a finger elsewhere.

And there was the matter of the witness, registered in record as one "John Colley, of St. Giles." Actually, it was St. Giles Rookery, where the alleys lent themselves to every sort of vice and degradation. The man's address alone ought to be useful in prejudicing a jury, pitting the word of a wealthy businessman against that of a pimp, even if the pimp's statement rang the truer.

But there were also the London mobs, coupled with an irate citizenry, who already were demanding Rand's head in a noose. And with each new newspaper revelation, their cries got louder, something that would certainly affect a jury intent on its own survival.

The hackney stopped, and the driver hopped down to open the door. As Patrick stepped into the street, the fellow reached for the string-tied box.

"Get that fer ye, sor," he offered.

Patrick proffered a half-guinea. "Just take it inside, and leave it with Mr. Cranston at the door, will you? He'll keep it for me."

"Aye."

Glancing up at the sculpture of the Recording Angel held up by Fortitude and Truth above the Bailey entrance, Patrick settled his shoulders and turned the other way to Newgate, where the scaffolds conveniently sat outside Debtor's Door. Today, the street was uncrowded, probably due to the rain. On a good day, he'd seen it fill within minutes with a rioting, surging mob eager to watch a hanging. Eighty thousand riffraff, the papers had estimated the last time, which made one wonder if England were half so civilized as its government would have it.

Above, in the windows of houses, were printed signs offering "a fine breakfast and a good view of the gallows, ten pounds." It cost more to properly see a hanging than a good play in Drury Lane, Patrick reflected, well aware of the irony of that.

Going round to the keeper's gate, he asked for permission to visit Rand.

" 'E's been moved agin, sir—to the keeper's apartments." A knowing grin split the jailer's face. "Fer 'is pertection 'til 'e's 'anged."

"At a cost, no doubt," Patrick observed dryly.

"Thirty guineas a week," the fellow acknowledged, "and extra fer 'is board."

"He can afford it."

"Aye—and oo'd begrudge 'im a bit o' ease ere 'is neck is stretched, eh?"

"Precisely."

The jailer motioned to a man standing against the wall. "Show 'im ter Bat Rand, eh?"

"Aye."

Rand's cell proved to be a single, well-appointed room, complete with a featherbed, a chest for his clothing, a small table with chairs for meals, and a writing desk. Not to mention a window with a view of the street.

"I see you have come up in the world," Patrick murmured from the doorway.

"Eh? Oh, collect you was meaning the room. Aye, 'tis better, ain't it?"

"Considerably."

"It ought to be—I'm paying dearly for it."

"Thirty guineas."

"Fellow told you that, eh?"

"Yes."

"Well, it ain't home, but it suffices, I suppose." Rand eyed him shrewdly. "Came back, did you?"

"Yes."

"I thought mebbe as Ellie could persuade you."

A surge of anger rose within him, but Patrick managed to control the urge to hit the old man. His jaw working, he managed to say tightly, "She spoke to me, if that is what you mean."

"Aye. Taking little thing, ain't she?"

"You, sir, are offensive," Patrick snapped.

"I got money, sirrah—so I don't have to be nice unless I was wanting to." Rand shrugged. "But it don't matter, does it? You are back, and that was what I was wanting."

"On condition."

One heavy brow rose. "Condition? What's that supposed to mean?"

"You are going to have to tell me everything, Mr. Rand. I don't intend to go into court playing hoodman blind with Peale."

"Aye."

"You are entitled to the best defense I can mount—whether you are innocent or guilty."

"Glad to hear it," Rand acknowledged.

"But I have to know whether you did in fact murder Annie Adams."

The old man looked up suspiciously. "I ain't a fool, Hamilton—no sirrah, not at all. I wasn't born under no three-penny planet."

"Mr. Rand—"

"Well, I ain't about to say I was guilty, sir—how the devil was that to sound, eh?"

"It would be privileged information totally inadmissible as evidence."

"Still, I ain't going to say I did it."

"Without your promise of complete candor between us, I shall simply walk out that door." When Rand did not respond, Patrick could not entirely control the exasperation he felt. "And given that you have managed to insult both Mr. Parker and myself, you will have whistled two of the best criminal barristers in London down the wind," he added irritably.

Rand peered intently into Patrick's face, then seemed to relent. "You are a man as knows how to lay the cards down, ain't you?"

"Yes."

"You got to understand, Hamilton. I didn't make m'money by being loose with the chatter, and I ain't used to letting anybody tell me how to go on."

"Your life is in my hands, sir."

"Aye. Then you'd best sit down, eh? It ain't going to be no easy thing to tell you all of it."

"All right."

As Rand sat down on one side of the table, Patrick took the opposite chair. "Now—tell me everything that you know, everything that has happened, beginning with Peg Parker."

"Parker!" Rand yelped. "Now I ain't charged with that!" He hesitated a moment. "Am I?"

"You might be. Did you know her?"

"Course not," the old man muttered testily. "Never laid eyes on the woman."

"You never frequented Maddie Coates's establishment? Before you answer, I might point out that the answer is easy enough to prove."

"Aye, I suppose so." Rand looked suddenly glum. "All right—I been there," he admitted grudgingly.

"When?"

"How the devil should I remember that? I been to lots of 'em."

"No doubt," Patrick muttered. "I would that you are precise in every detail, sir."

"I said I'd been there."

"When?"

"I dunno. Two or three times last year maybe," came the sullen reply.

"Did you see Peg Parker there?"

"Might've. Whores all look alike in the dark, don't they?"

"Did you ever purchase her services?"

"I told you—I might have. Between you and me, I ain't been one to look much at 'em. All I was wanting was someplace to put it."

"Then you could have bought Miss Parker?"

"There you go—a-callin' 'em misses like they was proper females," Rand protested. "I already said I might've had her."

"But you do not recall precisely?"

"No."

"Did you know Maddie Coates?"

"The old whore as took m'money? Aye."

"What about Thomas Truckle?"

"Who? Oh—collect you mean the butler as was in the papers."

"Yes."

"Well, if I was there, I must've seen him."

"Probably. Now, to be specific, how well did you know Maddie Coates?"

"I answered that."

"You were not a regular customer?"

"Damme if I ain't answered that also!"

"If Mr. Peale brings girls from the Coates establishment into court to testify, can they say you were there frequently?"

"I already told you—" Rand saw the impatience in Patrick's eyes. "Aye, I suppose they could," he decided finally.

"Maddie indicated that there was an old gent who

preferred Peg, but due to his misusing her, he was no longer admitted. Mr. Rand, were you that man?''

"I ain't never been turned away nowhere."

"All right. I suppose the females of the establishment would know that also."

Rand flashed him a look that bordered on dislike. "They might say it," he conceded. "They wasn't always wanting to do what I was wanting."

"Which was?"

"Now they ain't going to tell that in court, I'll be bound!"

"They will be under oath, Mr. Rand."

"Well, I was wantin' her to let me bite her so's she'd squeal a bit." The old man looked up. "At my age, it ain't so easy anymore to keep going, if you was to know my meaning."

"Did you bite her?"

"Aye."

"That scarcely seems sufficient to get you turned out, sir."

"Well, sometimes I drew blood and they howled as I was killing 'em. And I kinda liked it like that."

"There were bite marks on Annie Adams's breasts," Patrick reminded him.

"I said I was with her, didn't I?" Rand countered. "I ain't being tried for that, anyways."

"I expect Peale will examine the coroner's records for Peg Parker and Fanny Shawe also, as well as those for every other female found in the river during the past several years, so if there is anything you wish me to know, you'd best tell me now."

"Bitin' ain't exactly one man's vice," the old man retorted.

"You did not know Fanny Shawe?"

"How many times I got to say it? I might have, and I might not. Surely I ain't expected to remember every whore I put it to, eh?"

"No, if their numbers are legion, I suppose not," Patrick murmured dryly.

"You ain't meaning to tell me you ain't never visited no whores, Hamilton? Well, I'm not believing it."

"Mr. Rand, I am not on trial. Now—let us consider Maddie Coates herself," Patrick went on. "You knew her—you have admitted that already."

"Not in the biblical sense."

Rand chuckled as though he'd made a jest, but Patrick didn't crack a smile. "She would have recognized you, wouldn't she? If she had encountered you anywhere, she would have recognized you?" he persisted.

"Aye, she might, I expect."

"Have you ever frequented the Red Dragon?"

"Where is it?"

"A blind alley in the rookery."

"Then I expect I been to it, and if they got whores, I've probably been in it."

Patrick's expression grew pained. "It is an opium den, sir—the one where it is believed Mrs. Coates died."

"If I got any addiction, 'tis the females, not eating opium!" Rand snorted.

Duly noting he'd said eating rather than smoking, Patrick leaned forward to look directly into Bartholomew Rand's face. "Were you there when she died? Do you know anything about how it happened?"

"I thought you was my attorney, sirrah!" Rand fumed indignantly. "Besides, she wasn't killed, as far as I know it. The papers was saying as how—"

"Did you know she used opium?" Patrick asked, interrupting him.

"I told you I did not—the other day, I told you."

"And at the time you were lying to me about knowing her, so why should I believe you now?"

"Dash it, sirrah, but I don't—" The old man caught himself. Looking sheepish, he nodded. "Aye, I got to tell m'lawyer, don't I?"

"Yes."

"Where was we?"

"Maddie's opium use," Patrick reminded him dryly.

"Oh, aye. Well, I seen the pipes, but I cannot say as whether 'twas for her or the men as was visitin' her place."

"But you never saw her eating any opium?"

"If I did, I wasn't knowing what she was eating. It ain't like I ever ate any myself, you know. Stuff's too demned bitter by half! Why they's fools as takes it that way—fools!"

"But you know what a hookah is?"

"Aye, 'tis a Turkish pipe, ain't it?"

"Yes." His eyes intent on Rand, Patrick asked flatly, "Is there anything you can think of that Peale might use against you during your trial, Mr. Rand?"

"Nothing you ain't already said."

"No witnesses who can connect you to the deaths of Peg Parker, Fanny Shawe, or Maddie Coates?"

"No," Rand lied. "And you are the only one as wants to try me for them, anyways, ain't you?"

"I dislike surprises, Mr. Rand." Patrick stood up. "Very well, that will be all this time, sir."

"Huh? But you ain't done nothing but beat m'brow, Hamilton! You ain't told me as how you mean to get me off!" the old man complained loudly.

"If I can produce statements from acquaintances of Annie Adams's pimp to the effect that he misused her, I can probably discredit his testimony against you. More than that I am not prepared to discuss just yet. A great deal depends on what the chemist discovers in Maddie's opium."

"Well, I hope you ain't meaning to ask questions as will get me charged with the rest of it," Rand muttered. "Don't know why they are needful of a chemist anyways."

"To see if the seeds and bits of plant found in what was left were from the poppy or if something else was added."

The old man considered Patrick for a long moment, then sighed. "Aye, I suppose. But it don't make no sense to me, none at all. But I got you, so I guess I ain't supposed to worry none over it, eh?"

Patrick smoothed the sleeves of his dark blue superfine coat, then picked a small piece of lint off one of them before he spoke to Rand again. "I want you to be very careful in here. I do not want you to speak familiarly with the guards—and above all, I don't want you to ask them to procure a female for you. I don't want Peale to be able to call a jailer who can testify you have misused anyone in here.''

"Eh? Here now—that ain't right!" Rand protested. "I mean, they ain't offered, but if they was to—"

"I doubt that, sir. Girls are to be had here for a tuppence to feed their babes."

"And if I was to get me one, what's the harm to it? A man ain't supposed to live like no demned monk, you know."

"While you are here, you will. Otherwise, you can find yourself another lawyer."

The old man's face darkened. "The hell I will! Now, you listen to me, sirrah! I'll do as I want if I want—ain't nobody as tells Bat Rand he ain't getting laid when he's wanting it."

"Either you do as I say, or you can hang by yourself. Do you not understand plain-speaking, sir? One girl in here, and I will wash my hands of you."

"Aye," Rand muttered. "But I still ain't seeing no harm to it?"

"It will be a great deal easier to persuade the jury that you are the victim if it appears Annie Adams enticed you."

"Well, and she did. Asked if I was wanting to feel her, you know. And when I was squeezing the jugs, she offered the rest of it."

"Later on this afternoon, Mr. Banks will come over to obtain a deposition from you. I would suggest you make yourself look as green and gullible as you can."

"Dash it, but I ain't green!"

"No, but if you persist in appearing belligerent, you may be perceived as threatening. And while you are here—and when you are in sitting in court, you are going to appear as meek and self-effacing as you can. It is your duty to make yourself likable."

"Still don't see any harm," the old man muttered under his breath. "They ain't hangin' a respectable businessman over no whore, are they?"

"Yes. And I would that you did not drink either."

"What?" Rand fairly howled. "Now, see here, sir!"

"The same jailers that provide your wine can testify to everything you tell them."

"Oh, but they ain't—"

Patrick sighed. "All right, I'll put it in language you can understand, sir—their lips are oft as loose as the legs of the whores you have frequented."

"But I'm payin' em!"

"And the money stops when you are hanged," Patrick reminded him. "Good day, Mr. Rand."

He was halfway to the door when he heard the old man grumble, "Ain't going to be much good to it, if you was to have your way about it."

As Patrick emerged from Newgate into the dreary drizzle, he looked down to where Fortitude and Truth still supported the Recording Angel. Squaring his shoulders, he reflected wearily that he was going to need a great deal of the former to obscure enough truth to exonerate Bat Rand, for in his heart he was certain the old man had lied to him.

Nonetheless, he crossed Newgate Street toward the Bailey resolutely. After he met in chambers with Justice Tate on another matter, he would seek out Peale and try to weasel the man's strategy out of him. And then he would have to beard Dunster about Jane.

"Hamilton! Good to see you!"

Clapping Patrick's shoulder familiarly, the Earl of Dunster guided him toward the formal saloon in the front of the elegant townhouse. As he stepped back to let the younger man pass, the earl motioned to a liveried footman. "Break out my best claret," he ordered. Turning to Patrick, he smiled. "Jane tells me we have something to celebrate, sir."

"Well, I had planned to broach the matter a bit more properly," Patrick admitted.

"No need to stand on ceremony—none at all, I assure you. I've been following your career for years, sir, and I've liked everything I've seen."

"Thank you."

"Handsome girl, my Jane," Dunster murmured.

"Yes, she is."

"Got everything a man could want—good looks, good breeding, good manners. The sort of female to help a man's advancement."

"I have admired her for some time, sir."

"Of course you have! And I have seen that she has waited for you. I could've taken Dillingham, you know, but she had her heart set on you, for you are the handsomer, she says." Dunster noticed that the footman had returned. "Ah, yes. That will be all, Thorpe." Moving to where the man had set the tray, the older man poured hefty amounts of the claret into two glasses. "Well, don't stand there, Hamilton—come get your share, eh?"

As Patrick took one, the earl lifted the other, smiling again. "To the future of the Tories!" As their glasses clinked together, the older man sobered. "You are the future of the party, Hamilton."

"I hope so, sir."

"No doubt about it." Dunster sipped from his glass, then indicated two chairs drawn up to the blazing fire. "Sit down, my boy, for we've a great deal to discuss."

Patrick took a seat, then drank of his claret. "Quite good stuff," he admitted.

"I've been saving it, sir, for precisely the right occasion, and I should say this fits that bill, eh?" Dunster held his glass out to the fire, letting the flames reflect off the deep red of the wine. "Best stuff ever smuggled into England from Bordeaux," he declared proudly.

"As an officer of the court, I shall try to forget that, sir," Patrick murmured, smiling.

"Mean to talk about that also. But just now there are other things more to the point." The earl's eyes met Patrick's. "Settlements, for instance."

"I don't expect a great deal, my lord. Your patronage means far more than money."

"Oh, I mean to be generous," Dunster insisted, waving aside Patrick's words. "Jane wants you, and I want her to have what she wants. Of course, I shall expect your candor also. Between us, we want to see that she has the sort of life she has come to expect, don't we?"

"I assure you that I can afford her."

"Of course you can! I have made some preliminary inquiries, and I think I have a fair notion as to where you stand financially, dear boy." The earl smiled, then sobered. "You've come far in the ten years you have been in London, haven't you?"

"I've had my successes."

"And you've made a name for yourself, there's no denying that."

"Thank you."

"You've got a good rep, Hamilton." When Patrick said nothing, Dunster continued, adding, "But I must admit I was more than a trifle disappointed to see you defend the Coates woman."

"The jury found her innocent."

"Innocent!" the earl snorted. "An unapt description of the harpy, if I have ever heard one."

"Not guilty, then."

"Yes, well—" Dunster cleared his throat. "Well, I daresay it didn't hurt you in the end, for it will be long forgotten ere the elections. Besides, God got His justice, anyway, didn't He?"

"I don't know, my lord."

"Well, she's dead, in any event. And I have assured my colleagues in the party that you do not mean to make it a practice of rubbing shoulders or anything else with that sort of person."

"Mrs. Coates paid me a goodly sum," Patrick said evenly.

"Harrumph! I daresay when we are done, you will not need to concern yourself with such things. The short of it, my dear Patrick, is that I intend to make you a wealthy man."

"I do not count myself particularly poor now, sir."

"How much are you worth?" Dunster asked bluntly.

"I thought you said you knew."

"I think I do, but I'd like to hear the figures from you."

Patrick neither liked the earl's tone nor his manner, and yet he knew his political future, if he were to have one, depended on Jane's father. He sat rather still, staring into the red-orange flames, composing himself to answer.

"I have nearly seventy thousand pounds in the 'Change, and almost none of it was touched by the recent troubles, my lord. And I have recently bought Farmington's estate near Barfreston without touching my principal." He paused for that to sink in, then added, "I paid cash for it."

"Really?" Seemingly impressed, Dunster nodded.

"I have been considering marriage for some time," Patrick admitted, "and I thought it a rather snug place to rear a family."

"How many rooms?" the earl wanted to know.

"Twenty-seven—and Farmington has added several water closets." When Jane's father said nothing, Patrick murmured apologetically, "I am well aware that it is nothing like what your daughter is used to, but it ought to do very well for us."

"Dunster Castle is possessed of nearly one hundred rooms and nineteen chimneys, sir," the older man reminded him.

"And how many water closets?" Patrick inquired mildly.

"Well, there are but three inside," Dunster conceded irritably, "but they are centrally located."

"As Jane has already informed me there are to be but two offspring, I cannot but think twenty-seven rooms ought to suffice, my lord."

Perceiving the slight edge to the younger man's voice, the earl retreated, allowing heartily, "Of course there are enough, sir! It was not my intent to disparage the place—not at all! I am sure Jane will be content enough there."

"I hope so," Patrick murmured dryly.

"Yes, well, she can be a biddable girl if you put your mind to it, my boy. But we were speaking of settlements, weren't we?"

"We had not quite gotten to that, my lord. I need to add that I also have another twelve thousand pounds in the bank."

"Eighty-two thousand—and the country house, of course, which does not count your current dwelling here," Dunster calculated. "Most impressive, sir. But I daresay your father—"

"My father sent me off with nothing, sir," Patrick said. "It was the Duke of Hamilton who paid for my studies at Cambridge."

"Yes, of course," the earl murmured soothingly. "One could have wished it were Oxford, but I am sure Cambridge provides a fine education also. And Hamilton is a fine fellow—a good connection."

"I don't plan to draw upon that, sir. Indeed, but aside from my name, there is no connection at all there, I assure you."

"I see," Dunster said, seemingly disappointed. "Well, in any event, it would have been easier to promote you amongst my colleagues in the party had you gone to Oxford, and I cannot deny that, of course. One tends to identify with one's school, you know, and Cambridge seems to have delivered up a preponderance of Whigs.''

"I cannot very well go to Oxford now."

"No—what's done is done, isn't it? And you will do very well, I am sure. I have spoken to the Prime Minister, and Liverpool is agreed we are in need of new blood to revitalize the party. He suggests you stand in a safe district, and as Billingsly is withdrawing for his health, we think perhaps Wychott West would suit you."

Patrick sat very still, every fiber of his body absorbing the news he'd been waiting for years to hear. Dunster had already laid the road for him to follow to Parliament.

"I am honored," he managed finally

"Oh, I quite expect you will earn it. After the lengthy debates on the Corn Laws last year, we are decided we need a man of your oratorical abilities to persuade those who would waver. You have a gift there, sir—a divine gift for argument."

"I shall certainly try," Patrick promised.

"No, my boy, you will do it." Dunster regarded him soberly, then nodded. "I have had my eyes on you for two years, Hamilton, and if you would have the truth of it, 'twas I who brought you to my daughter's attention. Not that she was not in alt once she saw you."

"Oh?"

"Yes. Why should the Whigs have all the firebrands, I ask you?"

"Why indeed?"

"You remind me of Fox in his heyday—the man was as eloquent as any. But a Whig," Dunster recalled, frowning. Recovering, he straightened in his chair. "But we were speaking of settlements, weren't we? I'd hoped to surprise you greatly, but it would seem I have underestimated your worth by nigh to a half. Well, that doesn't signify, I suppose. It only means that you will be able to keep my Jane in style, after all."

"Yes."

The earl toyed with his glass, then looked up again. "I had in mind to settle twenty thousand on Jane—and of course I intend to purchase a suitable house for your wedding present. I should hope you will wish to settle another ten thousand on her also."

"Thirty thousand seems more than adequate for her, I should think," Patrick answered. "But I am rather attached to the house I have got, my lord."

"It does nothing for your consequence, my boy—nothing. A man who will need to entertain must have room for an adequate number of servants."

"It serves as a reminder that I have made my own way before the world," Patrick countered.

"And you will go a great deal further," the earl assured him. "But appearances must be kept up, Hamilton. A man's reputation is built on appearances as much as substance."

What had he told Elise Rand when he'd accepted her bargain? That Paris must be worth a Mass. And the same could be said for Dunster's offer. To stall long enough to control his irritation, Patrick finished his claret. Then, setting his glass aside, he nodded.

"It seems eminently fair to me, my lord," he said finally.

"From the first time I saw you, Hamilton, I knew you were a reasonable man," Dunster declared.

"Papa—?" The door, which had been opened tentatively, swung wider, and Jane peered inside. "Is he—?"

"Come in, my love." Beaming, the earl gestured to Patrick. "Your betrothed has proven most amiable, my dear, and I have persuaded him to take the house I have offered."

As she looked at Patrick, her mouth curved into a sly, satisfied smile. "Then all is settled?"

Dunster rose. "I shall leave it to Hamilton to tell you of it," he murmured. "And between you, you may decide when you wish to wed." Turning back to the younger man, he added, "We expect elections next spring, my boy."

She waited until her father was gone, then she

crossed the room to Patrick. "I knew you would be pleased—I knew it!" she said excitedly. "And I have precisely the house already picked out! All Papa must do is persuade Lady Brockhaven to sell it, and since the old baron is dead, I cannot but think that an easy task. I mean, what can she want with such a grand place, anyway?"

He stood politely and tried to smile. "Don't you think I ought to see it?" he asked quietly.

She stopped and looked at him blankly. "But you have—surely you must have passed it a hundred times and more. And you cannot have missed it," she declared positively. Then, seeing that he did not appear entirely pleased, she assumed a defensive posture. "Well, it is precisely what we need, sir, for the rooms downstairs are quite large and commodious enough for the most excellent dinners and parties. I vow that I could seat at least thirty in the dining room."

"It is a bit far from my office, my dear."

"Oh, but did not Papa tell you? He is hopeful that you will turn all your energies to Parliament. Once we are wed, you need never return to the Bailey."

While he himself had contemplated just such a circumstance, it somehow galled him that Dunster and his daughter had taken it upon themselves to decide his future for him.

"No," he said evenly, "I am afraid I am a barrister at heart."

Caught out, she tried to recover. "Well, I am sure Papa—"

"Jane, don't you think this is something to be decided between us?"

"Well, yes—of course it is, Patrick. But Papa—"

"No, I mean between you and me."

Her face fell. "You mean you do not want the house?"

"I didn't say that. I am willing to look at it, if it pleases you that much."

"Oh, but it does! And Papa will buy it for us." She moved closer to look up into his face. "Please, I should like it above all things."

There was no denying that she was beautiful, but as he looked into her dark eyes, he felt almost nothing. As guilt assailed him, he forced another smile.

"All right—we'll look at it tomorrow," he promised her.

"And if you do not like it, I'll tell Papa."

"Fair enough."

She smiled softly. "You have forgotten something, haven't you?" When he did not respond, she prompted him. "Well, we are engaged to wed now, aren't we? And you have not so much as kissed me today." As she spoke, she moved closer still. "Well?"

"I did not think it proper in your father's house, but—" Drawing her into his arms, he looked again into her dark eyes. "But I cannot think he would wish to call me out over it, would he?" he murmured, bending his head to hers.

"I am quite certain he would not," she whispered.

His arms closed around her, holding her, as his lips met hers tentatively at first, then with more ardor. She was soft and pliant in his arms, and he managed to tell himself that that was enough. But as his kiss deepened, she began to struggle, then when he released her, she pulled away from him.

"Really, sir, but you go too fast," she protested.

"Jane, we are to be married."

"Yes, but—"

"But what?"

"I am not that sort of female."

"What sort of female are you?" he dared to ask her.

"Well, I shall be the right sort, of course. I mean, I will grace your table, and I shall try to be witty and engaging before company, and I shall hope to make you happy."

"And sleep in my bed and bear my chidren?"

"Well, that of course, too," she managed, her face reddening. "Though I shall expect to have my own chamber."

"To avoid tempting my amatory instincts, no doubt," he said dryly.

"Now you are funning with me again," she retorted.

"No, Jane, I am not."

Seeing that he regarded her soberly now, she tried to reassure him. "It is my intent to be as good a wife as my mother, Patrick—and Papa has had no complaints."

"Ah, yes—the complaisant wife, as I recall."

Her color deepened. "Must you amuse yourself by twisting my words, sir?" she demanded. "You know very well that I am no match for you in that corner!"

"As a barrister, I twist words for my living, Jane, but if it offends you, I shall beg your pardon for it."

"No, there is no need." She came closer again, this time to stand on tiptoe to brush a chaste kiss on his lips. "I love you, Patrick," she whispered.

His arm closed around her, this time loosely, and he managed to smile into her upturned face. "Then we ought to be very happy, shouldn't we?"

"Yes." She leaned back into the circle of his arm. "Do you think we could go look at the house tomorrow?"

"With Lady Brockhaven still in it?"

"Papa will make her an offer she will not refuse," she answered. "Please."

"If you can gain an appointment, I suppose I can look," he conceded.

"And until we can get a suitable carriage of our own, we may use Papa's."

"I have a very serviceable tilbury, my dear, but I dislike trying to find a place to leave it standing."

"Well, I am sure we can use it also. Oh, I forgot— Papa intends to buy you a bang-up pair at Tattersalls when you have the time to go with him."

"I have horses also. But—" The wryest of faint smiles curved his mouth. "It is kind of him to let me see them first, I suppose."

"You are vexed, aren't you?" she asked anxiously.

"No," he lied.

"Are you going to puff it off to the papers?"

"Yes." He dropped his arm and stepped back from her. "I suppose it is the least I can do since I may be detained a bit longer in London than I expected." As he saw the disappointment in her face, he asked, "Is there any particular newspaper you prefer, my dear?"

She swallowed, then recovered. "I should like the announcement in all of them."

"Then all of them it is."

"Thank you." There was an awkward silence between them for a moment, then she smiled. "You are staying to dine, aren't you?"

"Not tonight, I am afraid. Actually, I am promised elsewhere," he murmured apologetically. "But I do intend to see that my clerk gets the notice fired off to every paper in London." Reaching out, he lifted her chin and bent to kiss her lightly. "Until the next time we are met, my dear."

"And when will that be?" she asked tremulously.

"When we look at the Brockhaven house," he answered.

He left her then, and made his way outside into the continuing drizzle. As he sank back into the hard hackney seat, he tried to tell himself he'd gotten precisely what he'd wanted. By marrying the Home Secretary's daughter, he was poised for a brilliant career where he could influence the making of the laws rather than the manipulation of them. And yet as he looked out the water-streaked window, the joy he'd expected wasn't forthcoming. In fact, rather than feeling triumphant about what he'd done, he felt as though he'd just sold his soul to the devil.

It was dusk, and in Bolton Street, Watier's was beginning to fill up with gamesters and dandies, with Brummell already playing deep at Macao. Feeling oddly detached and slightly disguised, Patrick carried his drink over to watch the usually impeccable Beau cover his eyes as Lord Alvanley raked in his money. Patrick felt a stab of sympathy for Brummell, for things had not been going his way lately, but then he considered that the Beau had brought it upon himself by continuing to play far too deep. That and the bitter estrangement between him and the Prince Regent had made him reckless.

"Prinny must not be coming tonight," he observed to Lord Sefton, who shook his head also.

"A sad breach, sir, a sad breach," Sefton murmured. "Not that Brummell does not deserve it. He ought to know where he can be cruel, and where he cannot."

"How far is he down tonight?"

"Several thousand more than he can pay." The earl looked Patrick over. "And you, sir, do you play?"

"Not this time."

"A pity. At least you could afford it." Drawing Patrick aside, he said casually, "I saw your cousin Hamilton—the duke, I mean—and he had a very interesting bit of gossip, old fellow."

"I shouldn't think my affairs worthy of his notice," Patrick responded noncommittally.

"I gather you are thinking of joining the Tories."

"Possibly."

"Then I hope you will take my advice and distance yourself as best you can from Liverpool."

"Why does it concern you?" Patrick asked bluntly.

"His days as P.M. are numbered."

"It does not take a seer to know that, my lord—but I doubt Prinny will cast his lot with the Whigs, given that they have made him a figure of ridicule."

"No, no—you mistake my meaning, sir," Sefton assured him. "The right Tories will come out on top." His eyes met Patrick's speculatively. "Are you one of the right ones? I wonder."

"What do you think?"

"I think you can ride Dunster's coattails anywhere you wish to travel—if you are willing to live in his pocket."

"I don't know." Patrick appeared to consider the matter, then shrugged. "We shall have to see, won't we?"

"But it surprises me that you aren't playing hazard at Crockford's. That is Dunster's usual hang-about, is it not?"

"I suppose it must be. I seldom see him here or at White's."

"Oh, but it is, my dear fellow. A place for 'government ministers, politicians, and war heroes,' Brummell calls it." Flicking open his snuffbox, Sefton held it out to Patrick. "Care to join me? It is a sample from Petersham's collection."

"Thank you—no. I'm afraid it makes me sneeze."

"So it does everybody," the earl agreed, taking a pinch for himself.

"Hallo, Hamilton." Before Patrick could turn around, Lord Brompton clamped a hand on his shoulder. "Ain't seen you in a whiles, eh?"

"And I daresay we shall see even less of him, for he means to stand for Parliament, I'm told."

"You don't say! Well, actually I *had* heard as we might be wishing you happy," Brompton conceded. "Any truth to the tale that you have offered for Dunster's chit?"

"Read the papers." Abruptly Patrick set his empty

glass on a passing tray, then he nodded politely. "Good day, gentlemen."

As he moved away, he could hear Brompton complain to the earl, "What maggot has he got in his brain? I wonder. It ain't like him to be uncivil."

"No, but I own he has surprised me, Charles. I cannot imagine him as a Tory."

Looking around him, Patrick felt as though he were as empty as those who sat hunched over their games pretending there was some purpose to every turn of card or roll of dice. No, he wasn't being fair to them, and he knew it. The problem lay within him, not them.

But he'd made his beds, both of them, and now he was going to have to find some way to lie between them. On the one hand, his future father-in-law was going to be exceedingly angry when he discovered that Patrick was going to defend Bartholomew Rand just before spring elections. And on the other, Elise Rand was going to pick up the newspaper and read where he'd engaged himself to Lady Jane Barclay. Hopefully, she would see that as he saw it—a political bargain between two ambitious people, and nothing more.

He looked back to where Brompton still conversed with Sefton, and he sighed heavily. Not so long ago, he'd have considered having his name linked with Dunster's rather heady stuff. Maybe if he were not so brain weary, he still might have, but somehow just now it all seemed rather hollow.

"Hamilton!" someone called out. "Come join us, sir!"

Looking back, he could see it was Rivington and Sedgley, a pair of respectable Tories, which ought to have pleased him, but not tonight.

"I was just leaving," he answered.

"Already? But the night ain't begun!"

"I am promised elsewhere," Patrick lied.

"Oh, aye. Well then, another time perhaps," Sedgley said.

Picking up his hat and walking stick at the door, he

waited for an attendant to procure him a hackney, then he stepped out into the cold, steady rain. Heaving himself up into the seat, he hesitated as the driver waited expectantly, then he made up his mind, surprising even himself.

"The Rand house in Marylebone."

"Aye, guvnor."

Telling himself that he went to apprise her of his visit to Rand earlier, he knew it for the weakest of excuses. No, it was to see Elise Rand once more. Closing his eyes, he leaned back, recalling her to his mind, feeling the overwhelming heat of desire.

He had no right to do this, none at all, he reasoned rationally. She'd paid her share already, and what he wanted to do was little more than the sort of extortion he abhorred. No, he argued within himself, he would merely see her and speak with her, nothing else.

But in the eye of his mind, he saw her red-gold hair tangled upon his pillow, her pale body naked upon his sheets. And though her blue eyes were closed, he could still see the ecstasy of union in her face. Giving in to the extraordinary effect she had on his senses, he allowed himself the luxury of remembering every movement, every word, every inch he'd explored of her. And it was as though every sense was once again alive to the feel of her.

Finally, when he could stand it no longer, he forced himself to think of Jane, and he felt utterly disgusted with himself, knowing he'd betrayed nearly everything he believed in to act upon the political stage.

The hackney slowed, then came to a stop, and his driver shouted something to a group of town latelies ahead. Patrick heard the pitiful yelp of a dog, and he looked outside to see the wet-eared would-be dandies playing what appeared to be bowls with a pup instead of a ball. Opening his door, he hung out, yelling at them.

"Make way! I am an officer of the court!"

Derisive jeers greeted him. Jumping down, his walking stick in his hand, he walked toward them. One obviously very drunk fellow laughed loudly.

"Ain't we got us a swell, James!" Putting up his fists, a boy gibed, "You wanna see some science?"

For answer, Patrick ducked and struck the fellow hard at the knees with his stick. The youth fell into the mud, a surprised cry on his lips.

"Here now—he ain't but one! I say we get him!"

They rushed him then, and he was in a tangle of arms, legs, and fists. As he stumbled into the mud with a boy on his back and two punching and kicking him, he fought back, throwing the one over his shoulder into the other, then grabbing another by his hair and slamming him into a lamppost. The third caught him in the stomach with a solid kick, nearly knocking the wind from him, and he pitched forward. The boy on the lamppost shouted, "We got to get out ere the Charlies come!" The kicker took one last vicious blow into Patrick's ribs, then ran.

"Ye all right?" the hackney driver asked timorously as he bent over to peer into Patrick's face.

"No, I have had the wadding kicked out of me."

"Yer coat—'tis ruint, ain't it?" the driver pointed out, reaching to help Patrick up.

"I don't need help now." With an effort, Hamilton rolled to sit, then staggered to stand. Looking down at the mud on his coat, his pantaloon knees, and Hoby's best boots, he shook his head. "Never a Charlie when he's needed," he muttered. He wiped the back of his wet hand across his cheek, then stared at the blood. "One of 'em tried to put my eyes out," he decided. His gaze swept the now empty street, then stopped on the whimpering pup huddled against a building.

Walking over for a closer look, he stooped to examine it. "I think they got the better of us," he murmured, feeling along its backbone with his muddy hands. Lifting it to stand, he watched as it took an unsteady step, then yelped in pain. "At least they didn't break your spine, did they?"

"Ye better get a-going," his driver said nervously. "Ain't nothing ter say they ain't coming back fer the dog."

Scooping up the frightened, bedraggled puppy, Patrick supported its hind feet as he stood. "Not this one at least," he decided.

"Here now—ye ain't putting the mongrel in me 'ackney!"

"I'll give you double fare for it."

The fellow looked at the dog, then conceded, "Well, he ain't big enough to ruin anything."

With an effort, Patrick walked back to the hired coach and thrust the puppy inside. Then, catching the door frame, he pulled himself up after. "You, my miserable little whelp, are a sad case indeed," he told the cowering creature. "But I think I know someone who will doubtless welcome you."

The Rand house appeared nearly dark, an odd circumstance given the earliness of the hour. Nonetheless, with the muddy puppy under his arm, Patrick mounted the mansion steps and banged the brass knocker against the strike plate.

The door opened scarce a crack as Graves asked cautiously, "Who is it?"

"Patrick Hamilton."

The butler stepped back just far enough to let the barrister pass, then he hastened to close it and throw the latch. Turning around, he got a better view of Patrick, then gasped.

" 'Pon my word! What has happened, sir?"

Before Patrick could answer, another door opened off the wide foyer, and Elise came out, speaking irritably before she saw him. "If it is another crack-brain come to throw something, I shall—" She stopped mid-sentence to stare, and the color drained from her face. "Oh."

He smiled crookedly. "Hello."

She swallowed, fighting the urge to flee from him, and came no closer. "Whatever are you doing here?" she demanded. Seeing the mud on his clothes, she recovered enough to say, "You look as though you have been in a mill, sir."

"Something very like it." His smile broadened as he held out the dog. "I have brought you something."

"A puppy? But why—? Oh, my—he's hurt, isn't he?"

"Well, he can stand up," Patrick answered.

"Yes, well, it is rather late for company." She hesitated until the small animal wagged its tail. "Oh, very well!" she snapped. "Bring him in."

"Thank you." He followed her into her father's bookroom. "Er—I don't suppose you have something to put him on, do you?"

"Yes." She picked up a newspaper from a refuse basket, then spread it out over a reading table. Looking down, she saw where she'd marked another story about her father. "I hope he does not mind standing upon a pack of lies," she muttered. "Joseph," she called out, "fetch me rags and water!"

"Perhaps I ought to stand on a paper myself," Patrick offered.

"No. If you get mud on the carpet, it will dry, and then someone can beat it out." Turning her attention back to the small, quivering animal, her expression softened. "You are in sad case, aren't you?" she told it.

"You'll get dirty if you touch him," Patrick warned her.

"As if I cared for that, sir." Bending over the puppy, she crooned softly, "Aye, but you will be all right now, little one." Her hand touched the animal's soft muzzle tenderly. "Did your carriage hit it?" she asked Patrick.

"No. Some young fools were kicking him about."

"And you stopped them? I must own you have surprised me, Mr. Hamilton. I thought Tories cared for nothing beyond themselves."

"Now that, my dear, was unworthy of you."

"I am not your dear!" she snapped. With one hand still stroking the puppy's head, she pushed back her straggling hair with the other. "Your pardon," she managed more civilly. "If I am out of reason cross, it is that we have been considerably harassed today."

"Oh?"

"Yes. Awful people have written the worst sort of things and shoved them under the door, while others have thrown filth at the house."

"That doesn't surprise me."

"Well, it does me," she retorted. "And had it not been raining, I daresay we should have been subjected to a great deal more of it. It is the papers' fault—they are doing naught but rousing the rabble!"

"I'm sorry."

"Sorry? It isn't your fault, is it? You are not amongst those that say drawing and quartering is not good enough for my father, are you?"

"No."

Hot, angry tears welled in her eyes. "If they could get at him, they would tear him apart!" Wiping her eyes furiously, she cried, "And he has done nothing worse than most of them! Why must everyone believe him guilty ere there is a trial? Already they would have it that Papa is some sort of awful ogre—as though he eats children!"

"I went to see him today," he said quietly. "I kept my bargain with you."

She stood very still, then stared at the floor. "Yes," she said finally. "He told me."

"Then you went also?"

"I could scarce stay away, I think. He must know that someone believes him." Not daring to face Patrick, she went back to stroking the dog. "But you were there earlier, so I daresay you do not yet know the whole of it, do you?"

"The whole of what?"

"Just before I visited, they took Papa out in shackles to an empty room, where they threw his cloak over his head." A shudder went through her, then she mastered herself. "They brought in the watchman who earlier said it was Mrs. Coates, and this time—" She stopped to suck in her breath, then let it out in a sob. "This time, the man said, 'twas Papa who dumped that woman in the river! But he is lying—probably rather than admit he cannot remember!"

"He said he saw Rand with Peg Parker's body?"

"Yes." She leaned over the table, grasping the edges until her knuckles were white. "But there is more also," she went on, her voice now toneless. "I think they mean to blame him for the deaths of every prostitute killed in the area for at least a year. They have told him he is suspected of the Shawe murder also."

"I expected that."

She whirled around. "Why?" she demanded hotly. "Because he is convenient? So that they can say they have solved everything? How very neatly they are wrapping all their linen!"

"Ellie, Ellie—" He moved closer and drew her into his arms. "There is nothing you can do about what anyone says," he whispered. "I shall just have to try to prove them wrong."

"Can you? Can anyone help him now?" she cried. "Or will they try to appease the public by hanging him?"

His arms closed around her as she began to sob. Smoothing her hair over her shaking shoulders, he said soothingly, "There will be a trial, Ellie—there has to be a trial. A jury will hear all the evidence."

"The justices can direct a verdict! Mr. Parker said they could!"

"Parker only wanted out."

"And you? When they are throwing eggs and all manner of filth at you, will you wish out, too?"

"No. No matter what the outcome, I will see it to the end," he promised. As he held her, he was acutely aware of every curve of her body, and desire washed over him. His palm smoothed her dress over her back as his mind remembered the feel of her bare skin against his. "Ellie, it will be all right," he whispered.

She rested her head on the solid hardness of his shoulder, seeking comfort from the masculine feel of wool superfine beneath her cheek, the strength of his arms about her, wanting desperately to believe his words.

"I am getting your gown dirty," he said finally.

"I don't care," came the muffled reply.

The pup, left unattended, wriggled to the edge of the table, then fell to the floor with a painful yelp before wriggling between their feet.

"Oh!" Pulling away from Patrick, Elise dropped to her knees to gather the animal close. Holding it, she cradled it much like one would a baby. Her hand smoothed its matted fur against its bony back. "When you are cleaned," she told it huskily, "there will be food for you."

"Oooh, 'tis a wee thing, ain't it?" Molly said, coming into the room with rags draped over one arm and a steaming pan of water in the other hand. Behind her, Joseph carried a bucket.

"Give one of them to Mr. Hamilton, and I shall take the other," Elise ordered. With the muddy puppy still snuggling against her neck, she managed to rise. "Put it there—on the table where you see the papers."

"Aye, miss. Er—was ye wanting me ter clean it?" the footman inquired dubiously.

"No. See to Hamilton, will you?"

"I brung ye soap," Molly added. "Good strong stuff from the laundry."

"Thank you."

Elise went to work, wetting the clumped mud, then soaping the matted fur carefully as she looked for wounds. As though it knew she meant to help it, the little dog sat patiently beneath her hands.

"I shall need more clean water."

Joseph, who'd watched curiously, agreed. "Aye, he's a dirty little bugger, ain't he?"

"Actually, I think he is a she," Elise murmured as she soaped beneath its tail.

"Ye ain't supposed ter say it," Molly admonished her.

"Fiddle—as if I do not know the difference."

Patrick, who'd washed his face and hands with water from the bucket, carried it to her. "Here—you'd best let me help before your clothes are ruined also."

Elise looked down on her wet and dirty muslin gown. "I think you are too late, if you would have the truth." She wiped her forehead with her hand, leaving a streak of dirt across it, then met his hazel eyes. And the acute memory of his touch brought the heat to her face, forcing her to turn away.

"Yes—well, I guess you'd better," she managed.

As Patrick submerged the wriggling puppy up to its floppy ears, Molly looked over Patrick's shoulder, declaring, "Well, if it ain't a taking little thing—would

ye just look at them eyes? Like little black buttons,
ain't they?''

Recovering enough to look at the animal, Elise nodded. ''Yes, she does. In fact, I think we ought to call
her Button, don't you?''

''Well, we **got** ter call 'er something,'' the maid
agreed.

Lifting it out of the water, Patrick put the puppy
onto the muddy paper, where it tried to shake itself.
Elise wrapped it in the towel and rubbed it vigorously.
She set it back onto the wet papers. ''Can you tell how
badly she is hurt?'' she asked Patrick.

''I'm a lawyer, not a doctor, my dear.'' Nonetheless,
he ran his hand over it, feeling for broken bones. As
his fingers found a knot on its side, the puppy whimpered. ''I think she may have a broken rib here, but
as the lung isn't punctured, it will heal.'' Supporting
its back, he probed its abdomen. ''Not much swell-
ing,'' he decided, ''so probably no harm done there.''
Reasonably satisfied, he straightened. ''She looks as
though she'll survive.''

''I daresay you are right.'' He was too close. She
had to move away, to turn her thoughts elsewhere.
''Joseph,'' she said, looking to the footman, ''you will
get her a basket and a pillow. And, Molly, if there
is any cold tongue, perhaps Monsieur Millet can be
persuaded to chop it finely and add it to a bit of
milk.''

''The Frenchy ain't going ter like it,'' Molly
predicted.

Elise picked up the pup and held it close to her
cheek, feeling the soft velvet of its muzzle. Looking at
Patrick from a safer distance, she noted his ruined
clothes.

''If you were to get out of the coat, I expect that
Papa's valet might be able to—'' Even as she said it,
she could feel her face flush. ''That is—''

''I assure you it is beyond repair.''

''Well, you could wear something of Papa's home.''
Still holding the puppy beneath her chin, she crossed
the room to pull the bell strap, and as another foot-

man appeared, she ordered, "Tell Mr. Simpson to come down, will you?"

"Aye, miss."

As Patrick regarded her skeptically, she said defensively, "Well, Papa was not always fat, sir."

"But I cannot think he was ever tall, was he?"

"Of course he wasn't, but at least his clothes are clean. So unless you mean to stop by one of your clubs, you ought to be able to wear short trousers home in the dark."

"Yes, miss?" A man capable of supplanting Old Starch in condescension looked Patrick over.

"See what you can do with Mr. Hamilton's clothes, will you? If all else fails, give him Papa's."

To his credit, the valet did not blench. Instead, he walked around Hamilton as though he measured him. "If you would follow me, sir," he murmured politely, "I am sure I shall contrive something."

"Really, but I ought to just go," Patrick protested halfheartedly. "There is no need to bother."

"Outside, sir?" Simpson asked awfully. "Oh, I should think not—not at all."

"Well, perhaps you can brush the coat at least," he murmured.

As Hamilton followed Rand's valet upstairs, Elise sank into a chair. Idly stroking the cuddling puppy, she stared into the fire, her thoughts in utter turmoil. She'd thought she'd have some time before she had to face Patrick Hamilton again, some time to distance herself from what they'd done. But he'd merely shown up, catching her utterly unprepared, making her feel somehow weak and foolish, a circumstance she despised.

She looked down at the pup in her lap, its soft muzzle burrowed against her muslin skirt, and she could not help feeling a tenderness for it. "Molly was right," she murmured softly, "You are a wee thing, Button." As she rested her hand on its tiny head, the animal nudged her palm, seeking to be petted. She stroked its still-damp fur, marveling that something so little could have survived such violence.

"Well, the monsoor says he ain't got nothing fer a dog," Molly reported, breaking into Elise's thoughts.

"Did you tell him I ordered it?"

"Aye, but ye know them Frogs, don't ye? Anyways, I brung some milk as I warmed fer it myself."

"I would that you ceased calling Monsieur Millet a Frog," Elise said severely. "I have enough to contend with without his giving notice, thank you."

"Well, I ain't calling him it ter his face," Molly grumbled. "And if ye was wanting ter avoid the brangles, ye ought not ter have sent Joseph neither. He and Missus Graves is a-going 'round and about o'er the laundry baskets. She said he wasn't a-taking one fer no dog—and no pillow neither. Here—ye best let me take the creature, else it'll be a-piddling on yer papa's rug."

Reluctantly, Elise yielded the puppy, who whimpered as Molly lifted it. "Come on, ye wee worthless creature," the maid told Button. " 'Tis out inter the hall we are going. And when yer done, that Joseph is gonna be a-taking ye outside ter do yer business."

"When Joseph wins the brangle," Elise said after her, "tell him to take Button and the basket to my bedchamber."

Molly turned back at that. "And I suppose ye think I'm going ter clean the messes?"

"Yes."

"Aye," the girl sighed. "I figgered so."

The room was so very empty then, so empty that Elise could hear only the sounds of green logs popping in the fire and the clock ticking on the mantel above. Bat Rand did everything on a grand scale, and now his huge house seemed utterly empty without him or her mother. Never in all her life had she ever felt quite so overwhelmed or alone, not even when Ben had died. She was not at all certain she could hold everything together until her father was acquitted, but she dared not give in to the bout of tears that threatened, else she'd never stop crying.

She would survive—she had to. For Bartholomew Rand's sake, she would survive, she told herself fiercely. Rising from the chair, she hugged herself with her arms and walked closer to the crackling fire, staring into red-orange flames licking life from the logs.

"Papa, I wish you were here to tell me how to go on," she whispered.

Glass shattered, followed by obscenities shouted into the house. She ran into the foyer, nearly colliding with Graves, who stood staring at the broken panes. She would have wrenched open the door to confront the knaves, but a footman grabbed her elbow to stop her.

"Let me go!" she cried. "Let me tell them! Let me tell them!" She pulled free and threw open the door. "Why are you doing this?" she demanded. "My father is innocent!"

Patrick ran down the stairs in his shirtsleeves and caught her arms from behind. She kicked and struggled, then sagged against him. "Why will none listen? Why do they want to see Papa hang?" she sobbed. "He is one of them! Do you hear me?" she shouted as Graves bolted the door. "He is one of you! He started with nothing! He is one of you!"

"You are all right—you are all right," Patrick murmured soothingly against the crown of her hair. Looking over her shoulder, he ordered Graves, "Get someone to make a punch, will you?"

"Yes, sir—something with rum in it perhaps?"

"Yes—something strong."

"You don't understand—I've got to make them know he did not do it!"

Patrick half dragged, half carried her back to the bookroom, where he forced her into a chair. "That was a deuced idiotic notion—they could have brained you with a brick ere you said anything," he declared flatly.

He was standing over her, his hands holding her down. She looked up into his hazel eyes defiantly at first, then she dropped her head into her hands. Helpless, he stroked her shoulder, trying to give comfort. Finally, she seemed to collect herself.

"I'm sorry," she managed low. "I must've sounded like a madwoman."

"No, you were frightened," he responded more gently.

"It has been like that much of the afternoon. They have come and gone at will, and we cannot catch them. Before you arrived, we counted five windows that the cowards have broken."

"You need to hire Bow Street runners to guard the house, Ellie. Either that or you should consider leaving until this is over."

"No, I cannot go anywhere." She sat very still now. "But you are right about the runners."

"As your attorney, I can engage them for you."

She looked up again. "No," she repeated more definitely. "I shall have to learn how to do more things than hand out pamphlets in Covent Garden, I think. Now that there is but me, I shall have to engage them myself."

"You cannot do it all."

"There is nobody else."

The firelight played upon her shining hair, making it seem more red than gold, and as he looked into her face, desire for her nearly overwhelmed him. He dropped his hand and moved away.

"Would you like for me to stay?" Even as he said it, the strained voice he heard did not seem like his own. "Merely as a guest, I mean?"

"No. No, that will not be necessary, sir." She swallowed to hide her embarrassment. "I am quite all right now."

"And what if they come back?"

"What could you do? You cannot stop them any more than Joseph or the others," she countered. "Indeed, but we had James sit in the carriage outside, but then we feared they should destroy it with him in it."

"I thought perhaps you might feel a little safer, I suppose. I know—it sounds foolish to say it."

"Yes, well—" She glanced at the fire for a moment, then sighed. "And who is supposed to make me feel safe from you?" She studied her hands in her lap.

"I have never thought of myself as a weak woman, Mr. Hamilton."

She was using the formality of his name to distance herself, and he knew it. "I don't think you weak at all," he assured her.

"You do not have to toadeat me, sir," she muttered.

Joseph and another footman reentered, one carrying a silver bowl, the other a tray with two cups. "Ye got ter do something about that Frog, miss, 'cause he ain't wanting ter do nothing fer anybody."

"He isn't a Frog," she said wearily. "He is an émigré."

"Well, he's a Frenchy, ain't he? Mr. Rand—"

"I don't care what Papa has called him—I don't wish to hear it."

"Aye." He set down the bowl and took the cups, dipping the heated mixture into them. "Now it's a mite stronger than what ye've had," he warned her. "Graves said ye needed more than as fit fer a lady."

"As I am not a lady anyway, I am sure it will be fine."

Patrick took the cup from the footman and handed it to her, advising her to sip it. As the servants withdrew, she took a gulp and nearly choked. As tears came to her eyes, she croaked, "What is it?"

After tasting his, he decided, "It has honey, rum, and lemons it it—possibly something else also."

She shuddered as the fiery mixture hit her stomach. " 'Tis rather strong, isn't it?" she managed.

"It grows on you when you get used to it," he murmured.

"I very much doubt that."

"Just take it a little at a time, and it will make you feel more the thing," he promised. To demonstrate, he sipped his own again. "See—nothing to it. Go on— keep trying."

"Yes, well—you are a man, and you are supposed to like this sort of thing." Nonetheless, she drank gingerly, making faces at him over the rim of her cup. "It could definitely use more sugar."

"In a little while, you'll feel more the thing," he predicted.

"Unless I drink myself unconscious like Papa, I won't feel much better about anything."

"You need to take your mind off your troubles."

"I cannot. I only wish I might do something useful to help Papa." She took another taste of her punch. Feeling the slow warmth diffuse through her stomach, she added, "You behold a desperate female, Hamilton. I have even considered trying to bribe the justices."

"I wouldn't recommend it."

"No, I suppose not."

"Ellie—"

Glancing up, she was all too aware of the warmth that seemed to lighten his hazel eyes. Rather than acknowledge it, she looked to the portrait of a young man over the mantel. "I cannot ever remember him like that," she said slowly, "but Mama said it was a good likeness."

He followed her gaze. "Who is it?"

"Papa. Sir Thomas Lawrence painted it before he was commissioned to do Queen Charlotte—I think it was shortly after he came to London, in fact." She drank again, then smiled. "Papa says it flattered him."

The young man who stared down at him was actually handsome in his loose cambric shirt and flowing stock, his red hair windblown above his piercing blue eyes. "I should think so," Patrick murmured finally. "But there is a certain resemblance between you."

"Actually, I am rather a compromise between them, I think. He was redheaded, she was blond; he was volatile, she was rather placid—and she was reared quite properly in the vicarage, while he was apprenticed so young he can scarce remember his parents."

"When I first met her, I thought you favored your mother more," he mused, still sipping his punch.

"I am my father's daughter, sir—much more like him than my mother in most things." She studied the painting again. "He had it made for her. Her father disapproved of him terribly, so when Lawrence did

Queen Charlotte and became exceedingly famous, Papa sent it to the Binghams with his marriage proposal."

"And that lightened the old gent's objections?"

"Not entirely. I think those were dispatched with money."

"Gold is usually persuasive," he murmured. Leaning forward, he refilled her cup, then his.

She looked down at the steaming punch. "I've never been foxed, you know," she murmured. "But I don't want to think about being alone just now."

"You aren't alone."

"No." She sipped, then held the cup in her lap. "I mean, before Ben, Papa and I were so very close that I could say anything to him and he could say anything to me. Then I met Ben at the Lord Mayor's house, and nothing was ever the same. Papa was determined to despise him, you see, and Ben was the kindest, most generous person I have ever known. You would have thought that after the way the Binghams had treated him, Papa would have been more inclined to tolerance, but he wasn't."

He didn't want to hear about Ben Rose, so he tried to turn her thoughts from the dead man. "Are you feeling more the thing?" he asked.

"I feel like I am somebody else," she admitted, her voice low, husky. "I feel like my mind could float away from my body." She drank again. "But I was telling you about Ben, wasn't I?"

"One man never likes to hear about another, Ellie."

"But you are nothing like Ben. Ben," she pronounced definitely, "wanted to do everything right. He thought if we waited, Papa would come around, but I knew he wouldn't. I begged Ben to elope with me, you see. He considered it dishonorable," she added sadly. Looking directly into Patrick's eyes, she said, "You have never worried about such things, have you?"

"Not often."

"But then I expect you have never loved anyone like that, have you?"

"No."

"And you cannot have ever hurt like I have, Hamilton. And now I shall lose everything—Ben, Papa—even Mama, for I cannot forgive her, you know." She brushed halfheartedly at wet eyes. "There I go again, Hamilton, feeling sorrier for myself than for Papa," she managed huskily.

"Patrick," he said softly.

She blinked again. "What?"

"My name is Patrick."

Her gaze dropped to her hands. "If I said it, I should have to concede intimacy between us, sir, and I don't know if I am prepared for that."

"Even after last night?" he dared to ask her.

"Particularly after that." Her fingertip traced the punch where he'd spilled a few drops of it. "I feel terribly ashamed, you know. Now I am no better than those women Papa has frequented."

"You are nothing like them, Ellie—nothing at all like them."

"Then why are you here?" she cried. "Did you come for another tumble?"

"I don't know why I am here," he answered quietly. "I was going home until I got into the hackney. Then the words just came out when I gave the driver the direction."

She drained her cup, and her mood changed abruptly. "I think you came to get foxed," she decided solemnly.

"Perhaps I did." She was too tightly strung to press just yet, he told himself. "So—shall we get foxed together?"

Looking across to him, she held out her cup. "Yes—and I shall take some more." For a long moment, her blue eyes were fixed on his face. "You know," she said slowly, "were it not for everything else, Hamilton, I should have liked you. But God ought not to have given you those eyes. It was most unfair of Him."

"Oh?"

"They are far too enticing for a man to have."

"That's not very discouraging, Ellie."

"No, it isn't, is it?" she admitted. "All right, then let us speak of the stage. You did say you wished for the stage, didn't you?"

"When I was fifteen or sixteen, I wished for it more than anything."

"I would that you told me about it."

"Only if you tell me what it was like growing up with all this," he murmured, lifting his hand to sweep the room. "I was a younger son in a house in sad need of repair. And I'd hear of how you came to be a female reformer."

"Is that why you don't keep a fancy carriage or a pair of high-steppers?" she asked, ignoring the latter. "Or why you do not have a big house in Mayfair?"

"I don't know. I spend what I want, but my needs have never been as great as the money that came my way, I suppose."

"Well, when Papa spends money he says it is because he never had anything when he was young. I have often thought it could go the other way also—that one might be inclined to hang on to one's fortune if one had but lately come into it."

"I do have a tilbury and a pair," he admitted, smiling. "But you asked about my acting ambition, didn't you? You may very much wish you had not."

"No, I'd like to hear it." She held out her cup. "After you pour me some more."

They sat together before the fire, talking of nearly everything from his disappointments to her concern for those beneath her. One by one, sleepy servants dutifully appeared to ask if anything more was needed, until Elise finally sent them up to their beds, leaving the two of them quite alone.

As he filled her cup with the last of the punch, he murmured, "I have the distinct feeling that you are getting the better of me."

"How so?"

"You know all my secrets now."

"All of them?"

"Most anyway."

She looked at him, seeing the warmth in his eyes,

daring to wonder if this were the way she and Ben would have been if they'd wedded. Two people together in the closeness of one fire-warmed room, sharing hopes and fears so deeply buried it took rum to expose them. And yet beneath everything they'd said, there had been a constant, intense awareness of him, of his every gesture, of the way he moved, the way he held his body.

"Is something the matter?" he asked, reaching to take her hand, holding it.

His skin was warm, almost hot, where his fingers grasped hers, making her want to pull away before they burned her. Afraid he could see the effect he had on her, she closed her eyes to hide it from him. She swallowed and tried to compose her thoughts.

"Ellie—"

"Please—" Despite the rum, she felt tauter than a bowstring now, as though she would break into pieces if he touched her further. "I think you had best go. It grows late, and—and I—"

"Kiss me, and I will leave," he said softly, lifting her up from the chair.

"I cannot."

"I know what you feel, Ellie," he whispered, drawing her into his arms. "I can feel it also."

"No, you—"

She got no further as his lips met hers softly, gently, nibbling at the corners of her mouth, tempting her. His hands moved over her body as though there were no clothes between them. Her own lips parted, and as he possessed her mouth, she knew a hunger greater than any shame.

When at last he released her, his eyes were dark with desire. "Do you still want me to go?" he asked harshly.

The very air between them seemed to crackle. And it was as though every fiber of her being cried out for what he offered. For answer, she twined her arms about his neck, clinging to him as though he were life itself, raising her head for another kiss.

It was still dark when the puppy began licking her hand. As she drew her arm back from where it had hung over the side of the bed, she came awake with a groan. For a moment she lay there, aware first of the ache in her head, then that Patrick Hamilton slept soundly behind her. And everything came back to her with an almost painful clarity—the dog, the punch, the whispered words of surrender.

The puppy whimpered. Easing her body from beneath Hamilton's arm, Elise turned to pick the animal up. It wriggled and snuggled beneath her chin as though it sought its mother. She held it close, stroking its soft fur absently, thinking of the man beside her, remembering the intensity of the passion between them.

She'd not meant to let him stay—that had been the rum, she supposed. No, she wasn't being truthful, and she knew it. She'd wanted him to hold her, to ease the ache of loneliness, the terrible fear she felt. But most of all she'd wanted to feel again the heat of his desire, the ecstasy his body gave her.

She was a sinful, wanton woman. She knew that also. And yet as she'd lain beneath him, panting, writhing to slake her own desire, it had seemed so right to be there. As though that were at least part of what she'd been made for.

Somewhere, a clock broke the night silence, striking the hour of four. Startled, the puppy broke free to fall from the bed, and it fled to seek refuge underneath. Outside, the watch called out, " 'Tis four of the clock!'' loudly, repeating it thrice, as though there was someone awake to hear him.

Elise turned over, peering through the darkness into Patrick's face, wondering if his head ached also. Very gingerly, she touched his forehead, then traced downward with her fingertip over his straight, even nose, his sensuous lips, and his nearly perfect chin. His breath paused momentarily, then resumed its rhythm.

"You are awake, aren't you?" she said softly.

For answer, he caught her arms and rolled her over him. She squealed in surprise and tried to pull away, but his arms held her. Very deliberately, he nuzzled her neck, then eased his body lower to afford him access to her breasts. As her hair fell like a silken curtain over him, the warm scent of lavender enveloped him.

She was going to tell him her head hurt, but as his tongue touched her nipple, it tautened, and she forgot everything but the sensation there. His lips closed around it, teasing, sucking. As she shivered from the spreading heat, his hands moved over her bare shoulders and back, his fingertips barely touching her. She arched above him, savoring the feel of his mouth on the breast, his body hardening beneath hers.

"Let me love you again ere I have to go," he whispered hotly against her bare skin. As he spoke the words, his fingers slid between them to find the wet softness there.

"Ohhh," she moaned.

Now there was no heaven nor hell, only the exquisite pleasure centered beneath his hand. As he stroked, her whole body seemed to crave what he did to her. Closing her eyes, she threw her head back, and as he tasted first one breast, then the other, she moved with abandon. And when he withdrew his hand, her cry of disappointment dissolved into a long, low moan as he guided himself inside.

She moved her hips eagerly, taking rather than giving, luxuriating in the feeling of power he gave her. Beneath her, he bucked and thrashed, straining, driv-

ing harder to stay inside as she sought almost franti-
cally to ease the unbearable, aching need within her.
Her breath came in gasps, and her whole body seemed
wet with her effort. Finally, he grasped her hips, holding them while she came, and the shudders of her
ecstasy carried him home.

She was still, silent now, and as the lavender-scented
veil of hair lay like silk over his face, he sought to
regain control of his breath. His arms came up to
hold her, imprisoning her over his chest.

She lay there, her head just above his heart, listening to the beat of it, nearly too exhausted to move.
One of his hands smoothed her hair where it fell over
her shoulder, stroking it tenderly.

"Don't get off," he whispered. "I could stay like
this forever."

His words were scarce out when the doorknob rat-
tled, and Molly called inside, "Was ye wantin' me ter
take the dog? I thought I was hearin' the creature
trying ter get out." She jiggled the knob again. "Ye
got yer door locked, miss!"

Patrick put a warning finger over his lips, and Elise
nodded. "It is all right," she called back. "I was but
frightened—and I did not want her to wander."

"But yer Button was a-crying—I guess it must've wa-
kened ye."

"She's all right also. Go on back to bed, and I'll
take care of her. In a little while, I shall take her
outside."

"Aye. I thought she was a-bringing the house down
about ye," the maid muttered.

They listened as Molly padded back up the stairs to
the servants' quarters, then Elise reluctantly rolled
away from Patrick. As he reached for her again, she
shook her head.

"If she had any notion, I should die of mortifica-
tion," she said.

"At least I locked the door."

"Yes, well—" She paused awkwardly, scarce able to
meet his gaze now. "You'd best go." As she spoke,
she pulled the sheet up to cover her nakedness.

He leaned to kiss her, murmuring wickedly, "I'd say you are a bit late for that now." Nonetheless, he sat up. "This is the part I hate, Ellie."

He had his back to her, and for that at least she was grateful. "I daresay you have had a great deal of experience leaving, haven't you?" she managed painfully.

"I suppose I've had my share," he admitted. "But for what it is worth to say it, there's been no one I'd compare to you. No one," he repeated.

"If I am suposed to feel flattered, I don't." She swallowed, trying to hide her embarrassment. "I did it for Papa, you know."

He turned around. "Now that, Ellie, is a lie," he declared flatly. "That was the first time, I'll admit that. But last night and this morning were for you, and you know it."

"And you also," she answered nearly too low for him to hear.

"And for me—I don't deny it." Rising from the bed, he lit a candle in the embers of the nearly dead fire, then searched for his clothes. "Damn," he muttered.

"What?"

"I don't think Button needs to go out." He bent over and picked up his wet sock, holding it up. Smiling wryly, he looked at her. "How does the rhyme go? Diddle, diddle, dumpling, my son John—one shoe off, one shoe on? Well, my dear, I shall make it one stocking off, one stocking on, I think."

The way he said it made her dissolve into laughter, relieving the tension between them. He regarded her sardonically for a moment, then grinned. "You are a complete wretch, Ellie."

She watched from the bed as he found the clothing he'd strewn in haste but hours earlier. As he sat on a chair to pull on the dry stocking, Button dared to peek at him from behind the safety of a bedpost.

"And you are a wretch also," he murmured. "A damned ungrateful one, if you want the truth."

As if it could understand him, the puppy retreated

and came up next to Elise's side, where it attempted to jump onto the bed. Bending over, she picked the small animal up and cuddled it, rubbing her cheek against the small, wet nose. Button's tongue lapped eagerly at her face.

"I'd say by the looks of it, you are up for the morning," Patrick observed.

"I hope not."

"I expect she's hungry, don't you?"

"Yes, of course."

"Then why don't you come down to see me out? While Button eats, I shall merely slip out the back door—unless you want me to walk her for you."

"How are you getting home?" she asked nervously. "I cannot very well have our carriage put to without everyone knowing."

He appeared to consider that, then shrugged. "If my poor hackney fellow isn't still waiting, I shall just have to walk until I can hail another."

"And what if you are accosted—or worse?"

He smiled crookedly. "Would that worry you?"

"Of course it would!" she snapped, exasperated. "If anything happens to you, who is to defend my father? Besides," she added truthfully, "I should probably miss you."

"I should hope so." He stood and tucked his shirt into his dirty trousers, then brushed at the dried mud on the legs. As his bare foot found his shoe, he slipped it on, then put on the other. Moving to the cheval mirror, he regarded his reflection askance before combing at his disordered hair with his fingers. Turning around, he smiled again.

"Sometime, Ellie," he said softly, "I'd like to have a whole night with you. I'd like to wake up when it is light enough to see you."

As she flushed to the roots of her hair, she turned away, seeking the wrapper Molly had laid out for her. Pulling it on, she hastily tied it closed. When she started around to pick up the puppy, she faced Hamilton again. Before she could avert her still flaming face, he lifted her chin with his knuckle, forcing her to look into his eyes.

"God, but you are beautiful. You have no notion what you do to me—no notion at all."

She closed her eyes and swallowed. "Please, Patrick—There—I have said it, haven't I?" she managed. "I would that you just left before any of the servants come down."

"You still think God is going to get you for this, don't you?"

"Yes."

"Well, He won't. Do you think He cares what you or I do, Ellie? Do you think He cares what happens to any of us?"

"Yes."

"If He did I should be trodding the boards at Drury Lane, emoting before an appreciative audience rather than wearing a damned robe and wig to argue the finer points of law in front of a jury who cannot understand them." When she still refused to look at him, he bent his head to hers, brushing her lips. As an involuntary shiver went through her, he dropped his hand. "And if He cared one whit, Ellie, you'd be wed to Ben Rose instead of standing here with me."

"I have to think you are wrong," she whispered.

"How can you look at the misery around you and see some grand design to it?" he countered. "All right then—why *are* you standing here with me?"

"I could ask the same of you."

"Because I want you. And you?"

"I don't know. Because I am weak, I suppose—is that good enough for you? Because Papa believes that without you he will hang. Because—"

He stepped back, and his manner softened. "It will have to be, won't it?" Turning back to the rumpled bed, he picked up Button and scratched its ears. "Come on—if we leave, I daresay she'll follow us," he told the animal.

"We'll have to go down the back stairs," Elise decided, pulling her wrapper more tightly about her.

He took the candle and went ahead to light the way

into the deserted hall. As they crept down the steps like thieves, the puppy wriggled beneath his arm. At the bottom, Elise hesitated, then reached for Button.

"You will find the back door that way," she whispered.

"Aren't you going to latch it after me?"

"Yes, but—"

"What sort of lover are you? You are supposed to cling to me and beg to know when you will see me again," he said lightly.

"Well, not being as experienced in this sort of thing as you obviously are, I plead my ignorance. Now—will you just go?" Afraid that he meant to kiss her again, she stood on tiptoe to plant a quick, almost chaste kiss on his cheek. "Good night, Hamilton."

As he opened the door, she could feel the cold, damp air. "Lud," she muttered, "you cannot go out in that." Turning quickly, she went down the dark hall to a closet, then came back. "Here's one of Papa's greatcoats, and you cannot say it won't go around you," she declared, handing it to him.

"Ellie—"

"Thet you, miss?" one of the servants called out sleepily from above.

"Yes, but there is no need to worry, I assure you," she answered hastily. As Patrick handed her the candle and slipped outside, she barred the door. "I was but going to feed the dog, then I intend to go back to bed."

A footman, his nightcap still on his head, peered over the rail. "Thought I heard voices," he mumbled.

"I was talking to Button—to the dog, that is."

"Ye want me ter walk it fer ye?"

"No—you can sleep another two hours."

He went on back up the stairs, leaving her to find something for the animal. "You know," she told it, "you are certainly a patient little creature."

Like the rest of the downstairs, the kitchen was deserted when she passed through it on her way to the cold cellar. Opening the door, she heard rats scrambling for cover below.

"Yes, well," she declared resolutely, "they don't like light much, do they?"

Moving gingerly down the narrow steps, she descended into the depths of the cellar and crossed between the assorted sacks to the corner pit. Fastening the candle into a holder, she lifted the cover and felt beneath the damp straw for the milk jar. Pulling it out, she looked about for a cup, then went to the sacks. As she looked into one, a mouse ran out. Undaunted, she found the crockery cup inside and shook the flour from it.

"That ought to serve," she murmured as much to herself as to the pup. Setting Button down, she poured some of the milk into it. As the animal drank eagerly, she returned the jar to the cold cellar. When she turned back, Button was licking the last vestiges of milk from the cup. "Greedy, aren't you?" she said, tucking the creature back under her arm. "And I suppose you are wishful of going out also."

Its bright little eyes watched her soberly.

"All right. I expect Molly will thank me for it."

She stood shivering in the walled garden behind the house while Button explored every plant before finding one suitable. As soon as the animal finished squatting, Elise scooped it up quickly and returned inside, where she encountered one of the tweenies, a girl of probably no more than fourteen.

"What are you doing up?"

"I 'eard the door and I thought they was a-coming again," the girl explained.

"I was taking the dog outside."

"But I 'eard it twiced."

"She was reluctant, so we had to go back. But I don't blame her, for it is cold outside."

Reaching to touch the dog's muzzle, the girl peered at it. "Oooh, ain't ye a wee creature," she crooned to it. "Why ye ain't big enow to be weaned, are ye?" She looked up at Elise eagerly. "If ye was a-wanting ter sleep, I'd watch o'er 'er fer ye. I'd be real careful, I would."

"Yes, well—"

The tweeny's expression was wistful. "Me mum wouldn't let me 'ave no dog. Said as she 'ad enow mouths ter feed." As she spoke, she continued to rub the sober puppy's head and nose. "I got a mite o' bread fer 'er."

"I don't suppose it would hurt anything," Elise decided. "But she mustn't run loose. And you may have to mop up a puddle or two."

"I wouldn't mind it," the girl assured her.

"She might sleep if you wish to go back to bed."

"I'll take 'er ter bed wi' me."

A clock struck the three-quarter hour. "I'll send Molly for her before breakfast," Elise told her.

"Oh, thankee, miss." The tweeny bobbed a quick curtsy, then ran up the stairs with the dog peering over her shoulder.

Rubbing her arms to warm herself, Elise walked more slowly, climbing to her own bedchamber. Once inside, she poured water into the china washbasin, removed her wrapper, and wiped herself clean before putting on her nightgown. Fastening the tiny satin-covered buttons to her chin, she returned to her bed. She leaned over to blow out the candle stub, then she lay down again.

The sheets were already cold, as though he'd not been there at all, but as she closed her eyes in the early morning darkness, she could still feel the heat of his mouth on her breasts, the strength of his body beneath hers. And despite the dull ache in her head, she felt utterly, completely, sinfully sated.

E lise came awake slowly, then stretched languorously as Molly threw open the window sash, declaring, "Ah, and a fine day for October it is, miss—truly it is." The maid breathed deeply before adding, "It don't look like it means ter rain."

"What time is it?"

"Past eleven." Molly closed the window reluctantly and turned around. "Ye was sleepin' like the dead, ye was. I tried to bring that Button up ter ye, but ye wasn't answerin'."

Elise turned over and yawned. Seeing the depression in the other pillow brought forth a flood of night memories that left her nearly weak. Then she spied Patrick Hamilton's wadded stocking on the floor, and her heart paused.

"Yes—well, perhaps you ought to bring her up now. I daresay Lizzie must be quite tired of her."

"No, she ain't. And I wish ye'd been up ter see that monsoor when we was a-taking the creature out the back door ter do 'er business."

"Oh?"

"She ain't but a mite, but she fair jumped outer that tweeny's hands, and there she was a-barkin' and squeakin' at the Frenchy's foot like she was a-goin' ter bite 'im." Molly grinned. "Aye, ye'd a-thought her was big as one of them mastiffs, ye know."

"But she didn't bite him surely?"

"Oh, her tail was a-waggin' the whole time. But ye know what?" Before Elise could respond, the maid went on. "He was a-laughin' at her. Picked her up in his hand, he did, and gave her a sausage ter take out wi' her. Course we didn't get her out in time, and she piddled on his floor, but he said as one of the fellows could get it up. Ye got her named wrong though," Molly declared. "Button don't fit her. Flirt'd be more like it. All the men is liking her, and James says she's got ter be some sort of spaniel, 'cause her ears is floppin'."

"I have no idea." Seeing that Molly was about to move around the bed to straighten the disorder of her hastily discarded clothes, Elise rose quickly to block her path. "Why don't you bring her up to me?"

But the maid was not easily deterred. "Aye, and I will, but I got to get yer things up from the floor." She eyed Elise askance for a moment. "Ye ain't usually one as makes a mess, ye know."

"It was the punch—I could scarce find my way to bed."

"Oh, aye."

Elise took a long step to cover Hamilton's stocking with her foot. "Actually, it gave me quite a headache."

"I told Joseph as they was givin' ye too much of it," the maid murmured, bending to gather the muslin dress and lawn petticoat. Holding up the dress, she sighed. " 'Tis ruined, it is—ain't no ways as I can get it cleaned fer ye."

"I have others, so you might as well throw it in the fire."

"Be more like ter make rags of it," Molly decided. "And if ye was ter move, I'd get yer shoes and stockings up also."

"I'll pick them up myself later. Just now I should rather have a tisane for my head, thank you."

The girl nodded sympathetically. "Aye, ye was weasel-bit then, wasn't ye? I ain't never seen ye dose yerself fer anything." Folding the soiled clothes over her arm, she started for the door with them, then as Elise started to step off the stocking, the maid turned back. "Er—was ye wantin' a hair o' the dog mebbe? Or was ye wantin' what Simpson gives yer papa?"

"I don't care—whatever you think is best."

"Aye—ye miss yer mum, don't ye?"

Elise didn't answer. Molly sighed, then left, closing the door. As soon as the maid was gone, the girl lifted her foot and picked up the soiled sock, looking for somewhere to put it. As new footsteps could be heard coming up, she hastily opened her writing desk drawer and shoved the stocking inside.

"Miss?" Joseph asked as he knocked.

"I am not dressed," she answered through the door.

"Ye got a caller downstairs as says the More woman has sent her."

"Hannah More sent her? What does she want?" she asked cautiously.

"She wasn't saying."

"Yes, of course." She could not very well spurn anyone Hannah sent, and she knew it. Not when the woman had taken care of seeing Pearl decently buried. "All right," she decided. "Put her in the blue saloon, offer her tea or something, and tell her I shall be down directly."

She washed her face and hands, then dressed quickly before pulling a comb through her tangled hair. Taking pins, she pulled the worst of it back and fastened it atop her head, leaving a few straggles to frame her face. Making a face at her image in the mirror, she went down.

As she entered the reception room, a black-clad female rose to greet her, holding out her black-gloved hand. "Miss Rand, I am Mrs. Barrow." Looking down at her dress, she murmured rather sadly, "The Widow Barrow now."

"I'm sorry," Elise said politely.

"Yes—well, Mrs. More thought perhaps we could help each other."

"Oh?"

The woman brought up her other hand, showing a small Bible. "She rather felt as though you might wish to pray with me."

"Oh."

"A terrible business about Mr. Rand—utterly terrible."

"Yes, it is."

"Prayer is good for the soul, you know." Mrs. Bar-row stepped back self-consciously. "I daresay we are not at all acquainted," she conceded, looking at the rich elegance of the room. "Indeed, but I cannot say I have moved in your circle at all."

"I am not precisely certain what my circle is," Elise murmured. "But do sit down. Er—did Joseph offer you anything? Tea—or coffee perhaps? Or a sweet bun?"

"The footman? Yes, he did. I believe he is gone to get something just now."

"Good."

The woman smiled wanly. "As if anything could make me forget my loss."

"How long has it been since Mr. Barrow passed on?"

"Last March." The woman looked down at the Bible in her lap. "But it seems as though he has been gone forever. Hannah—Mrs. More—said you had suf-fered a bereavement also, but I cannot think it quite the same."

"I was betrothed once, but Ben died before we were wed."

"I'm so sorry."

"Yes—well, so am I."

"We must believe that God's plan, however ob-scured from the eyes of man, is best, my dear."

"Somehow I cannot accept He meant Ben to be murdered."

"No, of course not. And your poor unfortunate fa-ther—shocking, utterly shocking. Of course, I am sure he did not do those terrible things."

Mercifully, Joseph interrupted them by carrying in a tea tray. A junior footman followed with a silver plate of sugared buns. After they left, Elise dutifully poured two cups, asking courteously, "Sugar and cream?"

"Yes, but not too much."

Elise settled back with her tea, sipping of it, wishing the other woman at Jericho. "You must tell Mrs. More I appreciate her concern—and yours, of course."

"She thought it a very good thing if I should find someone to pray with besides her, particularly as I am not overly fond of her place at Cheddar." Mrs. Barrow set aside her cup and reached for a bun. "Mmmmm. These are quite good."

"Thank you. Monsieur Millet supervises the baking also."

"A Frenchman?" the woman said, sniffing. "Well, I have always thought perhaps we do not properly appreciate our own English food, but I expect it is not at all fashionable to say it."

"My father likes almost everything."

"Oh, the poor man." The woman popped the last of the bun into her mouth, then washed it down with her tea. "Now—where were we? Speaking of prayer—yes, that was it." Looking at Elise again, she shook her head. "You poor child. Hannah says you are possessed of such a goodly heart." When Elise remained silent, she went on, "When she told me of that unfortunate person who died alone in that hospital, I knew I should like you." Holding out her Bible, she said, "I have found divine sustenance in this. Indeed, but one has but to open it anywhere to discover the truth, and I have made a practice of trying to divine God's message to me through it."

"Sometimes God's message is difficult to fathom," Elise murmured.

"Oh, I assure you it is not—not at all. Here—you shall see precisely what I have discovered." She pushed the gold-stamped book into the younger woman's hands. "Go on—open it anywhere, and you will see. Whatever page it is, we shall consider it a divine revelation of the Almighty."

"Perhaps you ought to do it."

"No, no—I am here because of poor Mr. Rand. Now, close your eyes, open my Bible, and let the Lord guide your hand. Then when you look, you will have your comfort in Scripture."

"Yes, well, I cannot see how anything can help beyond direct divine intervention." But under Mrs. Barrow's determined gaze, Elise sighed and closed her eyes. Her fingers grasped the edge of the Holy Book, feeling along the top of the pages, then opening it. Her finger moved down halfway, then she dared to look at the printed words. As a chill went all the way to Elise's marrow, the woman leaned closer to see.

Elise read silently, then said tonelessly, " 'The wages of sin are death.' "

"Oh, dear. Well, perhaps we have not gone about it quite right. Perhaps we ought to pray for guidance first," Mrs. Barrow decided nervously. "I am sure that cannot be quite right." She took her Bible back and bowed her head. Closing her eyes, she prayed silently.

But Elise sat very still, turning her thoughts not to her father, but to Patrick Hamilton. The wages of her father's sin could not be death—Hamilton was going to save him—he had to—he had to. Dear God, but he had to save Bat Rand from paying the wages of his sins.

When she looked up, the woman's lips were moving as she carefully opened her Bible. Her thin, black-gloved hand traced slowly down the page, then her finger pointed and stopped. As Elise watched, she looked down, then reddened.

"Well, I cannot say this is going to help at all," she said uncomfortably.

"What is it?"

"Ezekiel, chapter 16, verse—well, 'tis either 38 or 39, but I am sure it does not signify in the least."

"May I see it?"

"Yes, but—" She handed across the open book.

Elise's eyes scanned the page, then stopped at "Wherefore, O harlot, hear the word of the Lord." Her eyes dropped lower and the words seemed to accuse her. "And I will also give thee unto their hand, and they shall throw down thine imminent place, and shall break down thy high places: they shall strip thee also of thy clothes, and take thy fair jewels, leaving thee naked and bare." Her finger moved down the page, finding more. "And they shall burn thine houses with fire, and execute judgments upon thee in the sight of many women: and I will cause thee to cease playing the harlot, and thou shalt give no hire any more.''

She scarce heard Mrs. Barrow say, ''Well, I am sure that cannot apply to Mr. Rand, for it speaks of a woman.'' She took the Bible back and shook her head. ''Unless, of course, it concerns those women, explaining how they came to die. Yes, that must be it,'' she decided quickly. ''It was by God's hand.''

''I rather think that God does not stab and strangle harlots,'' Elise answered dryly.

''No, but perhaps He has allowed it to happen. Perhaps your father was but the instrument—''

''My father did not kill those women! And this is but a game, not revelation!'' Taking a deep breath to calm herself, Elise managed to say more evenly, ''There is no justification anywhere for what happened to those poor females.'' Taking back the Bible from the affronted woman, she quickly thumbed through it, finding the verse she wanted. ''There—'God is love'—see that? A loving God does not destroy. Even Hannah will allow that He hates the sin and loves the sinner.''

''Well, I am sure I did not mean—''

''Yer pardon, miss,'' Molly said apologetically from the door. ''I brung yer hair o̅' the dog—Joseph said it was the best fer what ails ye.''

As the maid gave her mistress the cup, Mrs. Barrow unbent enough to ask curiously, ''What is it?''

''Rum,'' Elise announced baldly. She gave the appearance of drinking deeply, then smacked her lips. Looking across to the stunned woman, she nodded. ''It is, after all, the only cure for being weasel-bit, isn't it?''

''I am sure I do not know,'' Mrs. Barrow responded faintly. Putting her plate on the table between them, she stood up. ''My dear, I fear I have already stayed far too long. No, no—as I have my pelisse, there is no need at all for you to accompany me to the door— none, I assure you.''

''I will tell Papa of your concern,'' Elise murmured without rising.

As the front door closed, Molly stared after the woman. "Well, she ain't one as lingers, is she? And ye—well, ye was downright brassy! I vow I ain't never seen ye like that before—never."

"She was an encroaching female—one of those who pretends sympathy but is spurred by curiosity."

"Oh. Well, ye scandalized her." Molly reached for the cup. "Why, ye ain't drunk any of it."

"I don't want it. I'm afraid if I drank it, I might not stop with one."

"Ye going ter eat? If you was to want, I'd tell that monsoor to coddle some eggs fer ye."

"No. I am overlate as it is." Elise stood. "Papa will think I have forgotten him if I am not there before two."

Still angry with the foolish Barrow creature, she went out into the foyer and started up the stairs. Looking down, she saw the stack of her father's newspapers piled neatly on the reception table next to the empty card basket. She'd promised herself she wasn't going to read any more of their lies, but there was that within her that had to know what they said. Retracing her steps, she went back for the papers.

Reading, she climbed the stairs absently. The first story in the *Gazette* was of Lord Liverpool and the government rather than Rand, and for that at least she had to be thankful. Her eyes moved down the page, scanning for his name, then stopped. She stood there, too transfixed to move, as she read the announcement of Patrick Hamilton's engagement to Lady Jane Barclay, daughter to the Earl of Dunster.

"Is summat the matter?" a footman asked behind her.

"Huh? Oh, no," she managed to answer. "Nothing that was not expected—nothing at all."

Somehow, she managed to finish her climb and seek the solitude of her room. She sat down at her writing desk, feeling utterly, completely empty. The wages of sin, her mind echoed. The wages of sin.

But it wasn't as though she loved him, nothing like that at all, she reminded herself. And it wasn't as though he'd ever said any words of love to her. It had been a simple bargain—her body for his defense of her father. That was all, and there'd been no pretense of anything else. Except he'd acted as though he cared whether she liked it or not, as though he'd wanted her to enjoy what he did to her.

But somehow she still felt betrayed. She looked down at the newspaper on her desk, seeing again the small, boxed announcement. No, if any ought to feel betrayed, it was Lady Jane Barclay, for at least he had promised her something. At least he must have led Dunster's daughter to believe he loved her.

She felt sick inside. And suddenly everything he'd done with her, every caress he'd given her, every whispered word she'd heard, came to mind, mocking her for a fool. How he must have laughed at her even while she panted beneath him, knowing that the rich Miss Rand was playing the whore for him.

That was what she was, and no matter how great the cause, the inescapable fact was that she'd traded herself like a harlot. And he'd let her do it. And she, who prided herself for honesty in all things, had let herself become not only a whore, but also a liar, for the pleasure of his touch.

A raw, bitter anger welled within her as she opened the desk and saw Hamilton's stocking. Taking it out, she balled it up and threw it toward the fire, missing. Looking down, she saw the back of her watercolor of Ben Rose, and she wanted to cry. Sweet, gentle Ben had never suspected what a sinner she was.

Well, it was better this way, anyway, she told herself, for what if they'd continued to play the game—what if she'd have conceived a child of him? Now that was a sobering thought, for unlike the promiscuous wives of the *ton*, she had no complaisant husband to cover her shame. No, then the world would know what she was, and she'd be bringing forth a bastard. Maybe she already was. No one spoke of such things, only whispering occasionally that so-and-so's maid had disgraced herself. But surely it did not happen so quickly. Briefly she considered the chilling possibility of a child, then thought of her father, of the jeering mob outside Newgate Prison, of the scaffold just outside Debtor's Door. No, no matter what the cost or risk, she'd had to gamble with whatever means she could. And Patrick Hamilton had not wanted money.

The door opened behind her, and Button bounded across the floor, its tail wagging, to bark and nip at Elise's legs. She brushed it aside furiously.

"Get away! Get away from me!"

The puppy sank down on its haunches, looking up at her with soulful, reproachful eyes. Its tail thumped tentatively a couple of times.

"I thought ye was wantin' her," Molly said apologetically, bending down to collect the dog.

"I was." Sighing, Elise reached out to scratch the floppy little ears, then took the animal into her arms. "It isn't your fault, after all, is it?" she said to it.

"Ye look queerlike, miss. Ye know, ye oughter not let that woman overset ye."

Still cradling the dog against her shoulder, Elise walked to where the discarded stocking had fallen. Reaching down, she retrieved it, then dropped it directly into the flames.

"What was that?" Molly asked.

"Nothing—nothing at all." She turned around. "I am quite all right now, I assure you."

"Oh, I nearly fergot—Simpson was asking as ter what ye wanted ter do with the coat as Mr. Hamilton left. Was ye going ter send it? Or was he going ter come back fer it?"

"Burn it." As Molly was taken aback by the vehemence in the two words, Elise nodded. "It is ruined, isn't it?" she countered reasonably. "I cannot think he would want it."

"Aye, I suppose not. I was just a-thinkin' ye might be wantin' fer him to come back fer it."

"No."

"And we was believin' ye was likin' him."

"He is Papa's barrister, that is all."

"Aye. Well, then I got ter tell Simpson, ain't I? Was ye wantin' me ter take the dog?"

"No."

She waited until Molly left, then she carried Button to bed with her. Lying down, she held the puppy close, letting it snuggle beneath her chin. As Button licked her neck happily, Elise stared absently, composing in her mind the letter she intended to write Patrick Hamilton, wondering if she dared send something like that to him. Or if she ought to let the matter lie until the next time he wished to bed her.

Patrick sat there, trying not to yawn as he listened to Banks going over the files he would need for the afternoon. Two pleadings and a meeting in chambers with Justice Russell, Prosecutor Peale, and a magistrate. The pleadings were like rote to him, for he merely had to declare his clients' innocence and request the trials be held the next session.

It was the meeting that made him uneasy because it concerned Rand. If it was to consider binding the old man over for a quick trial, perhaps in hope of quieting the unrest, Patrick would not be grouse hunting with Dunster at all. Yet if it was to seek agreement for a postponement to possibly the January or February session, there would be even greater consequences, for the ensuing outcry might prove too great a liability for Patrick to overcome before the spring elections, causing Dunster to abandon him in favor of another more viable candidate.

With the unpopularity of Prime Minister Lord Liverpool, the Tories did not need so much as a breath of scandal, much less an avalanche of it. No, Dunster was not going to be pleased either way, but at least if everything happened quickly, perhaps Patrick's notoriety would be over before the elections.

"In the Rand matter, I have taken the liberty of engaging Mr. Thompson, and—" Seeing that his colleague appeared distracted, Banks cleared his throat to gain attention. When Patrick looked up, he repeated himself, "I have taken the liberty of engaging Mr. Thompson to seek information for us."

"Mr. Thompson?"

"Billy Thompson, then—surely you must recall him? He was the coachman charged with cracking young Lord Fellowes's head during a mill in Covent Garden. Not your usual case, I must say, but I believe he claimed to be a relation to your Mr. Hayes."

"Yes, I remember him. Go on."

"In turn, Mr. Thompson has enlisted the aid of a man merely known as Weasel—not Mr. Weasel—in St. Giles Rookery."

"That ought to make for an enterprising pair," Patrick murmured. "Thompson and Weasel, eh?"

"Yes—well, I have hopes so, in any event. I gave each of them twenty pounds that they may show it about and buy information about Mr. Colley, the—"

"Annie Adams's pimp," Patrick acknowledged impatiently. "Did they discover anything of note, or were they merely lost souls on my money?"

"Mr. Thompson has listed his expenses to date, if you should wish to see them."

"No. If you are satisfied, I am prepared to rely on your judgment, old fellow."

Patrick leaned back and laced his hands over his waistcoat. Closing his eyes, he listened as the solicitor carefully enumerated every rumor or tale to be had about Annie Adams and John Colley, none of which helped Rand. Apparently there had been little strife between the two, and poor Johnny had planned to marry his golden goose and take her out of the rookery as soon as she earned them a nest egg. Definitely the sort of thing to add weight to Peale's case against the old man. Poor Colley had had no reason to kill her.

"They have frequented the brothels and dens to some advantage, sir," Banks went on, "and there is some disturbing information, possibly fictitious, brought on by the scurrilous tone of the newspaper reports, but some of it warrants further investigation, I think." He paused. "Whether it is because the public wishes to believe Mr. Rand guilty and therefore needs to feed upon such things, I cannot yet say, but this man Weasel claims to have heard of Rand's involvement with a number of impures."

"A predilection some of the jury might share. Visiting harlots is reprehensible, not illegal," Patrick pointed out.

"Nonetheless if what is said is taken into account, it might prejudice your case, sir. Apparently, Mr. Rand is not above providing opium for certain acts."

"Opium." Patrick digested that, then shook his head. "Hearsay merely. Unless the individual females involved are called, I won't allow Peale to admit the testimony. Anything else?"

Banks turned a sheet of paper over and scanned the notations he'd made on it. "Only that a female called Cathead Mary said Mr. Rand regularly crawled the streets in St. Giles, and that the women who knew of him generally avoided him." He looked again at the paper, then flushed. "To quote the woman, she described him as 'a mean old bugger as was always hurtin' 'em—'e 'ad ter 'ave 'elp ter keep the wee thing up, if ye ken.' She further told Weasel that 'if 'is carrot don't pop off, 'e's a nasty man,' whatever that is."

"Nasty man?" Patrick sat up. "A nasty man, my dear Banks, is a member of a garroting gang—the one who does the strangling."

"Oh." For a moment the solicitor was taken aback, then he recalled his purpose. "Well, obviously she did not like him very much, in any event."

"If she even knows him." Favoring the solicitor with a lifted eyebrow, he added, "Cathead Mary, old chap?"

"I collect that means she is an ample female, doesn't it?"

"At least she has heavy breasts."

"I cannot imagine how you can understand the low cant," Banks said, "for I am sure I do not."

"You have no notion of what I have heard in the course of my practice. Before I could afford you, I had to do this myself."

"You? But you are the barrister!"

"I came to town with naught but empty pockets and

a paper that said I was a lawyer," Patrick admitted flatly. "For the first year at least I earned my bread by cadging cases where they happened. And whenever I saw the watch arrest rich young dandies on the riot, I was there to get the fools out." Seeing that Banks did not quite believe him, Patrick smiled wryly. "There was a time, old fellow, when I represented pickpockets who had to lift another purse to pay me."

"And you knew it?"

"I had a notion. But times have changed, and I have now prospered to the point where I am considered utterly respectable."

"I should say so, sir. When I sought a position, you were highly recommended to me. Why, even Justice Tate's clerk suggested this as a place for proper advancement."

"Did he now?" Abruptly Patrick's smile faded. "Is there anything else you have discovered? For if there is not, I've got to get on over to the Bailey."

"Perhaps I ought merely to give the rest of it to you to read, sir," Banks said, handing his report across the desk. "And while I certainly cannot credit all of it, I do think you ought to take a rather careful look at it, for there seems to be an alarming pattern where Mr. Rand's relationships with those women are concerned. Cathead Mary claims to know of one who showed her the marks on her neck and said it was Rand who'd done it."

"No doubt an equally charming female," Patrick murmured dryly. "But I don't entirely discount it—not at all. From the first, Rand has tried to hoax me about one thing or another."

"Well, I am sure you must have your reasons, but I must say I cannot think why you are defending him before elections, if you are considering standing. Of course he *is* very rich," Banks conceded.

"As you say, I have my reasons." Patrick shoved the report into his drawer, then looked up. "What else do you have there?"

"The usual sort of thing. Statements, precedents,

and speculations pertaining to the other two hearings."

"In case Peale attempts to put the double on me and distract me with Bat Rand, eh?"

"Precisely."

"Sometimes, my dear Banks, I cannot think what I should do without you." Patrick stood and stretched. "And someday I intend to get enough sleep," he added. "But before then, there are Russell and Peale to plague me." Walking to the peg hooks on the wall, he took down his robe and pulled it over his head. "Just leave those on my desk, and I'll take them with me." Fastening the front of the black gown with one hand, he reached for his wig with the other. "I am out of time at the moment."

"But you will read about Mr. Rand? If for naught else, the woman was rather graphic enough to provide enlightenment as to what he liked to purchase."

"First thing in the morning," Patrick promised. Smoothing back his hair, he pulled the wig on, then straightened it in front. "There ought to be a law against this damn thing," he muttered. "I despise it."

"Oh, I almost forgot—do I have your leave to advance Mr. Thompson and this Weasel fellow further expense money?"

"I thought you said you gave them twenty pounds apiece."

"Yes, but it was ten for the service, the rest for an assortment of females, nine pints of stout, three bottles of gin, five of rum, and four of hock. Rather a bargain, I should say."

"Are you quite certain they did not drink themselves through Covent Garden?" A faint smile played about Patrick's mouth. "I wonder that they are able to account for any of it."

"Mr. Thompson says it was necessary for them to drink and carouse with females to gain the information," Banks answered with a straight face.

"The poor, dedicated fellows," Patrick observed wryly.

As Banks left, John Byrnes nearly collided with him

in the doorway. Seeing that Patrick was already ready to leave for the Bailey, he murmured apologetically, "I thought perhaps you might wish to read this on your way today."

"What is it?"

"A note from Lord Dunster."

"I'll take it."

"If any comes, shall I say when you will be back?"

"Tomorrow, but there won't be any time for appointments as I am attempting to get everything in order before adjournment. As for today, I won't get out of Sessions much before four-thirty, then I intend to visit Rand again."

"You'd best request an escort around to the back then, for I am told there is an ugly crowd there again today. I had it of his clerk that Mr. Wilcox's carriage was very nearly overturned in the mistaken belief that 'twas he who defends Mr. Rand. Someone cried out, 'There he goes,' and 'twas a near thing—a very near thing."

"Thank you for the warning." Picking up his worn leather folder, he sighed. "There's not much I can do about a mob, John."

Patrick was nearly out the door before his clerk remembered something else. "Oh—may I be amongst the first to wish you happy?" Byrnes called out. "I saw the announcement in the *Gazette*."

"Thank you."

So the paper had already printed it. Well, by nightfall everyone of note ought to know of his good fortune, he reflected soberly.

As he climbed into the waiting hackney, Patrick had to remind himself that Jane was the means to an ultimately desirable end. But what he truly wanted was Elise Rand. He had but to close his eyes to see her, to feel the warmth of her skin, to smell again the lavender in her hair. Even as he thought of her, he felt an intense guilt for what he was doing to her. She deserved better of him, and yet he knew he didn't want to give her up for Jane.

* * *

The mood of the milling mob was ugly, so much so that Patrick had to borrow the keeper of the Sessions House galley's cloak for the walk to Newgate. As he skirted the crowd, he could hear someone at the front shout, "We don't need no 'earing to 'ave a 'anging! Kill the old puddin' poker ere 'e flashes 'is way out with 'is gold!"

The rest caught his spirit and chanted, "Kill 'im— kill 'im!" rhythmically. Then, as the prison doors were secured, the chant changed to "We want Rand! We want Rand!"

There was no way through the mob, and to risk identification might well mean being torn apart. Patrick crossed at the corner and was retreating toward the Bailey when a contingent of Horse Guards rode past him, sabers slashing, straightway into the crowd. The taunts and jeers turned into outraged howls, then to screams of terror. The mob broke and ran, fleeing pell-mell in every possible direction, taking refuge in doorways and crannies, as the horses trampled those who could not get out of the way. A soldier came close by Patrick and would have struck at him, but he threw off the cloak and called out, "Officer of the court! I am an officer of the court!"

Stopping, the horseman backed his mount to block Patrick from the surging, fleeing Londoners, while his fellow guards drove them through the streets. When the last appeared to have passed, he clicked his reins and moved away, leaving Patrick to survey the carnage. Several blood-spattered fellows appeared dazed as they were arrested, while two men lay ominously still. At the other end of Newgate Street, a few stared sullenly at soldiers who now formed a protective line around the prison.

An officer spied Patrick and rode up, demanding to know his business, then apologized when another recognized him. He called out for escort, and two soldiers dismounted to accompany Patrick to Debtor's Door. In the shadow of the scaffold, he stopped for a moment to take a deep breath of the air, then he went inside.

"Ain't nuthin' like a Lunnon mob, eh?" a prison guard said cheerfully. "It don't do no good ter move 'em, 'cause they just come back when the soljers is gone."

"Or else they go elsewhere."

"They'll be back—they want to see old Rand swing, eh?"

"I am come to see Mr. Rand."

"Oh—aye. Jem! He's here fer the old man! The one as is in the keeper's rooms!"

A slatternly woman roused from over a half-empty gin bottle, then grinned evilly. "Worms is going ter get 'im same as anybody else," she predicted. " 'Is money ain't saving 'im!" Her voice rose in a high-pitched laugh, then she lay down again to cradle her bottle.

Another female called out piteously to him. "Eight pounds, sir—eight pounds and I'm out—eight pounds, sir!" He glanced at her, seeing her swollen belly, wondering if she'd gotten that way since she'd been there. As he walked on, he could hear her still crying, "Only eight pounds, sir!"

A vacant-faced man sat with two half-naked little girls clinging to his legs, while a thin woman of indeterminate age lay curled in fetal position upon a pile of dirty straw, a direct violation of the rules banning wives and children from living with men in prison. But so many had no place to go, and guards were lax in enforcing the prohibition. As he passed them, Patrick wished he'd chosen another door. Fishing in his coat pocket, he drew out coins left from his hackney fare. He stopped to toss them inside. The two small girls scrambled on their knees to reach them, then grasped the shiny silver pieces in grubby hands.

"How much?" he heard himself say.

The man roused. "Thirty pounds as I couldn't pay." He slumped again.

Patrick turned to the guard. "Remind me when I leave, and I'll apply to the magistrate for him."

"And what's he ter do then wi'out nuthing, I ask ye?"

It was a reasonable question, one for which Patrick had no answer. Nonetheless, he reached for his purse and took out thirty pounds in clean, new banknotes, then passed them inside. Hesitating, he added another ten.

As he moved away, Jem told him, "He'll be in gin fer a month, that's all."

"It smells better at Tattersall's than here," Patrick muttered. "At least there they muck up after the horses."

"Ye get used ter it."

"Never."

He found Rand eating, the table before him spread with a three-course meal, while a servant stood nearby. The old man looked up, then with his mouth too full for speech, he gestured to a chair. Reaching for a cup of claret, he washed the food down noisily.

"About time you was coming," he said. "Thought you'd be here ere before now."

"I was in chambers with Justice Russell and the magistrate."

"And taking your time, you was," Rand observed irritably. "Well, don't stand there—sit down, sirrah. You got news—I can tell it." As he spoke, he got another cup and filled it. Pushing it toward Patrick, he said impatiently, "Go on—spill the budget."

Patrick sat down, then nodded. "All right. The short of it is that the evidence is sufficient to try you, but I expected that. I was given the choice of presenting arguments in a hearing or going ahead to trial."

"I ain't understanding the difference," Rand muttered. "Six of one, and half a dozen of the other, ain't it?"

"No. If I agree to waive the hearing, you will be tried before Christmas. Otherwise, there will be a formal hearing to determine whether you will be bound over, which will be merely for show, I assure you."

"When will that be?"

"Monday, if I make that choice."

Rand appeared to digest that with his meat. "And the trial—when would that be, then?"

"During the first session of the new year, if you have the hearing. Without it, I would expect to go to trial next month."

"What? No, sirrah, I won't have it! By God, I won't! You got to get me out of here before then! Go bail—I don't care what it costs, go bail!"

"Mr. Rand, neither Peale nor the magistrate would recommend it," Patrick replied flatly. "They believe a conviction is inevitable."

"Then bribe the demned justice! No, sir, Hamilton—I ain't spending Christmas here. I ain't spending Christmas without Em and Ellie—that's all there is to it!"

"Then you wish to go ahead with the trial?"

"Of course I don't! I ain't ready to swing yet, am I? That's why I got you, ain't it? You are going to keep me out of the noose!"

"Then you prefer to go with the hearing and delay the trial?" Patrick persisted.

"What do you think?" the old man sneered.

"I think I'd rather try it now."

"You got enough to get me off?"

"No, but if you will cooperate with my solicitor, Mr. Banks, when he conducts the interview with you, I shall be prepared either way," Patrick lied.

Rand eyed him shrewdly, then shook his head. "Pulling the wool over my eyes, ain't you? It ain't my neck as concerns you—'tis the demned elections. And saying you are prepared ain't quite the same as saying you are getting me off."

"If you are to have a chance either way, you will have to cooperate with Mr. Banks," Patrick said patiently.

"I told you all I got to say."

"We are already pursuing information in Covent Garden and St. Giles, and I expect to have statements in a matter of days. It is my intent to compare those against what you tell my solicitor, and hopefully we will discover a possible perjury in one of them—or at least something that will cast doubt on John Colley's veracity. Otherwise you are as sunk as an anchor."

"They ain't going to tell no fancy fellow nothing," Rand snorted.

"Mr. Thompson can scarce be called a fancy fellow, I assure you. It is my hope that someone will be loose-lipped enough to tell him either that Colley tended to roll Annie's customers—or that he at least had a violent temper."

"Bribe 'em to say it."

"No."

"Mighty hoity-toity for a lawyer cove, ain't you?" the old man observed nastily.

"You will answer every question Mr. Banks puts to you with candor," Patrick continued mildly, ignoring the barb.

"Didn't hire him—hired you," Rand muttered. "And you got to tell the justice I want out."

"One does not in general tell Russell anything. In fact, one maintains an utterly respectful mien before him—do you understand that?"

"No."

"All right. Then perhaps I ought to restate the matter more plainly. Justice Russell believes the answer to ending crime is to execute everyone accused of any infraction whatsoever. This year alone, he has sent two children to the gallows for the theft of a bucket of paint in one case, a goose in the other."

"Ain't a man alive as cannot be bribed with something, Hamilton." But the old man's manner had sobered considerably. "He's got to want something."

"I don't intend to make the offer."

"Even you—you got your price, ain't you?"

"Mr. Rand, this isn't a mill conducted with our fives. I am tired of sparring with you, of playing games where you believe you can bluster and intimidate." Patrick's eyes met Rand's and held. "I am not a five-quid lawyer, sir—I am the best barrister to be had in London. Do you understand that?"

"Aye, but—"

"But I will not go into court with half a deck when you are hiding the other half. This is a game of distinct rules dealing with evidence, precedence, and the presumption of innocence. I don't have to convince Peale or Russell you did not commit murder, sir. But I do have to cast enough doubt in the minds of your peers to make them waver, to question what the prosecutor tells them. To accomplish that, sir, you must arm me with the truth."

"I said I didn't do it, didn't I?"

"You do not listen well at all, I'm afraid. You think you are too clever by half, that by obfuscation you may muddle through, but it won't serve."

The old man exhaled fully. "All right. What was you wanting me to tell them?"

"You cannot tell them anything—you cannot even sit in the witness box. All that stands between you and the gallows is myself and the jury I present my case to. So if you have killed Annie Adams, Peg Parker, or Fanny Shawe, I want to know it. If I find you are leaving me out to be blindsided, I shall withdraw from your defense—do I make myself clear on that head?"

"I ain't going to break my gel's heart, Hamilton."

"If you are asking if I would tell Miss Rand, I will not. Anything you tell me is between us and no one else."

"All I was wanting was to go home."

"Then you are a fool," Patrick declared bluntly. "If you left here, you would not live to get to Marylebone. Surely you are not deaf, sir."

"Aye, I heard. But I can afford the Runners."

"It took the Horse Guards to get me inside."

Rand drank from his cup, then wiped his mouth on his sleeve. "You are a cold man, Hamilton," he said sourly. "Cold."

"I hope not." Patrick rose without touching his wine. "I'm afraid I cannot stay, but you may tell Banks tomorrow whether you want the hearing or not. And if I have not heard by two o'clock, I shall inform Mr. Peale we are ready for trial next month."

"You already got your mind made up, ain't you? You want to try it, and the devil take me—I can tell."

"It would be better for me to try it quickly."

"But not for me."

"Either way, I mean to do the best I can for you, sir."

The old man waited until Patrick called for the guard, then he murmured, "Ellie was here to see me today." When Patrick said nothing, he added, "She read the announcement in the *Gazette*. She said—" He paused for effect. "She said as she ain't expecting to hear from you again, I should wish you happy for her."

Patrick felt almost sick as his stomach knotted.

"She's got a kind heart. Said I was to tell you the little dog is fine also," the old man went on slyly. "You ain't to worry over 'em—not at all. Not that you would, eh?"

As he followed Jem out, Patrick wondered how he ever could have thought of Bartholomew Rand as affable. He walked back toward the Bailey, his mind on Elise, knowing there was no way he could say anything to her that would excuse him. He couldn't expect her to understand that he still wanted her, but he was marrying Jane.

She said as she ain't expecting to hear from you again . . . As his mind echoed the message her father gave him, he was certain she'd told him good-bye. And he was equally certain that Rand knew everything. In his own way, the old man had played the pimp using his own daughter.

Despite the fact that it was supposed to be a happy occasion, conversation at Dunster's dinner table was stiff and lagging, and for once Patrick was in no mood to make up for the lack. Beside him, Jane attempted to engage everyone with plans for the Brockhaven house and her wedding. And her wedding it was going to be, for she informed Patrick that she wished to be married from her father's estate before they took a wedding trip abroad to Italy "where the weather is warmer in early spring." Moreover, she intended to entertain with "an elegant reception upon our return, which must include members of parliament and officials of the government, of course."

"Have you shown Mr. Hamilton the house you have picked out?" her mother asked mildly.

"Not yet, Mama, for he could not go as planned."

"Perhaps tomorrow then. Indeed, but I should like to go with you, and I believe we ought to tend to the matter before we go home to Scotland."

"Tomorrow I am in court, I'm afraid," Patrick murmured.

There was another silence, broken once more by Jane. "I was thinking perhaps of early March—or late February even for the wedding date. What do you think, Patrick?"

"I think we will be in Italy during Lent."

"Oh, yes—you are quite right, of course. They are mostly Catholic, aren't they? Well, that will not serve, for I should miss a good English joint."

"What do you think, sir?" Lady Dunster asked Patrick.

"I think I should prefer summer."

"One could almost believe you did not wish to marry me," Jane complained.

"Nonsense," her mother said. "He is being sensible merely."

Throughout the meal, Dunster seemed unusually preoccupied, almost distant, entering into the conversation only when directly addressed. Upon an appeal from his daughter, he allowed that he should like the matter settled before the election "so that Hamilton may benefit from the connection."

Later, Jane remarked wistfully that she had wished for the engagement earlier, for she had wanted to "bedazzle everyone with my betrothal ring."

"You haven't considered that, have you?" her mother asked, turning to Patrick. "Indeed, but if you are in need of an opinion, I shall be most happy to accompany you to Rundell and Bridge, sir—providing we go before next Thursday. I have seen some lovely ruby rings there."

"But I had hoped for sapphires, Mama."

"Nonsense, my love. Rubies flatter your complexion."

Jane looked to Patrick. "What do you think? Should you buy me sapphires or rubies?"

Having done nothing in that quarter yet, he managed to smile. "Actually, I was thinking of giving you the ring over Christmas."

Her disappointment evident, she said archly, "But you have not answered me—which is it to be?"

"It is my intent to surprise you," he murmured.

"Well, a family heirloom would be quite acceptable," Lady Dunster allowed judiciously.

"I'm afraid what there was of my mother's jewelry went to my oldest brother."

"Yes, of course. Quite proper, really. Well, then it will have to be something from Rundell's, won't it?"

"Yes."

Jane turned to her father. "Did your man of affairs contact Lady Brockhaven?"

"Yes." Dunster stopped eating for a moment to fix his eyes on his daughter's. "She wants thirty-five thousand for it."

"That sounds like rather a lot," Patrick observed.

"Oh, but it isn't!" Jane insisted. "You cannot have seen it! The rooms are commodious and perfectly situated for entertaining, Patrick. And we shall only have to redo the reception rooms. Besides," she added smugly, "Papa means to buy it for us."

"If Hamilton does not want it," her father ventured, "I am sure between you, you can settle upon something else."

"But I want it, Papa."

"Yes, well—" The earl coughed to clear his throat. "We shall discuss it."

"But there is nothing to discuss!" She appealed to Patrick. "You must tell him you want it."

"I have not yet seen the house," he murmured.

"But I have told you of it," she said, her voice coaxing. "I know you should like it."

"Jane, I am sure Mr. Hamilton does not wish to be badgered over his dinner." Lady Dunster gestured to a hovering footman. "I daresay Mr. Hamilton could wish for more sherry."

What he devoutly wished was to be elsewhere. But he reminded himself that Lady Jane Barclay was his entree onto the political stage, and therefore she deserved better of him. Sipping of the sherry, he schooled himself to pleasantness.

"Tell me, Mr. Hamilton," Lady Dunster asked, "how is it that you have chosen to practice your profession alone?"

"I am not precisely alone, my lady," he responded politely. "I am associated with a solicitor and we employ a clerk."

"But you have not joined a firm. One should think that with your outstanding reputation, you would perhaps have gone in with Parker and Jeffries, for I am certain they would have welcomed you."

"When I arrived in London, I applied to them and was roundly turned down," he admitted.

"Turned down? How so?" she wanted to know.

"I had no money—and no reputation as yet."

"Oh. Yes, I suppose that must signify, mustn't it?" Recovering, she smiled faintly. "But you seem to have rectified the problem, haven't you?"

Before he could answer, the earl intervened. "Of course he has, Bella. You are talking a great deal of nonsense, my dear, for Hamilton means to quit the practice of law in favor of the enactment of it."

"Well, I have not entirely made up my mind to leave all of it," Patrick demurred.

"Nonsense," Dunster declared flatly. "You have a brilliant career ahead of you, if you will but let me manage it. Follow me, and one day you shall have your own portfolio."

After years of wanting exactly that, it ought to have lifted his spirits to hear it, but Patrick felt strangely empty of emotion. He looked at Jane's fine, determined profile, wondering how he could have ever thought there would be no price to pay for what he wanted.

It was that he lacked sleep, that he was too tired to feel, he told himself. And it was Bartholomew Rand. Even as he thought of the old man, he felt an intense resentment. He disliked the notion that he'd been shamefully manipulated by an uneducated Cit, but there was no help for that either. He could not break his bargain with Elise and have a shred of conscience.

"When we are done, shall we play at whist for a while?" Jane asked him, breaking into his thoughts.

"You have already heard him say he has court tomorrow, my dear," Dunster reminded her. "And truth to tell, the fellow is utterly exhausted." He looked to Patrick. "What say you, sir? A brandy together, and then I shall send you home in my carriage."

"I should like that. And you are quite right, my lord—I've scarce slept this week."

"Of course you haven't," the earl murmured soothingly. "A gentleman was not made to work as you do."

"But you will go with me to look at the house?" Jane persisted. "If you delay too long, I shall be gone from town—or worse, she may sell it elsewhere."

"At thirty-five thousand?" her father asked dryly. "I very much doubt that."

"If it looks as though I shall be out before three, I'll send a note 'round," Patrick promised. "Perhaps Lady Brockhaven will not mind it if we come late."

"Tomorrow afternoon, I am to be fitted for a new riding habit."

"The next day, then."

"Very well, but beyond that, I shall be leaving London."

"Yes—well, now that the momentous things are settled, I should like to cose a bit with Hamilton in my study." As he looked at his daughter, Dunster's expression softened. "It will not be for long, my dear, and then he may take his leave of you."

"Well, I think you are appropriating him shamelessly, Papa, but I daresay it must be important."

"It is." The earl folded his napkin carefully and laid it across his dessert plate before rising. "Your pardon, my love," he said to his wife. "After you, sir," he said to Patrick.

"Well, dearest," Lady Dunster murmured to Jane, " 'twould seem we are *de trop* for the moment. Shall we withdraw to the blue saloon?"

The older man led the way to the dark-paneled room where a new fire had been laid in the grate. Walking to a massive desk, he picked up a box and flicked it open.

"I'd offer you snuff, but I abhor it," he admitted, smiling faintly. "But if you would care to smoke, I have had these from the Indies."

"Thank you, no. I cannot say I have either habit."

The earl moved to a sideboard. "Brandy? Or would you prefer a glass of Madeira?"

"Whichever you are having," Patrick said politely.

"Then brandy it is." Unstoppering the decanter, the earl poured two glasses before turning around. He held out one. "Yours, sir." As Patrick took it, Dunster lifted his in a toast. "To a future prime minister," he murmured softly.

"I would doubt that, my lord."

"Not at all." Taking a sip, the older man studied the younger one over the rim of his glass. "I can see it—I can see it. You have what I never had, sir—you have passion."

He'd used the same word Rand had used when he'd first come to the law office. Patrick managed to smile before he took a swallow.

"You are filled with fire and zeal, Hamilton—and when you speak, it is a wonder to hear you. No, no—no need to protest it, for we both know it is the truth." Dunster drank again. "Liverpool is on his last legs, and we Tories are fighting and blaming amongst ourselves. Oh, we shall win the next elections, but without new blood, the public is tired of us."

"It was the war."

"It was mistakes, sir—mistakes! And you are the new blood, Hamilton. You can be to us what Fox was to the Whigs, I tell you. Aye, you can."

"I hope so, sir."

"You *can*." The earl set down his glass, and his manner changed abruptly. "I encountered Mr. Peale at Crockford's this afternoon," he said casually. "He was with Lord Russell after court was adjourned for the day."

"Oh?"

"We spoke at length of you. Both of them hold you in highest regard, you know. They were falling over each other to be the first to felicitate me for my daughter's good fortune."

"Coming it too strong, my lord."

"No, no—I assure you they were. But while Mr. Peale was engaged in conversation with Lord Hurley, Russell was confiding in me that he believes you are making a serious mistake, Hamilton."

"He told you about Rand."

"Yes."

"I see."

"You cannot defend him. I'm afraid you will have

to withdraw—and the sooner the better. I expect you will do it tomorrow.''

Patrick did not like Dunster's tone or manner. "No," he said flatly. "I cannot."

Taken somewhat aback, the earl stared hard at him, then said evenly, "You cannot defend a man half of London wishes to see hanged, Patrick. If you do, you will not be elected to a seat in Commons." He paused, looking away. "I wish I could wrap it up in clean linen for you, but there it is. You may tell Mr. Rand you are giving up your practice of law for a career in government.''

"A man facing the hangman's noose is not likely to accept that," Patrick countered. "And particularly not since I have taken his money.''

"How much is he paying you? And do not invoke privilege with me, sir, for I will not brook it.''

"Enough."

"Whatever it is, I am prepared to match it," Dunster snapped.

"Even if it is half of all he owns?''

"Russell says he is guilty—that there can be no question of it," the earl responded, ignoring Patrick's answer.

"Then Russell ought to withdraw from hearing the case.''

"Damn it! Can you not listen? I don't mean to fence words with you, Hamilton! You cannot defend a man who has murdered God knows how many females, I'm telling you! Not if you wish to be elected! Have you not heard?—there are mobs ready to riot if he does not go to trial today, and even more if he does not hang! And with the current unrest, all that stands between thousands of rioters and utter anarchy is the Horse Guards, sir! If you do not distance yourself, I cannot aid you!''

Although he himself had been thinkking much the same thing, Patrick considered Elise. "I might well win it," he said finally.

"To what end? So that they will want your blood also?''

Patrick took a swallow of his brandy, then walked to stand over the fire. Staring into the licking flames, he said slowly, "If I can get the trial scheduled with the Recorder for next month, they will forget before I have to stand. You said you did not anticipate elections until spring."

"And if he is bound over until a later session?"

"As much as I dislike the notion, I will still have to defend him. I have given my word."

"The man is a murderer of the foulest sort!"

"If I win an acquittal, it will enhance my reputation rather than destroy it."

"May the Almighty save us! Even if I concede it will make you a sought-after barrister, I am telling you it will ruin your chances of standing for Commons!"

"And I am telling you that if the trial is over, the mob will have found some other cause by then—there is no memory in mass hysteria—it is of the moment, my lord, nothing more."

Dunster drew in a deep breath, then let it out slowly. "Then perhaps I have not made my concerns quite clear, Patrick. If you defend Bat Rand and lose, your rep loses also. If, on the other hand, by some miracle you should win, you will enrage rather than appease the populace. There is no way to win at this, sir—no way at all."

"I think you are wrong."

"Do you now?" the earl said with deceptive softness. "Well, let me remind you that I have nigh to thirty years of service to my party and to this nation, while you have but ten in the practice of law. If you were a betting man, Hamilton, which one of us would you put money on?"

"If I were a betting man? You, sir. But I am not a gamester."

"I would that you thought on it. If you persist, I cannot guarantee you a district to stand from."

"Are you telling me you intend to abandon me?"

"No, but I am telling you you may be standing from some village in Cumbria, and even then I cannot promise you will win it. You certainly will not be elected out of London." Once again, Dunster's manner changed. Walking over to Patrick, he dropped an arm familiarly about the younger man's shoulders. "Think on it—'tis all I ask. Now, enough's been said, I think, and no doubt Jane would like to bid you good night ere you go."

Knowing that Elise had read the announcement of his betrothal, Patrick was torn between trying to explain and merely brazening it out. In the end, while visiting a jeweler in Clarges Street, he chose not only a ruby and diamond ring for Jane, but also an exquisite sapphire bracelet for Ellie. The first he presented to his departing fiancée, the latter he dispatched to Marylebone.

After waiting for two days, he could stand it no longer. Using the news that Rand's hearing had been set for the next week and the trial itself for January as an excuse, he went to see Elise. And even knowing she must be feeling either hurt or angry, he could not help the exhilaration he felt at the thought of seeing her. He fairly bounded up the steps to pound the knocker.

The sober butler stood in the doorway to tell him "Miss Rand is not receiving today."

"Tell her it is of the utmost import," Patrick insisted.

"I'm sorry," Graves said stiffly, "but she is not at home to anyone, I'm afraid. However, if you would wish to leave a note, I am sure I can get you something to write with."

At that moment, a small ball of brown fur ran past Patrick's legs, its floppy ears flying as it bounded outside to jump and yip at his horses. Behind it, a young girl followed calling out, "Come back here, ye miserable creature! Ye'll be trampled!" But as she caught it, her actions gave the lie to her words, for she held it close, nuzzling the small face. "Button, ye'll be the death of me," she told it severely. Passing Patrick, she dropped a quick, bobbing curtsy. "Yer pardon, sir, but I was afeard she was going ter be gone afore I could catch 'er."

"What is it, Lizzie?" Elise came to the banister above them, then stopped abruptly when she saw him. As the color drained from her face, she said, "Oh, 'tis you."

He took off his hat. "Hello, Ellie."

Telling herself that she was not going to let his unexpected appearance overset her, she remained upstairs where he could not touch her. Crossing her arms across her breast, she regarded him steadily.

"Aren't you going to come down to hear what I have to say?" he asked quietly.

"No."

"I thought perhaps you would wish to know that the hearing has been set, and I wanted to assure you it is but a formality. I do, however, expect Rand will be bound over for trial, either before Christmas or after."

"Yes. Papa told me."

She was making it awkward for him, and he knew he deserved it. Nonetheless, he didn't want to speak with her in front of her servants. He moved closer to the stairs.

"Ellie—"

"You have told me, haven't you?"

"Not all of it."

"What else is there?"

He could threaten her with his withdrawal from Rand's defense, but he wanted her to come to him of her own free will, not because she had to. His hand caught the newel post as he took the first step.

"I have brought my tilbury and pair. I thought perhaps you might want to partake of fresh air."

"No."

"The leaves in the parks are quite lovely this time of year."

Despite the fact that she had no claim to him, she still felt a certain bitterness. "No," she repeated coldly. "I don't wish to go anywhere." Seeing that he had taken another step up, she fought the urge to run to her chamber and slam the door before he could reach her. "I would very much rather that you left."

"And I'd very much like to talk to you."

"About what?"

Seeing that both Graves and the girl were regarding him curiously, he dared not say what he wanted. "I'd hoped to discuss Rand with you."

"I'd suggest you go to the horse's mouth, sir, and discuss whatever it is you want with him."

"If you do not come down, I shall come up, Ellie."

"No."

"I need your help—I need to know the precise dates when Rand was robbed and the watch brought him home."

"Ask him."

"I have, and he says he cannot remember. He is not the most forthcoming client I have had," he added wryly.

"No, I suppose not. He does not think he should be tried at all."

He took four steps up. "Five minutes, Ellie—'tis all I ask."

She had the choice of calling Joseph or one of the other footmen and throwing him out or of being backed into her own room. And she knew she had no right to be angry, not when she had initiated the bargain between them, and yet she did not want him to ask her to play the harlot again. Not when he had already promised himself to Lady Jane. And yet when she looked down on his face, she could not help remembering how it felt to be held by him. And she knew she was just as afraid of herself as she was of him.

"Five minutes, and you will go?" she heard herself say.

"Word of a Hamilton. Now—do you want to come down—or shall I come up?"

"I'd rather come down," she decided.

She moved slowly, gracefully, as though she were a

queen. He backed down and waited. As she cleared the last step, she squared her shoulders.

"Is Papa's bookroom all right—or would you prefer the front saloon?"

"Whatever is suitable to you."

"The bookroom, then." Turning to the butler, she told him, "As Mr. Hamilton does not stay, there is no need for refreshment, and therefore you are not to disturb us." To the tweeny, she added, "Put Button back upstairs, if you please."

"She is a taking little thing—the dog, I mean," Patrick murmured, holding the door for her.

"She has the house at sixes and sevens, if you want the truth of it." She regarded him severely for a moment. "We all quite despair that she will ever be civilized, but wretch that you are, I daresay you knew that when you brought her here."

"But you like her."

"Yes. There are times when everyone goes on as always, and then I think I should go mad without her," she admitted. "Sometimes her madcap manners are all that keep me from thinking about what is happening to Papa. Or from dwelling on the fact that Mama has left both of us to go it without her."

"Poor Ellie," he said softly. "You have a lot on your shoulders, don't you? I would that I could help you, you know."

She moved to the fireplace and crossed her arms again, rubbing them as though she were cold. He was too near, too alive. She forced herself to think of the announcement in the paper.

"Did you get my gift?" he asked finally.

"Yes."

He came up behind her. "Ellie—"

"I pray you will not touch me."

"For what it is worth, I do not love her."

"But you are committed to marrying her. What would she feel if she knew you were here with me? At least one of us ought to be able to hold a head up, don't you think?"

He reached out, touching her shining red-gold hair

with the back of his hand. "It isn't a love match, I swear it. She doesn't even want to sleep with me, Ellie. Jane is but the political price I have to pay for Dunster's support."

She ducked away and spun around. "And you think I am your whore? Well, I am not!" she cried. "I don't want to be that anymore, Hamilton. I am the rich Miss Rand, not some back alley trollop as can be laid at will."

" 'Twas your bargain, Ellie," he reminded her. " 'Twas you who began—"

"And 'tis I who am ending it."

"Ellie—Ellie—it doesn't have to be. We can go on, and—"

"No." Swallowing hard, she walked to the window to put distance between them. "It isn't your fault for taking what I offered," she said, her voice low. "I thought I could do it—I made myself believe that since Ben was dead, it wouldn't matter—that my soul and my body were two very different things, and that you could touch one without hurting the other—that Papa's life was worth selling my person for."

"I don't think of you that way at all."

She clenched her hands at her side so tightly that her nails dug into her palms. "Hear me out, will you? I am trying to tell you that I don't want anything more between us."

"Because of Jane? I told you—"

"Because of me!" She bit her lip hard to still its trembling, then she forced herself to face him again. "It's wrong, Patrick—terribly wrong. I cannot look myself in the mirror without seeing what I am, and I cannot bear the shame. The cause was good, but—"

"I still want you—you are like some sort of malady that I don't want to cure."

"I'm afraid you will have to cure it with Jane. I'm asking you to defend my father, and I am asking you to do it for money rather than for me." When she looked up, the expression in his eyes nearly unnerved her. "Will you still defend him, Patrick?"

He knew he had it in his power to compel her, to

tell her he was walking out the door unless she kept her part of the bargain. But he also knew she would probably hate him for it.

"Yes," he said finally.

"Then 'tis settled, isn't it?" she managed. Exhaling, she told herself it was over, that she had survived. "Now—I am not precisely certain as to when Papa was robbed, but the last time was but a day or two before he brought you home to dine."

"Did he ever speak to you about opium?" he asked suddenly.

"Opium?" she repeated blankly. "Only that he abhorred it. Why?"

"There have been rumors that he might have used it—and that he might have lured prostitutes with it."

"Like everything else that is said, it is a lie. Why would he need to do such a thing, I ask you? He didn't need to use opium like that—he could buy whatever he wished with money."

"Fanny Shawe died the day before I came to dine," he said quietly.

She stared incredulously, then found her voice. "Whose side are you on?" she demanded furiously. "Surely you must know my father did not do such a thing!"

"I am merely saying what the prosecutor will say."

"Well, I would that you did not say it to me," she snapped. But as she realized he was utterly serious, her anger faded to fear. "You don't think he will be convicted, surely?"

"I don't know. I need help, Ellie—I need for him to give me answers rather than bluster."

"But if he did not do it, he cannot know any answers."

"I don't have a wand to wave over him, no matter how much he wishes to believe it. In his mistaken belief in my powers, he is fashioning his own noose."

"Can you not tear this Colley apart with words?"

He appeared to consider for a moment, then admitted, "As much as you have no wish to hear it, I'm going to tell you that I don't know about that either."

"But you are Patrick Hamilton! You are the best to be had—you told me that yourself!"

"Oh, I can make Colley look like a fool, but when everything is considered, will a jury believe he killed the woman who earned his bread? What was his reason? Jealousy? Greed? Rage? For everything, Ellie, there has to be a reason."

"Then what was Papa's supposed to be?" she countered angrily. "If she gave him what he paid for, why would he kill her either? Or why would he have murdered Fanny Shawe? Or Peg Parker?"

"Or Betty Wilkes. Or Kate Tilley. Or Bess Miller."

"Who are they?"

"Three other women taken from the river in the past year."

"Surely—*surely* they are not accusing him of those also? They cannot think he has murdered every dead female in London, can they?"

"Peale expects to charge him for those I mentioned tomorrow. And while perhaps each can be defended, the sum of all of them may well be overwhelming."

"But why? What has he done to deserve this? Is it jealousy that a laborer's son should get rich in bricks? Why is it that the streets before the prison are filled with those who would hate before one shred of evidence is presented?"

"When bellies are empty of bread, there is a tendency to seek diversion, I suppose. A London mob needs no excuse to pillage and burn, Ellie."

"What they want is a sadistic exhibition—with my father as the attraction," she said with asperity. "Indeed, but it surprises me that they have not been here today to shout insults and throw garbage at his house."

"Did the Runners come?"

She went to the window and lifted a hanging. "They are out there—across the street. If anything is to happen, they are to run for the authorities. There is not much they can do alone, after all, and I would not expect them to stand before rioters bent on committing mayhem."

"I would that you left here," he said soberly. "There is no accounting for the whim of a mob. And once the hearing is held, if he is bound over for a later trial, it could become uglier still."

"And where would I go? Papa never wished to leave the city for the country, saying he'd been born and bred here. No, I shall stay, I think. I do not mean to let street ruffians drive me from the house I was born in."

"You could remove to the Pulteney Hotel and be safer."

"And have every nob in the place look down his nose at me—or whisper behind my back? I think not." Aware that he was standing too close for her comfort again, she moved away. "But we are afield, aren't we? I wish I could be of more help, but I cannot. I do not know precisely when the watch has brought him home—it was not an entirely uncommon occurrence, you see."

"Oh?"

"Yes. Sometimes he was merely too drunk to stand, and twice at least it was because he'd been robbed and beaten. There is nothing else to tell, perhaps because I was too wrapped up in myself to note it."

"Can you tell him that if he is not prepared to assist in his defense, he is asking me to go into court with my hands tied at my back? Otherwise, I cannot help him."

"Yes. I can do that at least."

"There is not a great deal of time before the first hearing. And if he is bound over for the next few weeks, I can almost promise that a verdict will go against him."

"I shall go again this afternoon," she promised, sighing. As he looked like he might take another step toward her, she settled her shoulders. "Yes, well—it has been more than five minutes, hasn't it?"

"Yes, I suppose it has." Picking up his hat from the table where he'd laid it, he set it on his head. He started for the door, then turned back.

"I have hopes you will wear the bracelet."

She shook her head. "I have already sent it back to Mr. Byrnes in your office this morning. I hope you will disregard the note attached to it, for it is not terribly civil."

"It was the announcement in the *Gazette*, wasn't it? I should have told you of it, but I didn't want to. I'm sorry—truly sorry, Ellie."

"No, it was not the papers." She tried to force a smile, but it twisted. "It was Ezekiel."

For a moment he was nonplussed. "Ezekiel?"

"Yes. Chapter 16, verses 35 and 39."

"Oh—that Ezekiel," he murmured. "I shall have to read it."

"And if you are possessed of a Bible, you ought to try closing your eyes, then opening it up at random. You might be rather surprised at what it tells you also. What was it that Thomas Gray said?—that 'God works in mysterious ways, his wonders to behold'—or something very like that, in any event."

"Sometime I might try that, but just now I think I shall look up a fellow called Weasel somewhere in St. Giles Rookery and see what I am getting for my money," he decided. "Good day, my dear."

As the front door closed behind him, she sank into her father's high-backed chair, telling herself she had done what she had to do. But as her gaze swept the empty room, she felt so completely alone that she did not think she could stand it.

And outside, as Patrick climbed into the two-seater, he leaned his head back and closed his eyes, unable to deny the depth of his disappointment. For a moment he cursed himself for not compelling her to lie with him, then he admitted he wanted more than that. With the vanity he shared with every man, he'd wanted her to want him without regard for the right of it. He'd wanted her to want him as much as he wanted her.

It was the night before Rand's hearing. Patrick sat alone over his notes long after the house was quiet and all the servants had long since taken to their beds. Pushing back a lock of hair that strayed over his forehead, he reached again for his bottle of port, and drank directly from it. Leaning back, he loosened the neck of his shirt and stared for a time at the ceiling.

Nothing Thompson or Weasel had uncovered offered any hope—if anything, the gossip they'd gleaned accused Rand of all sorts of evil, but the most damning of it all were the interviews he himself had conducted in the doorways and alleyways of St. Giles, while Weasel had hovered nearby for dubious protection.

Between all of it, they'd discovered an alarming pattern of sadistic behavior, for Rand apparently made a habit of degrading and abusing the prostitutes he'd bought, seeking perverse pleasure in their pain until sufficiently aroused to complete the acts he paid for. But the ones they'd interviewed had lived to tell tales, Patrick reminded himself, and probably at least some of what they'd said had been colored by what they'd heard about the old brick maker.

He'd gone also to the Red Dragon to question the proprietor about Maddie Coates, and that had nearly proven a dead end. The man insisted he'd seen nothing out of the ordinary, nothing at all, the night that Maddie and Thomas Truckle had died. As far as Maddie's mysterious companion, he'd scarce seen him and could offer no description beyond saying it was a fellow in a hooded cloak. Which could have meant Rand or a thousand other possible men. And it wasn't Patrick's duty to prove the old man had killed anyone, he reminded himself. It was to cast enough doubt to make a jury believe he hadn't. But regardless of Rand, Patrick still wished to know how she'd come to die.

No, his concern for a connection between Maddie and Rand was irrelevant just now. Maddie was already dead, and unless Patrick chanced upon some miracle, Rand was going to join her.

His eyes burned and his shoulders ached, and yet he knew if he went to bed, he would not sleep. Straightening his body, he took another pull of the port, then returned his attention to the papers before him, sifting through them yet again, scanning them for something he could have missed.

The trouble, he supposed, could well be that he did not like Bat Rand enough to see what he wanted. Combing his hair back again with his hand, he reexamined John Colley's sworn statement, looking for some discrepancy to twist to his advantage, seeing nothing.

Both Rand and Elise were determined to believe he could make up something out of whole cloth, but this time he wasn't having much luck at it. Unless—he stopped to make a marginal note to have Weasel search for any other females Colley might have pimped for. As weak as it was, he still saw in Annie's Johnny the best possible key. If Patrick could rattle him into making some possibly damning admission— and if he could play upon the jury's probable dislike of the watch—he might yet be able to shake Peale's case, for how many people aside from a mob desirous of a good hanging could believe the wealthy brick maker would need to visit prostitutes? With his money, he could afford Harriette Wilson herself.

As Patrick saw it, the sheer number of charges might work to his advantage, for if he could cast doubt on any one of them, he might gain enough sympathy for Rand to get a dismissal. The trouble with that was that the old man wasn't the sort of fellow to elicit much sympathy. And if he went into the Sessions House with

the belligerence and arrogance he'd been showing
Patrick, he was going to slip the noose on himself.

"I should have thought you abed ere now," Hayes
said from the doorway.

Patrick looked up, seeing the man's nightgown and
cap above the candle he carried. "I could say the same
of you."

"The pickled tongue I had for supper has come
back on me," Hayes explained. "I came down for
some digestive biscuits, but they were not in the
pantry."

"I'm afraid I've got them." Pushing the tin across
the cluttered desk, Patrick murmured, "It did not set
well with me either." Picking the wine bottle up again,
he squinted at it and saw it was empty. Disgusted, he
dropped it onto the floor with the others. "Before
you go back up, I would that you got me another."

"Port and digestive biscuits, sir? I should think one
would negate the other."

"They probably do."

His butler glanced at the mantel clock, then shook
his head. " 'Tis nigh to three o'clock."

"And I have to be in court by ten."

"Yes, I have been reading about the Rand thing in
the papers. And a bad business that is, isn't it?"

Patrick squeezed his eyes shut, then opened them,
hoping to ease the soreness that came from too much
reading in too little light. "It may well be the first
murder case I have lost in five years," he admitted
tiredly.

"Do you think he did all those terrible things?"

"What I think, Hayes, is immaterial—the question
is not whether or not he is guilty, but rather whether
I can get a dismissal now or an acquittal later." He
sat back and linked his hands behind his head. "If
you were a juror, having read everything that has been
said, what would you think?"

"Well, I should attempt an open mind, of course."

"But you would believe him guilty, wouldn't you?"

"Yes."

"So you have a fair notion of where I am starting."

"I think so, sir."

"Not a very auspicous place, is it?"

"No, but you have found the means to win more often than most, haven't you?" Hayes said quietly. "With your wit and eloquence, I do not doubt your ability to succeed in this also."

"But you've never seen me in court."

"I have lived here and in your lodgings over the grocer's shop since you first came to town ten years ago, sir. If it can be done, you will do it."

"Thank you."

Hayes picked up the tin of biscuits. "Should I leave some for you also?"

"No. I'll just take another bottle of wine." But even as he said it, Patrick knew he did not need it, not if he were to be alert enough to cross swords with Peale. "Never mind the wine," he said, sighing. "I guess I ought not to go in weasel-bit, eh?"

"No. You ought to go to bed," Hayes said bluntly. "Good night, sir."

Too weary to think anymore, Patrick stood up and stretched, then walked around the room to clear his head. Stopping, he looked into the waning fire for a time, his mind not on Rand, but rather on his daughter, and the ache he felt nearly overwhelmed him.

Just now, he wished he were with her, not so much for passion, but for solace. Just to lie beside her, to feel her head upon his shoulder, her body within his arms. No, it did no good to think such things, he decided regretfully. He might as well get used to the notion of Jane.

Jane was more like him, selfish and cynical, more suited to playing the role he needed. In Lady Brockhaven's grand house, she would grace his table and preside over brilliant parties, being for all outward purposes the perfect Tory hostess. With her at his side and Dunster at his back, there was no limit to how far he could climb.

Elise, on the other hand, was still possessed of ideals, of the notion that one could do something worthwhile in this world. She believed and she spoke passionately, espousing causes when she did not have to, when she could be instead the rich Miss Rand. While he had moved about in the glittering, vacuous circles of the *haut ton,* attempting to climb upward, she had not only survived a broken heart, but she had also managed to turn her grief into something she believed useful.

And she had the audacity to think herself a sinner, while those who considered themselves her betters amused themselves with numerous lovers, never bothering to consider anything beyond their own pleasures. Even those few virtuous wives who counted themselves above such scandals were more than happy to turn blind eyes on their straying husbands as long as there was money to spend. At least that was the way Jane saw it. She probably would not intend to take a lover herself, lest her slender waist expand to stoutness.

The bracelet had been a mistake. He knew that now. It had been perceived as a token of payment for what Elise had given him, whether she would admit it or not. In her mind, it had validated that she was no more than any other fashionable impure, which was ludicrous. Cit-born or not, she was heiress to more money than any miss on the Marriage Mart.

But he needed and wanted more than money or even more than Ellie. With the intensity of an opium addict, he craved power, and not the sort that came with a portfolio of investments in the Stock Exchange, but rather from the portfolio of a minister. Well, he'd made his own bargain for that, and now he would have to live with it. It was, he knew, the price he had to pay for what he wanted.

He looked around the bookroom, seeing not just books, but the wealth that allowed him to have them. He'd come a long way from the day he'd stood, a boy in mended pants before a father too prideful to allow even a poor Hamilton to go on the stage.

His gaze stopped on a book of Gray's poetry. Odd that she should have mentioned Gray, for whenever he thought of the poet the verse that came to mind

ran something like—he tried to remember it without
opening the book—something like "The wealth of na-
tions, the pomp of power, await alike the inevitable
hour—the paths of glory lead but to the grave." Not
a very comforting thought at all.

Turning back to his littered desk, he stopped and
looked at the shelf. There amongst Pope and Dryden,
Boswell and Sam Johnson, Milton, Shakespeare, Mar-
lowe, and Ben Jonson was a large, gold-stamped, leather-
bound King James Bible. Curious, he picked it up,
wondering what on earth she could have read in Ezekiel. He didn't even remember that particular book.
Opening it, he tried to remember what she'd said.
Chapter 17, verses thirty-something. Finding that, he
scanned it and groaned.

He was about to put it back onto the shelf when he
recalled how she'd come to discover the damning
verses. It was a hoax of the worst sort, perpetrated no
doubt by one of those fanatics she admired. Nonetheless, he closed his eyes, reopened his Bible, then
looked down. It was Proverbs. He lifted his finger
and read:

"Pride goeth before destruction, and a haughty
spirit before a fall."

Not a very comforting thought at all. He shut it
again and returned it to the shelf, too tired to ponder
whether it had any meaning for him. Changing his
mind about working further, he blew out the brace of
candles that illuminated his desk, then he went back
to shovel ashes over the fire, suffocating it. Picking up
the last lit candle, he went up to bed. As he climbed
the stairs, he struggled with himself, knowing that his
own oath taken before the bar mocked him. Regardless of whatever reason, whether he liked the old man
or not, when he'd taken Bartholomew Rand's case, he
was constrained to provide the best defense possible.

And as the striking clarity of his obligation came
home to him, he knew he had to live up to it. Dunster,
Elise, Jane—none of them could affect what he had
to do. No, if it looked as though Peale was better
prepared than he was, then he'd have to ask to delay

the trial. Who knew? Given the uncertainties of life in the rookeries, maybe John Colley would die before he could testify.

Once in his chamber, he undressed, then crawled between crisp, clean sheets, where he lay in the darkness, staring into oblivion, trying not to think of Bat Rand or Dunster or Jane, allowing himself the luxury of remembering the scent of lavender in red-gold hair, the feel of warm, soft lips parting beneath his.

The gallery was packed, and outside the crowd surged and shouted, nearly drowning out the usually rote proceedings. While Prosecutor Peale presented his information, Patrick scanned the seats, looking for Elise Rand. Then he saw her.

She was clad simply in a dress and pelisse of Clarence blue trimmed with black braid. Her bright hair peeped demurely from beneath the upturned brim of a close-fitting bonnet trimmed rather plainly with black-dyed feathers and black ribbons tied beneath her chin. In her lap, her black-gloved hands clasped a black-covered book he suspected was her Bible. She looked as if she were going to church rather than to watch her father being set for trial.

Her eyes met his in recognition, and her lips moved as though she said something to him. He looked down at the sheaf of papers he'd brought with him, knowing that no matter what he did, he was going to ultimately disappoint her. Beside him, Rand sat staring first at Prosecutor Peale, then at Justice Russell, his face scowling, as though he thought he could intimidate them.

One by one, Peale's witnesses were presented, and each time Patrick did not bother to challenge them. Each answered Peale's clipped, precise questions, then Russell turned to Patrick asking, "Do you examine them, Mr. Hamilton?" And each time, Patrick rose, saying, "At this time, I have no questions, my lord."

A low murmur of disappointment rippled through the gallery, then was stilled when the keeper raised his hand. When Patrick looked up, Elise was on the edge of her seat, leaning forward anxiously. He knew she wanted him to say something, to tear John Colley or the uneasy watchman or the others apart with words, but he knew it wasn't going to matter. Not yet.

As the last witness to probable cause was excused, Peale stood to give his argument for a speedy trial, asking that it be set before the current session ended for the holidays. And then it was Patrick's turn to speak.

His heart pounding nearly as much as it had the first time he'd tried a case in the Bailey, Patrick rose, turned his notes facedown, and looked slowly around the gallery, then to Justice Russell.

"My lord," he said clearly, "this proceeding is not so much about justice for Annie Adams, or Peg Parker, or any of the other unfortunate victims of murder, but rather to provide a vehicle for the state to rush Mr. Rand willy-nilly to judgment. In the name of punishing one crime, it is not the right of any state to use its power in the commission of another, equally heinous act—that of taking the life of one of its citizens without providing both for the right to a carefully conducted trial"—he paused, then his voice rose again—"and to an unprejudiced defense of that right. To the lord justice, I must submit that given the addition of charges against my client, some of which were merely entered yesterday, it is not in the interest of justice to proceed further until I have had sufficient time to examine each and every accusation. I therefore must respectfully beg of this court that if a decision to bind Mr. Rand over is made, I should be given at the very least until the end of January to prepare a more than merely adequate defense."

Russell frowned, then looked to Peale. "And you, sir—have you no objection?"

"My lord, I see no need to delay beyond November," the prosecutor responded.

As those in the gallery clapped, Patrick addressed the bench again. "My lord, I should wish to be heard in chambers, if it please you."

"Mr. Peale?"

"No objection, my lord."

"Very well, then." Russell addressed Patrick. "But it is with the understanding that the matter of binding shall be retained by this court, and therefore the purpose of consult is merely to determine whether to postpone a trial, if such is ordered."

"Yes, my lord."

Amid jeers from the gallery, Russell, Peale, Junior Prosecutor Milton, and Patrick withdrew. As the court sergeant held the door, Peale leaned close to whisper to Patrick, "The date was set at Lord Dunster's request, you know. I did not wish to leave you hanging out before the elections."

"I am not ready to go to trial."

"Perhaps you ought to face the notion that the old man is guilty as sin itself," Milton suggested.

"There are six counts of murder against my client. I should like sufficient time to defend each one rather than merely respond to the whole."

"There may be another," Peale murmured apologetically. "The chemist has discovered a concentrated quantity of jessamine in Mrs. Coates's opium, which indicates she was killed rather than succumbed to an excess of the drug itself."

"There is nothing to connect Mrs. Coates to Mr. Rand—beyond a common acquaintance with Peg Parker," Patrick retorted.

Not addressing that, the prosecutor added, "That could be your out, you know. It could most certainly be argued that you cannot defend one of your clients against causing the wrongful death of another. We have but to bind Rand over for November, then you may discreetly withdraw, perhaps recommending Mr. Parker or Mr. Fisher in your stead."

"Gentlemen, am I to be privy to this dicussion at all?" Justice Russell demanded querulously. "Well, what is it to be?" he asked Patrick. "Do you wish to plead that you cannot represent your client? I am sure I am within my authority to discover sufficient connection."

He knew Dunster would expect him to bow out,

and yet he knew also that Elise Rand would never forgive him if he did. "No," he said soberly, "I am asking that when he is bound over, there is a later date for the trial."

Russell looked to Peale curiously. "But I thought you said Lord Dunster wished——"

"Lord Dunster does not defend this case," Patrick said dryly. "And while I have no wish to withdraw, I am respectfully asserting my right to adequately counsel Mr. Rand."

"If he should be charged with the murder of Mrs. Coates, it is my opinion you will have to withdraw in favor of unprejudiced counsel," Russell observed.

"Unless Mr. Peale or a magistrate has caught my client giving Maddie Coates the tainted opium, I respectfully submit that I should not be discharged on grounds that are tenuous at best, my lord."

"Oh, give over, Hamilton!" Ned Milton snapped. "Whether you deserve it or not, we have found you an out."

But a slow smile formed at the corners of the chief prosecutor's mouth as he regarded Patrick. "No, I think not, Ned," he said softly. "Obviously, Mr. Hamilton wishes to try this one himself, and I for one am willing to let him." Turning to Justice Russell, he nodded. "I have no objection to setting this one in January Session—or February even, my lord."

"Do you mean to charge Mr. Rand with the murder of Mrs. Coates?" Russell asked him.

"Not now," Peale answered. "As my learned colleague Mr. Hamilton has said, the connection between Mrs. Coates and Mr. Rand is arguably a tenuous one."

"Yes, very well, then is it settled? I shall direct it to be found that there is probable cause to sustain six murder charges against Rand. And I shall direct the Recorder to submit the order to the Lord Mayor and to discover a suitable date in January. Further than that I am not prepared to go."

"Thank you, my lord," Patrick murmured.

"You, sir, are a fool," Russell told him bluntly. "And I cannot think that Lord Dunster will be pleased—not at all. He does not usually exert himself to influence the setting of trials, but in this case, I am sure his intent was to help you.''

As they filed back into the courtroom, a hush fell over the gallery, allowing Peale to be heard telling Milton, ''I shall look forward to this one, I think, for Hamilton cannot win it.''

But later, when the decision had been directed and received, an indignant howl went up at the discovery that Rand would not hang before January. To protect the prisoner from crowd fury, a number of guards closed around him, but not before someone had managed to spit in the old man's face. Although in fetters, Rand lunged toward his attacker, shouting, ''I ain't gallows bait yet! D'ye hear that? I got Hamilton—and I ain't going to hang!''

Elise pushed through them and put her arms around her father, trying to soothe him. ''Of course you are not, Papa—of course you are not.''

The old man embraced her awkwardly, lifting manacled hands to hold her. ''You ain't going to let 'em do it, are you, Puss?'' he said thickly. ''You are the one as I could always count on, aren't you?''

''Yes.''

They pulled him away, and dragged him out of the courtroom under heavy guard to a holding cell beneath the Bailey itself, while the surging galley emptied, allowing the angry spectators to meld with the mob outside. She stood there for a moment, feeling the sting of hot tears burning her eyes. Then her chin came up as she turned back to Patrick.

''Why did you not defend him?'' she cried. ''Why did you not prove they lied? You did not even bother to ask them any questions, Hamilton! I could scarce believe my eyes!''

''I'd rather not answer that here, Ellie.'' He tried to take her arm, but she wrenched away from him. ''Let me take you home, and I will explain.''

''You cannot explain it!'' she shouted furiously. ''You did nothing!'' Whirling on her heel, she plunged into the crowd.

"Don't be a fool, Ellie!" This time, he caught her from behind and held on, pulling her arms back as she struggled to get away from him. "No, you don't—you'll be trampled or worse."

"You lied to me, Hamilton—you lied to me! When the time comes, you are going to let them hang him!"

He shook her then. "I told you I would discuss it while I am taking you home." He could feel her shoulders shake as her anger gave way to tears. Turning her around, he enfolded her in his arms, letting her sob against him. "I have not yet begun, Ellie, I swear it." Over her shoulder, he could see Justice Russell eyeing him oddly. "Come on—I've got to get you out of here." To Russell, he explained, " 'Tis Miss Rand, and those in the gallery have overset her. I would that you allowed me to take her out the other way."

Russel shook his head. "The sergeant tells me they are out there also. Perhaps she is better served by waiting in my chambers." Moving from the bench, he allowed, "I am thinking of staying awhile myself, for the mood is rather ugly out there."

Under most circumstances, Patrick had regarded the man as much an adversary as Peale, but in this instance, he released Elise and took her more properly, guiding her by her elbow, directing her after Russell and a bailiff. Inside, the justice indicated a seat.

"Do sit down, Miss Rand. Hamilton."

"Thank you, my lord," Patrick murmured politely. As Elise sank into one of the chairs, he added, "I think she could use something to drink."

"Well, there is port—and brandy, of course, but I cannot think either at all suitable."

"Perhaps the brandy—purely as a medicinal, I assure you."

Instead of answering, Russell gestured to the bailiff, who went to a cabinet and poured out a glass of the distilled wine, then returned to hand it to Patrick. Still standing over her, Patrick held it out for her, taking care to appear merely the concerned barrister.

"Sip it," he advised, "it will make you feel more the thing."

"Yes, of course." She tasted it obediently, then pushed it away. Looking to the justice, she managed to say, "I am all right."

"There was no need for an unseemly display of temper, Miss Rand," he responded. "Your father has not yet gone to trial."

"It was the crowd," Patrick explained. "I doubt she could hear anything over it."

"Yes—well, do sit down, I pray, for I have writs to sign just now."

As the older man crossed the room to sit at his desk, Patrick leaned close, speaking low for her ears alone. "I would that you said as little as possible, for he is not on Rand's side at all."

She nodded, then said aloud, "I do not believe I care for any more brandy, sir."

It seemed like an eternity before the angry threats and shouts abated enough for anyone to go near a window, and all the while Russell worked silently, looking up occasionally to survey them.

"What is he signing?" she dared to whisper.

"It isn't any commutations, I can tell you."

"They cannot all be death warrants surely. I thought that was the prerogative of the Lord Mayor."

"The mayor merely approves what the Recorder gives him." Patrick walked to the windows and looked out, then turned around. "I believe we can leave safely now, Miss Rand, providing you do not mind walking a bit to my conveyance. Not knowing if a hackney could get through, I took the precaution of standing my tilbury a street over."

"I can walk."

"I shall be taking Miss Rand home," he told the justice.

Russell waited until they were almost gone through the door before clearing his throat. "I shall, of course, have to tell Lord Dunster that you have refused, I'm afraid."

"I know."

As they stepped out into Bailey Street, she gasped, "Why they have wrecked nearly everything!"

"It is not as bad as it looks," Patrick assured her. "A few overturned carts and some refuse, that is all. This is nothing to when there is an actual acquittal, I assure you."

"They are naught but animals," she said with feeling. "Animals," she repeated. Then she looked up. "What did Justice Russell mean by what he said?"

"The Home Secretary will be displeased."

"Over what? I'm sorry, I ought not to pry, but I collected that it had something to do with my father."

"It did." Taking her elbow again, he crossed the street and tried to hurry her. "Lord Dunster was of the opinion that the trial ought to be held as quickly as possible."

"Because of the nature of the crowds," she murmured.

"Because of the possibility of spring elections."

"Yes, of course."

"He would prefer that I distanced myself from unpopular causes—or that I extricate myself from them altogether."

"Is that why you made no effort to examine the witnesses?"

"No."

He was walking almost too quickly for her to catch up. She caught her skirt, hiking it enough to lengthen her stride, but he merely moved faster. "Will you wait?" she said peevishly. "If not, I might as well break into a complete run."

"I beg your pardon for it." Nonetheless, he did not slow down much.

"The skirt of my gown is hideously narrow, you know."

"If any recognizes me and calls out, hang the skirt and run," he advised her bluntly.

"Why?"

"Because I am not precisely popular today." Reaching the corner, he looked both ways, then pushed her ahead of him into the street. "That is my rig over there."

"Well, thank heavens for that at least." Holding her hat, she hurried across.

He caught her at her waist and boosted her up, then climbed in after her. Fishing in his coat pocket, he drew out several coins and handed them to the boy who'd waited with the tilbury.

"They was feelin' the oats, sor, so I run 'em ter the corner and back," the fellow said expectantly. "Four times I done it fer ye."

"Thank you." Digging deeper, Patrick found another coin and tossed it to him. Taking the reins, he muttered, "For that I could have hired a hackney and not worried if it would still be there."

"Tell me, Hamilton," Elise asked, "are you always so cheeseparing?"

"No."

"You live in a rather ordinary house, drive a two-seat gig, and seem to enjoy doing almost everything for yourself. And yet by all accounts you are wealthy."

"I learned my shocking economies when I lived over a grocer's, I suppose. Good habits tend to die slowly with me," he admitted cheerfully. "And I did attempt buying you jewelry, as you may recall."

"Because you felt I expected payment."

"No, not at all. 'Twas guilt, I suppose," he admitted candidly. "I had rather expected you to be angry."

She looked at her gloved hands, saying nothing for a while, then when she spoke again it had nothing to do with Jane or jewelry. "You were going to tell me why you did not question Mr. Peale's witnesses, I believe," she said slowly. "You were going to explain why you did not defend Papa."

"There was no need, for he was certain to be bound over."

"That was it?" she asked incredulously. "That was the only reason?"

"Not entirely. I wished to delay tipping my suit to Peale. If he knows now what tack I mean to take, he is not only forewarned, but he is forearmed also. For every witness I can find, he can find an opposite one if he knows what he is looking for."

"Then you still think you can win it?"

"Not now, but I still have hopes of discovering something—either that, or that the witnesses will somehow disappear."

"Surely they would not hang an innocent man—they cannot!"

"It does not take much to convict of a capital offense, my dear." His eyes still on the street, he said soberly, "There are two hundred separate crimes punishable by death, the least of which is the theft of anything worth more than five shillings."

"But it is not applied thus surely? I mean, what of begging children in the streets?"

"When the census was taken last year, there were sixteen, five of them girls between the ages of nine and thirteen, in Newgate. And before you say we would not hang them, perhaps I ought to tell you that we have a definite appetite for hangings—in this one month, fifty-eight people went to the gallows in London alone, and before the year is out, I expect we will have executed nearly three hundred."

"Then why do they care about Papa?" she demanded passionately. "If there is that much to watch, what difference can one more make?"

"There are two things everyone wishes to see—the fall of the rich—and the fall of the powerful."

" 'Tis barbaric! 'Tis like the Roman circus!"

"Precisely," he murmured. "Everyone profits from the show. On a particularly busy gallows day, the Lord Mayor will host a banquet for the dignitaries come to watch, while the wealthy lease windows in the houses with a view, where they eat catered dinners and look down on the proceedings. The rest of the world pushes and shoves in the street, hoping to see it when the trap opens."

"I don't care how civilized they claim to be," she declared acidly, "they are every one of them barbarians."

"Even Byron?"

"Lord Byron came?" she asked incredulously.

"He hired a window and brought friends."

She was silent for a time, then she sighed. "Then I suppose it was rather brave of you to risk angering Lord Dunster."

"I have never played the puppet for anyone, and I see no need to begin now," he said simply.

Ahead of them, a cart turned over, spilling its owner's wares into the street. Patrick waited while the poor fellow scrambled about to retrieve bundles of cheaply made shirts from the dirty pavement, then he nudged his pair of horses forward, easing past the wrecked cart. When he reached the corner, he glanced at Elise.

"That is another reason why I prefer to be driven," he murmured, "I have to keep my eyes on the street rather than you."

"What fustian!" she retorted. But as she looked up, there was no mistaking the warmth in his hazel eyes. Her gaze dropped again to the Bible in her lap. "I would you did not say such things," she managed finally.

"I read Ezekiel, you know," he told her.

"Then you must surely know why."

"The Good Book can be used to justify or condemn nearly everything, Ellie. If you doubt it, look up the first two verses in Ist Kings, chapter 1."

Curious, she opened it up and thumbed to the place, where she read, " 'Now King David was old and stricken in years; and they covered him with clothes, but he got no heat. Wherefore his servants said unto him, Let there be sought for my lord the king a young virgin . . .' " She stopped. "Yes, well, I should have expected such from a lawyer, shouldn't I? You can even twist the Bible to suit you."

"A point of information merely," he said, smiling.

"Did you seek your own revelation as I told you?"

"Yes." His smile quirked downward at one corner. "And I found 'Pride goeth before destruction, and a haughty spirit before a fall.' "

"Well, that ought to tell you something."

He reined in. "Ellie—"

She looked away. "If you are wishing for someone to give you heat, Hamilton, I'm afraid I shall have to suggest Lady Jane Barclay, providing you wed her first, of course," she said flatly.

"Are you a jealous woman? I wonder," he asked softly.

"No, but I find myself feeling sorry for her."

"All right." He clicked the reins, letting his horses move forward. "I will not press you further."

As she sat there beside him, she tried to tell herself she was relieved, that those words were welcome, but as she glanced sideways at his strong, set profile, she knew differently. What she wished for was to be Dunster's daughter. To have Patrick Hamilton wish to wed her as well as bed her.

After he had set Elise down at Rand House, he drove home, where he dutifully wrote Lord Dunster, explaining that he could not in conscience rush Bartholomew Rand to trial. Nonetheless, he thanked the earl for his efforts to minimize the political liabilities associated with the case.

He leaned back in his chair, pondering his words, carefully composing his thoughts, then he dipped his pen again to add, "It is with great regret that I will be unable to join you before Thursday next, owing to the press of business. I would that you conveyed my continuing regard to Jane, for I know she will be disappointed. Indeed, I shall write her under separate cover, but I would that you explained my position here as gently as you can. Tell her that the preparations for trial are tedious but necessary, and assure her that she is in my thoughts often."

Hoping that it would mollify both Dunster and his daughter, he sprinkled sand over the letter to dry the ink, then shook it over a wastebasket before folding the single sheet. Sealing it with wax from a candle, he carefully addressed it in his neat, bold hand. Taking out another piece of paper, he dipped his pen again and poised it pensively.

He didn't really want to write to Jane, but there was no help for it. He sat there for a long time, then dipped his pen again and began with "My dear Jane, I trust your journey was a pleasant one and that you are arrived home safely. As for me, I fear there is not much to say. I have been sadly busy since you left, and given that I shall be defending an exceedingly difficult case, which will require my personal attention for another week at least, I do not foresee arriving in Scotland for several days beyond that. I do hope you will forgive what must surely seem inattentiveness on my part."

It was, he reflected soberly, not a very romantic letter. He stared into the fire, seeking inspiration, finding none. Closing his eyes, he tried to bring her to mind. It was no use. He wasn't the frivolous sort of fellow who could rhapsodize about a woman's eyes or the arch of her brow, at least not Jane's, anyway. Not that she was not lovely, not at all. But even if he'd been so inclined, she simply did not inspire him.

Briefly, he allowed his thoughts to wander to Elise Rand, seeing her, her eyes closed, her lips parted for his kiss, and the ache he felt was nearly unbearable. Resolutely, he returned to Jane.

His pen scratched across the page deliberately, adding, "It is that I am nearly too tired to think tonight, but tomorrow I shall try to do much better, I promise you. For my sake and for your own, I pray you will take care of yourself. Your servant, Hamilton."

It rather sounded like something he might have written his mother, but it would have to do for the moment. He reread it, wondering if perhaps he ought to have said he loved her, but he simply could not bring himself to write the words. Besides, with the exception of that one day in her father's carriage, she'd not said it to him either. And he suspected he'd been trapped, for since then she'd appeared much more interested in being married than in him. It seemed as though he were merely around to give her the consequence of being engaged. Not that he blamed her, for his part in the betrothal was nearly as calculated as hers.

He opened his desk drawer to look for another quill and saw the sapphire bracelet. Now if he were truly wanting to appease her, he ought to send that, but he couldn't. He'd bought it for Elise Rand.

Hayes cleared his throat behind him, and Patrick looked up. "What is it?"

"You scarce touched your supper, sir, and Mrs. Marsh was wondering if perhaps you wished your dessert served in here."

"No. Actually, I am rather at a loss tonight."

"It did not go well in court today?"

"No one was satisfied, if you would have the truth of it. Rand was bound over for trial after Christmas."

"It seems rather a long time away."

"You also, old fellow? Are you one of the legions unwilling to wait for him to hang? No, it isn't as long as you would think, considering there are poor souls who have waited in Newgate for years without being tried."

"Well, I am sure it does not matter to me, sir. Shall I bring your after-dinner port now?"

"No." Patrick heaved himself out of his seat, then stretched. "I think perhaps I may go to White's while I am still welcome. Once I stand as a Tory, no doubt I shall have to forgo the place for Brooks', eh?"

Hayes frowned. "I would that you did not ask my opinion of that, sir, for I quite favor the Whigs myself."

"I know."

"But no doubt you will improve the Tories immensely," the butler declared loyally. "For all that you would hide it, you have a kind side to your character."

"Doing it too brown, Hayes," Patrick murmured dryly. "And I pray you will not say it too loudly, for I am a lawyer."

"While you are readying, shall I send a fellow for a hackney?"

"No. I'll take my own gig tonight, so you may order the pair put to it."

But when freshly shaved again and in his evening clothes, he swung up into the tilbury seat, and started not for White's, but rather for Elise Rand's house. Not that he expected her to relent, but conversation with her held more appeal than drinking himself under the gaming tables. Besides, he felt incredibly lonely. Behind, on the back step, his coach boy whistled a mournful tune.

As Patrick drove the Marylebone Road, he could hear them, and his blood ran nearly cold. The glow of torches gave a deceptively rosy glow to the night sky. He flicked his whip, urging his horses to speed, hoping what he smelled and saw had nothing to do with Rand.

He heard the horses behind him, and then he was swallowed within the ranks of surging Horse Guards, leaving no doubt that he was not mistaken. They passed at full gallop. His heart in his throat, Patrick applied the whip and shouted at his horses. They broke into a run, and the tilbury careened after them.

Angry jeers taunted the riders, then shots rang out, and the acrid smell of gunpowder met the smoke of torches. Ahead of him, Patrick could see the fire, while behind him water wagons rumbled. All he could think of was that the mob had burned Rand's house. He dismounted and ran pell-mell for it, encountering a wall of dirty, screaming Londoners. Horses reared, and the troops continued firing, adding to the unbearable din.

He cut off at the corner, running for the side street, then coming around the back of the house. Frightened servants were pouring out of a service door, carrying what little they could save. Patrick gulped of the smoke-filled air, and ran harder. As he reached the lawn, he could see soldiers scrambling up the brick walls, trying to reach someone hanging out a window.

Scanning those who'd gathered outside, he saw Elise, and the relief he felt was indescribable. But before he could reach her, a small, soot-streaked tweeny broke away from the others and ran back inside. Elise screamed at her, then ran to catch her, disappearing into the smoke. Above, a window broke from the heat of a burning curtain.

The old butler turned to go back, but Patrick pushed him aside. A soldier caught at Patrick's coat, nearly tearing it off him, but he broke loose and plunged into the heat.

The smoke was so thick he couldn't see, burning his eyes, his throat, and his lungs. He dropped down to crawl on his hands and knees, shouting hoarsely, "Ellie! Ellie! For God's sake, answer me!"

Somewhere in the darkness, a child cried fearfully, "Button! Button, where are you?"

He looked up, seeing the girl outlined by the fire behind the smoke. Still on his hands and knees, he scrambled up the steps and caught at her skirt, pulling her down. She tumbled over him, and lay coughing at his feet. The soldier, who'd followed him, grabbed her dress and dragged her toward the door.

"Ellie! Ellie! Answer me, Ellie!" Patrick croaked out. "Where are you!" The banister above the foyer came crashing down, and a flaming piece of it nearly struck him. "Ellie!"

He saw her then. She was above him, the puppy in her arms, and she appeared dazed. Somewhere behind her, more glass broke, and the rush of air fed the flames. For a moment it looked as though she might go back, but she caught at the wall, choked by coughing.

"Down here, Ellie! Down here!" he shouted at her. "Get down! For God's sake, Ellie, get down!" His lungs were raw, and his breath nearly gone. "Roll down the stairs!"

It was obvious that she could not see for the smoke billowing up. But she dropped to her knees, out of his sight, then he heard rather than saw her hit the steps as she came down, rolled into a ball around the dog. He pulled her burning skirt off her and lay down beside her. With one arm tightly grasping her beneath her shoulder, he crawled for the door.

Someone caught him, pulling at his shoulders, dragging both of them, and he finally tasted air and felt the cool earth beneath him. He opened his burning eyes as a soldier knelt over Elise, lifting her arms above her head, pounding on her back.

"Got to get the smoke from her lungs," the fellow said, his own voice rasping.

Another soldier wiped at Patrick's face with a wet handkerchief. "We are taking you to a hospital," he reassured him.

Somehow, Patrick managed to sit up and look at his black hands. "No, I am all right. Ellie—"

She was coughing—a good sign, he hoped. The guardsman who'd been pounding on her sat back, nodding. "She ain't burned," he said, "but the dog's a mite singed."

"Lizzie?" she croaked.

"Silly little chit ain't hurt," someone told her, taking the limp puppy.

She sat up shakily, then felt of her hair, discovering she still had it. Then, whether from relief or exhaustion, she began to cry. Deep, whooping sobs wracked her body.

Heedless of those around them, Patrick pulled her into his arms, cradling her in his lap. His hand pressed her head into his shoulder while he said over and over again, "You are all right, Ellie—you are all right, Ellie."

"They burned my house, Hamilton!" she cried, her voice nearly too hoarse for speech. "They burned the house where I was born! They have destroyed Papa's house!"

"I know—we'll build you another," he promised.

"I got 'im!" a begrimed guardsman announced gleefully. "I got 'im!" In between shouts, he kept blowing into the dog's mouth. "Tough little cove, he is!"

"Oh, Button!" the tweeny cried as the pup wagged its tail.

"Did—did everybody get out?" Elise managed through her tears.

"Aye." Molly stood over her, shaking her head. "Ye was a fool ter go back, and ye know it."

"Lizzie—Lizzie went in—"

"And ye ought ter birch her fer it," the maid said sourly.

"I went atter Button!"

"Aye, and ye nearly kilt yer mistress fer a dog!"

Fighting the urge to turn her head into Patrick's smoky coat, Elise forced herself to look at what was left of her house. Flames were coming from broken windows, licking up the brick walls, while inside the whole place was an inferno. Something crashed loudly from within.

People made a line from the water wagons, passing buckets in an impotent attempt to save what was left. And then a piece of the roof caved in.

"Tell them to save the water," Elise choked out. "It is hopeless."

Still holding her, Patrick struggled to get out of his coat, then he laid it over her torn petticoat to cover her bare, soot-streaked legs. Looking up at Graves, he asked, "Is there anywhere you can stay?"

"Yes, sir."

"And the others?"

"Most of us have relations in London."

"I'll find a place for Miss Rand—and her maid, of course. If you need anything, you may apply to my office, and I shall leave instructions for Mr. Byrnes."

"I cannot go home with you," Elise protested. "A hotel—the Fenton—"

"No. I want you out of London. I'd take you where you are safe from this," Patrick told her.

"Ye'd best listen ter him, miss—he went into the fire fer ye," Molly added.

"But Papa—"

"Yer papa's going to want ye safe," the maid declared. "Ye got to listen to Mr. Hamilton."

Forcing a smile despite the awful ache in her breast, Elise looked into Patrick's smoke-blackened face. "I owe you my life, Hamilton. I couldn't see anything in there—if you'd not called out, I'd not have found my way down," she whispered.

His arms tightened about her shoulders. "I wouldn't have come out without you, Ellie. You are—"

A guardsman cleared his throat, interrupting Patrick. "If you are taking her with you, sir, you'd best leave by the back. She ought not to see what's out front."

"Aye, there's five as won't be settin' any more fires," another announced grimly. "And that's not counting the ones as trampled each other. Some of 'em is plain flattened."

Molly surveyed her streaked dress sadly. "But we ain't got nuthin' ter wear, fer there wasn't no time to save anything. E'en m'Sunday gown's gone. And ye— ye cannot go about without no skirt—" She looked about her helplessly. "Well, ye cannot, but—"

"Just now I am beyond caring about that," Elise countered wearily.

"I brung yer papa's money box," Joseph mumbled. "I thought you might 'ave need of it. I think we got all his boxes out, but I don't know what's in some of 'em."

"Thank you." Elise sat up and reached for the money box. It wasn't locked. "You are all going to need something." Opening it, she stared almost numbly into the neat stacks of banknotes and the small sacks of coins. "Will ten guineas each—? I don't know—you will need everything—"

"It ought to suffice for a few days at least," Patrick said gently. "After that, they may apply to my office, and Banks or Byrnes will see they have what they need." Looking to Graves, he directed, "Just take whatever of import that you have managed to save to my office. Later, when she is more able, Miss Rand will sort through everything." Seeing that the man hesitated, he added, "Mr. Byrnes will give you a receipt listing what you give him that she may have a full accounting."

"Aye, sir."

Elise handed out ten guineas to every one of them, then as most left, she finally struggled to stand, holding Hamilton's coat over her legs, while Molly stood behind her, shielding her from the soldiers' and servants' eyes.

Leaving them in the company of a solicitous lieutenant, Patrick walked the block and a half to where he'd left his tilbury, only to discover his frightened coachey had apparently fled in it. Disgusted, he walked back.

One of Rand's neighbors, a wealthy sugar merchant named Joshua Clark, came forward to offer the use of his carriage, but one of Rand's coachmen spoke up then, saying that the carriage house hadn't burned and that while the horses were a bit skittish, they'd all survived.

"Glad enough for that, at least," Clark declared bluffly. "Bat's demned proud of his horseflesh—always gets the best of everything, you know."

His wife, who'd watched silently with their servants, offered to provide Elise with clothes and a cloak, saying, "By rights, you ought to stay here with us, my dear."

"Here now—" Clark growled. "Hamilton's tending to that, ain't you, Mr. Hamilton? Bat's lawyer, after all."

"Yes."

"Well, the least we can do is see that she does not go off looking like the veriest ragamuffin," Mrs. Clark insisted.

"I don't—" Feeling at an utter loss still, Elise hesitated until the older woman took her by the arm and led her toward a pretentious sandstone mansion nearby.

"You, too, Mr. Hamilton," the sugar merchant said. "Best get off the street ere anything more happens, eh?" Falling in beside Patrick, he added conversationally, "Been an admirer of yours, sir—followed you in the newspapers. And if I wasn't to tell you it's in the coffee houses as how you are meaning to sit with the Tories, I'd be remiss."

"Oh?"

"Aye. Good thing if you was to do it, you know," Clark went on. "Too demned many reformers amongst the Whigs, as I see it—why, if we was to listen to them, I'd not make a profit, I'll be bound. Why, the Whigs is bad for business!"

Emotionally drained, Patrick had no wish to discuss politics just then. "You flatter me," he managed to murmur.

"Ain't no flattering to it," Clark assured him bluntly. "The Whigs is wanting in my pockets to make everything right—like it is Joshua Clark's fault as the

shiftless don't eat. No, sir—put 'em to work, I say—
and them as don't, well, they don't eat! Simple
enough, ain't it?"

"A lot of the displaced are soldiers come back from
the war," Patrick reminded him grimly.

"And we don't need 'em anymore. They was somewhere ere they went off to fight, wasn't they? Well, let
'em go back where they was come from!" Clark
paused and caught himself. "Not as we don't owe 'em
something, sir, but damme if it's coming from me,
that's all." His eyes raked over Patrick, taking in his
streaked face. "Best have Tinney—that's my man—
fetch you a cloth and bowl, eh? Margaret ain't going
to want you in any of her chairs like that."

"Thank you."

Aided by Clark's valet, Patrick washed up outside
the kitchen, then joined the old man inside. While he
waited for Elise and Molly in the front parlor, he
sipped brandy and listened to the man tell of the terror they'd all felt when the "mass of lowest humanity"
had descended on the street.

" 'Twas terrible, sir—utterly terrible," he said, shaking his head. "Poor Margaret was already gone to bed
with the headache, and for all we knew of it, they was
going to get this place also. Had to get her up, then
we all pushed the furniture against the doors. Why,
'tis a wonder we did not lose this house."

"Hopefully, the worst is over until the trial."

"Finer man than Bat Rand don't live, I can tell
you," Clark pronounced definitely. "This whole thing
is a travesty, it is."

"How well do you know him?" Patrick asked
politely.

"Lived beside him for years, twenty-three to be precise. Aye, I remember when the girl was born. Sad
business there, too, for Emmaline nearly died—almost
bled to death, you know."

"Did he drink quite a lot?"

"No more than most of us. Oh, he tippled a bit
much sometimes, I suppose, and the watch was having
to bring him home a time or so."

"Did he tell you about being robbed?"

"Aye, he did. Said I ought to be careful myself, for he was just walking down the street when the rowdies rolled him." Clark poured another glass of brandy. "I expect it will be a while," he told Patrick, "for Margaret ain't letting Ellie out ere she is cleaned up a bit."

"No, I suppose not."

"Guess you are wondering why I ain't offering to keep the gel, ain't you? Thing is, we ain't wanting any more trouble, don't you see? Margaret's heart's bad, and with them breaking windows and shouting at Rand's house during the night, I was afraid they'd mistake my place for his." Clark looked into his glass for a moment, then drank deeply. Smacking his lips, he turned his attention back to Patrick. "Besides, what if they was to come back?"

"Well, now that Rand's house is burned down, I cannot think that likely," Patrick murmured dryly.

"Eh? Oh, no—and with the place closed down and the girl gone, they ain't got no reason to, as I'm seeing it."

"Did Mr. Rand say where it was that he was robbed?" Patrick asked casually.

"That's the devil of it, sir—'twas near Carleton House once, he said. And if they are so bold as to roll a man there, there ain't a safe place left in London after dark."

"Carleton House?"

"Aye. Odd place, ain't it? Guess they ain't got all the riffraff as was in St. James out yet, eh?"

"Apparently not."

"Rand was a good man," Clark went on expansively. "I ain't supposed to tell it, but the war's over now, so who's to care?"

"Tell what?"

"Where I got m'brandy—aye, and m'wine also. And what with the lace trade shut down, he was able to get Margaret some of that also."

"Rand was a smuggler?"

"Lud no! But he knew some of 'em, and he wasn't above providing his friends with what was wanted."

"I see."

"No, you don't," the old man declared bluntly. "Bat Rand drove a hard bargain with the bricks, but he wasn't above taking care of things for his friends and his family. Why, Margaret was able to trim her petticoats when there was others as couldn't."

"How well does Mrs. Clark know Mrs. Rand?"

"Emmaline?" He appeared to consider that, then shook his head. "She wasn't right after the girl was born."

"She suffered a brain affliction?"

"No, but she wasn't like she was. Oh, she was pleasant enough, I guess, but she wasn't a goer like before. And when Miss Rand was old enough, Bat liked to take her with him to the Lord Mayor's dinners and things like that when Emmaline wasn't wanting to go." Clark drank his brandy, then licked his lips. "Good stuff, ain't it? Yes, sir, but Bat knew how to get things. The French devil never stopped him from getting what he wanted."

"Oh?"

"Aye, and it wasn't just things like brandy neither. When he got a boat in from China—or was it India? Well, it don't signify which, anyways, does it? Point is, Margaret's a hand at the gardening—does some of it herself even."

"He got her something for her garden?"

"Aye, he was into the plants himself, but what Brit ain't? But to make the long and short of it, he liked to give her stuff to try out. A couple of years back, he gave her yellow jessamine—she liked that, 'cause the blooms was showy."

"I see."

"Gave her oleander once, but it didn't prosper. If it was warm, I'd take you out to Margaret's garden, but it don't show well this time of year."

"I'm afraid I am that rare Englishman who cannot tell one flower from another," Patrick admitted. "Tell me—did you ever know of Mr. Rand's keeping a mistress?"

"Why he was devoted to 'em—Emmaline and the

girl, I mean. Oh, he might've drank a bit, and he might've been hard on them as made bricks for him, but he wasn't what they are saying."

Patrick leaned forward to set his empty glass on the tray. "Tell me, Mr. Clark—would you be willing to testify as to his character?"

"In court? And what if those folks was to come back for me? No, sir, I would not."

"He may hang."

"Aye, and I'd be sorry for it, but what can I do? I got a sugar business to look after—got ships coming in from the West Indies every month."

"Would you count Mr. Rand a herbalist?" Patrick asked suddenly.

"Well, he was always growing things."

"Did he ever use opium?"

"What? Of course he did not! Wouldn't even touch snuff!"

"Did he ever buy a quantity of sugar from you?"

"Well, of course he did! Gave him a good price, and he took it."

"More than a household would use, would you say?"

"Well, he's got—or rather, he had—a big house, sir."

"Yes, of course."

"What are you going to do with the girl?" Clark asked him.

"I had thought to send her into the country."

"You won't get her to leave him. Not that I approved it, but he treated her like a son, sir—a son rather than a daughter. Broke his heart when she was wanting to wed Sam Rose's boy."

"So I have heard."

The old man nodded. "He was wanting for something between her and m'son—and I cannot say I was adverse to it. But you know the saw, sir—what was it the Romans said? 'Familiarity breeds contempt,' eh? Well, it did. My Philip would have offered for her, but she let him know she wasn't having him."

"Oh."

"Ain't no, 'oh' to it. She met the Rose fellow, and there wasn't no one else. She and Bat argued over it—why, that summer, we could hear 'em over here. Finally, there wasn't anything Bat could do, so he agreed to it, but he wasn't happy." Clark reached for the brandy again. "But they was all right after the funeral, and he felt terrible for her. Terrible."

"I should think so."

"Just as well as she didn't take Philip now, ain't it? I wouldn't have wanted this business visiting my doorstep, you know."

"I suppose not."

"Wonder where they are at. Girl could've had a full bath by now, don't you think? You got a wife, sir?" Clark asked, changing the subject once again.

"No."

"Fortunate fellow, then. That's the worst thing about the females, Hamilton—they are always keeping a man waiting. More brandy, eh?"

As Patrick was about to decline, he could hear voices coming down from upstairs, and he felt relief. "Yes, well, it would seem Mrs. Clark found something for her." Rising, he went to peer out the door in time to see Elise come down.

"Frank!" Clark barked out. "Tell 'em to put Rand's team to his carriage! Hamilton, you was wanting the big carriage rather than something else, wasn't you? I mean, it ain't phaeton weather if you got any ways to go."

"The carriage."

The woman's dress hung on Elise, and with a remaining soot smudge she'd missed on her face, the rich Miss Rand looked the complete waif. But despite everything, she managed a crooked smile.

"If you laugh at me, Hamilton, I shall never forgive you," she said, her voice still low and raspy.

"Here now," Clark chided, "is that any way to speak to a man as went into a burning house for you?"

She sobered on the instant. "No, of course it is not."

Behind her, Molly carried an old portmanteau.

"Right generous the missus was," she said. "Got dresses fer both of us."

"Oh—Frank!" Clark shouted again. "Fetch a cloak for Hamilton!" Turning back to Patrick, he said, "Now you ain't going to refuse it, sir—and if I was wanting it back someday, I daresay I know where I can find it. Just glad to help a fellow Tory, that's all."

In the foyer, Margaret Clark embraced Elise, then kissed her on the cheek. "Do let us know how you fare, my love," she said.

"Now where was that you was taking her?" her husband wanted to know.

"The country."

"Where in the country?"

"South," Patrick answered vaguely. Taking the cloak that one of the Clark maids carried, he draped it over Elise, swamping her in it. "You may rest easy that she will be safe, sir."

"But that don't—"

"Good night—and thank you for everything," Elise told them.

Patrick held the door, waiting for her and Molly to go out, then he inclined his head politely. "Perhaps one day I shall see you in court, Mr. Clark," he murmured.

"What? What's this, sir?" the old man called after him. "No, afore God, I hope not!"

"What was that all about?" Elise asked curiously.

"Nothing of import." Taking her arm, he walked her toward the Rand carriage house, which was still standing.

A new, quiet crowd had gathered to watch the last of the fire, while Bow Street Runners stood guard to keep out any looters. The brick facade was intact, a silent, smoldering skeleton, gutted inside. As they walked past it, Patrick could feel her shiver, and thinking she meant to cry again, he put his arm around her.

"Ye fergot Button!" Lizzie called out. But as she said it, she rubbed her dirty face against the animal's nose.

"Don't you want to come with your mistress?" Patrick asked the girl gently.

"Oh, aye—aye, sir! Why, I can keep Button from messin', I can."

"If ye can, 'tis a miracle," Molly muttered.

"Where are the driver and coachman?"

"Here, sor! All of us is still here," a fellow responded.

"I need a driver and two coacheys. The rest can stay to guard what's left."

"Aye, sor—that'd be me and Will as'd come wi'ye, I s'pose." The fellow spat on the ground, then went inside.

"I don't know how I shall ever tell Papa," Elise said tiredly. "It meant so much to him—the house—Mama—everything. He was born poor, and he wanted everyone to see what he'd gotten."

"He'll come about." Leaving her briefly, Patrick went in to confer with the driver, giving him directions, then came back. "Well, we are ready, unless you can think of anything else you need."

"No. I can buy everything we need tomorrow."

The big, impressive carriage, with its glossy black body and lacquered maroon doors, rolled out, pulled by a team of four showy bays. As the coachman stood back, the driver climbed up onto the box. One of the others hastened to throw the worn portmanteau into the boot.

Patrick tossed the young girl up, then Molly gave her the dog before following her inside. After giving Elise a hand, he swung up into the seat beside her. It wasn't until the carriage passed several streets that the tweeny asked, "Where are we going?"

"Barfreston."

"Where's that?"

"Kent—between Canterbury and Dover."

Elise's chest and throat still felt raw inside, and her eyes were burning from the awful heat of the fire. She closed them and tried not to think, but it was impossible. Her father was in prison awaiting trial for murder, her mother had fled, and now she had no house to live in. It was as though she were caught in an endless nightmare. She wanted to cry, but there were no more tears.

It seemed she was deserting Bat Rand also, but she was beyond fighting it tonight. Tomorrow, she would be able to think more clearly, to collect herself and make arrangements for everything. But not now.

She felt Patrick Hamilton's arm close about her shoulder, and it no longer mattered whether he was promised to Jane Barclay or not. Tonight she merely wanted him to hold her. As he pulled her nearer, easing her beneath his borrowed cloak, she didn't even care what Molly or Lizzie thought. She turned into his body and laid her head against his chest, smelling the smoke on his clothes, hearing the steady, reassuring beat of his heart beneath his shirt.

He sat there, stroking her hair with his fingertips, wishing he had it in his power to shield her from the world that wasn't yet finished crashing down on her shoulders. For a long time he stared into the darkness, lost in thought. When the last street lamp was passed, when there was no sound beyond the rumble of wheels on macadamized road, he looked down to discover she slept. And he was nearly overwhelmed by the tenderness he felt for her.

With Bat Rand's coach and four, it ought to have been an easy journey to Barfreston, but somewhere past Canterbury, the driver became utterly lost. After winding through the rural countryside, over seemingly endless country lanes, at dawn he finally reined in and ordered the coachey to inform Hamilton the village was nowhere to be found.

Molly roused. "We ain't never getting ter it, are we?" she mumbled drowsily.

Patrick eased his arm from beneath Elise, shifting her sleeping form onto the seat, then jumped down for a look, finding nothing familiar.

"What is the last village we came through?" he asked finally.

"I dunno—'twas too dark ter tell, but the inn was the Cock 'n' Candle." Brightening, the coachman dared to ask Patrick, "How far d'ye think we got ter go?"

"I have no idea. Perhaps we should go back to the inn and ask for directions."

"Aye."

As Patrick swung back up into his seat, Elise sat up and yawned. "Are we arrived?"

"No."

"Oh." She rubbed her cramped shoulder, trying to ease her arm. "Where are we?"

"I don't know, but if you wish, we can take rooms at the Cock 'n' Candle back up the road a bit."

"Not unless you want to." She looked at the ill-fitting wrinkled gown. "I cannot think you would care to be seen with me."

"I'll engage a private parlor, and we can have break-fast at least. Then if you are too tired to travel farther, we'll stay there."

As the coach turned around in the narrow road, she felt rather self-conscious. But when he turned to her again, he smiled.

"Don't worry—I won't let any more harm come to you."

"Papa will wonder what has happened when I don't visit him today."

"He'll be all right. I mean to send word to him that it isn't safe for you in London."

"I don't want to worry him."

"You can write a letter, and I'll see it sent. He wouldn't wish you to risk facing that mob again."

"I suppose you are right." She leaned back and swallowed, closing her eyes for a moment. "But there is so much to tend to—the house, the servants, Papa—just everything."

"You need a repairing lease, Ellie."

"But I should not have left London," she said tiredly.

"A hotel wasn't safe, and I couldn't take you home with me," he reminded her.

"No, I daresay Dunster would not have liked that."

"I was thinking of you rather than me."

"Aren't you supposed to be going to Scotland? I thought you said—"

"I did, but just now I am not precisely certain of a welcome," he admitted wryly.

"Because of Papa."

"No," he lied.

"You cannot afford for him to be angry, Hamilton. You need his support with the Tories—you cannot stand without him, can you?"

"No. But I am so tired just now that I don't even know what I want anymore."

"You ought to have remained in London."

"No." He forced a smile. "No, I am in need of a repairing lease also. I need somewhere to think. Go on back to sleep," he advised her. "I'll waken you

when we are there." As she turned her head against
the seat, he slid over and gave her his shoulder again.
"Here—you'll break your neck that way."

Savoring the strength of his arm, the solidness of
his shoulder, she closed her eyes once more. "You
know, Hamilton, you have been a surprise to me," she
murmured dreamily.

"Patrick," he reminded her. He waited until he
thought she slept again, then he said softly, "And 'tis
a bonny lass ye are, Ellie Rand. I canna ever remember
another like ye."

She slid her arm around his waist and snuggled
closer. "I like it when you speak like that," she whispered huskily. "You have a beautiful accent."

"And to think I have spent half a life ridding myself
of it," he murmured.

"If I were Lady Jane, I should wish to hear it a great
deal more."

"Jane wouldn't."

"Well, she ought to take you as you are, if you want
my opinion, Hamilton."

"Patrick," he said again.

But as he looked out on the rose-cast hills, he knew
he was going to have to face Dunster. As soon as he
could bear to leave her, he would have to go to
Scotland.

After having eaten at the inn, then retracing their
route back to Woolage Green, the driver found the
right road. By the time the carriage reached Barfreston, it was nearly noon, and the village was bathed in
autumn sunlight.

Now seated more properly beside Hamilton, Elise
leaned to look out the window as they came upon the
stone church. Impulsively, she turned to him.

"How pretty it is," she said. "Can we not stop and
go inside?"

"If you wish, but it is only a short walk from my
house."

"Beggin' yer pardon, miss, but I'd as soon get where

I'm goin'," Molly protested. "And the dog ain't been out since we was at the Cock, ye know."

"Oh, she ain't mindin' it," Lizzie told her, stroking Button's back. "Right good her's been, if ye was ter ask me."

"Yes, she has. I suppose we ought to get her settled, then I can walk back," Elise conceded.

"The whole village is pretty and peaceful," Patrick observed. "I liked it here even before I saw the house."

"How did you come to choose it?" Then, realizing she shouldn't be prying, Elise hastily added, "I'm sorry—that really isn't my concern at all."

"Actually, I bought the manor when I decided to marry. It seemed like a good place to rear children."

"Oh. Yes, of course."

"But somehow I cannot quite imagine Jane here," he admitted wryly.

"Then she has not seen it."

"Jane rather fancies grander places, I'm afraid."

As they turned up the narrow lane leading to the white stone house, Elise could not help admiring it. "Oh, how lovely—why, it is like a picture, isn't it? Patrick, she will be completely taken with it once she comes here."

He sat up abruptly. "But even though I was the first to bring her up, I don't want to think about her or Dunster today. Suffice it to say they are in Scotland, and I am here."

But she longed to ask just how that came to happen. "Well, as soon as I write to Papa, I think I shall go back to the church," she said instead.

"You won't be disappointed, I promise you. And," he added, smiling. "I don't want to speak of Rand either. Not today."

It wasn't that the house itself was at all prepossessing, she decided, looking at it again. It was rather its setting, the gentle hills, the expanse of lawn, the small bridge over a brook, and the row of trees that lined the lane. It looked not like a grand country mansion, but rather like a home.

"It used to belong to Farmington," Patrick told her, "and although there are but twenty-seven rooms, he modernized it considerably, adding a number of water closets." When she said nothing, he admitted, "It cannot be compared to Rand House."

"No," she said simply, "but it is still standing. And growing up in my home was rather daunting, to say the least, for Papa used it to flaunt his success before the world. Whatever anyone else had, he required two to show he could afford it."

"And yet you loved the house."

She considered for a moment, then allowed slowly, "Well, I don't think it was because it was big, or because it displayed Papa's wealth so much. I think it was because Papa and Mama loved me there." Her eyes met his. "And you? Surely you liked the home you grew up in?"

"No. My house was a stark, ugly place in sad need of repair, I'm afraid, and I cannot say I was particularly happy there."

"I'm sorry."

"It wasn't your fault, was it?" he countered.

Feeling rebuked, she lapsed into silence. He stared out his window, then said finally, "It is my turn to be sorry, I'm afraid. I had no right to rip up at you for having a kind heart, Ellie."

"No, you didn't."

A rabbit ran across the yard, and Lizzie leaned forward to look, exclaiming, "Gor! They got real creatures—look at that, Molly!"

"Well, it ain't Lunnon," the older girl retorted. "A body'd think you hadn't been anywheres."

"I ain't," Lizzie admitted candidly. She held Button up to the window. "See that, eh? Ye'll have things ter chase, won't ye?"

"That has got to be the best dog I have ever seen," Elise decided. "There's been scarce a yip out of her the whole way. She does little besides eat and sleep."

"And piddle," Molly added dryly. "But fer what she is, she ain't no worse'n some and probably better than most."

The carriage stopped, and the coachman jumped down to open the door. Button, taking the opportunity, leapt out of the tweeny's lap onto the ground and ran across the grass, disappearing around the corner of the house.

"As you were saying, Ellie?"

"Well, I daresay she is rested from sleeping most of the way from London."

Patrick climbed down, then reached up for her. When she leaned out, his hands grasped her waist, lifting her to the ground, and as her eyes met his, there was no mistaking the warmth in them. For an instant, she felt her breath catch, then she was standing on the ground.

When he turned back, the two maids were already down and Lizzie was running indecorously after the little dog. Molly watched, her hands on her hips. Turning back to Elise, she sighed.

"Well, ye might as well give the creature to her, for 'tis all she's caring about." Then, realizing she sounded rather cross, she nodded. "Aye, but she ain't got much, anyways, ye know, fer her mum died and her papa put her in the poorhouse."

"Rand got her out of the poorhouse?" Patrick asked, surprised.

"No, I did." Twitching the skirt of the too-large gown into place, Elise smoothed it over her hips. "Papa let her stay because she dropped a curtsy every time he passed her, and he found that quite flattering."

"And no doubt you had something to do with that also?"

"Well, I allowed as it wouldn't hurt in the least," she answered, smiling. "Men are easily swayed when being toadeaten."

"What a baggage you are, my dear."

"Fiddle. I didn't want him to turn her out, that was all."

A stout woman came out, still wiping her hands on a starched apron. "Mr. Hamilton! Why, we wasn't expecting ye!"

"There wasn't time to write, I'm afraid," he said apologetically.

"Well, the place is in Holland covers, but I'll have 'em off in a trice." She stopped when she noted Elise. "Never say ye got yerself a missus, sir!"

"No. Miss Rand is merely rusticating for a while." Seeing that the woman was appraising Elise skeptically, he hastened to add, "And she has brought her maids with her."

"Maids, eh?"

"Her father is a client of mine. Miss Rand, Mrs. Pate—Mrs. Pate, Miss Rand. Miss Rand's father is in the brick business."

"Rand? Of the London brickworks?" the housekeeper asked, clearly impressed.

"Actually, the bricks are made at Islington," Elise murmured.

"Well, well—who'd a thought it?" The housekeeper's gaze dropped to the ill-fitting dress. "But how'd—?"

"Miss Rand's house burned, and nothing could be saved," Patrick explained.

"Oh, ye poor thing! Well, I got a woman as can take that up a mite fer ye—aye, and she's quick with the needle, if ye was to want her to make something up fer ye. A guinea ter the gown for the service."

"Thank you. I shall no doubt have need of her."

"Aye, and if ye was ter want, ye could ask the vicar's wife about Mrs. Thorne, and she'd tell ye as how she can copy nigh ter anything fer ye."

"I shall be happy to accept your word, Mrs. Pate," Elise assured her. "In fact, if you will give me her direction, I might call upon her today."

"No, ye won't, fer I'll have her come up ter ye. It ain't fitting fer ye to go to her when ye are a guest in this house. If ye want, I can send ter her now."

"Just now I should like a bath."

"Aye." Turning back to the door, the woman ordered, "Get yer body out here, Jack, and see ter the baggage. Aye, and tell Mr. Pate as 'tis Mr. Hamilton as has come." Returning her attention to Patrick, she explained, "What with the house in Hollands, there ain't but me'n Pate, two maids, the cook, and a foot-man inside, and the gardener and an ostler without. But if ye was wantin'—"

"No, it will be fine."

"And how long will ye be staying?"

"I don't know—possibly a fortnight or more," he answered evasively. "It depends on rather a lot of things."

"Aye, ye always got business, don't ye?"

"Yes."

As Lizzie came triumphantly around the corner of the house with Button securely in her arms, Mrs. Pate asked, "And now who would that be?"

"An orphaned housemaid," Patrick answered. "And the older girl is Molly, Miss Rand's maid."

But the housekeeper's eyes were on the little dog. "Well now, I ain't one ter like creatures in the house."

As the girl's face fell, Patrick intervened. "Actually, I said she could keep it inside."

"Oh." She looked to the girl. "Well, if it messes, 'tis yours to clean up." Then to the others, "Come on into the house, and I'll show you about—except Mr. Hamilton, of course, for he owns the place, though he don't get here often."

Having scrubbed herself from crown to foot to re-move the last vestiges of soot and smoke, Elise dressed and came down the stairs feeling considerably better. In the hall, Patrick was pensively studying a picture that hung over a small table.

As she cleared the last step, he turned around. "Well, you look much more the thing."

"I think I am."

She eyed him self-consciously, seeing that he'd not only bathed, but was freshly shaven, and in his snowy shirt, buff pantaloons, and black knee boots, he was even more handsome. And when he smiled at her, there was no mistaking the warmth in his beautiful hazel eyes. To be fair to the females around him, no man ought to have eyes like that.

"The dress fits better—never say you have already managed to stich a bit on it?"

"No. What you see, Hamilton, is merely the result of some judiciously placed pins." Heedless of propriety, she lifted the hem of the skirt, showing him. "Actually, if I were to pass a magnet, I should be in trouble." Her expression clouded briefly. "I wrote Papa."

"Good. Give it to Mrs. Pate, and I'll see she posts it."

She caught sight of the picture, and for a moment she looked at it, studying the small, rather delapidated house amid an altogether bleak and forbidding setting.

"Where is that?"

"Scotland in the winter—my childhood home, to be precise. My brother Jamie sketched it from memory somewhere in Portugal."

"Oh."

"Not very impressive, is it?"

"Well, I should not say that precisely."

"My parents spent what little money they had preserving the notion that they were relation to the Duke of Hamilton, which was distant enough to be laughable. My brothers and I scarce had shirts whole enough to cover our backs, but my mother wore silk dresses because she was wed to a Hamilton." He looked at the picture again. "As though everyone could not see the house and know we did not prosper," he remembered bitterly.

"And your father?" she asked quietly.

"My father was a hard man, given to violence toward those smaller than himself, but he too wanted to believe that the Hamilton name somehow made him better than his neighbors. He made great show of sending his sons off to Edinburgh to the university, until he got to me. I was the rebel he could not understand, I'm afraid."

"Oh?"

"I told him I'd die before I'd go there. I wanted to get as far away as possible."

"So you went to Oxford."

"Cambridge. Oxford was the seat of all things Tory, and my father fancied himself a Whig. But he never believed in any of the causes. I think," he mused, "it was that he was not prosperous enough for the Tories to claim him, and he knew it."

"At least he sent you to school."

"No. He managed to convince the duke that if I did not go to Cambridge, I should be the first Hamilton to trod the boards and blemish the family name."

"I see. And what happened to your brothers?"

"Kit has a church living in Cambria, David is a surgeon in Edinburgh, and Jamie died in the war."

"I'm sorry," she said quietly. "Losing him must have been terrible for your parents. And you also, of course."

"My father and mother were buried at Bothwellhaugh before it happened."

"How awful for you."

"I suppose I ought to have mourned them, but at the time I felt nothing beyond what they'd done to me. Had Papa died earlier, I would have chosen the other path."

"And yet you have prospered in your profession," she reminded him gently. "You *have* prospered, Patrick."

"At first I only wanted to repay the Duke of Hamilton—I didn't want to hang on his sleeve by the tenuous thread of diluted blood. Then I decided if I couldn't be a Kemble upon the stage, I would have to be the best barrister money could buy. I wanted to be rich enough to have what I wanted, only to discover my wants were more modest than anticipated. I don't suppose that makes much sense to you, does it?" he asked ruefully.

"Having been born rich, I daresay you will think it foolish to say it, but money never meant much to me. There are only so many gowns and so many jewels that one female can wear, Hamilton, and when I look about and see the pain and suffering that abound, I feel rather guilty for what I have been given."

"When we were young, we dreamed of what we should have, swearing we should never be improvident like Papa."

"And your other brothers—do you see them often?"

"Almost never. Kit is married to a Friday-face who views me with great suspicion—and as he is under her thumb, I don't relish being in his company either."

"And the doctor?"

"David?" He appeared to consider, then sighed. "David is too much like our mother. He earns a good living, and yet he cannot keep any of it. The only times I hear from him are near quarter day when he must settle with the tradesmen."

"How very sad."

"I don't know—the only one I have missed is Jamie. We wrote to each other rather often, and when his captain went through his belongings after he died, he found the picture and a note that said, 'Should I perish, I would wish that you give this to my brother Patrick, that he may see how far he has risen above it.' " He stared absently, as though he could see something within the space before him, then he settled his shoulders. "We were the younger two." Abruptly his manner changed, and he smiled. "Do you still wish to see the church?"

"Yes."

"Now?"

"Yes. I thought I should walk there and give thanks for my life. When the curtains caught from a torch thrown inside, it was like tinder. I have to think it divine intervention that everyone got out."

"But you went back in."

"Because of Lizzie. She was too young to die."

"You are a wonder to me, Ellie," he said softly.

"Stuff," she answered, coloring self-consciously. Taking her borrowed cloak from the hall tree, she wrapped it around her. "Being as you are a deist, I don't suppose you are wishful of coming with me, are you?"

"I'm not certain I should count myself as a deist,

Ellie." He waited until she looked up at him. "I may believe in Divine Providence yet."

"Oh?"

Instead of explaining, he reached for his own cloak and slung it carelessly over his shoulder. "Come on, Ellie, I promise it will be worth the walk."

The air was crisp and far cleaner than that in London. As she walked beside him with the autumn leaves crunching beneath her slippers, she felt as though London and Rand and her troubles were far removed from this present, peaceful place, as though they were a whole world away.

He held her elbow, guiding her down the path until she stepped on a rock and nearly slipped. Then, with no words between them, he slid his hand down her arm to clasp her fingers. And they walked thus until they came to the hill above the village.

"It is lovely, isn't it?" she murmured. "It is like going back in time."

"Yes. Sometimes I would that I could go back—not to Scotland, but to here," he admitted. His hand tightened on hers, squeezing it. "If I could have a wish, I should want to live here with you and never go back to London."

Unable to let him see what his words did to her, she fastened her gaze on the mossy trunk of a tree. "You cannot run away from Dunster any more than I can desert Papa," she said.

"I want you to stay with me."

Never in her life had she wanted anything as much, never had she wanted to believe as much as now, but she knew also that he was promised to Jane Barclay. And as foolish as she'd been before, she knew now that her heart went with her body, that she could not separate one from the other. And she could not and would not allow herself to love someone she could not have forever.

"No," she said finally, not daring to meet his eyes. "I shall tell you what Elizabeth Woodville told Edward IV in slightly different words: I am not good enough to be your wife, but I am too good to be your mistress. I don't want to share you with Lord Dunster's daughter.''

"Ellie—"

He was so near she could smell again the Hungary water he'd splashed on his face, and she could feel the warmth of his body. As he turned her to face him, she fought the urge to cry. And when his lips were so close that his breath caressed her cheek, she tore herself away.

"If I let you kiss me, Patrick, I will not want you to stop," she told him, her voice scarce above a whisper. "I beg you will not shame me further."

"You cannot tell a man you want him also, and expect to turn him away, Ellie," he said softly. Putting his hands on her shoulders, he turned her around once more. "I am telling you I want you above everything."

It was as though she were brittle, as though if he touched her, she should break, and yet she could not force herself to push him away again.

"Please, Patrick—do not—"

Her words died against his lips, and the heat that leapt within her was searing, melting her resolve. She clung to him, giving kiss for kiss, until she could not breathe. His hands moved over her eagerly, urging her desire, uniting them in need. His tongue licked the sensitive shell of her ear, sending a shiver through her, as his breath rushed hotly, urgently. "I know a place where we'll not be discovered," he said hoarsely.

"Patrick, I cannot—'tis wrong—"

"Love me, Ellie—love me," he whispered. "Let us not think of tomorrow."

Her whole body was fevered, wanting, as though there was nothing beyond his touch, and yet she had to deny what she felt for him. As his hands traced fire over her hips, she pushed at him. "Don't ask this, Patrick—I—"

"Ellie—Ellie—"

" 'Tis not fair to me or to Jane!"

"Damn Jane! 'Tis you I want, Ellie—'tis you!"

She tore away from him at that, and before he could stop her, she ran pell-mell down the path toward the church as though hell pursued her. For a moment he stared after her, trying to calm the desire that still raged through him, then he hurried to catch her.

"Don't do this to me, Ellie," he said, taking her arm.

"To you?" she choked out. "Don't do this to *me!*" Swallowing to calm herself, she looked away. "I'm sorry. I have no right to act thus—not after you saved my life—and not since you are trying to save Papa. You have kept your end of the bargain, and I know it, but I want more than this."

He dropped his hand. "I don't want you to be sorry," he said, his voice betraying his sense of defeat. "I want to make you happy, Ellie—I want to make both of us happy."

"You cannot. The fault lies within me, Patrick, and I am only paying for my folly. I did not know it would make such a difference to me." She dared to raise her eyes to his. "I had put the pieces of my life together after Ben, and it is as though they have shattered all over again." She swallowed visibly. "I cannot stand anything more, Patrick—I cannot," she whispered miserably.

"Don't." This time, when he drew her against him, it was to comfort her. For a time, he stood there, his arms folded around her, his cheek against her shining hair, aching for her. Finally, he forced himself to step back. "Come on—I'd still show you the church."

She wiped wet eyes with the back of her hand, then nodded. Trying to smile, she twisted her mouth awkwardly. "What a wretched, foolish creature I have become," she managed. "I wonder that you can stand me at all."

"You've had too much to bear, Ellie," he said softly. "I won't make it any worse for you."

They walked silently, each subdued by his own thoughts, until they reached the old village church. Once inside, she looked about her, seeing the elaborate carvings, the beauty of the rose window, feeling the silent wonder, the solace there.

It was as though he felt it also. "If God is anywhere, He ought to be here," he murmured beside her.

Moving away from her, he sat down on one of the benches, looking toward the altar. Closing his eyes, he felt the emptiness within himself. And the words he'd read in Proverbs seemed to echo in his ears.

"Pride goeth before destruction, and a haughty spirit before the fall."

What was it that Shakespeare had written in *Macbeth*? "Vaulting ambition, which o'erleaps itself / And falls on the other side." And his thoughts turned to Jane Barclay. The irony wasn't lost on him—he'd been led blindly by his ambition, and now he was looking into the pits of hell.

He opened his eyes, seeing that Elise knelt, her head bent in prayer, probably not for herself, but rather for Rand. The faint light from a window fell upon her red-gold hair. As he looked at her now, he felt not desire, but rather a hunger for her kindness, for her healing spirit, for her sense of right and honor. And for her passionate belief in justice.

Somewhere between Bothwellhaugh and here he'd lost much of that to his ambition. And now he was going to fall, he knew that. From the envisioned heights of a ministerial portfolio, he was going to plummet to the unenviable position of political pariah. But now that he faced it, it didn't seem to matter anymore.

For as surely as he breathed, he knew now that he wanted to spend his life with Elise Rand, to have his children grow up in Barfreston and be confirmed in this church, to know the love that had been denied him so long ago. He no longer wanted the perfect wife, nor did he wish for an heir and a spare dispassionately conceived for the greater order. He wanted sons and daughters born with their mother's red-gold hair, and he wanted those sons and daughters to carry the name of Hamilton.

He saw her rise, and he walked out after her. "Do you feel better now?"

"Yes." She looked up at him, her expression sober. "I asked God for Papa's acquittal."

It wouldn't happen, and he knew it. "Sometimes God in His wisdom does not give us what we ask," he said finally. Reaching for her hand, he tucked it beneath his arm. "Come on—we'd best get back to the house."

She could not sleep. Instead, she lay there, listening to the night sounds of the ticking clock, the dying fire, the soft, gentle rain upon the roof, telling herself she was being a fool. For hours she'd tossed and turned, torn between conscience and desire, until she could no longer stand it. What had seemed so clear to her by light of day was by no means so when she lay alone in the night.

Every time she closed her eyes, she relived Patrick Hamilton's kisses, his every caress, hearing again his whispered words. And as wrong as it was of her, she ached for him to hold her again, to make her whole, to love her despite his promise to Jane.

She knew now that the few chaste kisses she'd shared with Ben Rose were but as small sparks when compared to the blazing fire Patrick had kindled within her. With Ben, she'd been the blithe innocent so sure of happiness that she believed her love could move the world. How wrong she'd been. How very, very wrong she'd been. Instead of moving, that world had collapsed in ashes.

And what fate might yet bring she did not want to ponder. Not now. For if Rand were hanged and Patrick Hamilton wed, she would have nothing beyond her father's fortune and the feckless mother she could not forgive. And what was left of her pride. Which was nearly nothing now. What had Pope called it? "Pride, the never-failing vice of fools."

Despite everything that had warned her against committing her body to Patrick Hamilton, she'd done it, and whether she wished to face it or not, she'd been wrong there also. She'd been wrong to think she could separate herself from what she'd done, and now she had to face the fact that her heart had followed where her body led. And not even the resultant shame could blot out the searing memories of passion—nor the aching need to relive that passion over and over again. And no matter how fervently she prayed, she gained no peace from yearning.

What she wanted was to love Patrick and to be loved in turn by him. More than that she dared not ask, and he dared not give. It was as plain as that. Whatever happiness there could be in stolen moments would have to be enough.

Throwing back her covers, she rose and drew on her borrowed wrapper, then with candle in hand, made her way down the hall to his room. Knocking softly, she waited for his answer, her breath bated. Nothing. Perhaps God was saving her from her folly. She turned back, hesitated, then started downstairs. No, she was not ready to give herself over to her tortured thoughts again. She'd warm milk, then find a book to read after she drank it.

At the bottom step, she paused, seeing the faint slice of light from beneath the bookroom door. Drawn to it, she pushed the door open wider and stood there watching him.

He was in his shirtsleeves and breeches, sitting at a table writing so intently that she was almost afraid to disturb him. Instead, she waited while he consulted a book, then wrote something more. Finally, she could not stand the silence anymore.

"You are up rather late."

Surprised, he looked up, then smiled wryly. "I could not sleep."

"Neither could I," she admitted, setting aside the candle. Daring to move closer, she asked, "What is it that keeps you from your bed?"

"You."

The word hung between them for a moment, then she nodded. "I suppose that must make us even," she said quietly, "for I feel it also." Her pulse pounded

in her ears as he rose and walked toward her. "I came
down to tell you that I lied when I said I could not
share you with Jane. If the truth be told, I should
rather have some part of you than nothing at all."

His arms closed around her, and he bent his head
to hers. "Ellie—Ellie—" he whispered against her lips.
"God, but I want you."

She kissed him hungrily, feverishly, as the heat between them flared like fire. His hands moved over her
back, her hips, pressing her body into his. "Love me,
Patrick," she urged him breathlessly. "Just love me—
please. I don't want to think anymore."

For answer, his hands caught at the ties of her wrapper, loosening them, then slid upward to ease it from
her shoulders. As it slipped to the floor, she undid his
shirt eagerly, baring his chest, while he worked the
buttons of his breeches. Together, they sank to the
floor before the fire in the tangle of his half-
discarded clothing.

There was no leisurely exploration, no tender words
of love, only the all-consuming fire of passion. She
closed her eyes as he eased her nightgown upward to
explore her body with hands and lips. And when his
hot palm slid over her thigh, she parted her legs for
him wantonly, giving him access there. She moaned
when his fingertips found the wetness within.

Her back arched eagerly as she twisted and turned
beneath his hand, seeking more of the pleasure he
gave her, until she thought she must surely burst from
the ecstasy of it. She protested feebly when his hand
left her, then she felt his body ease over her, joining
hers, filling all of her.

Her legs opened and closed as her hips cradled
him, holding him, striving to keep him deep inside,
straining for the ultimate union until wave after wave
of ecstasy shuddered through her, and she heard herself cry out over and over again. Abruptly, he sought
to withdraw from her, but her legs held him tightly
and her nails raked his back. His whole body tautened,
then he moved again, bucking and thrusting hard,
and his cry of release mingled with hers.

As he collapsed over her, her arms tightened around him, embracing him as she floated to peace. For a long time he lay over her, his heart beating against hers, his breath harsh and labored.

"I'm sorry," he gasped, "I tried to stop, but you would not let me."

"I didn't want you to leave me."

He looked into her blue eyes, seeing the lingering vestiges of passion in them, and he felt utterly, thoroughly complete. Bracing himself with an elbow, he brushed stray strands of hair back from her damp temples. "Ellie, you are magnificent—truly a wonder to me," he said softly. "You make it impossible not to love you."

There was such warmth in his gaze that she had to turn her head away.

Thinking she was ashamed, he eased his body down beside her again, drawing her into his arms, holding her head against his shoulder, trying to put into words what he felt for her. His hand stroked her hair as he spoke.

"I think I've loved you almost from the first, you know. You've always had such a sense of right—something I never really had. I've always been the brash barrister, a fellow more intent on making a name for myself than in righting the wrongs of this world. Until you came into my life, I thought I wanted power—I thought I could trade whatever it took to get me onto that stage."

She could feel his heartbeat beneath her ear. "You have the ability to do a great deal of good."

"I don't even believe in much of what Dunster stands for, Ellie. But I don't want to speak of that, not now. What I'm trying to say—and making a botch of it—is that none of it matters anymore. Dunster—Jane—the grand ambitions—none of it matters. Only you."

"You don't have to say this, Patrick," she whispered.

He wanted to blurt out that he couldn't save Rand, but he was afraid she'd feel betrayed. "Ellie—" No, he was too much the coward.

Afraid he meant to say something more about Jane, she shook her head. "Please—I don't even want to think of tomorrow. I want to live for now, Patrick. I don't want to care about anything else tonight."

Reluctantly, he released her and sat up, his back to the warmth of the fire. "Come on—we'd best go up to bed." Standing, he reached down to her. "Your back must be broken from the floor."

After pulling on their clothes, they crept up the wide staircase as stealthily as two children afraid of being caught. When they reached the hallway, he put an arm about her waist to guide her in the dark, and somehow they managed to reach her room without wakening anyone.

He stopped at her bedchamber. "Good night, Ellie."

"Good night."

He waited until she closed the door, then went on down the hall. In his chamber, he tossed his shirt over a chair and sat down to remove his stockings. For a long moment he stared into the semidarkness remembering her touch, the soft lavender scent of her body, the heat of her passion. And then he thought of Jane, and he knew what he had to do when morning came.

But for now, he didn't want to think of anything beyond the woman down the hall. She was the one he wanted now. She was the one he wanted forever.

In her room, Elise lit a candle from the coals left in her fireplace, then she carried it to the washstand. With her other hand, she poured water from the ewer into the bowl, dipped a cloth into it, and lifted her nightgown to wash. Lost in her own tumbling thoughts, she did not hear the door open.

"Don't," he murmured, coming up behind her. "Not yet." Her breath caught as his fingertips traced lightly over the bones of her shoulder. He bent his head to nuzzle the nape of her neck, and his warm breath caressed her skin. "If you do not mind it," he said softly, "I should like to stay with you."

Unable to speak for the new wave of desire that

washed through her whole body, she closed her eyes and nodded.

Turning her around, he blew out her candle. "Love me again," he whispered as the cloth slipped from her fingers.

It was a long way from Kent to Scotland, and it seemed even longer than usual because he was going to face Jane. At Bothwellhaugh, he broke his journey long enough to visit the ancient cemetery, where he stood in a cold, driving rain to look down on the graves.

Janet Hamilton. William Hamilton. James Hamilton.

Even now, as much as he'd once tried to put them from his mind, he could see his mother dressed for church in her silk gown, her head held too high to know the ridicule of those behind her. And his father holding his head in his hands every quarter day, always wishing for better times, spurred on by his determined, ambitious wife, always trying to be what she wanted, always coming up short. As he looked down upon the sodden graves, seeing the carved limestone markers, he felt a sadness for them.

He'd always believed they had taught him nothing, but he'd been wrong about that. Until now. Now he was determined not to make their mistake, not to take a woman who prized ambition above love.

His eyes strayed to Jamie's resting place, and his thoughts turned to the uncertainty of life. Pure, soft-hearted Jamie, the best of the lot of them, gone from this earth ere he could know the love of a wife or the joy of children to scramble for his attention, to laugh and play games at his feet. Instead he had returned to the dust from whence he'd come, proving beyond any doubt that life could be too short for any of it to be wasted.

From this cold, dreary place Patrick had come with

dreams far beyond the genteel poverty that had surrounded him, dreams of playing upon the stage, of hearing the approbation of a crowd. How his mother would have burst at the thought that he now had within his grasp far more than merely money—he had within his reach power and prestige beyond anything she could have imagined for him. And he had to console himself that if it had truly meant to be, then she must surely have lived to see it.

Turning away, he jammed his wet beaver hat over his soaked hair and made his way back to the carriage he'd let at a posting house in Kent. No, he had not the time to waste, he mused as he climbed once more into the coach. Above him on the box, the driver and coachman huddled beneath oiled cloth as the team once again plodded northward on the muddy road.

Leaning back, he slid the beaver forward to cover his closed eyes. He was weary, so terribly weary, and yet he could not sleep. Even if he extricated himself from Dunster and his daughter, there was still Bat Rand. For perhaps the thousandth time, he considered the old man. He was tired of Rand's games, tired of the machinations. And it would not end until the trial.

Mentally, he reviewed the evidence, sighing. Guilty. No question about that, none at all. No mitigating circumstances. Nothing. Plainly and simply, Bartholomew Rand had murdered those women, and he had no remorse at all. But Elise believed in her father, and there was the rub.

For days, he'd been toying with the boldest gamble of his career. One that would guarantee that Rand never walked the streets of London again. One that might keep the old man alive. Or might see him hanged. And either way, Elise would probably feel utterly betrayed.

He couldn't sleep, and he ought not to even try. Reluctantly, he sat up and pushed his hat back. First he had to deal with Jane.

Some three hours later, when the rain had turned to a fine mist that lay like a blanket over the hills, shrouding them into dim, gray mounds, the carriage turned into the narrow lane, jarring him awake. He sat up and brushed his hand across his eyes.

Ahead, he could see the high towers of the castle, the broad expanse of gray stone walls, the formidable gate house Dunster had had restored. And he knew that his welcome was going to be brief, his stay exceedingly short. But no matter how much he wished to run, he knew also he had to face the earl and Jane.

The road narrowed again, this time into a hard, rock-packed lane scarce wide enough for the carriage. As he reached what remained of an ancient barbican, he noted the bright green moss growing between the stones, life amid decay. Above, he could still see the rust marks where the gate had rested against the wall. And he wondered how many mailed parties had sortied out to raid their English neighbors or to make war against their fellow Scots.

Inside the courtyard, he could see the ruins of the first peel tower, dead grass now where ancient Scots had once retreated to hold this blood-soaked piece of land. More than five hundred years the present earl could trace his lineage backward, to when John Baliol and Robert the Bruce had struggled for a throne long since gone.

The coach rolled to a halt, then the driver hopped down, stretching his legs before he opened Patrick's door. "Was ye wishful o' my boy announcin' ye?" he asked through a black, gaping grin.

"Aye. Tell them—" He hesitated long enough to take a deep breath. "Tell them 'tis Patrick Hamilton come to wait upon Lady Jane. And when I am inside, wait at least an hour ere you leave."

"Aye, sor." Beckoning the boy down from the box, the driver cuffed his ears affectionately. "Ye heard 'im, didn't ye? 'Tis Hamilton fer her ladyship."

"For Lady Jane," Patrick said, correcting him. "There are two of them."

"Oh—aye."

Stepping down from the carriage, Patrick waited, feeling nothing now. The heavy carved oak door opened and an elderly retainer peered nearsightedly out.

"Och, and who is it?" he asked.

"Hamilton, sor!"

"His Grace?"

The old man had started to turn back to make the announcement inside, when Patrick stopped him. "Er—not the duke, I'm afraid," he murmured regretfully. "The name is Patrick Hamilton."

"Aye."

Moving slowly ahead of him, the butler limped beneath the long row of impressive portraits, some four hundred years of Barclays, beginning with "John, Lord Barclay: 1414–1442," all the way to "John, Earl Dunster: 1754–1792."

"Not a long-lived bunch, are they?" Patrick observed irreverently.

The old man stopped and looked up, then nodded. "All but the present earl, sir. Lord Dunster is already fifty-seven."

"And in good health?"

"And in good health, aye. Though he is not at home at the present."

"Still hunting grouse?"

"I believe he has gone to London to attend to a pressing matter," the butler answered. Stopping before another ancient door, he rapped sharply with gloved knuckles, then went in, declaring tonelessly, "A Mister Hamilton to see you, my lady." Withdrawing to allow for passage, he murmured low for Patrick's ears only, "Her ladyship has been a bit out of curl lately."

Jane did not turn around, forcing Patrick to lay his hat upon the table, then walk across the long, dark-paneled room to face her. When she looked up at him, her expression was mulish.

"So you have finally come," she said.

"Yes."

"You have been with your trollop," she declared matter-of-factly.

"I don't have a trollop, Jane."

"The murderer's brass-haired daughter, then."

He could have denied it, but he didn't. The sooner the interview ended, the better for both of them, he decided. "I should rather count it copper than brass, I think."

"Then you admit it?"

"Yes. Do you wish to hear of her?"

"No, of course not," she snapped. Rising from the chair, she walked to the tall, narrow window, where she stood staring out into the gray mist. "Mama told me I should expect this, you know," she said finally. "But I would have thought you could have the decency to wait until we were married, Patrick." Settling her shoulders, she spun around. "But as you have not, I shall have to accept it, I suppose. Mama said I should not refine too much on such things."

"Your mother is wrong."

"Is she? What would you have me do—cry? Plead? Beg for your constancy? I assure you, sir, that I shall not."

He felt an intense relief, for she was going to make it easy for him to cry off. "I am glad for your understanding," he said simply.

"Yes—well, such things happen in our class, Papa says, so I have decided I can live with what you have done, Patrick, and if you have no wish to give her up, I suppose I can live with that also." She took a deep breath, then raised her lovely dark eyes to his. "You see, I shall have what she does not, for I shall wear your wedding ring, and it will be my son when she reads the christening notice in the papers. She can have all she wants of you, but I shall have your name."

He stared at her, too thunderstruck for speech at first, then he found his voice. "You do not care if I share myself with another woman?" he asked incredulously. "It means nothing to you?"

"I am civilized enough to know you will tire of her one day."

"I see. And if I find yet another?"

"I can bear that also. I will have my house, my parties, and your consequence to sustain me. I shall make a life for myself so long as you are discreet, Patrick."

She was going to hold him to the damned bargain, he could see it now, and it had nothing to do with him at all. "I see. You are an incredibly understanding female, Jane," he said dryly.

"Thank you. I have hopes I am, in any event. Mama says if I am to succeed amongst the tabbies in London, I must be."

The only thought that ran through his mind as he looked into her lovely face was that a gentleman could not in conscience cry off without the lady's consent. And Jane knew it. No, by fair means or foul, he would have to find the means to make her break the connection.

"Do you still love me?" he asked her bluntly.

She regarded him coolly for a moment, then inclined her dark head slightly. "But of course—we are betrothed, after all."

"What a sham you are, my dear," he managed while trying to control the impotent anger he felt.

"Then we shall suit each other admirably, I expect."

"Very well," he said tightly. Then he began to gamble. "I shall have to remove Miss Rand from Barfreston before I take you there."

"There is no need, I assure you. You see, I have not the least intention of living in a small house in Surrey—or is it in Sussex?"

"Kent."

"In any event, I don't mean to live there. When you are wishful of rusticating, I shall merely come to visit Mama—or perhaps we shall discover a place more suitable to your position, in which case I shall like presiding over the neighborhood."

"You make it sound as though I have a title."

"You will have."

"Probably not after Rand's trial, Jane." He had the satisfaction of seeing her dark eyes widen. "Did not Dunster tell you? I mean to see that to the end—whether Rand hangs or not, I mean to be there."

She lost her carefully cultivated control then. "But you cannot!" she cried. "If you are so foolish as to defend him, the party will disown you! For God's sake, Patrick—think! We shall be outcasts!''

"The man deserves a defense, Jane.''

"The man is a murderer of the worst order!'' Collecting herself with an effort, she attempted reasoning with him. "If you would have what Papa can give you, you will have to abandon Mr. Rand. Otherwise, Papa says you cannot be elected anywhere.'' Reaching out to him, she clasped his hands in hers. "You have always wanted this, you know. One day you could hold a portfolio like my father, Patrick. One day you could have it all,'' she coaxed. "Power,'' she said softly. "Papa can offer you power.''

"I gave Rand my word.''

Her nails dug into his hands. "You gave *me* your word! You pledged to marry *me*!''

"All right,'' he said suddenly, playing his last card, thinking she must surely throw him over if he could make her believe him serious. "If you are still determined to have me, let us make it today.''

Her face went blank for a moment, and she dropped her hands. "Today? Oh, but—''

"You may stay wherever you like until the trial is over, and then we shall perhaps leave the country,'' he said calmly. "If you prefer, we can go to France, or if you would have greater distance between us and the mobs, we might take ourselves off to America.''

"America?'' she gasped, disbelieving her ears. "*America?* I should think not! Patrick, have you completely lost your senses? I wish to live in London!''

"Well, I daresay everything will be forgotten within the year,'' he allowed.

"The elections will be over! Patrick, this is insane! You cannot want to throw your future away for the likes of Bartholomew Rand! Have you not read the papers? Can you not know what he has done?''

"He is paying rather handsomely for his defense, Jane,'' he countered. "And every English citizen deserves to be tried in a court of law rather than the papers.''

"I cannot believe this! You *have* lost your mind, haven't you?"

"No, I have found it." This time, he caught her hands and held them. "Come away with me, Jane. We shall take Rand's money and live like royalty in America."

She jerked her hands away. "Patrick Hamilton, if you persist in this nonsense, we are at an end!" she said furiously. "I did not choose you so I could live at the ends of the earth, I assure you! I did not spend months gaining your attention so I should be disgraced either! Papa told me you were a man on your way up, Patrick!"

"Do you want to wed me or not? Tell me now, and I shall ride for a Special License." Moving closer, he turned her around and took her stiff body in his arms. Bending his head to hers, he kissed her thoroughly until she began to struggle. "Come away with me," he whispered hotly against her ear.

"Don't do this to me—Papa—"

"He will be glad enough when we get our heir, which ought to be quickly enough if we apply ourselves to the task."

"But I don't want to increase! At least not yet!" Righting herself, she ducked beneath his arm and put a safe distance between them. "I think you are a madman, Patrick Hamilton! And what of your Miss Rand?"

"Oh, I mean to keep her also."

"Jane, whatever—?" Lady Dunster's eyes swept the room until she saw him. "Mr. Hamilton," she said faintly.

"Jane and I are determined to be wed as quickly as possible," he announced baldly.

"Well, I am sure we—oh, dear, but this is rather sudden, isn't it? But I daresay we can contrive something—that is—"

"Mama!" Jane wailed. "We are not at all decided!" Drawing herself up to her full height, she pointed an accusing finger at him. "He has not the least intention of standing for election," she announced awfully. "Nor does he wish to live in London."

"Oh, dear—but—"

"He wishes me to go to America! And it would not surprise me if he means to take Miss Rand also!"

"America?" her mother echoed feebly. "Whatever for?"

"He is determined to defend Mr. Rand! Mama, you must tell him he cannot!"

Lady Dunster sank into a chair. "Oh, but you must not, sir—the Tories have no need of a scandal—not just now."

"I gave my word," he said quietly. "But regardless of that, I shall still be able to provide for your daughter, so you need not worry on that head."

Both women stared at him, then Lady Dunster found her voice again. "But you will not to able to stand for the elections, Mr. Hamilton. Surely you must know that."

"I do, but the trial will not be held until January."

"January, sir, is too late. I thought my husband said—well, I thought he meant to persuade you away from this foolish notion." She looked helplessly toward her daughter. "Jane, you must reason with him."

"I have tried, Mama, but he is too thick-skulled to listen!" For a long moment, Jane continued to regard him balefully, then she decided. "It is clear to me now that Mr. Hamilton has preyed upon me to gain his advantage. But I do not mean to stand for it, I assure you." Still looking at Patrick, she declared flatly, "My engagement to Mr. Hamilton is quite at an end. You may write to Papa and tell him I should not wed the lunatic if he were the last man in England."

"Well, I scarce know what to say, dearest. Your papa will be vexed, I am sure."

"When he hears of Mr. Hamilton's folly, I am sure Papa will support me."

"I see," Patrick said, feigning a deep disappointment. "Well, I am sorry, of course, but I cannot very well force you into a distasteful marriage."

"I should not go as far as the village with you now," Jane said emphatically. "I only hope you know you are throwing a brilliant future away. Papa could have given you everything, Patrick—everything.''

"Yes, well, then there is not much left to say, is there, my dear?'' he managed soberly. "Shall I send the notice in, or would you prefer Lord Dunster did it?''

"I don't care. You may, I suppose. You may merely say we have discovered we shall not suit.''

"As you wish, of course.''

"Well, I must say you are both rather civilized about it,'' Lady Dunster observed.

Jane took off her ruby and diamond ring and handed it to Patrick. "All I ask, sir, is that you do not give this to your doxy.''

"Jane!'' her mother gasped.

"It is all right, Mama, for he is going.'' Spying his beaver hat, she moved to pick it up. Holding it out to him, she said with utter finality, "Good day, sir.''

As he left them, he could hear her mother say, "I fear your father would have wished you to consult him.''

"Not when I tell him what I have escaped,'' the girl said. "Besides, I shall say I mean to accept Dillingham, after all, and that ought to appease him. Though,'' she mused somewhat wistfully, "Hamilton is still far more handsome.''

It was all he could do to walk soberly from the house, and when he reached the safety of the carriage, he collapsed against the hard leather squabs, feeling as relieved as if he'd escaped the lion's den. Had he not felt a slight twinge of guilt for deceiving her, he would have been in whoops. But at least it was now over, and he was free to go home to Ellie.

After he saw Rand. With that thought, whatever euphoria he'd felt ended. There was still Ellie's father left between him and happiness.

After making the trip back to London, he found a letter from the earl already awaited him. Breaking the wax seal with his thumbnail, he scanned it quickly, reading:

My dear Hamilton,

I am in receipt of Jane's letter, which arrived by messenger today, and it is difficult to express the depth of my disappointment in what I can only consider your sad lack of judgment. To defend Bartholomew Rand at this juncture can only be counted an utter folly, something I had not expected of a man of your intellect and promise.

As you must certainly know, I have no choice but to wash my hands of you. The party is in need of those who can bring victory, not those who must surely carry it down to defeat. I make my decision with genuine regret, sir, for I was not alone in seeing great possibilities in you.

It was signed, "As ever, Yr. Servant, etc., Dunster." Behind him, Hayes watched as he consigned the earl's letter to the fire. "I beg your pardon, sir—is aught the matter?" the butler asked. "I had expected you to remain in Scotland a trifle longer."

"You behold a jilted man, old fellow," Patrick murmured. Walking to where a decanter sat on the sideboard, he poured two drinks and gave one to the startled Hayes. Taking his own, he clinked the glasses together for a toast. "To Lady Jane Barclay," he said softly. "May she make someone else the perfect political wife."

"I am terribly sorry."

"Oh, I assure you I am not repining, Hayes—not at all."

Thinking his master must have finally snapped beneath the weight of work, Hayes regarded him curiously. "Are you quite certain you are not ailing, sir?"

Tossing off his drink, Patrick shook his head. "Wish me happy, Hayes, for I am getting married."

"Well, I am sure—that is, if Lady Jane Barclay has cried off, sir, I fail to see how—"

"Pure luck, old fellow—pure luck, I assure you. The Almighty has delivered me in the proverbial nick of time," Patrick managed more soberly. "You see, I have hopes of Miss Rand."

"Miss Rand?" Hayes echoed, stunned. "You are marrying the murderer's daughter?"

"Yes." Pouring himself another drink, Patrick flung himself into a chair before the fire, then stared into the flames for a moment. "God, Hayes, but I very nearly went to hell."

"I collect you have decided not to stand for Parliament," the old man said.

"No. Instead, I am inclined to contribute money to the Whigs, for at least they are not afraid to stand for something."

Hayes eyed his glass dubiously, then sipped it. "Well, I am sure *I* have always thought so."

As tired as he was, Patrick still had to see Rand, then he meant to leave for Barfreston and Ellie, taking time to visit the archbishop's office in Canterbury. When he went home, he wanted to present her with a Special License to marry. After that, she would never again have to feel ashamed for letting him love her. After that, she would be his wife of name as well as body.

He forced himself to sit up. "I don't suppose Banks or Byrnes has sent by any messages, have they?"

"If they did, the letters probably went to Scotland. Indeed, but I thought you had cleared your calendar for the hunting trip."

"I did—of everything but Rand."

"Terrible business about his house," Hayes observed. "The *Gazette* said the crowd numbered in the hundreds before the Guards came."

"At least. His neighbors ought to be thankful they are not in the City itself, for then there should have been ten times as many, maybe more."

"Aye. How many was it as witnessed the last execution?" Hayes asked. " 'Twas nigh eighty thousand as came," he murmured, answering himself. "Aye, but we Brits do love our hangings."

"With a passion," Patrick acknowledged dryly. "The circus for the masses."

"Well, I have only gone once, of course, and the pasties I bought did not set well at all. Not to mention that the poor fellow kicked far too long, and the hangman had to pull at his legs to end it."

"As odd as it may seem, given my profession, I have never been once."

"Not even when they hanged the doctor as was poisoning his patients?"

"No."

The butler stared into the fire also, then finally asked, "Will Mr. Rand go to the gallows, do you think?"

"Probably." Patrick studied the dregs of his wine for a moment. "Unless he is willing to risk his neck, the hangman will break it for him."

"Poor Miss Rand."

"I know." Setting his glass aside, Patrick heaved himself up from the chair. "I suppose I shall have to visit him and get it over with," he said heavily. Looking at the curled wisps of fire-blackened paper, he added matter-of-factly, "Two down, one to go."

Patrick walked outside Newgate Prison struggling within himself. For nearly ten years, he had practiced law more as an art than an instrument of justice, telling himself that the one resulted in the other. But this time, had it not been for Elise Rand, he could have easily walked away from the old man, saying that he had no wish to defend him.

But did not, by the nature of the judicial system, every defendant require the best counsel a lawyer could give? Or were there some crimes so terrible that every just feeling must demand vengeance? What then? Did one turn one's back on a man like Rand?

For once, he didn't have an easy answer. Most of what he'd wanted, most of the ambitions he'd cherished were gone now, replaced by the conviction that what he needed out of life was the love of a murderer's daughter. For a moment he closed his eyes, seeing her as she'd looked kneeling in the old Norman church that moment when he'd realized he loved her. Now, if only he could somehow protect her from the anguish that was sure to come, he was convinced he could make her happy.

"Hamilton! Patrick Hamilton!" someone called out to him. "Wait up!"

Pulled from his reverie, Patrick stopped and half turned to see Peale hurrying after him, his black robe billowing, his hand holding his wig. Patrick managed to smile wryly, knowing that when the older man heard the earl had abandoned him, he would think him a complete fool.

"I thought I'd caught sight of you," the prosecutor said breathlessly. He straightened the curled peruke. For a moment he regarded Patrick soberly, then he nodded. "Couldn't take any more of Dunster's managing, eh?"

"It would seem that gossip travels faster than a coach and four," Patrick murmured noncommittally.

"All over the Bailey. In fact—" Peale leaned closer as though he shared a secret with him. "In fact, Lord Dunster summoned Russell and myself to attend him earlier today, and I cannot say he was pleased at all."

"I know."

"You've got no defense, my boy—Rand is certain to hang."

Not wanting to discuss the case, Patrick turned the

subject. "I suppose Dunster told you I have been drummed out of the Tories ere I was in?"

"He said Lady Jane had cried off," Peale admitted. Once again, his eyes met Patrick's. "You weren't meant for the Tories, Hamilton. Men like you need challenges—you'd be bored beyond reason amongst them. And it would be a waste, sir—a terrible waste."

"Look, I—"

"Don't want to hear it, eh? Well, I'm going to say it anyway, for I have seen it with my own eyes," the older man went on. "You have the eloquence and fervor of a Charles Fox and the charm of a Dick Sheridan, Mr. Hamilton. I know, for I remember both of them well. Better Whigs have never sat in Commons—never."

"You flatter me."

"Lord Palmerston agrees with me. You, sir, are a born Whig—heart and soul. Anything else is prostitution, plain and simple."

"Odd words from a Tory, Peale."

"Me? Oh, I don't count myself much of anything other than a survivor," the prosecutor assured him. "I doubt even Mrs. Peale could say for certain which way I lean. But we are speaking of you."

Patrick smiled faintly. "Are we?"

Peale nodded. "Palmerston said I ought to tell you to come 'round when you have the time. I'd advise you to go."

"Maybe I will."

The older man looked toward Newgate before sighing. "You are possibly the best barrister I've faced—but I've got you on Rand, I'm afraid."

Patrick followed his gaze, then shrugged. "We shall have to see, won't we?"

"Man's as guilty as sin itself," Peale countered. "Never has anyone so deserved to hang. Fellow's an utter madman, Hamilton—a madman."

"Precisely." Patrick inclined his head. "If you will pardon me, I expect to see him now."

"Of course." The prosecutor held out his hand. "Until next we are met in court, sir."

"Until then."

Peale waited until Patrick had turned back toward the prison, then he added, "If ever I should be charged, I should wish you to defend me, you know."

As the older man's footsteps receded, Patrick stood there for a moment, digesting his words. So Palmerston might welcome him—an intriguing thought to say the least, but then the Whigs were never strangers to scandal.

A slow smile came to his face as he contemplated Dunster's certain chagrin if he were to stand for election as a Whig. Even as he thought of that, he could see himself speaking out in Commons, espousing Elise's causes with relish. It would be a novel role for him, that of accuser rather than defender, but he did not doubt he could excel at it.

After he spoke with Rand, he'd pay Palmerston a call and lay all his cards upon the table. Then if the viscount thought the party could stomach the son-in-law of a murderer, he'd fight to gain a seat in Parliament. And with all her passionate views, Elise ought to make him a damned fine political wife.

But first he had to see her father. Squaring his shoulders, he straightened his cravat, and walked up to greet the guard. For the brief moment it took to gain admittance, he looked up and saw the shadow of the scaffold on the wall. If he were a superstitious man, he would have counted it an inauspicious omen.

Rand looked up from his cards when Patrick was let in. "You ain't precisely looking well, Hamilton. In fact, you are appearing as though you have eaten something as don't agree with you."

"No. I am merely tired beyond reason, for I have but arrived from Scotland this morning."

"How's m'girl? Or did you take her with you?" Rand asked slyly.

"As well as can be expected, given the fire and all else that has befallen her. I took her to Barfreston, where she will be safer."

"So Graves said when he brought m'boxes to me. Ought to have put her up in a hotel, you know. It ain't like I ain't got the blunt for it. Now you got her

where she ain't even able to come see me." Rand
tossed down a card in disgust, then nodded to the
jailer who sat across from him. "Been winning
though—he's into me for nigh to fifty pounds."

"If you do not mind, I should like to see you
alone."

"Eh? Oh, I collect as you got news for me. Don't
suppose as you are getting me out, eh?"

"No."

"Well, go on with you," Rand told the jailer dismissively. "I guess I got to talk to my lawyer. But if
you was to bring me back a pint or so, I might forget
a pound or two of what you are owing me."

Patrick waited until the jailer left, then he sat down
in the vacated seat, where he regarded the old man
soberly.

"Well, ain't you a Friday-face, sirrah! I don't suppose
as you have even tried to get me out, have you?" he
demanded sarcastically. "Or was you too busy puttin' it
to m'daughter?"

"What a fond parent you are."

"Well, that's the lay of it, ain't it? If you ain't, you
ought to be, eh?"

He wanted to reach across the table and lift Rand
by the neck, holding him while he punched the arrogance out of the old man's face. But he held his temper by saying nothing.

"Your fool of a solicitor was here while you was gone,
spitting questions at me until I sent him packing. Aye,
that's why you are come, ain't it? Well, I ain't answering
any more, and that's all there is to the matter," Rand
declared truculently. "This is Bat Rand, the fellow as has
made more money than most of the nobs, and you got
me sitting here like I was nothing, Hamilton—nothing!"
When Patrick still didn't answer, he snapped, "Well,
that's what you want, ain't it? You want to ask me something as I don't want to answer."

"I don't need any more answers, sir," Patrick said
evenly. "None."

"Eh?"

"Do you recall that I told you that it didn't make

any difference whether you were innocent or guilty, but that you had to tell me the whole?"

"And I did—damme if I didn't!"

"Peale isn't a fool, sir—nor am I."

"What's that supposed to mean?"

"He's going to hang six murders around your neck and choke you with them." Patrick paused a moment, waiting for Rand to meet his eyes. "And I think it ought to be eight or more."

"Eight?" the old man howled. "The devil it is!"

Patrick nodded. "Maddie Coates and Thomas Truckle."

"What? Whose side are you on, anyways?" Rand demanded angrily. "It don't mean nothing if she was to kill herself with the demned opium! Nothing, Hamilton—nothing! Ain't a decent body anywheres as misses her!"

"Have you ever seen a cake of opium?" Without waiting for an answer, Patrick went on. "When it is pressed, it looks something like raw sugar, only there are bits of leaves and seeds in it sometimes."

"So?"

"But usually they are from the poppy itself rather than from jessamine."

"What? Here now—what's your lay, sirrah?" But even as he blustered, Rand paled.

"Jessamine. A rather showy plant, but deadly if eaten. According to the chemist's report, it makes the muscles weak before it causes convulsions and paralyzes the lungs."

"Never heard of it," Rand snorted.

"And when combined with the already dulling effect of the opium, the combination is probably overwhelming, possibly making the victim feel exceedingly drowsy, so much so that there are no convulsions. How did you explain that to her? I wonder. Did she know what you did to her, or did she think she was merely going to sleep?"

"I don't know what you are talking about."

"I think you do, for you gave Mrs. Clark some jessamine to plant in her garden."

"That don't mean as I knew it could kill anyone, does it?"

"It means you are a liar, but I am afield just now. Going back to the murders, you were the old gent who visited Peg Parker in Mrs. Coates's establishment, weren't you? Only when you got too violent with the girls, Maddie refused your custom."

"If she told you that, she was lying!"

"Poor Maddie. No doubt she thought if she had Truckle with her, you would not dare to harm her. She didn't know that you were going to leave her to die, then induce him to try it also, did she?"

"Damme if you ain't way wide of the mark, Hamilton!"

"I'm not asking anymore. I'm telling you what I believe happened. But again we digress—you wanted Peg Parker because she was one of the few who could make the pistol fire, didn't you? And then when it took longer and longer until you couldn't do it anymore—maybe even when she laughed at you, you got your pleasure from hurting her—and the others. When she ran away from Maddie's, you asked until you found her, didn't you? I have an informant who says you were with Peg the night she died—or so my source told Weasel."

"Weasel?" Rand's eyes narrowed. "Who the hell is that?"

"But the watch was mistaken about who threw Peg's body into the river, because of the cloak you had pulled about your face. As you heard in court, he has now decided it was you. Now—do you want me to guess about Fanny Shawe—or Annie Adams—or any of the others? Once you convinced yourself they were nothing, it was an easy thing to do, wasn't it? How many were there, sir? Eight? Ten? Twenty?"

"You are just wanting to throw me to the hangman, ain't you?" the old man sneered. "You ain't wanting to hurt your chances with the Tories, eh? Well, let me tell you something, Hamilton—you go trying to cut me loose, and I'll ruin you!"

"If you don't help me, I can all but guarantee you'll hang."

"Devil a bit, and I ain't. I told you—you are getting me out, else your rep's in shreds and you are ruined."

"How many women, Rand?" Patrick persisted.

"Women! They was dirt, I tell you—every one of 'em was dirt! Why, they wasn't nothing!" Collecting himself, Rand leaned forward, staring malevolently. "And if you think you ain't getting me off, you got something else to know. I ain't above telling the world as how you made a whore out of my daughter, sirrah! And what do you think Dunster is going to make of that, eh? While you was smiling at his girl, you was a-puttin' it to mine!"

Patrick's hand snaked out, catching the white stock, twisting it beneath his chin until Rand clawed at it. It wasn't until the old man's face purpled that he released his grip and let him fall back.

"I ought to have finished you," Patrick muttered. "How did it feel? Did Annie Adams claw at you like that? Did she fight for her life like Peg Parker did? Damn you! Why can you not admit the truth?"

"You are getting me out, I tell you! I don't care if it takes a hundred thousand pounds to the justice—or to Dunster himself, if you got to pay 'em both! He's the Home Secretary, ain't he? Tell him as I want out!"

"It came to me last week why you thought you had to have me," Patrick said. "It wasn't as much for my vaunted rep as for the connection to Dunster. You were making mistakes, but you couldn't quit crawling the streets for girls, so you thought you could get a bit of insurance after nearly getting caught with Fanny Shawe's body. You knew that if the watch had to keep bringing you home, they would eventually suspect you were either incredibly stupid or else you were the man they wanted."

"Much good it's done me," Rand growled. "You ain't done nothing for me."

"I am still representing you."

The old man eyed him suspiciously. "And why

would you want to do that? You have already said I am guilty."

"I'm a barrister, not a jury. If for once you will tell me the whole, I can still attempt a defense."

"Who's to keep you from telling it?"

"I cannot give testimony against you."

"And if I was to plead guilty to all of it?"

"You will be sentenced to hang."

"And if they was to try me?" Rand demanded sarcastically. "What then? I'm just as dead, ain't I?"

"Probably."

"Then you, sirrah, are worthless! The great barrister Hamilton," he sneered. "The one as has such reputation as the Tories is wanting him to stand with 'em."

"If you confess to all of it, I might be able to save your life."

"You said if I pled guilty I would hang!"

"It is my intent to prove you insane." As Rand glared at him, Patrick explained, "There is some precedent, sir—in rare instances, insanity has been used as a defense, although as yet there are no rules of evidence for it. But it has been ruled that if you are determined to be so insane that you have no control over your unspeakable acts to the extent that you commit them in a frenzy, utterly without cognizance of the right or wrong of your deeds, it may be found that you cannot be hanged."

For a long moment Rand stared. "I got to say I am mad?" he asked incredulously.

"No, I shall say it. I shall take your confession to a number of consulting physicians, and if they agree, we shall petition the court to have you adjudged incompetent to assist in your defense. We may not have to go to trial even, but if we do, then a jury will decide whether a sane man would have committed such acts."

"You are telling me I got to gamble with my life! No, sir, I ain't doing it! You can bribe Dunster! Ain't a man alive as don't want a hundred thousand pounds!"

"For all that we disagree on principle, Lord Dunster is an honorable man."

"Then offer it to the Russell fellow!"

"Mr. Rand, there are two hundred capital crimes, sir—and bribery of a judicial official happens to be one of them." Patrick stood. "If you need time to consider the matter—"

"No." The old man shook his head. "I ain't going to say I am mad." He looked up at Patrick balefully. "I still got Elise, and I am directing you to defend me. You got the tongue—you can make 'em believe Colley is lying."

"You are making a mistake."

"I still got you, ain't I? If you ain't doing it for me, you'll be doing it for Ellie, eh?"

"If you want the best opinion I can offer, I honestly believe an insanity plea is the only hope you have. But you don't have to decide today. I expect to be in town until Wednesday."

It was as though it had finally sunk in, for the old man sat silently for a time, then his shoulders sagged. "I ain't mad," he said finally, "but I'll do it."

"Thank you."

"Do you still want to know everything?"

"Yes. Is there anything I have not already surmised?"

"If you are wanting to count the old whore and the flash cove as was with her, there's been ten of 'em. Mebbe eleven—I don't know, for there was a gel as was still breathing when I left her."

"Where?"

"In an alley over near Carleton House—when it was still the market, you know."

"St. James?"

"Aye. I was throttling her when some fellow was stumbling out of one of the dens. But she could've lived, I suppose."

"And the other two?"

"I ain't got no names for 'em. But they was in the rookery, just like the Adams bitch."

"I don't suppose you remember the dates, do you?"

"Aye—every one of 'em," the old man acknowledged. "I put 'em all down in m'journal."

"You kept a diary of the murders?"

"Aye," Rand answered smugly. "Sometimes I read it when I couldn't go out—when the weather was bad. I liked to remember every one of the bitches and how I did it with 'em."

Patrick's skin fairly crawled. "Do you still have it?" he asked with a casualness he didn't feel.

The old man looked up at him slyly. "Why, you got it, Hamilton—right under your nose."

"Where?"

"Graves said you got m'boxes as was in m'house." Rand reached beneath his coat to draw out his watch fob. "And I got the key here." He fumbled a bit, then managed to get it off. "I don't suppose as you can keep m'gel from knowing about it, can you?" he asked, handing the key over.

"No. But I would to God I could."

"Aye." Rand sighed heavily. "My poor Ellie, she ain't going to understand. She loves her papa, you know." His eyes teared, and he wiped them with the back of his hand. "She always was a beauty, Hamilton—even when she was small, she was a taking little creature." His lower lip quivered, then he mastered it. "You got to keep her from knowing, sir—you got to."

"Right now she is at my house near Barfreston, where she will miss much of the news," Patrick said quietly. "But there's no way I can keep her from the trial. She'll have to hear it—and even if she didn't, she'd be certain to read about it in the papers."

"Aye. Ain't no help for that, I suppose. I just didn't want her to know everything I did, that's all. I didn't want her to be like Em and leave me." Again, he looked as though he would cry, then his lip curled. "The Binghams!" he snorted. "They was poor, and they had the gall to call themselves Quality! Why, my Ellie's got more Quality in one hair than Em had in her whole useless body!"

"I know." Patrick pocketed the key. "Good day, sir."

"Wait." Rand licked his lips nervously. "What's to happen to me? If I don't swing, I mean?"

"I expect you will be incarcerated in an asylum."

"With the demned lunatics? No, afore God, I ain't!" the old man blustered.

"I suppose you could count yourself more fortunate than Maddie or the others."

"Where are you going now?" Rand demanded querulously. "You ain't going to turn m'book over to Peale?"

"I'm going home to read it."

This time, Rand waited until the jailer had been summoned to let Patrick out. "You going to take care of m'gel, Hamilton?" he asked suddenly.

"Yes."

"Guess Dunster ain't going to be so hoity-toity when you got my money, eh? You can buy a lot of Tory votes with it, you know."

Patrick didn't answer.

As the door was closed and locked, Rand let his head fall to the table, and for a time, he was still as he contemplated his fate. He could almost feel the collar of rope about his neck, the bulge of his Adam's apple, the panic of being unable to breathe as the trap dropped from beneath his legs. A cold sweat poured from his brow.

No, Hamilton would save him—for Elise's sake, Hamilton would save him. And he'd be clapped up in Bedlam all the rest of his days on earth, alone and reviled. And once she knew what he'd done, Elise would turn away also. Just like Emmaline, she'd turn away.

He sat up. No, he wouldn't let it happen. Rising, he stumbled toward the corner where he kept his possessions. Throwing open the lid of his trunk, he rummaged through it until he reassured himself that the small cake of opium was still there. His hand closed over it, drawing it out so he could see it.

He'd see his daughter one last time. His hand shook as he put it away again. First he had to get a message to her, first he had to see her one last time ... then he'd part from her, and she'd never have to know the monstrous creature he'd become. Aye, it would be for the best.

Patrick was tired, so very tired, and yet as he stared at the locked box on his desk, he was drawn to it with what must surely be a macabre fascination. Rand had said it was all there, the record of unspeakable crimes put down in black and white.

He rose and removed his coat and cravat, then went to lock the bookroom door. Coming back, he poured himself a glass of Madeira and sprawled again in his chair. Taking a deep drink, he glanced at the fire, then he settled his shoulders. In his years at the Bailey, he'd seen and heard nearly everything, he told himself as he reached to turn the key in the lock.

Gingerly, almost as though he expected to recoil, he opened Rand's box and looked inside. On top was a journal, rolled to make it fit. As he lifted it out, he could see an odd assortment of seemingly useless items. He closed the box and set it aside, then he opened the old man's diary, and leaning forward on his elbows, he started thumbing through the yellowed pages.

Surprisingly, it went back several years, beginning with sparse entries, mostly notations about prices and services available in various brothels, with an occasional marginal remark about a particular girl he'd found. "Betty—Pretty enough, but greedy. Paid 20s.5d. for the favor."

He kept going, looking for later dates, trying to remember when Peg Parker was murdered. The candlelight flickered over the pages, making it look as though Rand's scrawl moved. Reaching to adjust the candle's position, he looked down, catching Ben Rose's name.

"Told her she could have the Jew, but won't let it happen. Already taking care of the matter. Costing fifty pounds and good opium, but worth everything when done."

He turned the page. "Boy's a fool. Thinks I mean to give my flesh and blood to him. Wants to talk settlements, but I got better in mind." The old man had skipped a space, then made a chilling entry. "Done, but botched. All I could do to say the right words to Sam Rose. Ellie in a taking, but she'll recover, no matter what Em says. Duncan wants more for it—got that business to tend also." Then two days later, he'd written more. "Duncan was a fool also. Went easy and none the wiser, poisoned by his opium. Must remember that."

As the import of Rand's words sank in, Patrick's skin crawled. The old man had paid for Benjamin Rose's death, then had killed his murderer, apparently without regret. He closed his eyes, remembering the pain Ellie still felt for her good, gentle Ben, and he was nearly overwhelmed by his own anger.

The entries continued, betraying Rand's growing tendency to violence as he distanced himself more and more from what he did. By the time he'd begun murdering prostitutes, he'd already convinced himself that they weren't really human, that by virtue of their acts, they'd somehow relinquished the right to live.

They were all there, every one of them, and unlike Ben Rose, their final moments were recounted in detail, as though Rand wished to remember, to relive their pathetic pleas, to enjoy the brief power he'd had over them. Peg Parker was the worst, for he'd been obsessed with her from the first notation where he'd noted the "snugness of her pudding pot." And when she finally had denied his custom, he'd stalked her, caught her, and tortured her. He'd even recorded how she begged first for her life, then to die. And how when it was done, he'd ripped her earring from her ear, a grim keepsake.

That was what he'd kept in the box—something to remember each victim by. A hank of hair. A piece of cloth. Anything that had struck the old man's fancy.

Patrick had always considered himself a strong man, but he was utterly, thoroughly repulsed by what he'd read. It was too awful, too much to absorb, and yet there it was. Concrete, dispassionate proof that bluff, genial Bat Rand was a man without conscience, a vicious murderer who richly deserved to die.

Patrick sat back, trying in his mind to reconcile the doting father with the calculating man who'd plotted to kill Ben Rose. Why had he done it? To destroy a rival for his daughter's affection? To control her life?

Only Rand could answer that, and maybe the old man didn't know himself. But he'd managed to lead two very different lives at the same time, and he'd very nearly gotten away with everything. He'd very nearly thwarted justice.

Patrick poured himself another glass of the potent wine, then sipped it pensively, thinking that Ben Rose and Rand's other victims cried out for that justice. But there was Elise to consider. There was no way to spare her the pain of learning at least part of what her father had done. It would come out in court, one way or another. It had to—whether Rand hanged or whether he rotted in an asylum, the world would know him for a murderer.

Elise was going to take it hard, he knew that. She might even feel he betrayed her when she heard his defense. But it was the only thing he could think to do short of giving the old man up to the gallows.

It was no use. He'd already agonized over it a thousand times and more, and there was nothing else. Just thinking of the horror she faced filled him with a hot, impotent anger at the old man. And at her mother. Where the hell was her mother? It was one thing for the woman to desert the old man, but quite another to leave her daughter.

Unable to think further, he gave it up. Tomorrow he would lay out the precedents. Tomorrow he would read the opinion that had saved George Gordon after the Gordon riots. Tomorrow he would call upon Dr. Whiteside, the physician who'd given testimony in a less successful case. And tomorrow he would try to bargain with Peale in the slight hope that between him and Peale and Russell perhaps they might discover the means to avoid a public trial. But tonight, he was going to drink the whole damned bottle, and he was going to feel sorry for himself, for Elise, and for damned near everybody but Rand.

As the carriage barreled through the heavy mists, Elise unfolded and reread her father's short message, perplexed by the urgency of it. "I pray you will come in all haste, and I beg you will not tell Hamilton I have asked to see you."

At first, she'd been inclined to think it but another of his queer starts, but the more she read it, the more it worried her. Had he and Patrick quarreled? If so, Patrick had written none of it to her.

Well, it didn't make any difference. She'd known all along that she couldn't sit idly by at Barfreston with naught to do but wait for Hamilton to return to her. She needed to be in London, to know what was happening, she told herself. But that was only part of the truth, and she knew it. She also wanted to be with Patrick.

Tucking the note back into her reticule, she picked up the *Gazette* to read the small boxed item yet again. "The Earl of Dunster wishes to announce that the engagement between his daughter, Lady Jane Barclay, and Mr. Patrick Hamilton is at an end, as both parties have discovered they shall not suit." Every time she repeated the words to herself, she could not help the hope she felt.

The carriage slowed as it passed through outer London, and she stared at the rows of chimneys barely discernible through the fog. She'd asked her driver to go through Marylebone first that she might have a glimpse of the house that had sheltered her since birth, and then she would see Patrick and surprise him. She leaned back against the squabs, wondering if he'd be displeased when he learned she'd not stayed at Barfreston. Or if he'd understand that she could not, not when Rand needed her.

Water condensed on the windows, forming rivulets that coursed at an angle toward the corners of the panes. Now the carriage wended through city streets, past fine houses. She straightened up, recognizing the landmarks as traffic about her increased.

Finally, the carriage turned the corner, and she had to force herself to look at what had been her lifelong home. Ugly black streaks of soot shot upward from every broken window, tracing the paths of flames. And in the carriageway at the side, the charred remains of tables and chairs were still piled for disposal. Had she had any tears left, she would have cried.

As the coach halted there, she could still smell the smoke, and for a moment she closed her eyes, fighting the nausea. Then she was all right. Possessions were not important, she told herself sternly. They were but bits and things collected, nothing more.

A coachey swung down from the box above and pulled open the door. "Was ye wantin' ter tarry a bit?" he asked doubtfully. " 'Tis wet out, it is."

"I'll go in with ye," Molly offered.

"No. There's nothing left that I wish to see."

"Where was ye wantin' ter go next?" the coachey inquired.

"I shall register at Fenton's, then proceed to Newgate to visit Papa."

"Well, I think ye ought ter tell Mr. Hamilton first," Molly said. "A prison ain't a fittin' place fer a decent female."

"Nonsense. I have been there before."

"But ye got Mr. Hamilton ter do it for ye now."

"I am following Papa's expressed wishes," Elise declared with a finality that brooked no further argument.

"Well, if it was me, I'd tell him," Molly countered, uncowed. Seeing that her mistress stared again at what was left of Rand House, she relented. "Aye, but ye got ter do what ye think best, don't ye?"

"Yes. Ten to one, it is but that Papa wants to bullock me, but in the event it is not, I have to see him. Besides, he must be feeling as though I've deserted him."

"Still, it wouldn't hurt none to leave a card at Mr. Hamilton's—just so's he'd know ye was in town," the maid suggested slyly. "He don't have to know as ye're going to the jail, does he?"

For a moment Elise closed her eyes, seeing Patrick in her mind, and the now familiar longing washed over her. "Most gentlemen are not at home in the afternoon," she said finally.

"But if ye was ter do it, he could be over at Fenton's fer supper, don't ye know? Otherwise, he'll be going ter one of the clubs," Molly pointed out reasonably.

She wanted to see him, there was no denying that. "I don't supposed a card would hurt anything," Elise conceded, her hands smoothing the skirt of her new gown.

"Ye look fine as fivepence, ye do," the girl reassured her. "And as soon as we get ter Fenton's, I'll have the blue dress pressed in case he should come ter dinner. Though," she recalled reluctantly, "I oughter be going ter Newgate with ye."

When they arrived at Patrick's house, it was as expected—he wasn't home. But Hayes informed Elise that "While Mr. Hamilton is out just now, I expect him back shortly. If you would care to wait—"

"No, that will not be necessary, but I should like to leave him a note, if you do not mind it."

"Not at all, miss," he assured her. "There is paper and pen upon his desk in the bookroom, and if you are wishful of warming yourself for a bit, I can have hot punch out in a trice."

"Thank you, but I am in rather a hurry," she murmured.

He opened the door for her, then disappeared, leaving her alone in Patrick's cluttered study. As she looked around, the memory of how it had all begun nearly overwhelmed her. She could almost hear her voice offering herself again. And she could feel the touch of his hands, the warmth of his breath that night. Reluctantly, she forced herself back to the matter at hand.

His desk was still a mess. A guttered candle, its black, nubby wick reduced to a speck within a pool of congealed wax, indicated he'd worked long into the night. Moving behind the desk, she looked for a clean sheet of paper, and her eyes caught sight of the metal box. A small plate on it had been engraved "Property of Bartholomew Rand."

Curious, she pried it open and found an odd assortment of what appeared to be refuse. Her fingers sifted through a cracked brooch, a broken earring, beads, a scented handkerchief, a bit of lace, a small velvet bow, a stained bit of blue satin. They looked like the treasures a child might keep—broken and useless.

"Did you find what you need, miss?" Hayes asked from the door.

"Uh—no," she said quickly. "But I see where he has had one of Papa's boxes out. I cannot think why my father would keep such things."

"As to that, I am sure I do not know. Apparently Mr. Hamilton found something to like in it, for it's been there half the week."

"How odd. Yes, well, I'm afraid I shall have to rely on you to tell Mr. Hamilton that I've returned to town and shall be staying at Fenton's Hotel for a few days." Trying to sound casual, she added, "I shall be in later today, should he wish to speak with me."

For a moment Hayes forgot his place, and he smiled widely. "If I were a gaming man, I should wager he will, miss."

"I hope so—I sincerely hope so," she said. "You see, he did not know I was coming, and he may be rather vexed that I did not apprise him."

By three o'clock, she had registered at the hotel, tended her toilette, and changed her travel-creased gown. And now she was ready to see her father.

The guard unlocked the keeper's apartment and led her back to Rand's room. "Papa?" she said from the doorway.

He looked up. "Well, damme if it ain't m'gel! Here now—no Friday-face, for I ain't having it!" he said bluffly. "Aye, don't stand there, Puss—come give an old man a kiss!"

"I came as soon as I got your note," she murmured, bending over him.

His arm came up, embracing her awkwardly, and she could smell the rum on his breath. He held her for a moment, then let her go.

"Aye, I was missing you, Puss—no denying it. Just wanted to see you, that's all there was to it. Here—" He gestured to a chair across from him. As she sat down, his welcoming smile faded, and he appeared pensive.

"Is something the matter, Papa?" she prompted.

"Eh? No, no—of course not. Hamilton don't know you are here, does he?"

"I left a card that I was in town. He was not at home when I called."

"Guess the Barclay family threw him over, eh?"

"Yes." She glanced down at her folded hands, then sighed. "We have cost him rather dearly, I'm afraid."

"Ain't no way to look at it, Ellie—no way at all."

She shook her head. "No, we have cut up his ambition, Papa. Between us, we have seen that he is denied a career in Parliament."

"Stuff and nonsense!" He regarded her slyly. "Man's got you, ain't he? Head over heels for you, Puss, and unless I miss the mark badly, m'grandsons is going to be Hamiltons."

"Papa—"

"I ain't repining over it—picked him out for you, didn't I? Had m'eye on him for an age."

"Actually, you threw me at him rather shamelessly."

"But it worked out for you, didn't it?" he persisted.

"What a wretch you are, Papa," she murmured wryly.

"I always wanted the best for you, Puss—you got to know that, eh?"

"Yes."

"You going to take him?"

"If he offers."

"Good. It's a comfort to me knowing as you'll be taken care of. And don't you be worrying none about cutting up his hopes, you hear? When he's got my money, there's plenty as will look to him—aye, he can buy his votes, if he's a mind to."

"No, he's not like you," she said, smiling. "But you did not send for me to speak of Hamilton, did you?"

"Just wanted to see you, that's all. Proud of you, Ellie—demned proud of you, damme if I ain't. Wanted you to know it." His eyes fixed on hers for a moment, then he looked away. "You was always my little gel."

"Papa, are you *crying*?" she asked incredulously.

"Aye—mebbe I am, Puss. It's been hard for me being here, you know."

She leaned across the table to possess his hands. "You are going to get out, Papa. Patrick will find a way—he'll prove you innocent in court. I know it, Papa—as surely as I breathe, I *know* it."

"That's m'gel, Ellie," he said, his voice nearly breaking. "You always loved your papa, didn't you?"

"You cannot give up! You cannot! Patrick—"

"Here now—none of this, Puss," he managed gruffly. "Ain't no time for both of us to be maudlin fools, is it? I wasn't wanting you here so's you could cry, you know." He reached to lift her chin. "I was wanting you to know as how you are everything to me, that's all." He let his hand fall to the table. "But I ain't been feeling good lately, Puss."

"You've been ill?"

"Not ill, precisely," he murmured evasively. "Just got these pains in m'chest, that's all. Got to thinking as how a man don't know the day nor the hour, and—"

"I'll send 'round to Dr. Davis," she promised quickly. "Ten to one it is but something you've eaten, but—"

"I ain't seeing no quacks."

"I shall have him here in the morning."

"Waste of money!" he snorted. "Ain't no sense in healing what is going to hang, is there?"

"You are not going to hang! Please, Papa, I'd not hear you say such things—you are not going to hang! I won't let them hang you!"

"Ellie—Ellie—don't, Puss." He rose awkwardly and moved with an effort, dragging his irons with him. Coming up behind her, he laid a hand on her shoulder. "All right—I ain't going to hang. There—is that better?"

"Yes." She twisted in her chair, turning to bury her head against his waistcoat much as she'd done as a child. "Don't say such things," she choked out.

His hand stroked her hair. "All right." He looked down, seeing not the lovely woman she'd become, but rather the little girl she'd always been to him, and his resolve stiffened. "Go on with you now, Puss. You send Davis 'round tomorrow, and I'll see him. Until then, you go home and make yourself pretty for Hamilton, you hear? A man don't want a Friday-face—you remember that, eh? Now, give your papa a kiss ere you go."

She stood and turned to embrace him. "I'll be here in the morning, Papa. There'll be a way—you'll see. As long as we both breathe, we are not done yet."

"Aye."

As she left him, she felt an intense unease. Shaking it off, she told herself he was all right, that it was probably nothing more than the blue-devils brought on by his confinement. What he needed was to be free, that was all. Perhaps Dr. Davis could prescribe something for his nerves.

As her footsteps receded, Rand went to the window to watch the street outside. The rain came down steadily now, striking the deserted gallows. Tomorrow there would be a hanging, a guard had said, but he wouldn't be here to watch it.

Down toward the corner, he saw her dash toward his carriage, and he nearly lost his resolve. But then he thought of Sam Rose's son, and he knew he had to do it. This way, she wouldn't be leaving him like

Em had. This way, she could still believe in him. This way, he wouldn't have to see the revulsion in her face.

He waited until the coach disappeared, then he went to the trunk and took out the opium cake. The small flecks of ground jessamine beckoned to him, promising no pain. Carrying it back to his table, he sat down and broke it up, then put it into his cup. Adding rum, he stirred the mixture with his finger, telling himself that he had to be certain to drink all of it.

He swallowed greedily, downing it, then shuddered at the bitter taste. Refilling his cup, he swirled the telltale dregs, then drank again, taking the last trace. Oddly, he felt nothing, and yet the deed was done.

He rose again, this time to go to his bed. Lying down, he pulled his blanket up and waited for oblivion. His thoughts turned again to Elise. Hamilton would never tell her, he was sure of that. She'd mourn him properly, and it would be over. Maybe Hamilton would even let her name a son Bartholomew after him. Aye, that would be something.

His mouth began to tingle, and his tongue felt thick. He closed his eyes, seeing Maddie Coates again, remembering how eagerly she'd taken the tainted opium. It hadn't taken Maddie long, as he recalled. And it had been painless.

Slowly, ever so slowly, the numbness crept, taking more and more of his body, making it more and more difficult to breathe. He was suffocating now. He tried to cry out, but he couldn't form the words. Panicked, he struggled, but it was too late—they were waiting for him across the darkening chasm, all of them. Maddie, Big Tom, Peg, Ben Rose, and all the others—they were grasping for him, pushing him into the deep, black hole. And he was looking into hell.

Elise stood, staring out onto the street below, seeing the carriages pass by the street lamps, hearing the wheels spray muddy water. A careless pedestrian, his head covered by a newspaper, started across, then stepped back, cursing a driver for ruining his clothes. Another time, she might have been amused by the scene, but just now the blue-devils threatened to overwhelm her.

She hadn't heard from Patrick, and just now she wanted him to hold her, to tell her that everything could somehow come out right. That there was nothing to fear. That her father would not hang. That the jeering, mindless mobs would not come again.

Her thoughts turned to her strange visit with Rand. It wasn't like him to complain of illness—nearly everything else, but not illness. Ordinarily, he would despise the very weakness of admitting any ailment. But he hadn't looked well when she'd left him, not at all, and now as she waited, hoping Patrick would come, she wondered if perhaps she ought to have summoned Dr. Davis rather than delay until tomorrow.

Perhaps her father was merely as melancholy as she was. Perhaps it was his mind rather than his body that ailed. Not that she ought to have expected otherwise, she chided herself. After a month in Newgate, where his window faced the gallows, he had a right to be downcast.

"You going back to Barfreston after ye've seen Mr. Hamilton?" Molly asked behind her.

Elise dropped the curtain and stepped back. "Not for a while. Papa needs me just now."

"Aye. I s'pose Lizzie'll be all right, but that Pate creature ain't too fond of Button—if it wasn't for Mr. Hamilton, that dog'd never be in the house."

"I should have called Dr. Davis—I know it."

"Eh?"

"Nothing. I shall just have to send for him in the morning."

Molly moved closer. "Ye know what ails ye? Ye ain't taking care of yerself like ye was to need to. Ye ain't eating and ye ain't sleeping. And yer worryin' as Mr. Hamilton ain't coming, ain't ye?"

"I don't even know if he's been home to get my message."

"If he ain't here tonight, he'll be here tomorrow," the maid declared. "Man's head over heels." When Elise did not answer, she decided, "Well, I'm going down and get a supper fer ye, and then I'm going ter stand over ye until it's gone, I am."

"I'm not hungry. Maybe I am too tired to be hungry."

"And it'd be a wonder if ye wasn't now, wouldn't it? Yesterday ye was in Kent, and now ye're in London."

"Maybe I shall just retire early."

"No, ye ain't—not until ye've eaten. Why, they've got suppers fit fer the nobs—the girl as brought the linens was telling me Wellington himself has dined here."

"Fenton's has always been noted for its food." Elise stared into the fire. "I don't know—maybe it is the rain more than anything," she murmured absently.

"Ye could go down to eat," the girl said slyly. "Do you a bit of good, it would."

When Elise didn't answer, Molly sighed. "All right, but don't ye be complaining about what I bring ye— whatever it is, ye got ter eat it." Before Elise could refuse, she slipped out the door.

Halfway down the steps, she encountered a grim Patrick Hamilton. When he saw her, he didn't smile.

"Where is Miss Rand?"

"Second door on the left at the top," the girl told him. She hesitated, then blurted out, "I hope naught's amiss, fer she's already in a queer taking—right cast down, in fact."

"Rand's dead."

The maid stood stone-still. "Dead?" she echoed. "Oh, no! I don't know as how she's to take anything more!"

He nodded. "If you do not mind, I should like to go up to tell her alone."

"Aye. I was going ter fetch her dinner, but—"

"Go ahead and get it. Just don't come back for a while."

"She'll be in an awful taking, Mr. Hamilton."

"I know. I brought some laudanum in case she needs it."

He went on up, found the door, and rapped on it lightly. At first, he thought she may not have heard him, then she answered, "If you are come back to ask me again what I want, I shall say I don't want anything," she said tiredly.

He turned the knob and pushed the door inward. She had her back to him as she stood before the fire. He hesitated, feeling utterly helpless, knowing she would probably go to pieces when he told her. But he had to do it. He'd rather she heard it from him than anyone else. And he knew he loved her enough to lie to her.

"It is still raining," he said softly.

It was as though her heart paused. As she turned around slowly, her pulse quickened at the sight of him. Then her smile died with the realization that something was terribly wrong.

There was no easy way to say it. He waited only until he reached her. "Rand is dead, Ellie," he said gently. "It is over, and he did not suffer."

"Dead?" she echoed, not comprehending. "But— but how? I saw him but hours ago, and—"

"Apparently his heart gave out. God, Ellie, but I'd give anything not to tell you." His arms closed around her shoulders, drawing her to him. "He died in his sleep shortly after you visited him. The jailer who brought his dinner found him on his cot and could not rouse him.''

"No! But he cannot be—he cannot be!" Yet even as she cried it, she knew in her own heart it had to be true. Rand had somehow had a premonition, and he'd summoned her to say good-bye. "I *knew* I should have sent for the doctor! I should have made him see the doctor!"

"Don't, Ellie," he whispered, holding her, aching for her. "They said it wouldn't have made any difference."

She wept unconsolably against his rain-spattered coat, and he stood there, stroking her soft hair, her shaking shoulders until he could stand it no longer. Rand hadn't deserved her grief, but she must never know it.

"Ellie . . . Ellie . . ." he whispered. "He won't have to stand trial . . . he won't have to face the hate of the mobs . . . he's safe now, Ellie."

"He was afraid—at the end he was afraid—" she choked out.

"He's not afraid anymore, sweetheart. He went easily," he murmured soothingly.

"I suppose I ought—I ought to be grateful for that at least, but I loved him, Patrick! I wasn't ready for him to leave me!" She bit her lip and tried to control herself. " 'Tis selfish of me, I know, but—"

"He didn't want to go to trial, Ellie. He was spared that at least."

"But he was innocent! Surely—surely he would have been set free!"

"He's free now." Everything he said seemed so terribly inadequate in the face of her grief, but he had to try anyway. "The prison physician says his heart was weak—that it could have happened anytime."

"But it did not have to happen in prison!" She caught herself and took a deep breath. "I'm sorry. It is not your fault, Patrick. You have been nothing but kind and helpful to us. 'Tis just so sudden—so unexpected—and I—" A deep shudder went through her.

"You are right, of course," she managed, swallowing. "I just cannot believe he is gone, I guess."

"I know." She was calmer now, but he did not stop stroking her hair as he spoke as rationally as he could. "I have sent to your mother, telling her that I am taking you home to Kent as soon as a private service can be held. Rand and I had a rather lengthy conversation yesterday, and I know he would have wished for peace between those he loved best," he went on. "I have asked her to come to Barfreston to be with you."

"But she *left* him—when he needed her, she deserted Papa," she said miserably.

"I know, but we all deal differently with our disappointments, my love. She must've felt terribly betrayed at the time." Releasing her, he reached into his pocket for his handkerchief. "You are a great deal stronger woman than she is, Ellie—you have the courage to go on." Dabbing at her eyes, he managed to smile crookedly. "I have hopes you will go on with me, and that we'll have bright-haired sons and daughters lining a pew beneath the rose window. Rand would have liked that, you know."

She looked away. "Patrick, I cannot marry you—not now."

"I am not at all sure I can wait a whole year, Ellie."

"If you marry me at all, the Tories won't have you. It will always be said you wed a murderer's daughter, whether 'tis true or not."

He reached to lift her chin with his knuckle, forcing her to look at him. "It doesn't matter," he answered softly. "They can all rot in hell for all I care."

"But your hopes—your career—"

"All my hopes lie in you—every one of them. And I have gained enough notoriety to keep my practice healthy for the rest of my life." He smiled again. "I would have made a miserable Tory, anyway. You've seen to it that I don't believe in half of what they stand for."

"But you always wanted Parliament—it was to be your stage, Patrick. Indeed, but you said so yourself."

"I love you, Ellie—I love *you*. As long as I have you, I can do without the rest."

"But I shall cost you everything!"

"I don't think so. And later—when all this is behind us—who knows? It is not impossible that I could stand for election as a Whig. But just now I've far more important things to do." Reaching again into his coat pocket, he drew out a folded paper and handed it to her. "It was my intent to return to Barfreston with this, Ellie. I was going to wed you quietly before the trial."

She opened the paper with shaking hands. It was a Special License to marry without banns. She wiped her wet cheeks with the back of her hand. "Under the circumstances, we should create quite a scandal, don't you think?" she asked huskily.

"Oh, I'm prepared to concede it quite improper at the moment, but once everything is settled and your mother is with us, I mean to ask you again."

"It will be said that we ought to observe a year of mourning."

"Would Bat have cared?" he countered.

"No—no, he would not. Indeed, he said as much today," she answered. And it was as though she could hear her father's words again, telling her scandal be damned. Smiling up through new tears, she nodded. "I should be honored to be your wife, Patrick." As his arms closed around her again, she clung to him. "I want you to hold me forever," she whispered. "I want you to love me forever."

Barfreston, Kent: May 1816

Elise closed the book she'd been reading and rose to pace nervously about the small saloon. Her mother looked up from her knitting and sighed.

"We shall hear in due time, dearest."

"I cannot stand the waiting, Mama." Moving to lift up a heavy drape from the window, the younger woman peered anxiously into the darkness. "Surely they must know by now."

"It will happen."

"I would I were half so certain." Elise let the drape fall, then turned around. "Mama, what if I have cost him the election?"

"Nonsense," Emmaline Rand declared dismissively. "He would never even think it."

"But what if it is true? Have you not read what Mr. Cranston wrote to the papers? That the husband of a murderer's daughter ought not to be considered? That Patrick is buying the election with my tainted money? Or that we are an affront to decency because we did not wait the full year to wed?"

Her mother dexterously looped a strand of wool over her finger, then looked up. "Mr. Cranston is a Tory," she observed mildly. "And I for one do not believe the rantings of one desperate man will make one whit of difference." She cocked her head, surveying Elise for a moment. "Much more to the point is when you mean to tell Hamilton about a far more interesting situation."

"I don't know. I suppose I have held it back for consolation should he lose," Elise conceded. "Besides, it is early days, and I have wanted to be certain."

Outside, Button barked furiously, and the two women looked at each other. Elise hesitated, then tore to the window again. "Mama, it's Patrick—oh, lud, but I cannot see enough to know one way or the other." Reaching to smooth her hair, she tried to smile. "I suppose it is too late to pray, isn't it?" Before her mother could answer, she hurried out into the hall to await her husband. "Please, God," she whispered under her breath.

Lizzie came skipping down the stairs. "I'll get 'im fer ye, Missus Hamilton. That Button, I don't know what gets into 'im sometimes." Pulling open the front door, she called out, "Come here, ye mongrel cur! Here now, but ye are wakin' the dead!" As the little dog bounded past her, she saw Hamilton. "If he jumped on ye, sir, 'tis sorry I am fer it," she mumbled, scooping up the animal and retreating toward the kitchen. "Come on, ye miserable creature, ye got ter learn better manners," she scolded.

For a moment Elise's heart paused as she looked into Patrick's sober face. Then he grinned and opened his arms.

"Well, Mrs. Hamilton, would you like to be the first to kiss this member of Parliament?" he asked wickedly.

"We won? You defeated Mr. Cranston?" As he nodded, she felt an intense relief. "Oh, Patrick!" she cried, hugging him tightly.

He wrapped his arms around her, savoring the very feel of her body against his. "It was a near thing, Ellie, but we won," he told her. "You carried it for me."

"I? But I did nothing!"

"If the crowd in the pub can be believed, Cranston overplayed his hand when he attacked you. Most people think you've been through quite enough, you see." As she looked up, he grinned again. "To them, you are the woman they see in church every week, not the shameless hussy he tried to make them think you."

"Did Cranston concede?" she asked eagerly. "Did he admit you won?"

"As a matter of fact, that's why I am late. He bought

me a drink and asked me to convey his apologies to you. Said he wanted you to know it was politics, nothing more."

"And what did you say to him?"

"Oh, I thanked him for the help he gave me, of course."

"You didn't!"

"After what he said about you? The devil I didn't." His grin faded, and he sobered. "I've got it all now, Ellie—everything I ever wished for. You and Parliament—what else could any man want?"

She leaned back in his arms, then smiled. "I could think of something else," she answered softly. "I could think of a bright-haired son or daughter, Patrick. Hopefully one with hazel eyes just like yours."

For a moment he couldn't speak as he searched her face.

She nodded. "Our firstborn ought to arrive with the new year."

If he lived to be a hundred years old, never in his life would he feel again what he felt just now, he was sure of that. Overwhelmed, he could only hold her, thinking he had to be the happiest man on earth.

"I was so afraid I'd cost you too much," she whispered.

"And instead you have given me everything."

As he bent his head to hers, she sought to prolong the sweetness of the moment. "Promise me that I shall be the *only* one to kiss this member of Parliament," she murmured huskily against his lips.

"Mrs. Hamilton, you have my word," he promised.

Fleetingly, images of Ben and her father flashed through her mind, then disappeared in the heat of her husband's kiss. There was no dwelling in the past, no time for sorrow anymore. Now there was only a world of grand tomorrows to be shared with him and this child she carried within her.